CRYSTAL
LATTICE

Other Novels by Joshua Palmatier:

The "Ley" Series:

Shattering the Ley
Threading the Needle
Reaping the Aurora

The "Well" Series:

Well of Sorrows
Leaves of Flame
Breath of Heaven

The "Throne of Amenkor" Series:

The Skewed Throne
The Cracked Throne
The Vacant Throne

The "Crystal Cities" Series:

Crystal Lattice
Crystal Rebel
Crystal War

Anthologies from Zombies Need Brains:

After Hours: Tales from the Ur-bar
The Modern Fae's Guide to Surviving Humanity
Temporally Out of Order * Alien Artifacts * Were-
All Hail Our Robot Conquerors!
Second Round: A Return to the Ur-bar
The Modern Deity's Guide to Surviving Humanity
Solar Flare * Submerged * Guilds & Glaives * Apocalyptic
When Worlds Collide * Brave New Worlds * Dragonesque
The Death of All Things * The Razor's Edge * Portals
Temporally Deactivated * Galactic Stew
Derelict * Alternate Peace * Noir
My Battery Is Low and It Is Getting Dark
Shattering the Glass Slipper * Artifice & Craft * Game On!

CRYSTAL LATTICE

A Novel of the Crystal Cities by

Joshua Palmatier

Zombies Need Brains LLC
www.zombiesneedbrains.com

Interior Design (ebook): ZNB Design
Interior Design (print): ZNB Design
Cover Design by ZNB Design
Cover Art "Crystal Lattice"
by Justin Adams

ZNB Book Collectors #37

First Printing, Zombies Need Brains Edition, April 2024

Print ISBN-13: 978-1940709666

Ebook ISBN-13: 978-1940709673

Printed in the U.S.A.

PART I

THE LYCEUM

Chapter One

"If I fail this challenge," Devon Alamort said, "I'll only have four months to develop a new one. That's not enough time. It took me a year just for these seven questions. I'll be back on the streets of Iandolo, back to the gangs in the lower city, back beneath Carbolen's thumb."

"What makes you think you'll fail this challenge?" Arrend asked. His mentor at the Lyceum, he'd pulled Devon from his jail cell after the disastrous Presidium job and brought him to the college. "Are your questions not strong enough?"

"No."

"Then why are you so anxious?"

They stood in the antechamber of the Inner Sanctum, where the challenges were held. Devon tugged at the constrictive folds of his white uniform, wiped the sweat from his forehead, tried to ignore Arrend's question.

His mentor placed a hand on his shoulder. "What's bothering you, Devon?"

He met his mentor's gaze. "It's Favian."

"Ah." Arrend's hand dropped from his shoulder. "Because Proctor Favian is the Master of the Board for you challenge?"

"He wants me to fail. I can see it in his eyes when I pass him on the quad or in the halls."

"That has nothing to do with you and everything to do with me. Favian and I have been at odds since long before your arrival here. He doesn't approve of my recruiting students from the lower levels of Iandolo. He feels that the Lyceum should be exclusive to mid-level and above, especially the towers. In this respect, he is small-minded."

"The other students told me he'd try to sabotage my chances of graduating, that he'd done it to others. But now…"

"He has control of your board." Arrend glanced at the double doors that led to the sanctum. "Favian will attempt to sabotage your challenge. He'll try to get beneath your skin. You need to ignore him, Devon. Focus on your questions. He can do nothing if the other members of the board find your solutions sound."

A rustle came from behind the doors and Arrend caught Devon's arm. "Don't let him break you."

One of the doors creaked open. An acolyte—a servant of the Lyceum—motioned them in without a word.

The inner foyer was dark, but Devon did not pause to let his eyes adjust, taking three steps forward, until his hands brushed the heavy cloth curtains that obscured the true sanctum. He thrust them aside and stepped into blinding white light.

The circular chamber of the Inner Sanctum stretched up into apparent eternity. Hundreds of narrow columns scattered throughout the room reached toward the heavens and the source of the light, the vertical bands of marble flecked with green and gray along the walls heightening the effect, but Devon had been here twice before and the illusion no longer awed him. He knew now that the light came from an ancient lucent crystal embedded in the ceiling and had calculated that the chamber was a mere four stories high, a third of that in diameter, even though it appeared twice that.

His gaze fell toward the center of the room, where between the columns six members of his Board of Proctors stood behind an arc of seven podiums, one for each of the schools of the Lyceum. Arrend moved to join them. All of them wore stern expressions, including his advisor. Devon kept his eyes Proctor Favian, from the School of Mages, who raised a hand and motioned him forward.

Devon drew in a steadying breath, then moved down the three wide steps to the sanctum's floor, heading straight for the podiums.

His footsteps echoed in the silent room and he felt a drop of sweat begin to trickle down his forehead.

"That's far enough," Favian said, his hand falling.

Devon halted, ten steps from Favian's podium. The challenge hadn't even officially started and already the tips of his fingers had begun to tingle with numbness. He clenched both hands into fists and focused on breathing.

"Devon Alamort, sixth year student in the School of Science, you issued the Board a challenge one week ago consisting of seven questions that you claim you have resolved."

"Yes."

"In the event that the Board, in its wisdom, cannot resolve these questions on its own, you attest that you can explain their resolutions to our satisfaction?"

"Of course I can. I've been here twice before. Do we really need to go through all of this again?"

Out of the corner of his eye, Devon caught Arrend shaking his head.

Favian gripped the sides of his podium. "The formalities are here for a reason, sixth year. They must be observed. Perhaps if you payed closer attention to such things you would have passed one of your first two challenges, like most of our students."

Devon bristled, but bit his tongue, thinking of the streets, the gangs, Carbolen. He couldn't end up back there; if Carbolen didn't kill him, the lower levels would. "I...apologize. I'm...anxious to get started."

Favian pushed back from the podium. "Where were we? Ah yes, your challenge." He pulled a sheet of paper from his podium and flicked it dramatically. "Seven questions, all pertaining to mathematics. I believe I shall hand the remainder of this challenge over to Proctor Arrend."

Favian looked directly at Devon. With a sickening twist in his gut, Devon knew the result of his challenge, even before his advisor stepped around his podium to where two acolytes were wheeling a free-standing slate board forward. The tingling in Devon's fingers grew, began to touch his hands, edge up his arms. His chest felt constricted. Numbed, he barely listened as Arrend cleared his throat and began.

"In the matter of the first question, regarding the sum of two cubes and how they can be broken up into a product, a simple three-dimensional diagram should prove sufficient." Arrend began sketching two cubes on the slate. "If we place the two cubes corner point to corner point and fill in the rest of a much larger cube with side length the sum of the two sides of the cubes, then consider the volume of the resultant larger cube, it's obvious that this volume must equal the sum of the volumes of the individual components inside it." He began scratching out an equation, shifting figures around. "Manipulation of the components will yield that the sum of two cubes must equal the product of the sum of the first and second side lengths with the product of the same subtracted from the sum of their two squares."

"Devon Alamort," Favian interrupted, "does this resolve your first question?"

Devon didn't even look at the slate. "It does."

"Continue, Proctor Arrend."

Arrend hesitated, as if about to say something, then returned to the board, erasing the cubes and rectangular boxes before beginning again. "In the second question, you claim…"

But the numbness that tingled through Devon's arms and now legs grew into a low but incessant hum that drowned out Arrend's words. Favian appeared attentive, confident, smug even, but the other proctors looked bored. As if decisions had already been made.

"Don't let him beneath your skin," Devon muttered. "He can do nothing alone."

His fists clenched tighter.

Favian asked if his second question had been sufficiently resolved and Devon responded flatly. Arrend moved on to the third.

The board would have already discussed their solutions, would have already formed an opinion about whether he would pass the challenge or not. There would only be doubt if they couldn't answer some of his questions. The proctors were too disinterested, which meant there hadn't been any doubt. He was going to fail. Again. With no time to recover. He'd be out on the streets. And he couldn't return to the gang that had taken him in. Carbolen would never trust him again, not after Devon had ditched the gang for the chance to attend the Lyceum. Carbolen may have pulled him from the trash before he died in the lower levels, but all loyalty had been quashed the moment he'd been captured when the Presidium job went bad.

He'd warned Carbolen the job sounded too easy. But Carbolen had insisted. As soon as Devon had cleared the outer perimeter, the job had cracked and splintered. Carbolen had shouted something about Devon triggering an alarm. Devon knew he hadn't—the crystal lock hadn't been that complicated—but there hadn't been time to protest, only run. Two other gang members had been caught. Devon hadn't said a word while he was in custody, but there was no way Carbolen would believe that.

That's where Arrend had found him, where he'd offered him a chance at the Lyceum.

But now the dreams were crumbling down around him. Six years of sweat and stress and an untold amount of paper filled with scratching and scribbling, nervous inspiration and mind-numbing failures, all leading to two failed challenges and now a third—

"Devon Alamort!"

He jerked back to the present. "What is it, Master Proctor?"

"Have you not been paying attention? We asked you if our resolution to your fifth question was acceptable. Is it?"

Fifth question? Had he responded to the previous two? He couldn't remember. He must have. They wouldn't have moved on without his acceptance.

He drew himself upright. "It doesn't matter. It's obvious that the Board finds my challenge weak and unacceptable. Rather than suffer the humiliation of the remaining questions, I will withdraw and attempt to come up with another challenge instead."

He turned to leave, walking purposefully toward the black curtains that concealed the entrance. His entire body felt numb. He couldn't breathe. He needed air.

"Withdraw?" Favian shouted after him. "You haven't seen our resolutions yet! You are a sixth year, with only four months of tenure left. I doubt you will construct a new challenge in that amount of time and, if you do not, you will be banished from the Lyceum!"

Devon didn't look back, shoving through the curtains and stumbling out the still partially opened doorway. Once in the audience room, he exhaled harshly and bent over at the waist. He tugged and pulled at the odd folds of his uniform, until he'd released enough of the constricting fabric that he could breathe again.

He didn't hear Arrend exit behind him until his advisor was close enough to place a hand on his shoulder.

"Breathe. You're fine. Just breathe."

"I'm not. Favian's right. There's not enough time to come up with a new set of questions. I put my best on this one."

"And a few of them were non-trivial."

"Ha!"

Arrend's comforting grip tightened. "You didn't stay for the last few. The proctors have the advantage, remember. You're working on your own; we have the entire Board and the resources of our library to help us. Yet even with that, the Board wasn't certain we'd resolved your final questions correctly."

"Favian seemed thrilled I'd be failing my third challenge."

"He was bluffing. He knew the School of Science had issues with your final questions and tricked you into sabotaging your own challenge."

Devon didn't believe it. But here, in the cooler air of the audience chamber, he realized all Favian had done was stand and stare.

"Proctor Arrend."

Both Arrend and Devon turned to the acolyte standing unobtrusively at the Inner Sanctum door.

"Yes?"

"The Board requests your presence."

"I see." Arrend faced Devon. "I'm certain they want to discuss your actions today."

"Favian will want me expelled immediately."

"He will, but this isn't unprecedented. Many students have fled the sanctum during a challenge, for various reasons. He won't be able to enforce it." Gripping Devon's shoulder again, his advisor said, "Go. Return to your rooms and then go out into the city. Get away for the rest of the day. We'll meet tomorrow, at third hour, in my office. You can present your solutions to your questions and we'll see if there's an avenue of research for you to explore from the results. As I said, the last few questions were challenging to the Board. There may be something there."

Devon didn't trust himself to respond. He waited until Arrend had reentered the sanctum, then spun on his heel and headed toward his room.

He wanted out of the damned uniform.

And he needed a damned drink.

* * *

The Shandy Quad sat on Fulsom Street, twenty blocks closer to the hub. It catered to everyone, but had become a standard hangout for Lyceum students over the years. Devon sat down at the bar and immediately noticed there was a new bartender. Short, not too thin, scruffy little beard and bedraggled hair mostly hidden by a generic cap, keen eyes and a quirky, intriguing smile. Definitely Devon's type.

Arch, the owner, saw him and sidled down to his spot. "The usual?"

"No. I'll have a crystal moon with Everlight, not that cheap juice from the lower levels."

Arch's eyes widened. "You sure you can afford Everlight?"

"Don't argue. Pour."

"That kind of day, huh?" Arch pulled a chilled glass from the ice casket beneath the counter and began mixing as Devon eyed the new bartender. "His name's Nic. Started two days ago. Not sure he's into student types, but hard to tell. Decent bartender so far."

Devon gave a noncommittal grunt.

"What color?"

"Whatever you've got."

Arch took a flat lucent chip from a stash against the back wall and dropped it into Devon's drink. As soon as it hit the alcohol, it began to glow a pale green, strengthening as it drifted to the bottom. A cheap trick, but Devon didn't mind.

Arch handed it over. "Want to talk about it?"

"No. Yes. Just let me drink myself into oblivion."

Arch stood back, crossed his arms over his chest, and squinted one eye at him. "The last time you were this prickly, you'd failed one of your challenges."

Devon didn't answer him, taking a sip of the sour drink as he scanned the rest of the bar's customers in the dim candlelight that Arch thought of as ambiance.

Arch's palms slapped onto the bar top. "You failed your third challenge!"

"Not so loud! The entire upper city doesn't need to hear. Besides, it's happened before, to other students. I still have time."

Arch leaned in close enough Devon could smell his lunch. "You're a sixth year. Not much time left."

"I know! Leave it. I'll figure it out."

Arch shoved back, grabbing a rag and polishing some glasses. Nic glanced their way, but stayed distant. The closest person to them—a woman Devon vaguely recognized from around the Lyceum grounds—studiously stared into her drink, clearly listening in.

Devon ignored them all.

"I don't understand," Arch said, breaking the tense silence. "You helped me fix the bar's lucent cooler when it started acting up, just dove right into the crystal pathways and found the problem. Not many can do that. No one knows how the sodding things work anymore. So how come you can't pass this challenge?"

"It's not the same thing."

Arch waited.

Devon set his drink aside with a sigh. "Listen, I don't know exactly what I'm doing when I'm messing with the lucent crystals, all right? I just…see the pathways, see how they're structured, and make a guess as to what they do. I don't understand how it all works. It's too complicated. The challenges are different."

"How so?"

"The proctors aren't interested in what you can do, they're interested in what you can prove. You can't just say this is how it works, you have to explain exactly why it works that way and prove that it will always work that way. That's why there's no one at the Lyceum who specializes in the crystals. Everyone knows how to use them for things like light and heat and other practical—" he glanced down at his drink "—and impractical uses, but no one can explain why. They just work. In the challenges, I have to come up with something I can prove will always be true that's never been proven before, something the proctors haven't seen. And I don't have full access to the library like they do. They keep most of that for themselves. Finding something that they don't already know how to do, that's not already in the library, is not as easy as it sounds."

The woman near them gave a curt laugh and said, "Tell me about it."

Both Arch and Devon turned to her, Nic edging closer.

"What do you mean, Lane?" Arch asked. "Have you even issued a challenge yet? You're only third year."

"No, I haven't, but at the rate I'm going, I won't even reach the challenge stage."

"Why's that?" Devon asked. "What school are you in?"

Lane glanced at him, her brow pinched in irritation. She had the straight black hair and thin pale face of the Luminesque Province. Devon was surprised, given the political tensions that had been escalating between their two provinces; most of those from Luminesque kept a low profile. There had been recent attacks on the wayfares between their two capital cities of Iandolo and Brovetto, rumored to have been by Luminesque forces, though the official word from the Council and the Towers was banditry from the Flatlands.

"Not that it's any of your concern, but the School of Mages. I'm having problems with the Sigils." She waved one hand in an intricate yet frustrated pattern, thumb pressed to her two central fingers, her index finger extended. Devon had seen the odd hand position and similar gestures before; the window of his rooms overlooked a small section of the mage training grounds. "I can't seem to get the patterns down right."

Now Devon was truly intrigued. He shifted two seats closer, Lane pulling back from him as he settled. Arch and Nic drifted closer as well. The magerium was the reason the Iridesque Province kept its dominance over all of the Crystal Cities. Iandolo was the only city where those with the talent for magecraft could learn to use and control it. When disputes between the cities escalated into violence that couldn't be controlled by Iandolo's army, the Iandolan mages were sent to subdue the uprising. To have someone from Luminesque training at the Lyceum as a mage meant Lane or someone close to her had some serious connections to the proctors or to the councilors themselves.

It also meant Lane would be under significant scrutiny.

"How did you manage to get into the School of Mages? You're Brovettan!"

"I am not!" Lane fidgeted in her seat, glancing around the bar. "My father was Brovettan, but my mother is Iandolan and I was born and raised here, not there."

"Oh." Devon settled back into his seat. That wasn't half as interesting as he'd hoped.

Arch must have felt the same way. He motioned Nic toward a customer and stepped away to help someone else.

"I suppose that makes it difficult for you," Devon said. "Dealing with the other mages."

"Yes, but I can handle them. That's not the problem. It's the damn Sigils."

"Oh, right." Devon waved his hand in imitation of what she'd done earlier.

Lane rolled her eyes. "Yes, those. I can't seem to get the patterns down. One small imprecision and the entire construct fails. If I don't pass the principal qualifiers by the end of this year, I can't continue."

"Sounds familiar."

They sat in commiserating silence. Devon was beginning to feel the effects of the Everlight when he turned to her and asked, "If you become a mage, though, won't you be tied to Iandolo? Mages take a binding oath to the city."

"So what?"

"Don't you want to visit Brovetto? See where your father grew up? Visit relatives there?"

Lane finished off her drink in one large swallow and stood up. "My father stayed in Brovetto. Didn't care enough to come to Iandolo once I was born. I hardly know him. So no, I have no desire to see Brovetto. Or my father."

"Sorry. I didn't mean—"

"Don't. It's nothing." She turned, obviously anxious to leave, but paused and forced a tentative smile. "Thanks. Not many people stop and talk to me, especially those from the Lyceum."

"Maybe I'll see you back in here again sometime. We can catch a drink."

Lane's gaze slid toward Nic. "If I didn't know better, I'd say you were asking me out on a date."

"I just meant—"

Lane laughed, the first time she'd appeared relaxed and natural all night. "Don't worry. I know what you meant."

"Good." She'd nearly made it to the door when he called out, "Good luck with your Sigils." He exaggerated a hand wave in the air and she laughed again.

After she'd left, he stared into his crystal moon, brooding, until Nic sidled over with an easy smile.

"Care for another?"

Devon pushed his empty glass forward with his fingers. "Certainly. That first one didn't go nearly far enough."

"I thought I heard Arch say something about failing a challenge?"

"Ha! Third one so far. And the kicker is if I hadn't gotten so twisted up inside of myself and left, I might have passed."

Nic set his drink down in front of him. "What do you mean you left?"

Devon took a hefty swallow and held the glass up as if in a toast. "I fled the challenge halfway through. Because I thought I was going to fail again." He dropped his arm, slamming the glass onto the bar harder than he'd intended. "It's my own damned fault. But I have to pass. I can't go back to the lower levels. The grit, the grime, the gangs. I just can't."

Nic grabbed his wrist, squeezing tight, and he looked up. "The lower levels ain't so bad."

Devon gave a weak grin. "I suppose not. Not if you're there."

Nic pulled back but didn't step away. Devon continued to flirt with him to distract himself, but when Nic asked if he wanted a third, he waved it off and left. He couldn't afford it and he was already drunk enough he'd have to be careful walking back to his room. Besides, he had a meeting with Arrend tomorrow.

That thought sobered him considerably. He stumbled out of the bar, then wove through the nearly-empty streets back toward the Lyceum. Shops were shuttered, lucent glowing in the walls of scattered buildings, lantern light flickering in windows above. Two War students challenged him at the northern entrance of the college, but let him pass through the narrow corridor between the high walls of the Mage and War practice yards to either side. He detoured past the school dormitories and quad and entered the Tower.

It was one of the oldest and tallest buildings on the grounds of the Lyceum, with bands of lucent crystal worked into the stonework. As Devon climbed the stairs toward the roof, he trailed a hand over the wall, his fingers scraping across the grit of the stone, then gliding over the slick surface of the crystal. He contemplated the dimly lit lucent. On campus, it glowed a light green in color. Out in the city, it came in a variety of colors—blues and golds and purples, even a few reds and yellows. Not for the first time, he wondered who the Founders—who had constructed these seven ancient cities of crystal—had been. Who were they? Where had they gone? Had the crystals been flawed in some way, abandoned because they were decaying? Or had the decay come later, after the Founders had left?

He paused at a band of crystal that was dark, the translucent material filled with tendrils of black, like smoke trapped in glass. One hand on the stone wall to the side to steady himself, he peered closer, his nose almost touching the lucent's surface, trying to see the pattern in the smoke. He thought there was one, even when they were lit, but it refused to resolve into anything meaningful. Yet the nagging sensation that there was meaning persisted.

His vision grew blurry and the world around him began to list to one side.

He closed his eyes and rested his forehead against the crystal before pushing himself away and continuing up the stairs.

When he stepped out onto the roof, the wind slapped him full force and he shuddered at its intense cold. When it died down a moment later and he moved out toward the roof's edge. The apex of the Tower was made entirely of lucent, the footing treacherous, but he'd come here hundreds of times. He headed to a section where the lip of the outer wall curved down, creating a narrow view of the city beyond.

Iandolo, like all of the Crystal Cities, rose from the Flatlands like shards of glass and fingers of stone thrust up through the barren earth. The three spires near the center were the highest, stretching up twenty levels above that of the Lyceum. That was where the powerful in Iandolo resided—the councilors, the richest merchants, even a few members of the army. The crystal glowed bright and healthy against the sky, a beacon in the center of the Flatlands. Other towers, five to ten levels in height, were scattered around the rest of the wide flat mid-level, among an amalgam of plazas and parks, walkways and balconies. Pinpricks of red and orange lucent were visible, even an entire streak of yellow up one side of the central, tallest tower. The combined light was strong enough to block out most of the stars immediately overhead and to illuminate the large circular swaths of farmland on mid-level to the south.

Yet even amid the glory of the lucent, Devon could see blotches of darkness where the crystals had failed. At the highest levels, they were merely strands here and there. As his gaze dropped lower and lower, the darkness grew and spread. Just west of the Lyceum, an entire section had gone dark—a full tower and half of another adjacent to it. He knew of additional sections where the crystals had decayed. Those in the upper city ignored the signs of the lucent's failure, pretending those areas didn't exist, just as they ignored those who lived in the twenty-four levels beneath them, where the majority of the crystals had failed and the citizens relied on lanterns and candles for heat and light.

Devon leaned out over the edge of the Tower and contemplated the tiers of the lower city. He didn't need his eyes to visualize what was down there. He'd grown up there, first with his parents in a section where perhaps half of the lucent crystals worked, but then later, after their deaths, much, much lower. When he'd been part of Carbolen's gang, they'd resided in a section only faintly lit by active crystals, the dead ones making everything appear black and sooty.

There, the water was tainted and the streets and alleys overrun by refuse and rats.

He couldn't go back there. Not because Carbolen might kill him. No.

Because, after the Lyceum, any existence he could find there would crush him.

Chapter Two

Devon woke with a groan and a thudding headache. He didn't remember descending from the Tower or falling into bed.

He blinked and bowed his head as he rolled up into a sitting position, sunlight glaring through his window, then swore.

Sunlight in his window meant...

"It's already past the second hour!"

He leapt up and hastily changed clothes, using the water in the pitcher and basin on top of his dresser to wash his face and armpits as a makeshift bath. Still bleary, he pulled on his shoes, then paused before his window.

From his vantage on the fourth floor, he could see over the high wall into the mage's practice field. Three mages were visible, dashing back and forth, their heels throwing up sand as they dodged each others' handiwork. When possible, one would pause long enough to snap out an intricate gesture with one hand, as Lane had done the night before in the bar, except with these students the motions were precise and yielded results. Most of it happened invisibly, the affected student flung backwards by an unknown force, or the sand exploding upwards in a blinding sheet.

For the first time, Devon paid attention to the mages' hand motions. He'd lived here six years and, aside from the initial curiosity when he'd first moved in, he hadn't thought about the mages at all; he'd had his own studies to work on. But now—

A chime sounded, reverberating out from the peak of the Inner Sanctum, signaling the third hour.

Devon bolted from his room, his door crashing closed behind him. He charged down the hall and stairs beyond, other students from the School of Science stepping out of his way. One or two called out after him or shouted in anger, but he didn't stop. He sprinted across the first-floor great room, then out the dormitory's large oaken doors, down the entrance steps, and across the quad toward the Master's Hall, skirting the large finger of amber lucent that jutted up from its center. He slowed briefly to admire the boys from the School of War practicing combat moves shirtless in the grass near their own residence, then picked up the pace until he noticed Proctor Favian watching him with a frown from where he stood on the walkway to one side.

"Proctor Favian."

Favian merely shook his head.

Devon arrived at Proctor Arrend's door a quarter after the third hour, composed himself, then knocked.

An acolyte opened the door, glanced over him in disapproval, then motioned him inside. "Proctor Arrend has been waiting for you," she said. "He's in his office."

Devon thanked her and made his way across the receiving room toward the pocket doors on the left, carved in an intricate pattern of tree branches with inlaid chips of lucent for leaves. Everything in Arrend's rooms—those that Devon had seen—was made of fine wood, leather, and lucent, from the chairs to the desks and lamps. The lucent leaves on the door flared briefly as he drew near and Arrend called out from inside, "Enter."

Arrend sat behind his desk, glancing over sheets of parchment with complex sketches on them. Two large slate boards behind him were covered in similar diagrams, obscuring the three windows along that wall. Devon recognized the drawings as two of the larger Wardings within Iandolo—sections of the city that had at some time in the past been encased in growths of orange lucent. No one knew why or how it had been done, but everything inside the crystal had been locked away, frozen in time. In a few of the Wardings, people were visible, as if going about their everyday lives, but trapped in mid-motion.

Arrend tossed the paper he was perusing onto the desk and looked up. "You're late."

Devon stepped up to the desk, where he could see that the pages littering its surface were all diagrams of Wardings, from the smallest to the largest, copious notes made along the margins regarding size, placement, shape, and what could be seen inside from different vantage points. "Why are you studying the Wardings? Isn't this something the mages have looked into? They didn't find anything."

"And that's the definitive answer?" Arrend asked as he stood. "That there's nothing to see here?"

"That's the accepted answer."

"Yes, I suppose it is. But I don't accept it. There is something to see here, we simply don't understand it yet. Obviously the Wardings are related to the lucent. Something happened at each of these locations and the lucent reacted."

"Reacted how? To do what?"

Arrend shrugged. "I don't know. I've spent years looking at them, observing them, taking notes, developing theories, risking the wrath of the mages, but I'm no closer to understanding them or their purpose—if they have one—than before." He began gathering up the parchment into a neat stack. "It's a private project of mine, one that has borne no fruit." He slid the pages into an inlaid wooden box and began to set it aside, but paused. "Have you seen one of the Wardings?"

"Yes. In the lower city. It enclosed an entire street and the two buildings on either side."

"And? What did you do? What did you see?"

"I looked inside. The street was immaculate, the lucent vibrant, the buildings clean. Nothing like the dirt-smeared, lucent-dead alley where we stood. And the people...they wore slick, oddly archaic clothes."

Arrend leaned forward. "Did anything else appear odd or out-of-place?"

Devon reached back to that memory, felt the sweat from the heat of the level, two other gang members waiting impatiently for him to finish. "A few of the people were beginning to look upwards. They looked vaguely worried. One mother was reaching for her daughter, as if she were going to snatch her up and run."

"What from?"

"I don't know. It looked like there were streaks of lightning overhead, but this was deep inside that level. It couldn't have been a storm."

Arrend settled back. "The Warding on Level Ten." He tapped the box containing his research. "Perhaps what this project needs is a new set of eyes." He handed the box over to Devon. "You should take a look, if it intrigues you. But you aren't here for that, are you?"

"No."

"There's no need to feel despondent, Devon. As I said at the challenge, if you'd stayed, you may have been surprised by the result. There was an intense argument among the proctors after you left that involved others besides those on your particular board of review."

Devon had never heard of other proctors partaking in a review board's discussion. "What about?"

"Whether the challenge was sufficient for a pass."

"A...pass?"

"I told you, our resolutions to your last few questions were weak. Some of the other mathematics proctors, along with others from the Sciences and even the Schools of War and Merchants, felt that you should receive a pass based on the last three questions alone. Even if our resolutions are correct, they presented enough of a challenge that, had the presentation of your resolution been found acceptable, most of your board would have recommended a pass.

"But you didn't stay. You let Favian influence you. I could see it even before I finished our resolution of your first question. You'd already given up. And then you bolted."

"I can still present my resolutions! I could—"

"It's too late. The Board considered that, but in the end they voted the challenge a failure. The decision is final."

Devon reeled. "Then...then it's over. I'm out of the Lyceum."

Arrend moved from behind his desk, taking Devon by the shoulder, steering him toward the side of the room, where standing slates like those used during the challenge had been wheeled into Arrend's office.

"Not quite. You see, because the Board never presented our own resolutions to the last two questions, it was decided that you could use those two questions again on your next—and final—challenge." He handed Devon a piece of chalk. "I want you to present your resolutions to me, so that I'm certain you've solved them in a manner the Board will accept."

Devon set aside the box of Warding notes and took the chalk. "But then you'll have seen my resolution. The Board can present it as its own, which will disqualify that question."

Arrend squeezed his shoulder in reassurance. "I've removed myself from your Board and promise not to disclose whatever you show me to them. They'll have to figure it out themselves."

Devon stared hard into Arrend's eyes. His time in Carbolen's gang had taught him not to trust anyone—not his fellow gang members or even Carbolen himself. His instinct was to hand the chalk back and walk out of the room.

But Arrend had saved him from the lower city, had fostered him through those rough first years when he'd lashed out in his struggle to fit in.

"I'll show you the key steps, but not the details."

"Very well."

Nearly two hours later, with three additional slate boards brought in by the acolyte, Devon stepped to the side of the last slate. "And that's my resolution for the last question of my challenge."

The back of his neck felt gritty with sweat and his arm ached from writing. Arrend's acolyte had appeared on two different occasions with a tray of light food and decanters of water and of wine. Devon reached for the wine now, his throat raw from speaking. He drank the first glass without pause, then poured a second.

Arrend, now ensconced in one of the leather and wood chairs, contemplated the boards, hand on his chin, one finger tapping his cheek. His brow was creased into furrows.

"This is unlike any approach I've ever seen," he finally said, leaning forward. Then he stood and drifted toward the boards. "The way you handled the substitution here, reducing it to a previously solved equation, is elegant and simplifies the calculations significantly. The method of transference here is inspired. There's some room for improvement in a few areas, but overall I don't see anything that the Board will be able to counter or disprove." Arrend faced him. "I'd say these two questions are ready for defense."

Devon swallowed his bite of pastry, the meat dry in his throat. "Then all I have to do is come up with five additional questions for the challenge in the next four months. Easy."

"You have nothing else? No other questions you've been working on, partially resolved?"

"Nothing that's close to being finished."

Arrend turned back to the slates. "There are new techniques in these calculations that may prove useful on other, as yet unproven, hypotheses. I suggest we both work on extending these results to see what we may discover."

Devon nearly choked on his wine. "You can help me?"

Arrend had already shifted to one of the slates and begun erasing Devon's calculations. "I cannot help you resolve a claim or conjecture, no. But I taught you the basic theories of mathematics for four years and I have guided you in your own research since. Helping you organize your thoughts and directing your inquiries in a particular direction is skirting the boundaries of what the Board would find acceptable, but at this point I'm willing to risk it."

"What about Favian?"

Arrend faced Devon. "What do you know of Favian? From before his time here at the Lyceum?"

"I thought he'd always been here."

"No." Arrend returned to the slates. "None of the proctors from the Schools of War or Mages began at the Lyceum. They were all part of the army. Most of those who are now proctors came to the Lyceum by choice—they retired from the army and were appointed here. But not Favian. He never intended to be a proctor, never intended to teach."

"What happened?"

Arrend set the cloth eraser aside. "It's not my story to tell, but if it will give you some perspective... Favian was rising as a battle mage in the army, one of their best. It appeared he would become a prefect, the highest rank in the army, but then there was an uprising in Brovetto. Nothing serious—a rebellion over food resources that had turned violent. The officials in Brovetto asked for the Council's help and they chose to send Favian with a team of mages and an escort of soldiers. Success in quelling the insurgency would ensure Favian's prefecture. He would finally achieve the rank he felt he deserved.

"But the resistance in Brovetto was more intense than he—than anyone—expected. The attack soured almost instantly. The rebels managed to set off explosives, killing at least twenty of Favian's forces, including one of his prized mages, Terrial, the daughter of Councilor Martov. Favian's forces rallied and took down the insurgents, but the damage had already been done.

"When Favian returned, Councilor Martov was enraged. Any chance of Favian becoming prefect had died along with Terrial. The

Council gave Favian the option of retiring to the Lyceum to teach or be stripped of his rank entirely and incarcerated for the rest of his life. The rest of the contingent that accompanied him—both soldiers and mages—were reduced in rank and sent back to the army. Favian chose the Lyceum.

"That's why he's so bitter. He does not want to be a proctor, does not want to teach, but he has been left no other choice."

"But why does he hate you so much?"

"Because I am the exact opposite of what he aspires to. I come from the lower levels—Level Ten, actually."

Devon had been down to Level Ten, but no lower. He had not lingered. Too dangerous. All he remembered was how dark it had been, most of the lucent dead. And the Warding, of course.

"I have no influence in the towers, especially the Council. I come from nothing and so to Favian I am nothing. And yet I have enough influence at the Lyceum that I can affect those who are allowed into the college. There are only so many placements made in each School each year. Favian would have them all given to those from mid-level or above, those who may be able to help him in the future. I—and a few others—have thwarted him in this respect. We feel that the placements should be given to those with the intelligence and creativity to learn and to advance our understanding of the world, whether they come from the towers or the lower levels."

"And so he tries to thwart your chosen students where he can."

Arrend shifted forward, suddenly stern. "He didn't force you to run from the challenge. You did that yourself."

"I know."

"That said, if he learns I am helping you, he will use it against you."

"But you're only helping me organize my thoughts."

"Precisely." Arrend stood and shifted back to the slates. "Let's start by listing some conjectures and proposals that have yet to be resolved that are somewhat related to the topics in number theory that you've explored here. Then we'll branch out into other subjects where the techniques you've used might be relevant."

"You're really going to help me? Right now?" It was already the seventh hour. This time of year, there were only eight hours of daylight.

As if reading Devon's thoughts, Arrend did a circuit of the room, brushing his hand along the veins of lucent in the walls to increase their light. In addition, he shook a few shards of crystal he had sitting on his desk and oriented their lights toward the slates, even though sunlight still streamed through the three windows. "That should cover us, if we happen to work late."

Devon stared at his advisor a moment, then poured himself more wine and picked up the chalk.

* * *

He stumbled into the Shandy Quad well after dark, the place crowded with people, most of them students of the Lyceum. Music blasted through the small room from a group of four who'd staked out one corner, the drummer and fiddler overly enthusiastic, at least for Devon's already pounding headache. He almost left, but spotted Lane sitting at the bar.

He shoved in next to her and caught Nic's attention, Lane glaring at him as he jostled her drink.

"I'm surprised to see you here," she said, speaking loudly to be heard over the music. "Don't you have a failed challenge to recover from?"

"Ouch. You don't pull your punches do you?"

"It's the truth, isn't it?"

Nic sidled over. "Another Everlight?"

"Cracked no, I can't afford that. My usual swill, that juice from Radimansque."

Nic winked and stepped away. Lane gave Devon a significant look.

"What?"

"He winked at you."

Devon waved a hand. "It's nothing. The truth is, I spent the last seven hours with my advisor looking at problems and possible ways to resolve them. I can't think straight right now." He glanced around in annoyance. "Why are there so many people here? It's never like this."

"It's the musicians," Nic said, handing Devon his drink, scooping up the chits of bright Devon set on the bar. "Arch is trying out music as a draw for patrons."

The fiddle screeched and half of the crowd roared in encouragement.

"I'd say it's working."

But Nic had already moved off. Devon watched his retreating back with regret, but then the man sitting next to Lane vacated his seat and Devon grabbed the opening.

"Did you find any problems for your challenge?" Lane asked.

"I can't say. It's all a jumble right now and I'm too exhausted and stressed to sort it out. I need to sleep on it, look at it fresh in the morning."

"So you came here?" She raised a quizzical eyebrow.

"I wasn't expecting this." He swung the hand holding his drink around to encompass the entire bar—the people, the musicians, the noise—but halfway his arm struck someone on the shoulder. Alcohol sloshed from the glass and spilled all over the woman's shirt. She shrieked, her voice piercing through even the fiddler's current jig, which ground to a halt with an ear-jarring crunch.

The woman spun as the entire bar fell into rustles and the jagged ends of conversations. Her eyes settled on Devon, then narrowed.

"What did you do?" The words were low and strangled.

Beside him, Lane half stood. "Quinn, it was an accident."

Quinn glanced toward Lane. "The Brovetto Bitch. I should have known." Her gaze flicked back to Devon and she barked out a laugh. "And the Gutter Wretch! I hear you've failed yet another challenge. Word around the quad is you'll be back in the lower city in another four months." She leaned in close, her breath reeking of ale and garlic. "Perhaps even the Flatlands, where you belong. How does that feel, Wretch?"

"His name is Devon."

Quinn held up an admonishing finger in Lane's direction. "Hush. I'll deal with you in a moment."

Lane ignored her. "It wasn't even ale. It was Radimansque clear. You can whisk it out of your clothes with a crook of your finger."

Quinn's attention slid toward Lane, the raised hand snapping into the familiar pointed index and circled finger-thumb of a mage getting ready to draw a Sigil. "Do you mean this crooked finger?"

Gasps filled the bar and the tension escalated. Students were forbidden to use the Sigils outside of the practice yards and their own dormitory. No one of consequence had been around to notice when Lane had done it yesterday. Besides, she was only third year.

Quinn was sixth. She knew more than the basics, could do serious harm with the right form. If anyone reported this, she could be thrown out of the Lyceum without so much as a trial.

"If I recall, you haven't yet mastered the basic patterns." Quinn jabbed her finger toward Lane and several people drew in sharp breaths; Lane stiffened, mouth pressed into a thin line. "Perhaps you haven't had the right teacher. Someone who can drill the patterns into you."

Devon swallowed, throat dry. "I don't think—"

But someone—one of the School of War students, taller than Devon, huskier, with a planar jaw and piercing dark eyes—pushed Devon aside. "Quinn, what do you think you're doing? You haven't passed your qualifiers yet. You could be expelled for simply crooking your finger here, let alone handing out threats. Your father wouldn't appreciate that. Isn't he still angling for a place on the Council?"

"Stay out of this, Dalton. It's a Mage issue."

"It involves War if it may eventually involve the city guard."

Quinn hesitated. Her teeth ground together and her poised hand twitched.

Devon didn't know if she'd intended to trace out a Sigil or not. She never had the chance to complete it, if so. Someone slammed into her from the side, dragging her shrieking to the floor. The three mages who'd been with her turned on those around them, fists flying, and the entire bar exploded. No one attempted to crook their fingers into the mage's hand position though. Dalton bellowed for everyone to stop, but was forced to duck when a glass flew toward his head. He crouched down near the protection of the bar and spat curses. The rest of the bar broke into a melee, more glasses and even a few chairs suddenly airborne. Devon grabbed Lane by the shoulder and hauled her down beside Dalton.

"We need to get out of here!" Devon shouted.

Lane looked at him as if he were stupid. "How?"

"Here!"

Devon glanced up to see Nic leaning over the bar.

"Up here! Get behind the bar. I'll let you out the back."

Devon grabbed Dalton's arm. "Dalton! This way!"

Dalton was facing the riot. "Are you joking? I'm School of War! I trained for this! You two get out of here. I'll do what I can until the city patrol arrives."

Devon and Lane stood and scrambled over the bar, Nic hauling on their shirts, Dalton urging them on from behind. They crashed to the floor on the far side amid shards of glass and spilled alcohol. Devon was certain he was cut somewhere, but he didn't take the time to find out. Nic motioned them both toward the back, but Devon paused.

Dalton plowed into the crowd, punching, elbowing, and tossing bodies aside. He began bellowing the mantra of the city guard as he knocked people unconscious.

Lane dragged Devon by the arm into the back room, where the noise dropped to a dull roar. Nic slammed the door closed behind them. Arch was already there, mumbling something about this being the last time he brought in musicians. He hooked a thumb toward the outer door. "Go on, get out."

Devon and Lane spilled out into the back alley and ran.

Two blocks later, Lane broke out in raucous laughter and staggered against the nearest building, one arm holding her stomach. Devon lurched toward her as she scraped down the wall into a seated position.

"Lane! Are you hurt?" He crouched down next to her and began checking for wounds, but she batted his hands away, still laughing.

"Did you...did you see her? She was...so serious. So intense." Her laughter began to die. She wiped at the tears running down her face. "I'm fine, Devon. Just some cuts from the glass and some bruises."

Devon sat down beside her and inspected his own wounds. A thin slice the size of his thumb on the pad of his palm; a few splinters of glass in his fingers. He began teasing them out. "I thought she was going to work a Sigil. You didn't seem worried though."

"An advantage of being a mage. It takes time to create the form. I'd have punched her in the face before she'd completed it if she'd tried. That's why mages are always accompanied by the army. The guards are there to buy us enough time to create the forms."

Devon had never thought about it. That must be why the Schools of War and Mages worked so closely together, why they trained in adjacent yards. "You would have paid for it later."

"Paid for what?"

"Punching her."

"It wouldn't have mattered. There would have been something else. There's always something else. Quinn's had it in for me since I arrived, because I've so obviously got Luminesque blood in me." She waved at her face, the skin so much paler than Devon's or anyone else from Iridesque. "She doesn't care that I've never been outside Iandolo." She paused. "You've clearly had run-ins with her though."

"Why do you say that?"

"She called you 'Gutter Wretch.'"

"Oh, that." He stared out at the street and the few citizens strolling along the crystal-lit paths on either side. None of them paid the two any attention. "It started when I first came here. I don't know how, but someone found out I was from the lower city, that Arrend had recruited me from a city watch cell." Lane quirked an eyebrow in curiosity, but he didn't elaborate. "The others in the School of Science began harassing me, but I'd dealt with that kind of crap in the lower city. I ignored it, kept to myself, and eventually they grew tired and stopped."

"And what would you have done if they'd continued?"

He looked her in the eye. "I'd have taken care of it."

She hesitated, but left it. "Unfortunately, Quinn's right. I haven't mastered the forms yet. Which means in another four months I'll likely be back with my mother in her gilded tower in the upper city." The words were tinged with bitterness.

"Wait, what do you mean 'in her gilded tower'? You live in one of the towers?"

"Haven't you heard? My mother is one of the Councilors. According to Quinn and everyone else at the Lyceum, that's the only reason I've been allowed to study as a mage—her influence. No Brovettan would be allowed in otherwise."

Devon didn't know how to respond to the heat in her voice. "But…the towers. Would being sent back there be so bad? You'd have everything you needed. Food, water, clean air. And the majority of the lucent still works."

"But it's a prison. There's so much more…space down here. I was hoping when they discovered I had the talent to be a mage that I could escape. But I don't think that's going to happen anymore."

"You can't give up. There are still four months left."

Lane didn't respond.

They sat in silence, the harsh whistles of the guard reaching even here. Devon assumed they were converging on the Shandy Quad. He wondered if there would be consequences for what Quinn had done. Except she hadn't done anything, had she? He wasn't even certain she'd started to draw a Sigil before she'd been tackled.

Nothing would come of it. Nothing ever did for people like her.

And then there was Dalton. He'd come forward to help when clearly everyone else was itching for Lane and Quinn to fight.

Beside him, Lane stirred. "We'd better get back to the Lyceum." She winced as she stood, clutching at her side again.

"You are hurt."

"I hit the side of the bar hard when we were scrambling over it. It's just bruised. It feels better if I keep moving."

Devon didn't argue with her.

They meandered back toward the grounds, circling wide around the Shandy Quad. Devon tilted his head back and stared up toward the spires of the upper city, lit with the glow of the lucent. He had a hard time thinking of it as a prison.

They parted at the shard of amber lucent in the center of the main quad.

"Good luck with your new challenge," Lane said as her figure faded into the shadows.

"And you with your Sigils."

He thought he heard laughter.

The amber crystal caught his eye and he placed a hand on it, his palm tingling slightly.

Then he turned and headed back to the School of Science's dormitory.

Chapter Three

Devon sat hunched over his desk, scribbling furiously at a piece of parchment. It was already filled with diagrams and calculations, just like every other piece of paper scattered about his room. The scratch of the nib of the quill was the only sound. He'd had an epiphany that morning. After nearly three weeks of frustrating failures and false starts, he thought this latest idea might prove fruitful. He'd already spent hours tracing down the paths of logic, headed toward the goal of proving at least one of the unanswered questions he and his advisor had come up with. He had answered a few trivial questions along the way, but nothing of significance, nothing that he could use as an additional question in his challenge. He needed something deeper, something with weight behind it. If he could find a way to connect this new approach to his already proven theories...

The scritch of the quill slowed and then halted. He stared down at the paper, then rubbed his sweaty forehead. He'd hit a wall, the calculations not coming together like he'd thought they would. Had he missed something? His eyes darted up to his previous work, scanning each line, double-checking the logic, the numbers, the variables. But there was nothing wrong with what he'd written so far. Perhaps he'd made a mistake earlier, on a previous sheet?

He began sifting through the pages beneath, all neatly numbered. As he worked his way backwards, a pressure began to build inside his head. He'd been sequestered in his room since the confrontation with Quinn at the bar, trying idea after idea, working on one problem until he'd grown frustrated, then turning to the next, cycling back and forth through them all. But nothing worked. Every attempt led to a dead end, to an equation that didn't make sense or that he couldn't resolve. He only had a little over three months now. Three months until he'd be forced out of the Lyceum back onto the streets, back down to the lower city with its lucent-darkened alleys and tainted water and vermin-infested pathways.

His entire body went rigid, one hand seizing into a fist, paper crackling beneath his fingers. "I can't go back there. I can't."

The headache grew and suddenly he couldn't contain it anymore. He leaped to his feet, the chair scraping a few inches before catching and toppling to the floor. With one sweep of his arm, he flung all of the papers, the quill, the ink bottle—everything covering his desk—to one side. The bottle shattered against one wall, throwing splinters of glass, staining the stone black. He spun and kicked the chair, sending it flying toward the wall beneath the window. With a heave, he shoved the desk away. It came to a skewed halt, too heavy to move far, so he reached for the plates from his hastily eaten meals, tossed them aside, the fired clay breaking with satisfactory cracks as he cursed Arrend, the Lyceum, the Board, and especially Proctor Favian. But the anger only grew, an inarticulate roar starting deep in his chest.

He'd reached for the shard of greenish crystal used as a lamp when something in his throat tore, as if he'd swallowed a chicken bone and its splintered ends had lodged back behind his tongue. He choked, began to gasp, unable to draw breath, and leaned heavily over the desk. After what felt like an eternity, his throat clicked and he heaved in air, began coughing—harsh, wracking coughs. He staggered from the desk to the window, managed to right the chair, and then collapsed into it.

As the coughing fit subsided, he heard shouts from the hallway outside. He thought at first it was concern over the noise. He'd made few friends with the other science students, but there were one or two he thought might care enough to be worried. However, after a moment he realized there was something else going on.

He rose and yanked open his door. Someone had posted a "Do Not Disturb" sign on it. Someone else had scrawled "Madman at Work" beneath.

A fourth year—everyone called him Itch—came tearing down the hall, headed toward the stairs.

"What's going on?" he shouted at Itch's back.

Itch paused at the top of the stairs, clearly surprised to see him. He ran a hand through his blond hair, his eyes wide. "There's been an attack on the edge of the city. They're calling out the sixth years from War and Mages."

Before Devon could form a coherent response, Itch charged down the steps, vanishing around a corner.

Devon cursed, looked back at the shambles of his room, then shut the door and followed.

He ran into others immediately, the stairs becoming choked before they all reached the first floor. It appeared the entire dormitory had descended to the great room, everyone milling about, trying to talk at once, excitement—tinged with a little bit of worry and dread—thrumming in the air. The hall's resident steward stood in the center, blatantly trying to calm everyone down and having no effect. Devon stepped to the side, back against one wall, and listened, but it was clear no one in the immediate area knew anything.

He began making his way toward the outside door, following the wall. Itch saw him and began to follow, along with a few others.

They'd almost made it to the entrance when a discordant chime rang from the quad outside. Unlike the soothing tones that marked off the hours of the day, this chime sank into Devon's bones and made his teeth ache. Everyone quieted.

And then everyone made for the quad.

Devon, Itch, and the rest spilled out onto the steps but they were quickly shoved forward onto the stone walkway and then the grass, spreading out to either side among the scattered trees between the buildings. Students were also emerging from the dormitories for Arts, History, Humanities, and Merchants, and proctors were taking more tentative steps from their own residence hall. In the center of the quad, near the plinth of amber lucent, students from the Schools of War and Mages were assembling, some of the proctors from both attempting to bring them into order. One of the proctors from War held an oblong dark blue crystal up over his head, the lucent emitting a flashing light. Some of the older students were gathered around him, those from War dressed in battle armor. Not the formal armor used for ceremonies, but actual hardened leather with all of the protective metal pieces near joints and around the neck. Real swords were strapped to their sides or backs. A few even wore helmets. Acolytes were hastily helping other students into their armor and arming them to one side. On the other side of the amber shard, another proctor held a pulsing red crystal over his head, mages in dark gray battle robes nearby.

Devon picked out Quinn amongst the mages, her eyes alight and eager. Then he spotted Lane—not among the sixth years, but in the group of younger mages standing in a large clump to one side.

The proctors from the remaining houses were beginning to spread out, heading toward their own students' halls, obviously intending to rein everyone in so the War and Mage students could finish.

Devon bolted across the quad toward the mages.

"Lane!"

Lane turned in confusion. "Devon?"

He ground to a halt in front of her, the other mages giving him odd looks. "Do you know what's going on?"

"You look like hell. Have you been sleeping?" Her nose wrinkled. "Or bathing?"

He grabbed her shoulders. "What's going on?"

"I don't know, they aren't saying much. But supposedly there's been an attack on Iandolo, near one of the wayfare gates. The Council is pulling the sixth years to help the army and the city guard in that area."

"It's that bad? Who attacked us?"

One of the other mages said disdainfully, "I heard one of the proctors say it was Luminesque when they yanked us out of training. The bastards." He suddenly remembered who Lane was. "Oh, sorry, I didn't mean—"

"Of course you meant it," Lane snapped. "How many times do I have to say it? I'm not from Brovetto! I'm not Luminesque!"

The proctors were beginning to separate the schools, herding their own students back toward their separate dormitories. One of the mage proctors caught sight of Devon and headed toward him.

He snagged Lane's arm again to catch her attention. "Wait for me by the Tower once they let us go again."

"Why?"

Devon began backing away, the proctor almost on them. "I know a place where we can go and get a better view!"

Before the proctor could say a word, he hustled back toward the Science dormitory. On his way, he saw Dalton donning a helm, the War student's expression as serious as it had been at the bar brawl. He halted in his tracks, nearly ran to Dalton's side. But then the War student was surrounded by his fellow sixth years and Devon lost sight of him.

The Science proctors ushered their students into a rough circle before the dormitory, some of the more adventurous climbing up on the stone balustrades of the steps or the trees for a better view. Even more scrambled to the upper floor windows and the roof.

On the quad, the first through fourth year War and Mage students were also herded toward their own dormitories, but the fifth years were allowed to work with the acolytes to finish girding the sixth years for battle. Proctors yelled commands and the sixth years eventually fell into lines, ten across and twenty deep. The two center columns were composed of mages, the four columns on either side War students, to protect the mages in between. Quinn held position near the front of the ranks; he couldn't tell where Dalton was, not with the helm in place.

When it appeared that everyone was in order, the proctors holding the two crystals each struck them with one hand, the discordant chime grinding into Devon's teeth again. Then four proctors appeared, Devon startled to see them in the same battle armor as the students. One of them was Favian.

"Did you think the proctors from the Schools of War and Mages simply cowered here on the grounds of the Lyceum in times of need?" Arrend asked.

Devon hadn't heard his advisor approach. "I hadn't thought about it much."

"As I explained before, all of the proctors from War and Mages served in the city guard or the army, most for a minimum of ten years. The only exception is if they are wounded in some manner, then they may become a proctor earlier." Arrend let that sink in before adding, "Favian served for nearly twenty before being forced here. That was ten years before your arrival."

Which placed Favian's incident at about the same time that the Crystal Cities had signed an uneasy peace treaty with Luminesque that ended nearly twenty years of hostilities. Devon wondered if the incident—in particular, the death of the councilor's daughter, Terrial—had prompted the peace treaty. Not that the antagonism had died out completely. Attacks on shipments and caravans on the wayfares, like the one that had killed Devon's father, had continued. Only within the last few years had there been incidents within cities.

Like what had apparently happened this morning.

Favian and the rest of the proctors dressed for battle took the blue and red crystals, mounting them atop wooden staffs. Horses were brought forth and the four mounted, those bearing the staffs placing them in holders in the saddles near one foot and controlling them with one hand, their free hand taking the reins. Orders were shouted down the column and without any speeches or proclamations the battle proctors led the sixth years in a march down the length of the quad, between the walls of the War and Mage practice halls, and out into the streets of Iandolo.

Arrend immediately turned to the students around him. "All right. Everyone back inside. You've seen enough."

Protests broke out but Arrend ignored them all, motioning everyone toward the stairs and entrance. Devon saw the other proctors doing the same. He shot a glance toward the mage dormitory, then tugged on Arrend's sleeve.

"I can't go back inside," he said urgently, "I need to go to the scriptorium. This interrupted my research!"

Arrend took in his disheveled clothes and hair. "It looks to me like you could use the break, perhaps get some sleep. Your eyes are practically bruised."

"I don't have time to sleep. I've only got three months left!"

Arrend waved him away. "If I find out you left the Lyceum..." he shouted at Devon's retreating back.

Devon had no intention of going into Iandolo. Or to the scriptorium.

He skirted the quad along the outer stone walkway, not wanting to draw attention to himself, then bypassed the library doors and entered the base of the Tower instead. The lower halls felt strangely empty, the majority of the proctors out on the quad. Even the acolytes were eerily absent. Devon's footsteps echoed off the marble floors as he crossed the high-ceilinged foyer and atrium toward the stairs. He didn't see Lane anywhere, began to wonder if she'd been unable to escape as he had, but as soon as he was within earshot of the steps he heard a hiss and saw movement from the shadows.

He hurried over, Lane stepping out into the atrium.

"How did you know to meet me by the stairs?"

"You aren't the only one who knows about the Tower, Devon. Now come on."

When they emerged on the roof, they found they weren't alone. Three other students were there, two from History and one from War, all fifth years.

The one from War immediately moved back from the low section where the city could be seen. Gusts of wind tousled his black hair. His arms fell to his sides, hands clenched into fists. "Did you have anything to do with this?" he asked Lane.

"Don't be stupid," Devon said, pushing past him to the wall. "We don't even know who—"

A thick column of billowing smoke rose from where the wayfare shot out from the city below onto the red-brown colors of the Flatlands toward Luminesque. Its blackness was stark against the burnished ground beneath and the cloudless deep blue of the sky above. The city between—composed of jagged rooflines and spires, open marketplaces and parks—stepped down toward the waygate and the smoke in twenty-four staggered tiers, obscuring the cliffs that dropped vertically a thousand feet beneath Level One to the true ground below, a land of uninhabitable cracked rock and dry scrub. But that height could be seen beneath the wayfare, which bridged the Flatlands at the same height as the edge of the city. At the base of the rising smoke, where the wayfare met the city, flames flickered. It was too distant for them to hear the fire, but Devon swore he felt an occasional hollow thud of sound, like a drumbeat, deep in his chest.

"Now do you see why I asked?" the fifth year War student said. "That's the waygate to Brovetto."

Devon glanced up from the smoke and fire long enough to catch the faintest glint of light where Brovetto would be on the horizon. "That doesn't mean the attack came from Brovetto."

"Are you saying that one of the other Crystal Cities—Balnis or Kerpez, perhaps—managed to sneak a large enough force through Iandolo's streets from their own waygate to cause that?"

The roof of one of the buildings near the waygate in the midst of the fire collapsed, belching thicker smoke and embers into the sky. One of the History students gasped and brought a hand to her mouth; the other's lips were pressed into a thin line. He held a board and parchment, quill moving as he recorded the events he witnessed.

A heartbeat after the collapse, Devon felt another of those drumbeats in his chest.

He thought of the streets and alleys of the lower city. "There may be more people in the lower city than above," he said, "but there are thousands upon thousands of buildings down there, most of them dead and abandoned. It's possible a force could be moved through there unnoticed, especially in smaller groups." He faced the War student. "I know. I lived there."

The student's incredulous face twisted with uncertainty.

"They could have crossed the Flatlands as well," Lane said.

"The Flatlands? Seriously? Nothing can live there. The land is poisoned."

"What about the bandits?"

The War student waved a hand in dismissal. "There are no bandits. Certainly none organized enough to do that."

Everyone turned back to the distant fires, which appeared to be spreading. More of the drumbeats thrummed in Devon's chest.

"I don't think they called the sixth years to help clean up," Lane said. "I think they're still fighting down there."

They grew quiet, watching, even the scritch of the historian's quill pausing. Devon's hand clenched into a fist as he thought of Dalton heading into that fire.

"I don't understand," he said. "I thought there was a peace treaty between Iridesque and Luminesque."

"There is," one of the History students said. "If this attack is by forces from Brovetto, then they've violated that treaty. There will be consequences."

"We'll retaliate," the War student said. "The Council won't let this affront stand."

"But why break the treaty now?" Devon asked. "Everything was stable."

"It's not as simple as that," Lane said. "Iandolo is the center of the Crystal Cities. The other cities have always harbored resentment toward us. And that resentment has only grown over the decades, because for some reason Iandolo has remained strong while the other cities have been failing."

"What do you mean failing?"

"They're falling apart, decaying—from rust and minimal upkeep, or pure negligence. From the simple fact that no one remembers how to repair half of what runs mechanically. And then the lucent is dying. Ultimately, everything is powered by the lucent. But no one knows how to repair the crystals either."

"All of that is happening here."

"Not like in the other cities. It's worse in Brovetto and Balnis, Kerpez and the rest. Towers have collapsed. Entire districts have gone dark. The citizens are getting desperate. They all know that Iandolo is better off, that most of our lucent still works, that we still have viable cisterns, that our city still functions, even if we have lost some of our technology, like the rails. It creates tension, a tension that grows every year as more and more of their own cities fall apart. They don't see that it's happening here."

"How do you know all this?" the War student asked.

"I'm a councilor's daughter, remember?"

He scowled and turned back to the fire.

Devon sidled closer to Lane. "Why is the decay in Iandolo happening at a slower rate?"

"No one knows."

"It may be because Iandolo was the founding city," one of the History students said. She hesitated when they all looked at her. She had the rounded face, slight stature, and narrow eyes of those from the Opalesque province. "After the Founders arrived, they built it first, raising it from the stone of the tell, above the wasted Flatlands. The other six cities came later. Because of that, they've never been as powerful as Iandolo. The heart of the lucent, the heart of all power, is here."

"You know about the Founders?"

The two History students shared a startled look, but the girl answered sharply, "Only what is generally known, nothing more."

Devon drew breath to pursue it, but another thud in his chest brought him back to the attack. "If the other cities are failing, why don't those from the other Provinces come here?"

"They can't," Lane answered. "The Council restricted immigration to Iandolo decades ago and it's only been tightened since. The few who manage to make it here are sent back with army escort. Those that are allowed to stay are chosen because of their abilities, either in the sciences or agriculture, or for political reasons. Besides, where would we put them? In the lower city, where nothing works? We can't let them live at mid-level or higher—we're already overcrowded. According to my mother, we're barely taking care of our own."

Devon thought about all of those people living in the lower levels, not just those immediately below mid-level that were controlled by gangs, but those even lower. They weren't being taken care of by the Council. They were barely surviving on their own.

"Technically," the second History student said, "all of the cities are supposed to be equal, according to the Founder's Pact, the agreement signed by all of the leaders of the Provinces at the time of the Founding. But it has never been so in practice. Iandolo has always dominated the Provinces. What began as a Council of Equals degraded over time—through political maneuvering, alliances, and betrayals. It's evolved into the Council we have today, where the other six provinces are merely represented by members of Iandolo's own elite."

"Like my mother, Councilor Varenov," Lane said. "She's a citizen of Iridesque, but she represents Luminesque."

The History student nodded. "None of the other six provinces have direct representation on the Council anymore."

"Is that why the Luminesque hate us so much?" Devon asked. "Why they've been attacking us so relentlessly for decades?"

"Partly," the History student said, half of his attention still on the attack below and his notes. "Note that the other Provinces haven't attacked us recently though."

"So what happened between Luminesque and Iridesque to cause this hostility?"

"Don't you know?"

"In the lower levels, we rarely take an interest in the activities of the towers and provinces. We were more concerned with finding our next meal."

The History student's eyes widened slightly at Devon's tone.

Lane interceded. "There was a coup on the Council. The Luminesque councilor was assassinated. The suspected organizer of the attack was the Iridesque representative, but nothing could be proven. In response, the Brovettan delegation withdrew from Iandolo, vowing retaliation. The Council replaced the Luminesque councilor with its own representative and Brovetto has held a grudge ever since."

"It was the first usurpation of provincial power on the Council by Iandolo, but it held with the support of the other Provinces," the History student said. "Luminesque had always been viewed as unusually aggressive and violent. The coup brought stability to the Crystal Cities…for a time."

"How long ago was this?"

"Seventy-two years."

"That long?"

"Yes. And now that, along with the economic tensions between the cities and the failing infrastructure, have brought us to this."

They all turned back to the billowing smoke below.

Devon lost track of how long they all stood, staring, as the fire spread, then halted and receded. Hours, based on the sun's arch across the sky. Occasionally, there were flashes of light, like lightning, or explosions. He caught Lane whispering beneath her breath at each one and he realized they must be the results of Sigils, ones she recognized. He also noticed the tension in her arms and hands, her knuckles white where she gripped the roof's edge.

The last of the visible fire in that area faded as the sun began to set. Trails of smoke remained but it was clear that, whoever had attacked, the army and city guard now had it under control.

The War student pushed back from the edge, cast both Devon and Lane an angry look, then departed. At some point, one of the historians had left, but the girl remained, now holding the board. She shrugged at Devon's confused look and said, "He clearly wanted to be down there with them. That's why he's angry. It had nothing to do with you."

Devon wasn't certain, but knew the History students were trained to be diplomats, to read emotional states, to be perceptive. They often picked up on vital clues others missed, so that their interpretations of events were more accurate.

"I think it's over for now. We should head down."

Lane allowed Devon to draw her toward the stairs. He paused and looked back at the History student. "Are you coming?"

She smiled, but held up the board and the papers with her scribbled notes. "I have to stay and record whatever might happen next."

Halfway down the stairs, Lane asked, "Do you think the sixth years had to fight when they got there?"

"The fighting went on long enough I think they did."

Lane's hands clenched. "I need to figure out what I'm doing wrong with the Sigils."

"I wonder if it was the Luminesque who attacked."

"If so, then my life just got infinitely harder."

"Dalton will know. We'll ask him as soon as he returns."

"If he returns."

Devon wouldn't even let himself consider that.

Neither one of them wanted to return to their dormitories, so they waited in the shadows of the School of War's practice yard. Hours passed before Devon caught sight of the blue and red glow of crystals. He nudged Lane awake as the four proctors appeared, Favian in the lead, back rigid with dignity, the sound of their horses' hooves echoing between the yard walls as they plodded forward. The sixth years trudged in behind, all of them spilling out onto the quad.

Someone must have been put on watch because a chime began to sound—not the grating of the call to war, but a softer tone. Proctors and acolytes emerged from various halls, racing forward to help the sixth years from their armor. Devon and Lane joined them.

"What happened?" Devon asked one of the War students as he helped him unlace the leathers along one side. He kept an eye out for Dalton. "Who attacked?"

The student coughed harshly, the silence they'd arrived in breaking apart as conversations escalated into shouts for the Humanities students as the proctors realized some of them were wounded. "It was the Luminesque." He spat, then winced and clutched at his side after Devon pulled the armor up over his shoulders. "They attacked the waygate first, utterly destroyed it, then began an incursion into the city. By the time we arrived, they'd already set fire to or destroyed nearly an entire sector. They pushed into three others before we managed to stop them and force them back out onto the wayfare. We would have hounded them all the way back to Brovetto, except they fled down to the Flatlands."

Devon had removed enough of the pieces of armor to see that his fellow student's entire side was bruised an ugly purple-black, even beneath the loose undershirt. "You need one of the healers."

The student tried to shrug it off, but coughed and spat again. In the light that was growing on the quad as the acolytes brought out more and more crystals, even Devon could see that the phlegm was bloody.

"Perhaps you're right," the War student said weakly.

Devon left him to work on the rest of his armor, caught Lane's gaze, verified from her grim expression that she'd heard who'd attacked, then headed off to snag one of the healers from the School of Humanities. As soon as the healer saw the bruise, she motioned to Devon.

"Help me move him to the outer hall of War's dormitory. But be careful. He's likely cracked a rib and it's caused a laceration inside somewhere." The healer carefully maneuvered the War student's arm on his wounded side up over her shoulder, leaving Devon to take the other. His gut turned just thinking about the cracked rib scraping around inside the War student's chest, but he swallowed back the queasiness and tucked himself into the sixth year's armpit.

They made it halfway to the hall before the student passed out from the pain, at which point the healer began to move faster. The interior of the dormitory was total chaos, War students shifting chairs and desks and tables out of the way so that the wounded could be laid out on the floor. Humanities proctors were directing the work, their older students already kneeling next to the wounded. Devon helped lay the unconscious sixth year on the floor, then backed away, noticing there were some wounded mages mixed in with the War students. The entire chamber reverberated with shouted orders, grunts and groans, curses and moans.

Suddenly, the enormity of what had just happened—an attack on the city, an act of war—hit him. He'd watched it happen from the roof of the Tower, but it had been distant, almost surreal. This was not. These students—students just like him—had been there, had been hurt, some perhaps even killed. And what would happen next? He couldn't imagine the Council of Iandolo not reacting. What would they do?

They'd send a force to Brovetto to retaliate, of course. Would that force include the sixth years? Perhaps even the fifth?

He began to back out of the hall, even as the healer he'd helped rolled out a cloth beside her, scalpels and needles and other tools clinking as they were revealed. She cut away the War student's undershirt and began to gently prod around the bruise.

Two healers carrying a mage bumped into him from behind as they entered the hall with a gruff, "Out of the way!" The mage's battle robe and the lower half of his face were covered in blood and his left arm was scorched and blackened.

Devon fled the hall, back onto the quad. Most of the activity had shifted into the temporary infirmary, but there were still students helping others out of their armor. None of those remaining appeared significantly wounded, which meant less than a dozen had returned harmed.

His panicked feeling eased. He drew in a few deep breaths to calm himself and began searching for Lane or Dalton in the sea of students and proctors still on the quad.

"Get your hands off him, you pale-skinned bitch!"

Devon spun in time to see Quinn grab Lane by the shoulders and throw her away from Dalton. Dalton looked startled—Lane had been helping him with his armor—but Quinn didn't notice. She stood over Lane, chest heaving, her battle robes stained with soot, strands of her hair falling across her face. With grim determination, she punched Lane in the face.

Devon charged forward, along with Arrend, Favian, and two others. Dalton struggled to his feet before anyone else arrived and grabbed Quinn, hauling her back, but she shrieked, began struggling in Dalton's grip.

"Let go of me! She's one of them! Don't you see? She was sent to the Lyceum as a spy!"

She tore out of Dalton's grasp and lunged toward Lane, but Dalton tackled her from behind, driving them both to the ground, where he held her down with his weight. "She's not a spy," he said through clenched teeth. "She's one of us!"

Arrend and Favian arrived, both of them standing between where Lane sat stunned and the other two grappled with each other. Devon came to a halt on his knees near Lane's side.

"Are you all right?" both he and Arrend said at the same time.

Favian raised both hands above his head. "Those of you who aren't wounded enough to need the healers, please head back to your rooms. The acolytes will help you with the rest of your armor. Everyone else who isn't needed in the infirmary, please head back to your dormitories. We thank you all for your help."

He didn't wait to see if everyone complied, merely crouched down next to Quinn and Dalton, speaking in a low, soothing voice. Those on the quad hesitated, then stood and dispersed. The remaining proctors helped some of them along.

Devon turned back to Lane. "Are you all right? You're bleeding."

Lane brought a hand up to her bloodied lip. "I'm fine." Her voice shook. "I just…wasn't expecting it to start this soon."

"It shouldn't start at all," Arrend said harshly. "You are a member of this community of study, as well as the daughter of a respected councilor. Your loyalty should be above question."

"Should it?" Favian stood. Quinn had calmed enough that Dalton no longer had to hold her down. "I beg to differ. Councilor Varenov's loyalties came into question the moment she returned from Brovetto bearing this child."

"Varenov's actions have nothing to do with Lane."

"They have everything to do with her! She has influenced Lane from birth, molded her into who she is today." Favian turned his focus on Lane herself. "Lane should be watched more closely, now that Brovetto has made its intentions toward Iandolo clear."

Lane's jaw set and she stood. "My mother may have raised me, but I make my own decisions. Over the past three years, how much contact have I had with her? With anyone from the upper city? Almost none. I don't need them. I can find my own path."

"Not if you don't master the Sigils."

"Enough." Arrend held up a hand to forestall any more comments. "Unless you plan to bring up specific charges against Lane, Quinn, there is nothing here to discuss."

Quinn, Devon, and Dalton all stood, Quinn never taking her eyes off of Lane. "I have no formal charges."

"Then this conversation is over."

Favian bristled, turned on Arrend, but in the end merely said, "Return to your room, Quinn. Dalton, you as well. And Lane…tread lightly."

Quinn and Favian headed across the darkened quad toward the Mage dormitory, Favian resting a hand on Quinn's shoulder, pointedly leaving Lane behind.

Dalton glanced at Lane. "I'm sorry. That shouldn't have happened."

"It's not your fault."

"No," Arrend said, "it was not your fault, Dalton. The fault lies firmly in Quinn's hands. But I'm afraid the sentiment will spread, after what I heard happened at the wayfare gate this afternoon. And it won't be just you, Lane, it will be all of those with Luminesque blood residing in Iandolo. Unfortunately, I agree with Favian's advice— tread lightly. Not only here at the Lyceum, but out in the city as well.

"Now, head to your rooms. After today, I think we all need some rest."

All three headed toward their separate dormitories. The quad was dark now except for the amber light of the shard at its center and a few scattered crystal lanterns brought out by the acolytes.

It wasn't until Devon opened the door of his room that he remembered he'd essentially destroyed it that morning. But he couldn't summon the energy to clean it up. Instead, he fell into his bed face first without even removing his clothes.

Chapter Four

Devon woke when sunlight struck his face again. He blinked in bleary-eyed confusion at the window, then shifted into a seated position.

Something clattered to the floor and he glanced down. His quill. He reached down to pick it up and realized he was still in his clothes from the day before—

And that his room was still a shambles.

He groaned and flopped back onto the bed. "I've not had enough sleep for this."

Odd noises filtered into his consciousness and he tilted his head toward the window. Standing, he picked his way through the scattered papers, shattered glass, and disheveled furniture so he could see out into the practice yards. Mages were practicing in the small section he could see from his window, but that was to be expected; they were always practicing at this hour. Maybe there were more mages in the yard than usual. He watched for a moment, then realized that the odd sounds weren't coming from the mage yard, they were coming from the quad.

If he leaned far enough out the window, he could see a portion of the quad through the trees. For a moment, he thought the mages had simply expanded their practicing to the quad, but then he realized there were War students among the mages. They were practicing together, the fifth and sixth years, formed up into groups, the mages either in the center, surrounded by the War students, or at the back, the War students in front, protecting them.

Devon listened to the clash of swords and spears and the shouts of the proctors to halt, to reset, to do it again, then ducked back inside his room and headed for the door.

The Science great hall was surprisingly empty but he discovered why as soon as he stepped outside. Most of the students were on the steps, the narrow landing in front of the building, or on the edge of the quad, watching the War and Mage students mock-battle each other. Even the dormitory's steward and a few of the black-clad acolytes stood entranced by the scene.

Devon caught Arrend, moving purposefully across the southern end of the quad. He shifted down the steps, edging toward where Arrend was headed. The two schools had taken up nearly half of the quad, the last few groups in positions near the amber shard. A small group of War and Mage proctors stood huddled there, conversing and pointing to the field, occasionally calling out new orders. The sets of twenty War students and ten Mages had been paired off against each other, one group attacking, the other defending. The War students were actively sparring with weapons or bare fists, but the Mage students appeared to be waving their hands in the air with no visible effects, unlike what Devon had seen in the sands of the practice yard from his window.

Devon positioned himself close to the War and Mage proctors a few heartbeats before Arrend arrived.

"What is the meaning of this?" the Science proctor asked, coming to a halt behind the group.

The proctors shared a look, one of them turning and heading toward the walls of the Mage practice yard. One of the proctors faced Arrend. Devon recognized him—Gallean, the War proctor assigned to the Board for his most recent challenge.

"After yesterday's call to aid the army and the city forces at the gateway, we decided the War and Mage students needed more practice."

"Using the quad? You have practice yards set aside specifically for that purpose, so your practice would not disrupt the other Schools and their studies and so the secrets of the magerium and its powers can be kept safe. Isn't that the imperative? To keep the Sigils and the mages exclusive to Iandolo? And since when do both War and Mage students practice together here at the Lyceum? I thought that was reserved for after they graduated, when they begin their service in the army or the guard."

"We decided that if our sixth years were going to be sent into the field, they should begin practicing the forms now, not simply studying them on paper."

"Who decided?"

"I did."

Everyone turned to see Favian approaching from the direction of the Mage yard, the proctor who'd left when Arrend arrived trailing behind him.

Favian halted next to Gallean. "I decided that such practice should not be forestalled and I suggested we begin immediately. After what happened at the gate, I felt it necessary we start now."

"The sixth years were only supposed to support the army at the waygate, not become actively engaged in the fighting."

"As anyone who's ever been on the battlefield knows, not everything goes as planned. The army was outmaneuvered. The sixth years found themselves caught at the edge of the most intense part of the fighting. You saw the consequences of that last night. Three of our students died in our own city streets, Arrend. Another dozen were seriously wounded, the rest battered and bruised, before the fighting shifted away from us. All because they were unprepared. You don't want to see that happen again, do you?"

"Of course not! But there has to be a better solution than training them in the quad."

"Such as? The practice yards are good for individual practice, for sparring, but they are far too small for battlefield tactics. We need the openness of the quad. We certainly can't have them practicing in the streets."

"What about the risks? Won't this reveal the Mage secrets to the other students?"

"I'm not incompetent, Arrend. The mages here on the quad have been instructed not to complete their Sigils. They are to do the basic form only."

Arrend glanced around at the rest of the proctors present, all of whom stood behind Favian and Gallean. "And all of you agreed to this?"

"Gallean and I are the Masters of our Schools," Favian said. "Agreement wasn't required, although there were no protests when I presented the idea to my fellow proctors."

"As for the School of War," Gallean said, "it was decided that the benefits of active practice with the Mage students far outweighed the risks of exposing our most basic tactics. Of course, we have less at risk than the mages."

"And none of you felt the need to consult with any of the other Schools?"

A few of the proctors fidgeted or glanced down at the grass, but no one spoke up.

Arrend turned back to Favian. "Continue for now. But we will discuss this further, with proctors from all of the schools present."

He stalked across the quad toward the proctors' hall, then abruptly changed direction when he saw one of the Merchant proctors. Favian watched with cold contempt until Gallean stirred.

"Should we continue?" Gallean asked.

"Most definitely."

"What about the mages? You were going to have them start completing their Sigils this afternoon, so the War students could get used to coordinating with their attacks."

"We'd better postpone that, until Arrend gets this worked out of his system. No need to escalate matters right now."

"My thoughts exactly."

The mock battles had ground to a halt while Arrend confronted Favian, but Gallean ordered everyone back to work. The students from the various schools who had been watching began to disperse with an audible sigh of disappointment. Devon contemplated returning to his room and his research, but the thought of cleaning up the mess and then facing yet another day beating his head against the stone walls kept him rooted to the grass of the quad.

At first, he analyzed the fighting formations, their structure and the benefits and flaws. All of them appeared to be based solely on protecting the mages from any sort of attack, mostly at the expense of the War students. Lane had told him that it took time for the mages to form their Sigils and that the War students were trained to give them that time, no matter the costs. He wondered how the attacks changed when the mages actually completed their spells, rather than cutting them short as they were doing now.

Bored with the formations, he began watching the mages instead, picking out Quinn, his thoughts dark as he replayed what had happened the night before between her and Lane. But the initial surge of emotion cooled and he found himself studying her form. Even though she wasn't allowed to complete the Sigils, she still fought with a particular intensity, more so than the other mages. Her mouth was pressed into a thin line, her brow creased in concentration. Her hand crooked into the mage form automatically, the Sigils—well, part of the Sigils—drawn in a smooth, fluid motion, nearly all of it in the wrist, her arm barely moving. Her body shifted with the rest of the unit, although the longer he watched the more he noticed that the mages tried to remain in one place. Movement tended to distract them. On rare occasions, Quinn herself would adjust to the War students' motions and lose track of her Sigil. She'd shake her head, fist clenched, mouth moving in what Devon assumed was a curse, then crook her hand and start over. Loss of the Sigil happened more often with the other mages. Devon could see how she'd risen in the ranks of the sixth years.

Feeling slightly traitorous to Lane, he shoved Quinn from his mind and focused on the other mages, letting his mind drift. His hands picked idly at the grass as the training continued, the rest of the school slipping back into its natural rhythms, the younger students rushing from the dormitories to the lecture halls in the southern part of the quad, the older students meandering around contemplating their own studies. Devon found himself slipping into the motions of the mages hands as they drew, some of them smoother than others. But they all had the same basic beginning—bottom, swipe up to a point on top, then swing around to the front, back, left, and right. After that, either the mage halted abruptly, as if their motion had been severed, or they started a new pattern inside the old, one that jolted to a halt just as abruptly later on. It was as if each Sigil had to start from the same basic form, or—

"Or the mages have to set up a framework before they can begin the true Sigil itself."

His entire body vibrated with the sudden thought, with the inherent correctness of it.

He bit his lower lip in doubt. After all, he'd thought he'd seen a pattern in his work for the past month and it had all led to nothing but frustration and a trashed room. So he sat back, closed his eyes, cleared his mind, and then began watching the mages again.

Ten minutes later, he scrambled to his feet and bolted back to his room. Slamming open the door, he swore and dove into the papers scattered underfoot, trying to find the few pages that were blank and his board. He grabbed his quill, yanked a drawer open to get a new bottle of ink, then bolted back down to the quad.

Throwing everything down on the ground near the makeshift practice field, he twisted the cork from the ink bottle and began sketching the mage's gestures. He didn't know what was important yet—if any of it was—so he started with the crooked hand they all made, then worked forward from there, trying to capture the nuances of each motion. He wasn't an artist, so the sketches were crude, but detailed enough he'd remember what the motions were later. After each sketch, he jotted down notes about differences between one mage and the next, even though the shape was generally the same. Then he made note of what a mage had done when they dropped the pattern in disgust and started again.

After a while, some of the proctors began taking notice of him. When one or two of them began to speak, gesturing in his direction, he stoppered the ink and collected his pages, heading back to his rooms.

Once there, he laid his sketches out across his desk in order, scanning from one to the next.

There was definitely something there. He could feel it.

Rubbing his temple, he looked around the room and sighed. It was too late to save the ink stain on the wall—that would be permanent—but he began cleaning up the shattered glass and scattered papers. He needed to think anyway. The basic form the mages were using was simply the beginning. He'd need to start there, determine what it was his mind told him he was seeing. But the true Sigil was what came after the form.

The last thing he did to straighten his room was to position the chair. But instead of setting it up in front of his desk, he put it in front of the window.

So he could see into the far corner of the mage's training ground.

* * *

The Shandy Quad had recovered from the brawl and aside from some newer stools didn't look much different than before. Arch stood behind the bar, polishing glasses. Nic served up drinks. The usual slew of patrons were spread around the tables.

Including Dalton.

Devon headed toward the bar and settled into the seat next to the War student. "You look terrible."

Dalton raised his head. "You have no idea."

"But I do. I've watched them drilling you and the mages on the quad the last few weeks."

Dalton sat back and scrubbed his face with his hands. "They're relentless. At first it was interesting working with the mages, even fun. But now it's just work. I feel like we've entered our service four months too soon. And then there are the nightmares. I haven't slept well since we were taken down to the gates."

"It was that bad?"

"It was…not what I was expecting. You'd think we'd have a clear advantage, since we're the only city with mages, but down there in the lower city, where the streets are a maze and with the confusion of the smoke and the fires…it was disorienting. It felt like the Luminesque were attacking from everywhere at once, even though they weren't. Our mages didn't know where to strike. Then something happened and we found ourselves right in the middle of real fighting. They hit us hard. And they were so vicious. Worse than the proctors led us to believe. I saw someone impaled right before me. Another had his arm hacked off. Just…brutal." He shook his head and took a long pull of his drink. Some kind of ale. Of course. All the War students drank ale.

Devon flicked a finger toward Nic, who nodded and began making him his usual. When he turned back, Dalton was regarding him with narrow eyes. "Where have you been? I haven't seen you here since the attack."

"In my room. Research."

Dalton cocked an eyebrow in disbelief.

"Seriously. I have to pass the next challenge. I can't go back to the lower levels, not the way I left things with the gang there. I don't know what they'll do to me. But I think I've figured something out. I've been working on it nonstop for the last few days. When I came out to head here, I was surprised it was already the ninth hour and getting dark."

"Your School is certainly different than mine. I don't think I've ever spent more than an hour a day in my room, aside from sleeping." He finished his ale and set the empty glass on the bar with a sharp sound. "Or at least attempting to sleep."

"Another?" Arch said, coming up to take the glass.

"I shouldn't, but hit me. It's not like I'd sleep if I left right now anyway."

Nic brought Devon's drink and they clinked glasses and took a healthy swallow.

"What made you leave your rooms now?" Dalton asked.

"I need some help. I came here hoping to find Lane."

The ambient noise of conversation in the bar suddenly fell silent. Devon and Dalton felt the change at the same time, glancing over their shoulders. Devon thought he'd spoken too loudly, that it was reaction to him mentioning Lane, but it was Lane herself.

She'd entered the bar.

He'd noticed a weird tension on the streets of the city on the walk over here, a strange vibration, as if the air were quivering. It reeked of fear, thrummed with anxiety. Everyone appeared drawn into themselves, shoulders hunched, wary. They shot glances over their shoulders and moved a little more quickly from place to place. The uneasiness was heightened by the additional city guards on patrol. They hadn't been doubled, but there were more of them and they were making their presence obvious. Instead of feeling safer, it was keeping everyone on edge. If they'd left the patrols alone, perhaps the city would have relaxed a little by now. When he'd entered the bar, that tension had sloughed off his shoulders, as if it were a haven from the outside world.

Now it had invaded the small, darkened space.

Lane glared around at the tables, then strode purposefully to the bar. She didn't notice Devon or Dalton, taking a seat by herself.

As soon as she sat down someone stood, their chair scraping across the floor, loud in the silence. A dozen others followed suit. Without speaking, they all departed, leaving only a half dozen people behind. A few of those remaining looked toward Lane with pity; most kept their eyes averted, as if Lane didn't exist. One of them was the History student they'd spoken to at the Tower while watching the fighting at the waygate.

"Bastards," Arch said, watching the door close. "Good riddance. I don't want judgmental racists in my establishment anyway."

"They were all students," Devon said.

"That doesn't mean anything. The entire city is like that right now. Those of Luminesque blood are finding it hard to walk alone on the streets. Even those who've lived here their entire lives."

"It may mean something to her," Dalton said, tilting his head toward Lane.

Devon slapped Dalton's shoulder. "Let's join her."

Lane glanced up with a grateful smile as they settled in around her. Arch poured a drink without taking her order and set it down in front of her. Devon was shocked at the lines of strain around her eyes and mouth; they made her look drawn and wasted.

"Ignore them," he said in dismissal, nudging her drink toward her hand as he lifted his own. "They aren't worth the stress and anxiety. They're less than filth."

"You haven't been living with them for the past two weeks." She downed most of the drink in one swallow, Arch's eyebrows rising in surprise as she wiped her mouth with the back of her hand. He turned to make her another without a word.

"Has it really been that bad?"

Lane gave him a look, but Dalton caught her attention. "He's been in his room since the attack. Researching. He doesn't know."

"All right! Fine. I've been out of touch. What else have I missed?"

"At the Lyceum? Not much. The proctors for War and Mages have increased our training, even for the third and fourth years. Your advisor, Arrend, brought our use of the quad before the entire assembly of proctors, but in the end Favian's plea for tolerance won everyone over and so the training continues. There's talk about us going straight into service after the graduation ceremony, rather than giving us two months off as usual, but that decision will likely come from the Council, not the proctors."

"And what has the Council done since the attack?"

"Nothing," Arch answered, handing Lane her second drink. "They're like dead crystal. Aside from adding to the patrols on the street, the Council hasn't called the army up to retaliate or issued a proclamation of outrage with a call for reparation demands. It's been absolutely silent, except for the sudden halt to all immigration into the city. No one from any of the other six Crystal Cities is allowed into Iandolo except for official Council business—no traders, caravans… no one. The waygates are closed to outsiders. Rumor has it that the Council is planning something big, a major assault on Brovetto itself. Their attack on our wayfare gate was unprovoked, after all. Thank the shards we were able to beat them back."

Dalton shifted uncomfortably in his seat, eyes lowered. Even Arch picked up on it.

"What?" he asked, setting both hands on the bar. "What did I say?"

"I—" Dalton halted and glanced around the bar, then leaned in a little closer, even though no one left was within hearing range except for Nic. "Everyone's been saying that the army and the city guard halted the attack and pushed the Luminesque from the city...but I don't think that's what happened."

"What do you mean?"

"I mean, we didn't push them out. They pulled out on their own."

Lane shook her head in confusion. "That's not how it looked from the Tower. After you left, the fires spread, much farther than they would have on their own, especially with the army and its mages there to help suppress them."

"No, I'm not saying they retreated immediately—" Dalton sighed in frustration, then started over. "When we first got down there, they were pushing hard. We lost ground, even with the mages there. But then something changed. Just before our group got caught in the main part of the fighting, the Luminesque forces halted and held."

"Because our own army stopped them."

"We hadn't been able to stop them before that."

"So what do you think happened?" Lane asked.

Dalton took a long pull of his drink, then set it aside and looked them all in the eyes. "It felt like they'd accomplished what they'd set out to do. And so they left."

"But they didn't do anything," Devon pointed out. "They just destroyed the gates and set fire to a few districts."

"I know. But I was there. We didn't push them out, they retreated on their own."

It didn't make sense. Devon hadn't been down as far as the gates while he was part of Carbolen's crew, but he couldn't think of anything the Luminesque army would be interested in down there. As Dalton said, it was a labyrinth of streets and alleys and buildings, most of them with dead crystals, their halls darkened, nearly all of them abandoned.

"Whatever happened," Arch said, breaking the awkward silence, "the Council needs to take some kind of action soon. The people of Iandolo may be stunned for now, but that will wear off. They'll demand the Council do something. And if they don't, it will get ugly."

More customers arrived—either not noticing Lane or not caring—and Arch moved down to help them. Dalton finished his drink and pushed himself away from the bar.

"Maybe I was wrong," he said. "I'm certain the Council has more information about what happened than I do." He placed a hand on Lane's shoulder. "If anyone at the Lyceum threatens you or hurts you, let me know. What they're doing to you is wrong. Those of us in War can take care of it."

"Thank you. But some of those who left tonight were from War."

"I know. Not all of us are like that though."

He left, only weaving a little bit as he made his way to the door. Devon watched him until the door closed, then turned back to catch Lane staring at him.

"What?"

"Shards, Devon, you like him!"

Devon fought back the blush, grabbing his drink. "Is it that obvious?"

"To me anyway." She glanced back toward the door in consideration. "He does have a nice body. Broad, muscular, tall, those dark eyes framed by dark eyebrows—"

"Stop it!"

She grinned and swung back to the bar. "You could do worse."

Devon was glad to see the grin, even if his cheeks still burned. "It would never work."

"Why not?"

"He's in War, I'm in Science. In another few months, he'll graduate, have a few months off, and then he'll be either a city guard or part of the army. I'll either be a proctor here at the Lyceum or...or I'll have failed and will be back to my old haunts in the lower city trying to keep myself alive. We'll be worlds apart."

"You'd still have those few months together."

"I don't think he's even noticed me. Not like that."

"You haven't really done anything to make it clear either."

Devon didn't answer.

Lane swirled her fingers in the rings of condensation their drinks had left on the bar. "I'll probably be back in my mother's ward by then, learning to be an assistant or clerk, safe and protected. She's probably already got my rooms readied. I'm surprised she hasn't sent bodyguards to bring me back after the attack on the gates."

"She could do that?"

"Of course she can. She's a Councilor. I wouldn't have a say in the matter."

Devon considered this. In the lower city, he'd always been free to do whatever he wanted, even as part of Carbolen's crew, within reason. Perhaps Lane's depiction of her previous life as a prison was more accurate than he'd originally thought.

It reminded him of why he'd come to Shandy Quad in the first place. He leaned slightly forward, noting they were still relatively isolated at this end of the bar, even Arch and Nic removed from them for the moment.

"You're still having problems with the Sigils?"

Lane stilled. "Yes. Why do you ask?"

"I may be able to help you with that."

"But?"

"But I'd need your help with something I'm working on in return."

Her fingers began to trail distractedly along the bar again. "What are you working on?"

He leaned in closer, back to the rest of the bar. "I've been working on the Sigils."

Lane's eyes went wide. "You're doing what? You aren't a mage! How can you—"

"Quiet," Devon muttered, though she'd already cut herself off. No one appeared to have taken any notice of them.

"Of course," she said to herself. "You've been watching the mages practicing in the quad." She pinned him with a look. "But that's only the base form. The mages there aren't working with the secondary forms. They haven't been allowed, because they're supposed to be kept secret, practiced only in the yard or used only in the field. We can't have the other cities learning how to produce mages. It would eliminate our most significant advantage over them."

Lane's voice hardened toward the end, changed timber, enough that Devon suspected he was hearing something her mother had recited to her over the years. It certainly sounded political. Or perhaps it was something her proctors had said.

"I learned the base form from those on the quad, yes. I learned some of the secondary forms from the mage practice yard. I can see a corner of it from my dormitory room."

She laughed. "Of course you can." Setting both elbows on the bar, she pressed her eyes into the palms of her hands, still chuckling. "So how do you think you can help me? I can't even complete the base form correctly."

"I think it's because they're making it too complicated. It shouldn't be that hard. Based on what I've seen, they're adding in flourishes and gestures that aren't necessary. But I can't test the theory—"

"Because you aren't a mage."

"Whatever it is that allows you to do what mages do, I don't have it. I've tried."

Lane remained quiet, long enough for Devon to start getting nervous, but then she dropped her hands. "Why not? I'm curious to see what you think you've found. If it helps me out, so much the better. How do you want to do this? Should I come to your room?"

"No! That would be…awkward."

"Then what? We can't meet in my room. The Mage's dorm is closed to all but mages. And we can't practice in the Mage's yard, where this should be done. So where?"

"I know a few places we can go in the lower city. Meet here tomorrow at the ninth hour—everyone knows we often come here around that time. We can leave from here."

Lane didn't seem thrilled about heading into the lower city, but she nodded. "We'll meet here then, ninth hour."

Chapter Five

When Devon arrived at the Shandy Quad shortly after nine bells, Lane hadn't arrived yet. He noticed an open seat at the bar and settled in with a nod toward Arch for a drink.

"Interesting what your War student friend had to say yesterday about the attack on the waygate."

Devon stilled and turned to see who sat next to him: the History student from Opalesque, the one who'd been on the Tower.

She smiled.

"You couldn't have overheard us," Devon said. "You were too far away."

"I have sharp hearing. Also, History students are trained to read lips." Arch arrived and set down Devon's drink before moving on. "Do you think it's true, what your friend said?"

"I don't know. I'm a Science student."

"Hmm. It makes one think though, doesn't it? If true, what were the Luminesque after?"

Devon looked away, took a swallow of his drink. Her questions made him uncomfortable. He didn't want to get Dalton in trouble. "You mentioned the Founders on the Tower. Do you know much about them?"

Now she looked uncomfortable. "As I said that night, only what is generally known, nothing more."

"I don't believe that. You're a History student. You have access to the histories in the scriptorium."

She gave a curt laugh. "Selective access, yes. We're likely more restricted than you are in the Sciences." She glanced sidelong at him. "But there are some texts we can read about the Founders."

"What do they say? Who were they? Where did they come from? Where did they go?"

She met his gaze, held it, long enough he thought she wouldn't answer. But then:

"They don't say where the Founders came from, only that they came. That they descended from the stars. That when they arrived here, they were trapped and alone. That something had gone catastrophically wrong and they were forced here. That they built the Crystal Cities in order to survive and that the lucent, the crystals, is something they found here and they made use of."

"Then why did they leave?"

"They didn't." She leaned in closer. "We are the Founders. We are their descendants."

Around them, the bar went mostly quiet. At first, Devon thought it was because of what she'd said, but then he noticed Lane had arrived.

"Your mage friend is here. Time for me to go." The History student slid from her stool.

"Wait! I don't even know your name."

She hesitated, then smiled again. "It's Jillian. Don't worry. I won't tell anyone what your War friend said."

Jillian passed Lane, who'd spotted him and had moved to join him. A number of the patrons left, but not as many as the day before. Lane didn't notice.

"Sorry I'm late." She dropped herself down into the seat next to Devon. "The proctors kept us after today. Extra time in the practice yard."

Devon stared after the History student, then shook himself and focused on Lane. "I was beginning to wonder if you'd decided not to come."

"You're going to help me learn the forms, right? Why would I pass that up? Nothing the proctors are doing is working."

Devon tapped the satchel tucked to his side. "I've got my notes right here. Among other things."

"Did you want a drink?" Arch asked Lane.

"No. We've already lost an hour. We should get to work."

Devon chugged the last of his drink and shoved the empty glass toward Arch. "Thanks."

They both stood, but Arch said, "You're going into the lower city like that?"

"Of course not. I have cloaks in my satchel, along with knives."

"Hooded?" He motioned toward Lane's face. "No one with Luminesque blood should be in the lower city right now."

"Yes, hooded."

He set his bar cloth down. "Come into the back room with me. Let me see."

He signaled to Nic to take over, then motioned them around the bar. Unlike last time, during the brawl, they weren't jacked on adrenalin, itching to get out, so had a chance to look around. The large room was stocked with glasses of various sizes, boxes of ales, bottles of alcohol from across the Crystal Cities, even some containers of fruit for garnishes. A small counter stood next to two large sinks, the smell of soap strong.

Against one wall, crates were stacked almost as high as Devon was tall. He didn't remember those being here the night of the brawl. They were unmarked and the wood used in their construction was old, marred with scrapes and stained with grime, as if from heavy use.

He'd shifted closer for a better look when Arch cleared his throat, eyebrows raised. "The cloaks?"

Devon pulled the two hooded cloaks from his satchel, the material a heavy dark gray. He handed one to Lane. "I grew up in the lower city, farther down than I expect to go tonight. Is this inspection really necessary?"

"Better to be cautious. You haven't been down there much in the last six years. It's worse off than you'd expect. And not just for the pale-skinned."

Devon pulled the cloak across his shoulders, let it settle as he secured it around his neck. Lane already had hers on, but Arch stepped forward and tugged her hood up and over her head. "That should work, but I'd keep your head lowered as much as you can."

"Shards, Arch."

"Let me see your blades."

Devon pulled out two basic knives, the blades about four inches long. He gave one to Lane, who said, "What am I supposed to do with this?"

"Just keep it. You never know when you may need it."

Arch gestured for Devon's knife, tested its weight, grunted in approval, then handed it back. He placed a hand on Devon's shoulder. "Protect her. She doesn't know what it's like down there."

He nudged them toward the outer door, shoved them out into the back alley, and closed up behind them.

"That was a little...odd," Devon said.

"Is it really that bad down there? Maybe we should find someplace else."

"No. I'm sure he's exaggerating. I know the lower city. We aren't going that deep."

Overhead, through the tangled walkways and buildings higher up, the sky brightened with a flash of far-off lightning. The Shandy Quad was situated closer to the hub than the Lyceum, which meant there was little sky overhead because of the surrounding buildings, but there was enough they could see storm clouds rolling in from the northeast, the stars vanishing as they raced toward them.

"We may need the cloaks for the rain though. Come on."

They pushed out into the city, moving swiftly, but not fast enough to draw undue attention. It was late, most of the streets empty, only the main thoroughfares with any citizens roaming about. The incoming storm had obviously driven even more inside. But there were patrols of city guards at every major intersection, seen in the night-dampened glow of the lucent. The closer they came to the center of the city, the less sky was visible and the more the buildings closed in on the street, until they couldn't see the sky at all and the street had become more like an exceptionally wide corridor. Lane drew closer to Devon, until she nearly trod upon his heels, but he said nothing. She came from the towers; the streets here near the hub had to feel claustrophobic to her.

They reached a platform of stone steps leading both up and down next to a wide shaft with a drop that reached all the way to the bottom of Iandolo. Over the years, some of the levels had built across it, so that if you fell over the edge now, you'd die hitting a platform or walkway five or ten levels down, rather than when you hit ground level. Four guardsmen eyed them as they began to descend, but Devon ignored them. He hadn't pulled his hood up. He was grateful

Lane didn't do anything obviously suspicious, like tug on the edges of her hood to keep her face hidden.

Devon halted three levels down. There were no guardsmen here—the lower you moved, the more sporadic the guardsmen became—and the streets were even emptier than above. Thunder rumbled, still distant, as he took them through a twisted set of back alleys around buildings covered with a thin layer of dirt and grime. Most of the lucent was still lit. Some of the War students ventured into the lower city, but few came more than a couple levels down. No one should recognize them here.

Yet he realized Arch had been correct: the streets were more dangerous now than before. His hand dropped to the knife as they passed doorways and niches cloaked in shadow and his skin prickled with the age-old warning that they were being observed. He hadn't relied on those ingrained instincts since entering the Lyceum, but they returned without prompting. He'd intended to go farther from the hub, but he changed his mind, circling the hub instead. All they needed was an empty building with enough space to begin testing his theories.

"Shouldn't we head outwards?" Lane asked as he again chose a street that kept them hubwards.

"There will be fewer people closer to the hub. Also, I think we're being followed."

Lane glanced behind them and edged even closer to Devon. They passed a few shops, one or two still open, and a dozen people, all in groups of two or three. Most kept their heads down, eyes averted. He counted at least that many watching from alcoves and windows, keeping themselves hidden. He didn't catch sight of whoever was following them. When they passed a building Devon knew used to be empty, he slowed, scanned the street for watchers, then ducked inside the half-open door, dragging Lane with him. He closed the door behind him.

The interior hallways were dark, the lucent in most of the building dead. Thunder growled again as he dug in his satchel and pulled out the crystal lamp he used for his studies, tapping one of its faces to bring it to life. Its soft green light fell across what had once been a grand foyer, rounded stairs climbing up from the tiled mosaic floor to the second and third level in a wide arc. A glass chandelier had once hung in the center of the foyer, but all that remained was a shaft of dead lucent jutting down from the ceiling and the shattered tiles where it had struck when it had fallen. The metal and glass had long since been stolen. The mosaic was covered in a layer of dust and debris and rat shit, the wooden doorways leading into the main hall on the first floor missing, also likely stolen. It had been an apartment complex, but now the windows were boarded up and the corners were full of debris. The interior had been ransacked ages ago, nothing of value left.

Lane drew breath to speak, but Devon halted her. He leaned in close to her ear. "Move to the far side of the door."

Devon set the lantern down in the middle of the floor, then shifted to stand back against the wall, door to his right. He held his knife ready. Lane's eyes were wide, her own knife drawn.

The door opened.

Devon snaked an arm around the intruder's neck, knife already at the man's throat. "Don't move."

The intruder's hands clamped down hard on the arm around his throat, but his body went still.

"It's me! Nic! From the Quad!"

Devon angled Nic into the light, then released him. "Why were you following us?"

"Arch sent me. He thought you could use the protection. He was wrong. You nearly lost me twice on the way here and could have killed me just now."

"I used to live down here."

"So Arch said. You haven't forgotten anything, it appears."

Lane shifted out from behind the open door. Her hands were trembling. "Now what? Should we return to the Quad?"

"No." Devon closed the door, then considered Nic. "You can keep watch while we work. I don't think anyone's here, but I should check before we go any further. Nic, stay with Lane."

He slunk toward the main hallway, keeping close to the wall, eyeing the stairs above. Nothing moved overhead. As he entered the corridor, he paused to let his vision adjust to the darkness. Multiple doors opened to either side, most of them missing or open. He entered each apartment, checked the inner rooms, then moved on. It went swiftly, the rooms empty.

When he returned to the foyer, he found Nic guarding the door, Lane crouched to one side. "Empty. Let's check upstairs."

He and Nic left Lane on the stairwell with the lantern as they investigated the second and third floors, but like the first, the apartments were stripped bare and empty. Taking the lamp from Lane, he led her and Nic to one of the back apartments. Setting the lamp down on the floor near the door, he moved to the far wall of the apartment's main room, where threads of lucent wove through the wood and stone.

"We can practice in here," he said, as he felt along the wall, counting threads of lucent.

"Why here?" Lane asked. "Why not any of the other apartmen—"

She cut off as one of the lucent threads abruptly came to life, branching upwards along the wall from a thick base, spreading out like a tree. Parts of it ran along the ceiling, all of it glowing a deep purple, filling the room with subdued light.

"Because some of the lucent still works here," Devon said. "Not many know that. The rest of the building is dead, which is why it's still abandoned." He faced Nic. "Can I trust you to keep this secret?"

"Why would he need to keep it secret?" Lane asked.

"Because working lucent is worth a lot of bright down here," Nic answered. "I won't tell anyone about the lucent or this room. Not even Arch."

Devon hesitated, still uncertain, but then strode to the center of the room, tossed down his satchel, removed his cloak—Lane doing the same—and pulled out his notes. Riffling through the pages, he picked out a particular set and spread them out on the floor.

"These are the pages dealing with the base pattern as I saw it being used by the mages on the quad. The form moves from here to here."

Lane knelt down next to him, scanning them with a slight frown. Nic settled into a position near the door, so he could look out into the hall and the stairs beyond, although still close enough to see what they were doing.

After a moment, Lane leaned back. "Yes, that's the base form, the one I've been struggling with."

"I think it's because they're making it too complicated." He set out another barrage of pages. "These are all variations I noticed the sixth- and fifth-year mages using. All of them appear to work in exactly the same way, but there are differences in the flourishes they use. If you take into account where the motions vary and eliminate those parts, you can distill the base form down to these six points—bottom, top, front, back, left, and right. I'm calling the six points nadir, apex, primary, secondary, tertiary, and quaternary."

"Why? Why not just call them bottom, top, and so forth?"

"Because it might get confusing once you go beyond the base form into the secondary forms. But don't worry about that right now. You need to learn the base form to get anywhere. My theory is you don't need any of the flourishes in order to initiate the base form. All you're trying to do is establish a field in which to work the secondary form. In essence, you're setting up a diamond-shaped boundary, and the secondary form is dependent on that boundary. If you screw up the boundary, nothing will work, no matter how precise you are with the secondary form.

"What I want you to try to do is establish the base form as you've been taught by the other mages. Maybe I can see where you're deviating from these six essential points."

"You're assuming that you're correct, that there really are only six points to the base form."

"I know. But we'll test that theory as we go."

Lane's shoulders hunched in indecision. She looked over Devon's notes, then sighed and stood, stepping back a few paces to give herself some room.

"You realize I'm not supposed to be revealing any of this to you, right? The School of Mages is very strict about keeping its secrets."

"We aren't working with anything they haven't revealed by practicing on the quad."

Appeased, she straightened, her hand crooking into the form Devon had become intimately familiar with over the past few weeks. She closed her eyes a moment, then opened them and began gesturing, starting with a jab down to the nadir, then a sweep up to the apex. Her hand dropped, then slid to the primary, secondary, tertiary, and quaternary positions, but when she finished she let her hand fall to her side.

"It didn't work. When I start, I can feel something beginning to build inside my chest," she laid a hand over her breastbone, "right here. A warm, tingling sensation. But about halfway through my form that starts to fade. That's how I know it isn't working, that I've done something wrong."

Devon thought he knew what was going wrong, but he said, "Do it again. Tell me when that tingling sensation begins to die off."

Lane repeated her form—nadir, apex, drop, then slide to the primary. "Here's where it begins to fade. By the end, I don't feel anything." She said it bitterly, the wistfulness when she'd first described the sensation gone.

Thunder rumbled, the sound muted by how close they were to the hub. All three of them looked up. The storm must be right overhead for them to hear it at all, this deep. Or it was particularly violent.

Devon turned back to Lane.

"I think the problem is when you drop from the apex, before you move to the primary. Your hand comes to a halt. I think that halt is acting like an additional point, one you don't need for the base form. Do it again, but go slower this time."

As Lane steadied herself, Devon stood and shifted forward. He watched her hand intently. As soon as she dropped from the apex and began to slide to the primary, he said, "There. Right there. You see? You come to a halt—a small one, but still a halt—as you begin to move toward the primary."

"I didn't feel anything that time at all. But the proctors harp on us about going too slow or too fast. The timing has to be just right."

"Interesting. Maybe that's why there are so many extraneous flourishes when they do it, so the timing is right."

"You still don't know if your theory is correct."

"Try it again, but this time, don't drop before you move to the primary position."

She rolled her eyes, but started the form again. The first few attempts, she immediately began the drop, cutting herself off with a growl. It was obvious she'd practiced with the drop, the motion already ingrained. Devon opened his mouth to give her a suggestion, but her look cut him off. He moved back to his notes.

She started again.

This time, instead of starting the drop, she swirled from the apex around to the primary in a smooth arc, continuing on to finish the form.

"Did it work?" Devon asked.

"No. But it was too slow. I need to speed it up."

She practiced it slowly a few more times, then began increasing the pace, swirling down from the apex through to the primary and secondary and the rest. She repeated it multiple times, then swore in frustration.

"What's happening?"

"Something else is wrong. It's not the speed—they drill us with a little mantra to give us the correct timing. The new form fits the mantra, and the tingling builds a little longer than before, but it still fades after I've passed the primary."

Devon sat down, notes spread before him. "Keep trying. Let me think."

"But if it isn't working—"

"Isn't that what you've been doing for months now? Practicing a form that wasn't working?"

Her mouth clamped shut, her body bristling. But she began the form again, jabbing the nadir and apex with perhaps more emphasis than before.

Devon rested his head in his hands, elbows on his knees. His gaze flicked from one page of notes to the next, at the forms he'd seen on the quad. He knew the six points created the base form. He knew it. So why wasn't it working? Of course, he hadn't known about the timing issue; that was new. He didn't see how it affected his general theory though. It did explain the flourishes. It gave the mage's hand something to do between base points. Otherwise, they'd likely just let their hand relax, like Lane had done with her drop, and that would—

He cried out, jolting upright. "I know what's wrong. It's your sweep from the apex to the primary." He motioned Lane to continue her form. "Let me show you."

"But we just adjusted that. And it seems to work."

"The problem is that you continue the sweep from the primary to the secondary, uninterrupted. You need to halt at the primary and change the motion. Then halt at the secondary and change it again. There needs to be an abrupt change in direction after each base point. That's what establishes it as a point of reference."

Lane's eyes widened in understanding. "Show me."

Devon took position next to Lane, tentatively tracing out a new pattern. It was harder than it looked. After a few passes, Lane began to mimic his motions. Their first few attempts didn't work, the gestures too smooth around one or two of the key points, but after a while they came up with a pattern that flowed, almost natural.

They began working that form, speeding it up. Their motions began to sync, hand and arm movements, even their breaths. Devon relaxed. A strange calm enveloped him, the connection between them strengthening. Sweat broke out on Lane's forehead, but after a while her eyes began to widen. Her gestures became more emphatic and her breathing quickened, Devon's doing the same, as if they were inextricably linked.

Then, suddenly, Lane sucked in a deep breath and held it, her hand trembling in the air before her. Devon trembled as well, his heart thudding in his chest with exhilaration. They both exhaled explosively and with a slight wrench Devon felt the connection between them break.

"It worked. My entire body is tingling, as if—as if energy is coursing through me. And I can see it." With her free hand, Lane reached toward something in the air before her. "It's a diamond, the six points glowing a harsh white, with pale blue lines connecting them. It's just…hovering there."

"A pyramid stacked on top of another upside-down pyramid, right? Base to base?"

"Yes."

"Congratulations. That's your base form. Everything else you do must happen inside that diamond."

"But how? I don't understand. They won't teach you anything more until you can create the base form. I don't know what to do now."

"Based on what the mages have done on the quad, you don't need to do anything, just let it go."

Lane let her hand drop. "It's…it's dissipating." Her obvious pain at letting it go twisted in Devon's gut.

"You can bring it back."

She faced him. "Did you see it?"

"I didn't see anything."

Lane turned to Nic. "You?"

"Nothing."

Devon hated her disappointment. "I felt something. When we were doing the forms, it felt like we were connected somehow. The more we practiced together, the stronger the connection became."

"I felt it, too. Some of the other mages—the fourth years and above—have mentioned it. That's how they're taught some of the more advanced and dangerous forms. They work with one of the proctors, form this connection, and then the proctor shows them the advanced form, the student's motions tied to the proctor's. It's called a bond. It keeps them from accidentally blowing up the school by getting the form wrong during training."

"Why don't they use it on third years, like you, to help you learn the basic form?"

"They could. But part of the test for third years is to be able to learn the basic form—and other third year secondary forms—without such help."

"Even if a student is struggling?"

"Especially then. Passing the third year is crucial."

"That seems...wasteful."

"The School of Mages is obsessed with control. And they only want the best mages. If you can't learn the basic forms on your own, then you don't deserve to be there."

Nic stirred. "It sounds like your challenge, Devon. Don't you have to present something you discovered all on your own?"

"Yes. But that's during our sixth year."

"We don't have a challenge like that in the sixth year," Lane said. "Instead, we have to prove we can control the forms during a mock battle on the practice field. They bring in mages and soldiers from the army to act as our opponents."

"You don't have to create something completely new? A form or defense or something?"

"Research is left up to the proctors."

"That hardly seems fair." Devon began collecting his notes.

"Why are you packing up?" Nic asked. "Are we leaving already?"

"Shouldn't we try something else?" Lane protested. "There must be something else we can do."

"Isn't this supposed to be part of your next challenge?" Nic added. "You don't have much time left."

Devon hesitated. The excursion into the lower levels had reminded him forcibly of where he'd come from, of what he could look forward to if he failed this last challenge. He needed to solidify his thoughts about the mage forms, test some theories. If Nic was willing to keep up his watch and Lane was willing to continue working...

"I have some ideas," he said, "but you need to practice that base form until you can do it without thought. Why don't you work on that while I see if there's something in my notes that's simple and easy to try as a secondary form."

Lane had already crooked her fingers.

Chapter Six

"Try shifting the third point in the second form a little to the left."

"What will that do?" Lane asked. They were in the makeshift practice room in the lower city, the purple light from the lucent tree glowing along one wall, Devon's green lamp shining from a position near the door. Nic hadn't been at the Quad, so they'd come down alone.

"Remember what I said a few days ago, that the diamond is a set of points?"

"You called it a lattice."

"I'm thinking of it as a structure of nodes or points confined inside the diamond, all connected. The secondary form selects a certain number of those nodes from the bottom pyramid. Based on what you've told me you see happening inside the diamond after you've completed that second form, I'd guess that there's one and only one point above those specific nodes in the upper half of the diamond. If you shift that third point, it will change the resulting node in the upper half."

"I wish you could see it," Lane said, her eyes focused on empty air a few feet in front of her, her crooked hand tracing out the base form, then shifting into the secondary form. It was one Devon had seen the mages using in the practice yard visible from his window. If done correctly, it created a wall of shimmering light in the air ten feet across and four feet in front of the mage. It was more of a distraction and was generally used to allow the mage to change position without the adversary knowing in which direction they were moving. It didn't appear to be harmful in any way.

Lane finished her secondary form, her hand dropping. "It's beautiful."

"Describe it for me."

"Like a swarm of bees, all made of colored lights. They spring up from the points of the form, swirling around each other, like a dance, converging in the upper part of the diamond until they all flash and then wink out. And then—"

Light flared in front of where Devon sat and he scrambled back. It began as a shaft of vertical deep blue light that elongated until it was four feet tall. Then it expanded horizontally, undulating like waves on water. When it reached ten feet in width, it halted. It wasn't completely opaque—Devon could see Lane's shape behind it— but that could be because of the placement of Lane's point in the secondary form.

This was the first time Lane had successfully created the wall. Before this, there had been sparks and sputters of light and one flare that had blinded them for a full minute. Nothing more.

The wall of blue light began to fade. When it vanished completely, Lane rushed forward and hugged Devon before he could completely stand.

"I did it!" She thrust him away from her so she could pace around the small room. "I did it. And now I know I can do more. So much more."

"You need to be careful. If you show too much progress, or use a secondary form they haven't taught you yet—"

"I know, I know." She paused and closed her eyes, tilting her head toward the ceiling, obviously trying to calm some of the pent-up energy inside her. When she exhaled, her gaze dropped back to him. "What should we try next?"

"How about this flame Sigil?"

"Perfect!"

"We should start it with the bond, so I can show you the secondary form."

They stood side-by-side, both of them tracing out the base form until they felt the connection between them forming. They'd practiced with the bond multiple times since that first tentative experiment, knew that once they were bonded they would repeat each other's actions precisely, even say the same words if it was solid enough, as if both were in control at the same time.

"I think we're ready," Devon and Lane said together, and then both nodded in answer. "Here goes."

Devon traced out the basic form and then moved directly into the Sigil he'd seen the mages using on the practice yard to create a whirl of fire. Lane mirrored him. Their breaths heightened as they neared the end, then held as a swirl of fire appeared in front of Lane, larger than Devon had expected, at least five times as large as the ones he'd seen produced on the practice yard. He began to yell a warning, but then the flame shot away from them, slamming into the far wall and bursting outwards in all directions.

A wave of heated air shoved both of them back, snapping the bond and throwing them both to the floor. Devon crawled to his knees, noticed the charred wood and stone of the wall, a few flames flickering around its edges. He scrambled for his discarded cloak and beat the flames out, then turned to Lane.

"Well, that was unexpected," she said. "Should we try it again?"

Devon was about to suggest they continue practicing the blue wall when something rattled outside the room.

Lane gasped, but Devon held up a hand and she stilled. He'd already turned toward the door, listening intently. He heard nothing, but his skin prickled, the fine hairs on his arms standing on end.

Without a sound, he shifted to his satchel and removed his knife. Then he eased up to the door, motioning Lane to stay where she was. A quick look revealed that no one stood in the backwash of green and purple light from the room, but the hall was pitch black beyond that.

Instincts from his time in the lower city kicked in. He slid out the door and down the hall, into the darkness, away from the glow of the lamp and lucent. Beyond it, he halted and crouched down, letting his eyes adjust.

Trotting forward, he ducked into the nearest rooms briefly, but his sense of where the noise had come from indicated it was farther down the hall. He slowed as he neared the wide opening looking down on the curved stairs and the foyer below. The stub of the lucent chandelier was barely visible, along with the first twenty steps down; the second and first floor below were an empty void.

A whisper of noise came, nothing more than a brush of fabric against a wall, then a gray figure in a hooded cloak emerged from below, moving tentatively, one hand against the wall for guidance.

Devon readied his knife. "Nic? Is that you?"

The figure stumbled on a broken step and swore, reaching down to the injured foot.

Devon stilled, then stood. "Dalton? What are you doing here?"

The figure looked up, but in the darkness Devon still couldn't recognize his face. "Trying to find you. Don't you have a light or something? I'm blind down here."

Devon lowered his blade. "Lane, it's Dalton. Bring out the lamp."

"Dalton? What's he doing here?"

Devon didn't answer, waiting until Lane emerged from their practice room with the shard and joined him on the landing. They both stared down at Dalton, the War student's face clear now in the greenish light.

"Well, can I come up or not?"

Devon shared a look with Lane, who shrugged. "Come on."

Dalton limped up the last fifteen steps and halted in front of them, arms crossed. "So…what are you two up to?"

Devon bristled at the interrogatory tone. "You don't want to know."

"Why not? Is it illegal?"

"Of course not!" Lane cried, affronted.

"Then what? I see you two meeting in the Shady Quad, leaving after only a few moments, sometimes with Nic, ducking into an alley and returning with hooded cloaks. Then you descend into the lower city. What am I supposed to think?"

"What a minute," Devon cut in. "We've been practicing here for at least an hour. If you followed us, where have you been all that time?"

Dalton's stolid front faltered. "I…lost you in all the twists and turns to get here. It took me a while to figure out where you'd gone. But that doesn't matter." He rallied, pointing a finger at Devon. "What are you two doing here?"

"Practicing," Lane said flatly.

"Practicing."

"Yes, practicing. Devon found a way to help me learn the mage forms. We come here to work on them, where those from the Lyceum won't know about it. Because the mage forms are supposed to be a guarded secret."

Dalton stared at her, then abruptly turned to Devon. "You're helping her? How? You aren't a mage."

Devon motioned them back toward the practice room. "I figured out the base form the mages use to start all of their Sigils," he said as they entered. The smell of smoke was sharp.

Dalton appeared skeptical. He eyed the charred wood to one side.

"Go ahead," Devon said to Lane, "show him. We've told him everything else."

"What should I do?"

"Not the fire. Try the defensive wall again."

Lane stepped away from them both, her back against the wall opposite the door. Dalton sidled up to Devon's side, close, and Devon's chest tingled. He sucked in a short breath. Dalton shot him a questioning look, but Devon shook his head, fighting back a blush. Dalton didn't notice, his gaze returning to Lane.

Lane began the base form, hitting the six points precisely. Her hand flew into the secondary form, more confident than before, then dropped.

The vertical shaft of blue light appeared, Dalton stiffening as it expanded into its full width. Devon noted that it was less translucent than her previous one.

"That's Paterni's Wall. Mages learn it in their fourth year."

Lane stepped through the wall as it began to dissipate. "I learned it today. From Devon."

Dalton looked at him.

"I can see part of the mage practice field from my dormitory window."

Dalton glanced between both of them, then strode toward the door. "I have to tell Proctor Gallean."

"No!" both Devon and Lane shouted, Devon lurching forward and grabbing him by the arm.

"You can't," Devon continued. "I'll be kicked out of the Lyceum."

"And I'll be sent back to my mother. Dalton, without Devon's help I wouldn't even be able to do the base form, let alone create this...this Paternack's Wall. Nothing was working! Until now."

Dalton pointed at Devon. "And what about you? What do you get out of this?"

"I'm going to use what I find as part of my next—my last— challenge."

"Don't you see," Lane said. "If you go to Gallean now, they'll remove both of us. They'll find out about Devon when he issues his challenge. And I don't intend to use anything Devon teaches me that hasn't already been taught by the proctors when I'm at the Lyceum."

Dalton didn't say anything, but he hadn't moved.

Devon swallowed. "Please, Dalton. This is all I've got that's worthy of a challenge. Without it, I'm back to fending for myself in the lower levels."

"Fine. We'll see what the proctors say when you issue your challenge. I'll keep quiet until then. But you owe me." He glanced around the practice room. "I think you should call it a night. I'll escort you both back to the Lyceum."

Neither Devon nor Lane argued. Lane touched the lucent, the purple tree fading back into darkness, while Devon gathered up his scattered notes and tucked them into his satchel. Dalton took the lamp and led them out into the corridor and down the stairs.

"If you lost us in the alleys here, how did you end up finding us?" Devon asked as they moved. "It's a labyrinth near the hub here."

"I knew you had to be close, so I began checking the vacant buildings—or those that looked vacant. If I hadn't found you within the next couple of streets, I was going to turn back. But then I looked into this building. There were fresh footprints in the dust and dirt on the floor downstairs."

Devon silently cursed himself. They'd have to wipe out their tracks before the next practice session. "That was dangerous. This level isn't as safe as it once was. You could have run into trouble in any one of these buildings. They aren't all abandoned."

"That's what I found out." He shrugged at Devon's look. "I won't be much of a city guardsman if I can't handle some lower city thugs."

They'd reached the outer door. Lane pulled her hood up over her head and they stepped out onto the street. Dalton led the way, lamp held up. It made Devon nervous; the lamp would draw unwanted attention. Few in the lower sections of the city had such luxuries. He kept his hand on the handle of his knife inside his satchel as they moved, picking out the figures in the shadows that withdrew into the deeper darkness as they passed by. Dalton wasn't wasting any time, heading directly toward the main thoroughfare. It wasn't until they reached the street safely and Dalton turned outwards that Devon realized the War student didn't intend to go up the stairs they'd descended to get here. He was going to use the much safer—but much less discreet—set of parks, walkways, and stairs at the city's outer edge.

Slowly, the buildings improved and the shadows receded, the ceiling overhead rising and then disappearing entirely, revealing a field of stars and a fat moon low on the horizon. They'd emerged above the wayfare that led to the Radimansque territory, the lucent crystals along its length shooting out across the darkness of the Flatlands toward the city of Balnis in a straight line. The scattered lucent of the lower city glowed beneath them.

The upper city rose much brighter above, the plinths of buildings and the walkways that connected them lit like the wayfare. The ascent to the Lyceum was less direct than the descent at the hub, but it passed through parks interspersed with fountains and art sculptures, statues wrought of iron and stone and even a few of lucent. There were more people here, strolling the walks. Horse-drawn carriages clopped by on the larger streets. A few ambitious street vendors had wares displayed on carts or blankets spread out in the open plazas, typically bouquets of flowers, jewelry, and other romantic trinkets appealing to the late-night couples or those on their way to assignations. Devon spotted a few pickpockets lurking beneath willowy tree branches or leaning casually in the alcoves of doorways, but the contrast between the walkways here and the alleys farther down and closer to the hub was marked.

They'd swung eastward as they rose and were nearing the Lyceum when a commotion on the street ahead caught their attention. Those on the street with them glanced toward the main thoroughfare ahead and the rhythmic sound of thousands of feet following the slow beat of a drum.

"What is that?" Lane asked.

"It sounds like an army," Dalton answered.

The three of them angled toward the main thoroughfare. The end of the street was lined with a small crowd of onlookers. Devon was too short to see what was going on beyond them, but he wormed his way through the press of people until he was near the edge, Dalton calling out for him to wait in disgust. Being small and thin rather than broad and brawny had its benefits. He heard Lane following him.

When he came to a halt, he realized it was an army—the Iandolan Army—the soldiers dressed in their full maroon and white armor, the mages lined up in the center of the column in the same colors but wearing tightly-wound battle robes. The sound of the march was much louder here, a heavy tread that Devon felt through his feet, punctuated by the drum. Both the soldiers and mages kept their eyes locked forward, their expressions grim or resolute. Every twenty or thirty lines or so, the column was broken by five men on horseback, the two soldiers on the outer edge carrying staffs with blue crystals on top, the mage in the center carrying a red crystal. The other two were either healers or Historians. Those on horseback were obviously of higher rank.

The woman behind Devon stepped aside with a curse and Lane appeared, muttering an apology. The woman rubbed her arm as Lane slid in next to Devon.

"What's going on?" she asked.

"The army is marching on Brovetto," the grizzled man next to Devon replied with relish.

"It's about time," someone else muttered. "After what they did at the wayfare gate?"

The others around them rumbled in agreement.

"We should have sent them the day after the attack," the grizzled man said, his voice raised. The crowd stirred. "They had the balls to come to our gate, to our city, raze a part of it to the ground, and the Council does nothing for weeks afterwards, acts as if nothing has happened? Those Brovetto bastards deserve whatever they get."

Someone shouted, "Yeah!" and Devon felt the curiosity of the crowd shift toward anger, the change subtle, like a tide.

He reached out and caught Lane's arm. "We need to get out of here."

She glanced toward him. "Why?"

He gave her an "Are you joking?" look, but the grizzled man suddenly shouted, "Hey!" and shoved Devon aside hard enough he fell out of the edge of the crowd into the street. Pain shot up his arm into his shoulder, but he lurched into a sitting position as the grizzled man snatched at the front of Lane's cloak and hauled her close. "What are you doing here? Spying on us?"

"No!" Lane shouted, then began to struggle, her hands closing on the grizzled man's wrist. "Let go of me. I'm a student of the Lyceum."

"I don't think so," the grizzled man said. Those around them looked puzzled, but then he reached up and yanked the hood back from Lane's face. "Why would a student of the Lyceum be out here, cowering behind a hood?"

Devon reached into his satchel, fingers closing over the handle of the knife, then shoved himself upright.

At the same time, Dalton thrust his way through the angry faces of those closest, his hand falling heavily onto the grizzled man's shoulder. "What's going on here?"

Devon slid up to the man on the other side, knife concealed by their bodies. He pressed the blade into the man's back, just beneath his ribcage, near his spine, and felt him tense.

"Nothing, Dalton, nothing," Devon said with a chuckle. "Just a misunderstanding, right?" He nodded at the grizzled man, who was glaring at him, his jaw tight, his scraggly beard jutting out in outrage. "Nothing for a sixth year War student to worry about, right?"

The man shot a look at Dalton, who wore an exemplary expression of a city guardsman on the verge of hauling troublemakers in for questioning. He let his grip on Lane relax.

"I thought she was a spy," he said, "being…pale-skinned and all. But she says she's a student."

"And she is," Dalton said. "A mage, actually."

Devon nudged the man with the knife.

He ducked his head, grinding his teeth together before saying, "My mistake then, eh?"

Dalton frowned, as if he knew something wasn't quite right, but let his hand drop from the man's shoulder. "All right then." He glanced up, above and beyond Devon. "Everything's fine, Prefect."

Devon stepped back, startled to find one of the soldiers on horseback standing a few paces away, one hand on the reins, the other holding up the staff. The horse snorted and tossed its head, but the prefect—face stolid, beard neatly trimmed, eyes like crystal—said nothing. His gaze dropped from Dalton, to the grizzled man and Lane, then to Devon.

Devon realized the prefect knew about the knife, even though he'd tucked it into the sleeve of his shirt when he turned.

Without a word, the prefect flicked the reins and the horse returned to his place in the column.

Everyone broke into babbling conversation, the column continuing to march past. When Devon turned back, he wasn't surprised to see the grizzled man was gone.

He asked Lane if she were all right and she nodded curtly, her entire body stiff with anger. "I could have handled it myself."

Devon didn't want to touch that, so he turned to Dalton. "Is it the entire army?"

"It would appear so."

"The Council would send a significant force," Lane added. "As a political statement and warning to the other cities, if nothing else. That incursion into the First Level was a clear violation of the peace treaty. The governors of Luminesque must be getting desperate to have committed such a force to an attack that clearly would not succeed."

"That depends on what they were attempting to accomplish," Dalton countered. "I still think they retreated, that they weren't driven back as everyone believes. Maybe they did succeed."

They watched for another ten minutes, the rest of those in the crowd keeping their distance. Then the column changed. The mages vanished, replaced by soldiers, and another contingent of men and women on horseback appeared, surrounded by an entourage of prefects in ceremonial regalia and a slew of servants bearing banners.

"Oh, no," Lane said, pulling back behind Dalton.

"What is it?" Devon asked.

"Some of the Councilors, including my mother."

Devon craned forward, searching those in the center dressed up in court finery. Not as ostentatious as the prefects, but close. Two were men, one older with a full beard and rotund body and face, the other thin. Lane's mother rode between them, back straight, eyes focused ahead on the army marching before them. Her hair was a light brown, long like Lane's, but except for some of the angles in her face she looked nothing like Lane.

"Who are they?" he asked.

"The man with the beard is Councilor Martov, representing Scintillesque. The other man is Councilor Iriarte. Those behind them are prominent merchants and courtiers seeking to gain influence with the Council."

"Are they going to Brovetto with the army?"

"I'm certain it's just an escort down to the waygate."

Lane shifted position as they passed, her eyes fixed on her mother. But the councilor never looked toward the crowd.

"She doesn't look so overbearing to me," Devon said.

Lane shot him a glare. "You haven't lived with her protecting you your entire life."

"Protecting you from what?"

"Everything."

The councilor's entourage ended, the last line of men and women bearing banners from the seven Crystal Cities tramping off down the thoroughfare toward the wayfare gate.

"What about their support? Their food and such?"

"It probably left days ago," Dalton said. "It would have looked like just another trade caravan headed toward Brovetto. We don't like to announce the movements of our army ahead of time."

The crowd was beginning to disperse, although Devon didn't like some of the angry looks shot their way. "We'd better get back to the Lyceum before things turn ugly again."

As they headed up the now empty thoroughfare, Devon glanced back over his shoulder—to where the army had vanished, and where the lights of the wayfare shot out toward the glow of Brovetto on the horizon.

He wondered how many of those in the army wouldn't return.

Chapter Seven

Devon sat in the Shandy Quad and sipped his drink. He didn't remember what he'd ordered and he didn't really taste it as he swirled it around in his mouth and then swallowed. He was vaguely aware that Arch and even Nic had tried to talk to him earlier, but after he'd answered in bare monosyllables—too distracted for conversation—they'd given up and drifted away. He sat staring at the wall behind the bar, but all he could see, rotating before him, was the double pyramid structure with its six focal points and the lines within that connected the various nodes he and Lane had mapped out over the course of the last few weeks. If he focused on one of the nodes, the notations he'd made on his master copy of the structure popped into his head, telling him what the particular node was used for, what secondary forms used it, and how it interacted with the other nodes around it.

The lattice of focal points and nodes wasn't complete. There were obvious gaps in the structure, mostly in the upper half, what he'd come to think of as the Outcome. The bottom half, the Source, was more detailed. He didn't know if the gaps were because of his limited exposure to the secondary forms or if they were inherent to the structure. His basic theory that the Outcome was chosen by selecting specific nodes from the Source had proven true so far. With Lane's help, he'd discovered that changing the order of the selected nodes affected the final outcome, and that adding a node or forgetting one when performing the secondary form could have drastic consequences. They'd experienced that firsthand with the flame Sigil; the practice room still reeked of char. They'd decided to stick to the forms he'd seen clearly from his dormitory window since then.

Obviously, Lane couldn't help with filling in the gaps. She was only a third year; they'd barely moved her beyond the base form, once she'd proven she'd mastered it. And they couldn't ask for help from any of the other more advanced mages—Dalton's reaction to what they were doing in secret proved that. He'd hoped to catch the mages practicing something new in the past week, after he and Lane had exhausted what he'd already seen, but if the proctors knew of other secondary forms, they weren't teaching them to their students, not even the sixth years. Or at least, they weren't being practiced in the yard. Maybe they were taught after the mages had entered into service in the army.

"What are you thinking so deeply about?"

Devon started, choking on his last sip. He swallowed painfully, wiped at his mouth. "Hey, Dalton."

"Didn't mean to startle you." Dalton beckoned Nic over and ordered. The young bartender was sporting hair dyed a pale blue, a trend Devon and Lane had noticed in the lower city the last few weeks, although Devon was suspicious that it had more to do with gang affiliation than with fashion. He wondered how long it would take to catch on at the Lyceum.

When Nic returned with the drink, Dalton spun toward Devon. "So?"

"So...what?"

"What were you thinking about? You were staring at that wall as if it held the answers to all of the proctor's questions."

"You have been rather withdrawn today," Nic said. "You didn't even react when I came on to you earlier."

Devon sputtered and both Dalton and Nic burst out in laughter.

Nic gave him a mock slap on the cheek and tweaked his nose. "No need to sulk. I know who's caught your attention." He tipped his head toward Dalton, then sauntered away.

Mortified, Devon stared down at the bar's counter. Dalton had gone quiet. He flinched when Dalton's hand fell on his shoulder.

"Listen, Devon—"

"No, don't!" Devon lurched up off his barstool. He faced Dalton, tried to smile. "You don't need to say anything, it's stupid, I know. So just forget it. It's better that way."

"But—"

A group of three students burst through the front doors of the Quad, halting a few steps in. "The army has returned from Brovetto! They're marching up the Spoke toward the Central City!"

There was an uncomprehending pause as those in the Quad processed the words, then everyone began stampeding toward the doors.

Dalton snagged Devon's arm as he began to pull away. "You haven't finished your drink."

"It doesn't matter. Leave it." He tugged his arm free, looked Dalton in the eyes. "It's nothing. Now come on."

Dalton still looked uncertain, but he set his drink aside and followed Devon out the door.

They trailed after the main group from the Quad, everyone talking excitedly as they jogged toward the Spoke. It was the eighth hour, the sun low on the horizon. Shafts of sunlight cut through the buildings and towers around them, slicing across the Spoke in swatches. Hundreds of local residents streamed toward the thoroughfare, until they all came up behind a large crowd already gathered. Dalton and Devon struggled to get closer so they could see, but the crowd was too dense, nothing like the one that had gathered the night the army had left the city weeks before.

"It's no use," Devon said to Dalton. "There are too many people."

"Over there! The statue!"

They rounded the back of the still-growing crowd and shoved their way through to the edge of a steel sculpture of a rearing horse, its forelegs pawing at the air, its hind legs on a large block of carved stone. The top of the stone was too high for any of them to reach, but Devon cupped his hands and Dalton stepped into this holster, onto his shoulders, and up. The War student pulled Devon up with grunt.

The unworked stone on top was encrusted with years of dried bird shit.

"This is disgusting," Devon said, scrubbing his hands on his shirt.

"It is," Dalton said. "But it's also fun. Look!"

The army had returned, slipping past the opening of the side street in rank upon rank, file upon file, as they'd done when leaving.

Except they weren't moving as crisply as they had back then. The soldiers and mages looked exhausted, heads bowed, eyes weary and worn. Their uniforms were dirty with soot and smudged with the red dirt and dust of the Flatlands. A few had rips or were scorched and burnt away. Some were stained with blood.

One of the prefects appeared, accompanied by a mage, and both of them raised their crystal staffs into the air.

The crowd—boiling with uncertain excitement—began to cheer, the roar rolling back from the edge of the Spoke into the side street as word spread. The prefect and mage shifted forward, out of sight, as the procession continued. The cheering died down, replaced by babble. A moment later, muted cheering could be heard from the next cross-street.

"I'd say we won."

"Of course we did," Dalton said. "No one can beat us. We have mages."

"But not without cost," Devon added.

The prefects must have put those that had fared the best in the fighting at the front of the procession, for those passing by now were more seriously wounded. Faces were scraped and scarred, arms were in slings. Bandages wrapped heads, torsos, legs. All of the wounds had been tended, but as the march progressed the wounds grew gradually more grievous. Blood had seeped through many of the compresses, the stains black in the half-light of dusk.

The thrill of the crowd dampened and conversations stilled. Yet all of those marching carried themselves with stiff backs and heads raised, even though it was obvious a few of them were straining to keep up. After a long uncertain moment, someone near the front of the crowd began to clap, the gesture spreading, sporadically at first, but then thicker and more heartfelt. The cheering began again, and this time it didn't fade. A few of the soldiers and mages responded by placing a fist against their heart, or bowing their head in thanks. One prefect and mage pair out of those interspersed throughout the army paused to watch before moving on.

Then, abruptly, the column of soldiers ended, a line of prefects and mages bringing up the rear. The clapping died out as the Spoke emptied and the crowd began to disperse.

Devon settled down on the edge of the stone block. "It didn't seem like there were that many returning. Weren't there more when they left?"

"There were," Dalton said. "But I doubt they had everyone return. Some would have stayed in Brovetto, to bolster the forces on the wayfare between here and there. And any of those who couldn't endure the march up to the central tower and the barracks there would have been left behind at the waygate. They'll be seen to at the gates, then moved up later, probably in wagons."

They sat in silence as the crowd beneath them thinned. Then Dalton stirred. "Were you and Lane going to practice again tonight?"

"I don't think we need to practice anymore. We haven't learned anything new in the last few weeks or so. I think I need to take a day or two to formulate a set of questions off of what we've learned... and then I think I'll submit my challenge."

"You're ready to submit a challenge?"

"I don't think I should ask Lane to experiment any more with different forms. The last time we tried that, we nearly burned down the building. It's too risky. I've been meaning to talk to Lane about it, but I haven't seen her the last few days."

"That's...odd." Dalton frowned. "Now that I think about it, I haven't seen her around the practice yards lately either. She should have been at some of the lessons. There were other third years there."

"You don't think..."

They shared a glance, then Devon swore and made to jump off the pedestal. Dalton caught his arm.

"She may just be busy. We should check around first."

"After what happened with Quinn? Shards, she could have been attacked on the streets, simply for looking like she's from Luminesque!"

"You don't know that. She could be in her room, studying. Let's at least check at the Shandy Quad first. Agreed?"

Devon nodded and Dalton lowered him down to the street, jumping down after him with a grunt.

"What's the problem?" Nic asked when they returned to a much busier Quad.

"Have you seen Lane recently?" Devon asked.

"She hasn't been in for a few days."

Devon swore. "Neither one of us has seen her either. That's not like her. She hasn't left me alone since she learned the base form. All she wants to do is practice. Something's wrong."

"Don't jump to conclusions," Dalton said. "You're a mathematician, aren't you? You have no proof anything's happened."

Dalton was right, it had only been a few days, but he couldn't calm the uneasy churn in his gut. "Let's search the Lyceum, see if we can find her there."

They scoured the college grounds, including the Tower, the scriptorium, and the classrooms. When they tried to enter the Inner Sanctum and the administrative areas, they were kicked out by the acolytes. They watched the War and Mage students practicing on the quad, but she wasn't with any of the mock battle groups, even though they saw some of the other third years there. When approached, her classmates said they hadn't seen her, or shook their heads in confusion, until one of them muttered, "I think she's in her room. Sick, maybe?" Then he hurried off to the mage dormitory.

"No one seems that concerned," Dalton said as they stood next to the shard on the quad. The half-light of dusk gave the quad an eerie gray color as classes ended and students faded toward their rooms or the dining halls. "Maybe she is sick and has been relegated to her room so it doesn't spread. Everyone seemed to think she was there."

"Maybe." But Devon didn't believe it. All of the instincts he'd honed to sharp edges in the lower levels were screaming.

Dalton forced him to meet his gaze. "Go back to your room, Devon. It's far too early yet to raise an alarm. We'll find her tomorrow."

"And what if we don't?"

"Then we'll talk to our proctors. I'm certain it's nothing though."

Dalton nudged him toward the Science dormitory, waiting until Devon had begun moving on his own before turning and heading in the opposite direction, toward War's barracks.

* * *

For the next few days, Devon watched the mages' dormitory, but he never saw Lane entering or leaving. Any of the mages he asked, students and proctors, said she was in her room, working, or simply sick. No one would agree to pass her a note, either, one of the students finally snapping, "She doesn't want to talk to you, Devon, let it go!"

"If she doesn't want to see you, then perhaps you should let it rest for a while," Dalton said. They were seated at the Quad—not at the bar this time, at one of the tables in a far corner. "Don't you have a challenge to prepare? The term is nearly over."

"Do you honestly think she's working in her room? It's been almost a week. We should have at least seen her headed to the practice yard at some point." He gazed out over the patrons, not really seeing them.

He'd barely touched his drink, dropped off by Arch nearly half an hour ago. "I can't work on the challenge without thinking about her."

Dalton reached out and grabbed his hand. "Devon, look at me. Look at me!"

He was startled by the intensity in Dalton's eyes.

"You can't let this throw you. By all accounts, Lane is fine. Maybe her proctors have kept her busy because she fell so far behind learning the base form. Maybe she truly is sick. I don't know. But your challenge…you only have one more chance. You have to submit some questions. That can't wait."

Devon remained silent, paralyzed by Dalton's gaze.

Then he realized Dalton was touching him. Warmth flushed his face as he jerked his hand back, his skin tingling. The sharp movement jostled the table and they both grabbed for their drinks, some of Devon's spilling. He swore, shoved back from the table, and stood, holding the dripping hand out to one side, until he realized Dalton was chuckling, the sound low and deep and somehow comforting.

He drew in a breath and exhaled slowly, then deliberately wiped his hand on his pants and sat again. "You're right."

"About what?"

"About everything—Lane, the challenge…everything. I need to focus. The mage proctors said Lane was fine, so the challenge comes first. I don't want to end up back in the lower levels." He took a few large swallows of alcohol, the drink burning on its way down. He gasped and asked hoarsely, "What did you order for me?"

"Kerpezian whiskey. I thought you needed something mellow."

"It burns!"

"Of course it does, when you gulp it. It's supposed to be sipped." Dalton took a small sip, hiding his smile.

Devon tried it again, but Dalton was right. Sipped, it felt warm and tingly against his tongue, soothing.

"So tomorrow you'll work on your challenge?"

"I promise. But you have to keep watch for Lane. If you see her…"

"If I see her, I'll tell you straightaway."

* * *

The next morning, he forced himself to sit at his desk and pull out the master's copy he'd made of the double pyramid. On a fresh sheet of parchment, he began writing out his seven questions, the first few repeating the questions he'd used for his last challenge.

Then he began outlining new questions, ones based on the double pyramid's structure, on his theories on how the order of the nodes chosen during the secondary form produced certain outcomes, how changing the order altered the outcome, how selecting positions to either side of a node produced varying degrees of intensity. He phrased the questions as theorems and properties, statements he felt he could prove with the help of one of the mages.

It took three days. He worked non-stop, barely pausing for food, collapsing onto his bed for snatches of sleep when he could no longer keep his eyes open or when the intensity of the work caused a migraine. Food was delivered to his door, left outside after a discreet knock. He didn't know who had arranged it, but he ate whatever was provided gratefully.

Until, finally, he had all of the work done with Lane honed down to five questions, encompassing the Source and the Outcome, the known nodes and the lattice they created. He stared at the loops and whorls of the formal calligraphy that the challenge must be written in, so exhausted that the words they formed no longer held any meaning.

Then he gathered the papers up and slid them into a portfolio. Smoke from the candle burned his nostrils as he warmed a stick of red wax. His chair creaked as he leaned back into it.

Was this it? He still had time. He knew he was treading on dangerous ground, dabbling in the secrets of the magerium. It was a risky move. But he had nothing else. The questions he and Arrend had formulated had yielded no answers and there wasn't enough time to start with something completely new, like the Wardings, even with some of the work already done by Arrend himself.

He scrubbed at his eyes with his hands in frustration.

No, there was no other option. This was his only chance.

His last chance.

He leaned forward, snatched the heated wax, and with deliberate purpose sealed the portfolio, tossing the wax stick aside. Then he glanced around the room strewn with wadded up papers and a few discarded plates empty of food.

Not as messy or chaotic as when he'd destroyed it earlier; the black stain of ink on the wall was enough to remind him of that.

His gaze returned to the portfolio.

"I need a drink."

As soon as he stepped outside, he realized it was too early to go to the Shandy Quad. Mid-morning sunlight blinded him; he'd thought it was late afternoon. So he proceeded to the library. He shoved through the door and entered the scriptorium, a large room with a vaulted ceiling lined with podiums and tables for study and lit by columns of pale blue lucent. The library itself was off limits to students, except when they had permission to study a particular text or scroll. The scriptorium was where they came to request the tomes, and where they were watched as they perused them by members of the Arts who'd been assigned to the library after graduating. Aside from the books the few scattered students were looking through around the room, there were no texts or scrolls present. They were all kept behind the massive iron doors to the left of the scriptorium's entrance, guarded by four War students and presided over by Arts proctors.

Devon walked across the hall to one of those proctors now, his footfalls on the stone floor echoing in the ceiling overhead. Students looked up from their work at the noise, but returned to their books almost immediately. Their attendant Arts students watched him as he crossed to the proctor's massive desk, littered with papers, stacks of books, bundles of scrolls, and various writing implements and ink jars. A small table to one side held three candles and an open box that contained rectangular wax sticks in a range of lurid colors.

The current proctor—one Devon didn't recognize—looked up as he approached. He was older than any of the Arts proctors Devon had ever dealt with, with a thin face, sharp eyes, and a crooked nose supporting pinched spectacles. "What can we do for you? Do you have a signed petition to peruse a text?"

"I have a challenge," Devon said, setting his sealed portfolio on top of a stack of parchment.

The proctor reached out thin fingers to gather it up. "Ah, I see." He scanned the text on the outside of the portfolio, his gaze jumping back up to Devon's name, then toward him. "You attest that the contents are your own work, that you sealed this yourself, and that there has been no tampering with the portfolio since?"

"I so attest."

"Very well." The proctor stood and shifted toward the isolated table with the candles and sticks of wax. He scrawled his own name at the bottom of the portfolio, then began warming a stick of dark purple in a flame.

"This is your last attempt, yes?" he asked, removing the wax from the heat and leaning over the portfolio. "You've made other attempts and failed?"

Devon's hand clenched into a fist where it rested on the desk. "Yes."

The proctor looked up at him over the rim of his glasses. "Are you certain these are the questions you wish to ask for your final attempt? Once I seal this, there is no going back."

Devon thought he detected a hint of warning in the proctor's voice, but that couldn't be true. No one knew what questions he'd proposed, not even Lane.

"Those are the questions I wish to propose."

The proctor blinked. "Very well." He pressed the purple wax to the portfolio next to Devon's own seal, then stamped it with one of the many rings on his fingers. He handed it off to an Arts student, who retreated toward the iron doors. A small recess stood to one side with a handle. The Art student pulled down on the handle and slid Devon's portfolio into the empty space behind, then closed it.

"It will be delivered to your board by the end of the day."

Devon glanced back to the Arts proctor, who had moved back behind his desk. A strange emptiness filled his chest. It was done. His last chance to challenge was now out of his hands; his last hope of graduating now lay outside of his control.

He swallowed, feeling strangely lost, then stepped back from the desk and moved toward the scriptorium's door. His pace quickened as he crossed the room.

He stepped out into the bright sunlight and leaned back against the door. His arms were trembling, his fingers numb. His breath came in short hitches. But he closed his eyes, bowed his head, and forced himself to calm down.

"Is everything all right?"

Devon started at the voice, shoving hard away from the door, nearly stumbling into the Merchants proctor who stood before him. "I'm fine."

He headed toward his dormitory, his neck prickling under the gaze of the proctor, but halfway down the length of the quad he suddenly veered toward the mage dormitory. He didn't want to be in his room. Now that his challenge had been handed in, he wanted to see Lane.

The quad was oddly quiet, only a small group of War and Mage students practicing at the far end. But then, the end of the academic year was only a few weeks away. Most students were studying for their final exams and preparing to return home for the short break before the next term began. Devon wound around the few students scattered across the quad, brushed by the amber shard jutting up from the grass, and approached the Mage dormitory. He halted outside the wide stone steps that led up to the entrance. All of the dormitories had been built at the same time, using the same basic layout and architecture. The only significant differences were in the lintels surrounding the doorways and windows, each themed toward whatever group was housed inside. The Mage dormitory had images of wind and water and fire, along with crystals of different shapes.

Devon stared at the closed doors in frustration.

A group of mages walked toward him along the quad, coming from the practice yard.

"Hey! Do any of you know Lane? She's a third year."

The group of three second years stopped at the edge of the steps, the two girls on the right sharing a glance before the one in the middle stepped forward. "You're Devon, aren't you?"

"Yes."

"I thought we already told you, she doesn't want to see you. Or your friend Dalton."

He sighed. "Can you at least tell me if she's here in the dormitory or at the practice yard? I'll wait for her for however long it takes."

The boy opened his mouth to respond, the two girls shooting him warning looks, but then an older voice cut in with, "You again. I thought we'd already gotten rid of you."

Devon faced Quinn. The three second years used the distraction to escape up the stairs and into the dormitory.

"I don't give up that easily." Devon glanced toward the three mages behind Quinn, all fifth year or higher. "I don't suppose you'll tell me where she is?"

"Why would I do that?" Quinn began descending the steps, motioning to the three behind her without turning. "Come on, we have work to do."

She passed by Devon, close enough she nearly knocked into his shoulder. The others split to either side, hemming him in for a brief moment. One of them laughed.

When they were a few paces distant, he turned toward them. "Why do you hate her so much? What did she ever do to you?"

Quinn halted, back stiff. Then she spun and approached fast, grabbing his shirt and bringing her face so close he instinctively jerked back. "It wasn't her, it was her bitch mother, Varenov. That Council seat belonged to my family, to my father. But then Lane's mother returned from Brovetto, pregnant, with newly signed peace accords, and suddenly the seat that had been promised to my father was hers. Her mother ruined my family!"

She suddenly realized she'd raised her voice and everyone around them had fallen silent. The fist she'd wound up in Devon's shirt slowly unclenched and she shoved him away from her. "Her mother is a Luminesque sympathizer, at best. She has no right to be on the Council. As for her daughter...well, Lane doesn't have a chance here, even if she did manage to learn the primary form on her own."

Quinn began to turn away, but Devon grabbed her upper arm, held her back. "What do you mean?"

Quinn jerked her arm free. "Do you really think Favian would let a Luminesque graduate as a mage?" She leaned in close, said in a low voice, "Only Iridesque can be mages. It's how Iandolo stays in power."

Quinn pulled away, stalking through her entourage toward the practice yards, leaving Devon at the bottom of the steps of the dormitory. Could it be true? Quinn hadn't said so directly, but could the mages have been sabotaging Lane's attempts to become a mage? Not just Quinn, but the others around her, including Favian and the proctors?

He didn't want to believe it.

What could he do? Who could he tell?

"Arrend."

He headed toward the proctors' hall, not quite running. The sounds of the quad rang in his ears, overly loud. The world had tilted around him, skewed. He hadn't considered it at the time, too caught up in his larger theories, but what he'd done to help Lane had been rather trivial, a simple matter of timing and placement. The other mages, the proctors in particular, should have been able to correct it.

Which meant they had been hindering her.

And were they holding her prisoner now, since she'd learned the base form?

His shock began to transform into anger. He shoved through the outer doors of the proctors' hall and into the foyer that branched into the two corridors lined with living quarters. His knock on Arrend's door hurt his knuckles.

The door opened almost instantly, an acolyte barring entry.

"I need to see Proctor Arrend."

"Master Arrend is not here at the moment."

"Where is he? I need to speak to him."

"I do not know. He was called away by one of the other proctors."

"Do you know when he'll be back?"

"In general, Master Arrend does not apprise me of his plans, and even if he did, I would not be inclined to reveal them to a mere student."

She shut the door in Devon's face.

He stood, uncertain of what to do. Arrend could be anywhere on campus, or even outside in the city.

He drifted out of the hall back into the sunlight, raising a hand to shade his eyes. The quad was still dotted with students and proctors, but he didn't see Arrend anywhere. The shouts of the War students and mages sparring drowned out nearly all other surrounding sounds. He sighed, still agitated, then glanced up at the heights of the Tower.

By the time he reached the landing where he could see out over the city, his initial anger had died down. He stared out over the city, toward the barren reds and yellows and browns of the Flatlands, the lucent of the buildings gleaming in the sun, the heights of the wayfare to Brovetto a glint against the sand and rocks. A warm breeze tugged at his hair and he breathed it in, let it calm him further.

The sun had slipped past midday into afternoon when Dalton showed up.

"There you are." The War student moved forward and settled his elbows on the lucent, close enough he brushed up against Devon's side. "Itch said you'd left your room, but he didn't know where you'd gone."

"I handed in my challenge."

Dalton glanced toward him for the first time, eyebrows raised. "It's all done?"

"All done."

"Congratulations! Now all you have to do is wait."

Devon had expected to feel more elated, or at least nervous, but instead he was strangely ambivalent. What Quinn had said about what she and Favian and the others were doing to Lane had tainted his vision of the school and blunted his enthusiasm.

"We should celebrate tonight," Dalton said. "Hit the Shandy Quad, maybe even go higher up the Hub, closer to the towers, find a fancier bar there, my treat."

Devon attempted a weak smile.

"What's wrong?" Dalton faced him. "Something's wrong. Tell me."

He told Dalton about his run-in with Quinn, about what she'd said. "They never intended for her to graduate. They've been actively blocking her in her studies. And now I think they're simply holding her captive so she can't learn anything new."

"Quinn didn't exactly say that." But Devon could hear the doubt in Dalton's words.

"The suggestions I gave Lane for the primary form were relatively simple. Her proctors should have made those same corrections, but they didn't."

"Maybe it was just Favian and Quinn."

"Can you see Favian working with her on his own? There were others involved, probably the whole school of mages."

"I doubt that."

He was becoming agitated again. "No, you're right. Not all of them. But enough. If she hadn't learned the primary form, she would have been expelled at the end of this year. They didn't count on me helping her."

"Devon…"

"We have to do something, Dalton! We have to tell someone!"

"Devon—"

"I already tried to find Arrend, but he wasn't in his rooms and the acolyte there didn't know where he'd gone. He could be anywhere!"

"Devon!"

Devon jumped, and in that moment of shock Dalton leaned in and kissed him.

He stiffened at first, then weakened.

When it broke, he felt lighter.

Dalton cupped the back of his head, fingers tangled in his hair. "We'll find Arrend. He'll know what to do. I've known something was wrong for days now, ever since you asked me to find Lane while you worked. She hasn't been seen outside the mage's dormitory—I had a group of younger War students watching for her. That's not natural. Like you said, they're keeping her away on purpose, keeping her isolated."

"Maybe we should go to your War Proctor, Gallean."

"He's too busy dealing with the consequences of the Luminesque attack and Iandolo's response."

"I thought the Iandolo Army had dealt with that already."

"That was simply retaliation. I doubt we cowed the Luminesque at all. They'll be back, but this time we'll be waiting for them. Right now, we should try to find Arrend, and if that fails, maybe one of the other proctors. And we should go celebrate your challenge."

Devon managed to smile this time, although somehow the challenge didn't matter as much anymore.

They checked Arrend's rooms again, the administrative halls, the scriptorium, and the Science dormitory. Arrend wasn't anywhere and most people said they hadn't seen him since that morning. A few of the other proctors mentioned that he'd been pulled away for some kind of special meeting in the Inner Sanctum. Dalton brought up telling one of the other proctors again, perhaps from History or Humanities or Arts, but Devon didn't know any of the other proctors well enough to be comfortable approaching them for something like this, even the proctors who were on his own board.

So instead they retreated to the Shandy Quad, sitting in the corner table, ostensibly to celebrate Devon handing in his challenge. But they were both subdued, neither speaking much, their gazes meeting every now and then before breaking away.

Later, in the dark, on the empty quad, the amber shard glowing faintly to one side, Dalton said, "We'll find Arrend tomorrow, tell him about what Quinn said and our suspicions that they're holding Lane in her room. He'll know what to do."

"I've been thinking about what Arrend told me about Favian and how he ended up here at the Lyceum, and about what Quinn said about Lane's mother taking her father's place on the Council. What if it's all tied together?"

"How do you mean?"

"Favian was forced into this proctor position when that military expedition to Brovetto failed and that councilor's daughter died. He's been searching for a way to get out of here, back to the military, or at least back into the Council's good graces. Maybe he saw an opportunity when Lane arrived here. If he could force Lane out, embarrass her in some way, maybe even accuse her of working with the Brovettans, that would reflect back on her mother. A scandal like that might even force Lane's mother to step down from the Council."

"Opening up the spot for Quinn's father," Dalton finished. "That's how he enlisted Quinn's help, not that she wouldn't have made Lane's life here hell regardless. She would have brought her cronies in on it."

"And Favian could have used his influence over the other proctors to keep Lane from advancing as well."

"He would have spoken to Quinn's father as well, to make certain he was ready to approach the Council when needed. It's an interesting theory, but it's all based on supposition. We should let Arrend know what we're thinking and let him sort it out."

Devon nodded, glancing at the shard, the grass, up at the Tower. "Listen, Dalton, about what you did on the Tower—"

Dalton grabbed his hand and cut him off with another kiss, not as intense or as long, but more powerful. "I meant it, Devon. You can't take it back. Now get some sleep."

He turned and vanished into the darkness toward the War dormitory.

Devon lingered at the shard, a faint smile tugging at the corner of his mouth. Then he headed back to his parchment-cluttered room, falling into bed and sleep with thoughts of Dalton and Lane and the challenge swirling around his head.

Chapter Eight

"Devon, wake up!"

Devon rolled away from the voice and the hand shaking his shoulder. "Go away, Itch. I need to sleep."

"You don't have time." Itch leaned in close. "Proctor Arrend is waiting for you downstairs. He says the Board wants to see you immediately. It's about your challenge!"

Devon jerked upright, flinging the blanket aside. Itch lurched back.

"It can't be about my challenge. I only turned it in yesterday."

Itch swallowed, his blue eyes wide, his hair mussed and wild. "I know. But that's what Arrend says. He wants you to get into your whites right now. He's going to accompany you to the Inner Sanctum."

"He can't go to the Inner Sanctum with me. He removed himself from my Board."

Irritation flashed across Itch's face as he grabbed Devon's arm, dragging him up from the bed. "Go wash up! I'll get your whites."

He shoved Devon out of his bedroom, then slammed the door in his face. Devon stood still for a moment, shivering in his undergarments, then swore and headed for the washroom.

Twenty minutes later, Itch still tucking in the last folds of his whites, he was half convinced this was some kind of elaborate prank.

But when he descended the stairs to the dormitory's great room, he found Arrend standing to one side of the doors dressed in his formal regalia. His expression was stern, the rest of the Science students in the great room unusually silent.

As soon as Arrend saw him, he motioned him forward.

"Good luck," Itch said.

Devon turned to look at him, then strode across the room to Arrend.

"What's happening?"

"Nothing good. You've been summoned to the Inner Sanctum by your Board." He pushed through the massive doors of the dormitory into lackluster sunlight. Scattered clouds moved swiftly through the sky, but the wind smelled of rain and darker clouds blackened the horizon to the west. "They want to speak to you about the challenge."

"But I just handed it in yesterday!"

"I know. As soon as Favian got his hands on it, he summoned your Board. I only heard about it because your Arts proctor, Illiam, sent one of his students to my office to warn me of what was going on. I went to the Inner Sanctum immediately, even though it's against policy. I've been there since yesterday afternoon." They were crossing the quad, Arrend moving at a fast clip, Devon barely able to keep up without breaking into a run. But Arrend suddenly halted, catching Devon by the shoulder. "Did you honestly think that researching the mage's forms would be appropriate for a challenge? Did you think there would be no consequences? Why didn't you come to me? Why didn't you ask?"

A thread of anger had crept into Arrend's voice. That more than anything sent a cold spike of dread down to Devon's core. But he'd known he was treading on dangerous turf.

Arrend shook his head, nudging him back into motion. "It doesn't matter now, what's done is done." The anger had vanished, replaced by weary resignation. "I don't know how this is going to play out," he said as they entered the administrative building, accompanied by the first heavy gust from the incoming storm. "Unless asked a direct question by one of the Board, don't say anything. Let me do the talking."

They entered the audience chamber outside the sanctum. Arrend moved to the inner doors. "Wait here until summoned by one of the acolytes."

Then he entered, the door drifting closed behind him.

Devon stared at the cushioned chairs that lined the walls of the small room, but didn't sit. His arms were tingling again, his fingers numb. He cracked his knuckles and snapped his hands, trying to bring feeling back into them, as he scanned the banners that hung on the walls. The largest, depicting the crest of Iridesque, hung above the doors to the Inner Sanctum. On the two walls facing each other between the sets of doors were the school banners, one for each area—Science, Arts, Humanities, History, War, Merchants, and Mages—and one for the school in general. The symbols embroidered on each banner for the individual areas were the same as the symbols he'd noticed in the architecture of the dormitories while waiting for Lane.

Lane. Dalton. Arrend.

He'd taken a step toward the doors to the Inner Sanctum, intent on telling Arrend about what Favian and the other mages had done to Lane, but caught himself. He'd have to inform Arrend after this meeting, no matter what happened to him personally. If only he'd been able to find Arrend last night—

A ragged laugh escaped him. He and Dalton hadn't been able to find Arrend yesterday because Arrend had been here, defending Devon.

He flinched when the inner doors opened and an acolyte stepped into the room.

"You may enter now."

Unlike the three challenges before this, the acolyte did not precede him into the room, instead standing to one side to allow Devon entry. Devon felt his presence at his back as he took the three steps through darkness to the heavy black curtains and then pushed through into the blinding light of the sanctum itself. He remained at Devon's side, uncomfortably close, like a guard.

Arrend stood before the arrayed podiums of the Board, where the challenger usually stood, the representatives of each of the schools already in position. All of the proctors regarded Devon with expressions ranging from boredom to anger, Favian the angriest by far. Movement caught Devon's attention to one side of the podiums and he shifted to one side.

"Lane!"

His shout echoed strangely in the room, louder than it should have been, some of the proctors wincing. Lane glanced up at him, her face streaked with tears. Devon started toward her, but the acolyte caught his arm and shoved him toward Arrend instead. A second acolyte stood behind Lane.

His relief at finally seeing Lane immediately turned to anger. "Why is she here? She has nothing to do with my challenge!"

"She has everything to do with your challenge," Favian snapped.

"That has yet to be decided, Proctor Favian." Arrend's voice was shockingly calm. He nodded to the acolyte that deposited Devon at his side, then gave Devon a warning look before turning back to Favian. "If you have a grievance over Devon Alamort's challenge, he is now here to hear it."

"And why are you here, Arrend? You stepped down from Devon Alamort's Board after his last challenge."

"I'm here to defend this student against unwarranted allegations of misconduct."

"There are no such provisions in the codices of the Lyceum!"

"There are no provisions prohibiting it either."

"Enough!" Proctor Gallean slapped his open palm against his podium. "Proctor Arrend has been arguing in Devon Alamort's behalf since he stormed into the sanctum yesterday. I see no reason to force him to stop doing so now."

The other proctors on the board nodded or murmured agreement.

"Very well," Proctor Favian said, shifting his attention from Arrend to Devon. "Let's begin. Devon Alamort, sixth year student in the School of Science, you issued the Board a challenge consisting of seven questions that you claim you have resolved."

The formal wording, just like all of his previous challenges, caused Devon to falter. "Yes."

"Is it true that five of these questions pertain to the School of Mages? In particular, to the Sigils mage students are expected to learn as part of their studies?"

Devon looked at Arrend, who said, "Answer the questions truthfully."

"Yes, they do."

"Then as Master of this Board, and Master of the School of Mages, I declare this challenge invalid and demand that Devon Alamort be expelled!"

The rest of the Board appeared shocked, even Gallean. Devon bristled, but Arrend laid a restraining hand on his shoulder.

"Under what rule do you declare the challenge invalid?"

Favian gripped the sides of his podium. "Everyone knows what the mages practice is sacrosanct. Our art is to be kept secret. It's what keeps Iandolo secure from the other cities."

"But you chose not to keep it secret."

"What do you mean?"

Arrend took a step forward, pointed at Favian. "You chose to have your students practice in the quad instead of the more secure practice yards. You chose to reveal those secrets to the rest of the school. Devon Alamort is not to blame for your indiscretion." Devon's advisor turned to face him. "It was the practice on the quad that generated your initial interest in the mage forms, yes?"

"Yes. I started noticing the patterns then, began sketching them out."

"And your conclusions, the basis for your challenge, come from that work?"

"Yes."

Arrend spun on Favian. "You saw him. Both you and Gallean approached me about it, but by then he had stopped observing you. You cannot fault a student who bases his research on material that you've presented to him yourself."

Favian's eyes narrowed. "He could not have posed such questions based solely on what he saw on the quad. We only worked the primary form there. None of the students moved beyond that."

"But the study of mathematics is the study of patterns and extrapolation. Perhaps he learned enough to extend the primary form to what must logically come next."

"His questions are too deep! They delve far beyond the primary form. He must have had help."

Everyone turned toward Lane, Favian stepping out from behind his podium. The Master of the Board motioned and the acolyte behind Lane escorted her to a position a few paces before Favian.

"Did you help Devon Alamort with his research? Did you meet with him, in the lower city, violating your vow to keep what you learned in your studies secret?"

Lane hesitated, then said, "Yes."

Favian stalked away from her. "Devon Alamort went too far. He should never have solicited the help of one of our students to further his own studies, never have put her in such a position."

"But he helped me!" Lane protested.

Favian raised a hand for silence, his eyes on Arrend. "He stepped beyond the bounds of his school, regardless of how much he learned or could extrapolate from the quad. He went too far, Arrend. He must be punished. The only suitable punishment for this offense is expulsion."

A few of the other proctors on the board had shifted closer together, were conversing in low murmurs. Gallean glanced between Favian, Arrend, Devon, and Lane, then cleared his throat.

"I'm forced to agree with Favian, if this is true. To protect the city, to safely defend Iridesque, the secrets of the mages must be kept."

Arrend's gaze swept over the other proctors, all of whom had fallen silent at Gallean's words. Devon could tell they agreed. He tasted bile at the back of his throat.

But Arrend moved toward Lane.

"You said that Devon helped you. How?"

"This is nonsense!" Favian exclaimed. "How does that matter?"

Arrend ignored him. "How did he help you?"

"I was having problems creating the primary form. Devon thought he could help, based on what he'd seen on the quad, but he knew we couldn't work on it openly, so we went to the lower city to practice. He taught me how to do the form."

"So you're a third year?"

"Yes."

"And once you knew how to do the primary form correctly, what happened next?"

"I struggled with the secondary forms the proctors began to show me as well, and Devon helped me learn those. He also had a few theories he wanted to test out. I helped him with those."

"How many additional forms did you show him?"

"Not many. I didn't know any of them at first. They aren't taught until you've mastered the primary form."

Arrend stepped toward the proctors. "She's a third year, Favian. How could Devon have used her to 'delve far beyond the primary form' if she didn't know those other forms herself?"

Now the other proctors looked uncomfortable.

"If he didn't use this student as his source," Gallean began, "then how did he learn of these secondary forms?"

"We should ask him," Arrend said.

Devon fidgeted under their gazes. "I surmised some of them from what I'd already learned on the quad."

"But the others?" Favian asked.

Devon ducked his head. "I can see a corner of the mage practice yard from my dormitory window."

Gallean burst out in laughter. "He didn't cheat, Favian. He found a hole in our security."

Favian ground his teeth together, then said, "This oversight will have to be dealt with. But the fact remains that Devon Alamort should never have contemplated researching the mages' forms, especially using information he knew he should not be privy to. He knows his own guilt. He's flushed with it as we speak."

Devon clenched his fist, unable to stop the heat rising up from his neck. Arrend must have seen something in his eyes, for he suddenly began walking toward him, shaking his head.

"What about your own guilt?" Devon asked.

"What do you mean?"

"Devon," Arrend said. "Don't."

"Ask him why Lane was having trouble learning the primary form. She's a third year. She should have learned it weeks ago."

"Because she's incompetent," Favian said sharply. "She should never have been accepted into the program. If her mother hadn't been on the Council—"

"It's because they've been holding her back, sabotaging her forms. The primary form is simple. Anyone can learn it. But they didn't want her to succeed, so they taught her the wrong pacing. Not just the proctors, but her fellow students as well, the fifth and sixth years who were supposed to be helping her."

Devon didn't think Favian could get any angrier, but now his face turned livid.

"That is blatantly false! How dare you make such an accusation here in the sanctum!"

The other proctors had become animated, gesturing and conversing amongst themselves, the acoustics in the room blurring all of the conversation into a low rumble. Devon glanced toward Lane, who looked stunned. She looked up, mouthed, Is it true? He nodded and answered, Quinn.

Anger replaced the tears in her eyes and her stance grew rigid.

Then Favian shouted, "Enough!"

The turmoil died down.

Gripping his podium, Favian said, "Whether his accusation is true or not does not matter. We are here to decide whether Devon Alamort's challenge is acceptable and if not, what should be done about his transgression. Do you have anything to say, Proctor Arrend?"

"Only this." Arrend stepped forward, facing the other proctors, ignoring Favian. "There is nothing in the Lyceum's rules that forbid a student from researching mage forms. In fact, it is encouraged—"

"Among the mage students!" Favian said.

"That's not explicitly stated. Devon Alamort did nothing wrong. He saw a potential avenue for study—one presented to him by Proctor Favian and Proctor Gallean themselves—and embraced it. He may have used his rather singular access to additional information by watching the mages on the practice yard, but I wouldn't consider that spying. He didn't sneak into the practice yard. He didn't even compromise a mage student by having him or her reveal forms he wasn't privy to. By Lane's own admission, Devon helped her with the forms, not the other way around. I submit there was no wrongdoing here, that Devon Alamort's research was done properly and within the context of the rules of the Lyceum, regardless of its sensitive nature. His challenge should be accepted and should stand on its own."

A few of the proctors on the board glanced at each other, eyebrows raised. Others bowed their heads, troubled.

Favian asked, "Are you finished?"

Arrend nodded.

"Then everyone but the Board should leave. We have much to discuss."

The acolyte watching over Lane grabbed her shoulder. She wrenched free and glared at him until he stepped back. When he motioned toward another door on the far side of the room, Lane headed toward it, the acolyte following behind.

"We should leave," Arrend said, standing next to Devon now. "I know you want to speak to her, but now is not the time."

Devon relented, the acolyte escorting them both into the audience chamber outside. The acolyte left immediately, shutting the door to the Inner Sanctum behind him.

"Is it true?" Arrend asked immediately. "Your accusation about Favian holding Lane back—is it true? It wasn't something you made up on the spot to get a rise from him?"

Devon's entire body began to tremble, his arms and legs weak. He sank into one of the chairs. "It's true. I was trying to find Lane— she'd disappeared—but no one at the Mage School would help me. I was waiting for her to come out of their dormitory when I ran into Quinn. She let it slip."

"So Quinn is involved. Who else?"

"She didn't name anyone else. She made it seem as if the entire magerium was in on it."

"Proctors and students?"

"Yes. And they were holding her in her room, wouldn't let her out."

Arrend swore under his breath.

"Why does that matter?"

"Because it means it will be nearly impossible to prove, unless one of the proctors or students comes forward."

"They won't."

Arrend didn't answer.

"Quinn said she did it because Lane's mother took her family's place on the Council. And because Lane is Luminesque."

"That's Quinn's reason. What's Favian's?"

"Dalton and I think it's a ploy to escape his banishment to the Lyceum. If he embarrasses Lane, the scandal might harm her mother's position enough that she'd be removed."

"And then Quinn's father could step in. He could then influence the Council to rescind Favian's exile. Given Favian's past manipulations, that's certainly possible." Arrend stared at the banners over Devon's head in deep thought, but turned to the door into the Inner Sanctum when the faint sound of raised voices reached them.

"What do you think they'll do?" Devon asked.

"I don't know. The rules aren't clear, but Favian holds a great deal of sway over the other proctors."

When they heard raised voices again, Arrend moved toward the door. "Wait here."

Devon leaned forward in the chair, resting his elbows on his knees, the heels of his hands pressed into his eyes. After a moment, he scrubbed at his face and stood, began pacing. He thought about everything that Favian had said. On some level, Favian was right; he should never have begun studying the mage forms. He'd known the school was secretive about their studies and he knew why. So why had he done it, regardless? Why had he pursued it?

Because it was there, staring him in the face, and he'd never been able to turn away once something caught his interest. Only this time, it didn't affect just him. Lane was caught up in it; Dalton, too, if they found out he'd known and said nothing.

"Damn it. I should have stayed focused on the research I'd already done."

Except that had been going nowhere. He'd had no other option; study the mage forms or have no challenge and be expelled.

The door to the Inner Sanctum crashed open and slammed into the wall. Arrend stood in the opening.

"What's happened?" Devon asked.

Arrend swept past Devon with a curt, "Follow me."

Devon scrambled to keep up as Arrend entered the hall outside, heading toward the main doors.

"What's happened?" Devon repeated as Arrend flung the outer doors open and they stepped into torrential rain. Devon used an arm to protect himself from the worst of the windswept drops, but Arrend didn't even do that as he paused at the top of the administration building's outer steps.

"You've been expelled," he said, water dripping down his face, his hair already matted to his head. "Worse than that, Gallean warned me that he's being pushed to have War detain you, since you are privy to mage secrets that cannot be exposed. The War Master told me to escort you off campus immediately, before Favian wins over enough proctors that the order has to be enforced."

Arrend headed toward the Science dormitory, cutting across the quad. Devon remained at the top of the steps, too shocked to move. A bolt of lightning, close, jolted him out of the paralysis and he ran after Arrend.

"They can't!" he shouted at Arrend's back. "I didn't do anything wrong! It was a fair challenge! Those were fair questions!"

Arrend spun on him. "It has nothing to do with fairness! You of all people should know that. You came from the lower city. You came from the slums. None of this has anything to do with right or wrong. It has everything to do with politics. You and Lane simply had the misfortune of getting caught up in Favian's game, whatever it is."

Devon gaped at Arrend, who straightened, his anger now edged with regret. "Lane?"

"She's been expelled, too. Ostensibly for helping you. But based on what you said about Favian and the others, they were only looking for an excuse. Favian is obviously using Quinn's hatred of Lane to gain some kind of influence over Quinn's father. I can only assume his intent is to somehow use Lane to force Councilor Varenov to step down, either by embarrassment or scandal or simple suspicion of some kind of collusion with Brovetto. Quinn's father probably assumes he'll take Varenov's place. Then Favian would have a say in the Council."

Arrend gripped Devon's shoulder, tugged him toward the Science dormitory.

"There was nothing I could do—for you or Lane. Favian never intended for you to pass that challenge, not once he realized you'd violated the mages' studies." He ushered Devon up the dormitory's steps. "We need to get your things and get you off campus as soon as possible. Gallean said he'd hold off Favian's decree as long as possible."

As soon as they opened the doors into the great room, what had to be the entire dormitory along with assorted other students turned toward them. Dalton stood at the front.

"What happened?"

Devon glanced around at everyone assembled. "I've been expelled."

There were a few gasps, but mostly the students simply looked shocked.

Arrend pulled him toward the stairs. "We don't have time for this."

Dalton shouted, "Wait!" and followed them, Itch on his heels.

As soon as Arrend flung open his dorm room door, he said, "Grab what you can. Only the essentials."

Devon snatched his satchel up first and began stuffing papers inside. Notes from his studies, both magical and mathematical, ink, quills, charcoal. Arrend went immediately to his window, staring out in the direction of the mage's practice yard, the corner that could be seen if it weren't raining. Dalton hovered in the doorway, Itch behind him.

"What can I do to help?" the War student asked.

Devon grabbed another satchel, flung it at him. "Fill it with whatever clothes you can find."

"What about me?"

Devon stared at Itch, something hard and hot lodging at the base of this throat. "Food. Go to the kitchen and see what you can get for me."

Itch vanished.

He stood for a moment, Dalton scrambling around behind him, Arrend watching out the window. The lump in his throat refused to move and he felt the skin prickling around his eyes. He was leaving, being forced out. The Lyceum he had called home for the last six years was being taken from him.

And worse, he was going to have to hide. From Arrend, from Dalton...everyone.

He jerked back into motion, not letting himself think about it any longer. He reached for every scrap of paper, not looking to see what it was, just stuffing it into the satchel, grasping for every last vestige of this life.

Then, beneath a sheaf of pages, he found an inlaid wooden box: Arrend's notes on the Wardings.

He picked up the box and turned to Arrend. "I should probably return this."

Arrend met his gaze. "Keep it. I can reproduce the notes."

Devon hesitated, but stuffed the box into his satchel, papers crumpling beneath it.

Itch appeared at the door. He thrust a cloth sack into Devon's chest. "Someone's coming. It looks like Favian and Gallean, with some of the War students."

"Time's up then," Arrend said, motioning all of them toward the door. "Downstairs. Now."

They ran down the stairs, emerging into the great room, all of the students clustered to one side, a wide path leading up to the open doors. The steward of the dormitory stood at the entrance, but glanced back as they crossed the room. "They're crossing the quad. You'll have to run."

Arrend took the steward's place at the door, ushered Devon, Dalton, and Itch outside. Devon could see Favian and the others, figures blurred by the pounding rain.

"Head to the left, toward the practice yards," Arrend said.

Dalton handed over his satchel of clothes and Devon slipped the strap for both it and his notes over one shoulder, making certain the mouth of the one containing his notes was closed so the papers wouldn't get wet. He clutched the sack of food from Itch to his chest.

Then he ran.

A shout rang out behind him—Favian—and he picked up speed, feet squelching in the grass of the quad, then splashing in the puddles between the cobbles of the two walls of the practice yards, the runoff at least an inch deep. When he emerged on the far side, at the boundary of the Lyceum, he saw another group of War students and two other proctors standing before a carriage, the door being held open by a man in rigid servant's livery. Someone was stepping up into the carriage.

It took a moment for Devon to recognize her.

"Lane!" He would have run toward her, but he could hear Favian and the others behind, in the tunnel between the yards now, close.

She turned. He saw her face clearly—sad, reluctant, forlorn. But it brightened when she saw him.

"Lane! I didn't mean for any of this to happen!"

Two of the War students who'd escorted her began to move toward him.

She attempted to back out of the carriage, but a lithe hand emerged from the dark interior and caught her arm. She twisted free in disdain, then shouted, "I know!" before the servant and the two other War students closed in behind her and forced her into the carriage, slamming the door closed.

The servant stepped up onto a small ledge to one side and the carriage was in motion before Devon had drawn another breath.

"Stop him!" Favian shouted toward the War students and proctors who'd dealt with Lane. "He's not to leave the Lyceum grounds!"

Devon hesitated, the ties that had bound him to the college the last six years strong.

But then he bolted toward the lower city, toward Carbolen and the life he'd left behind, toward an empty future with dead crystal and the Flatlands looming before him.

PART II

THE LOWER CITY

Chapter Nine

Devon jumped, caught hold of a bar of metal, and hefted himself up to the next level of scaffolding, the only part of the building that remained at the top of the mid-level tower. Brushing rust from his hands, he settled into a crouch in the lee of a half-finished wall, the chill wind still tugging at the hood of the cloak he wore.

From this vantage, he could see the quad of the Lyceum and the crowd of students and families gathered there, too distant to make out individuals. During lulls in the wind, or when it blew just right, he could hear the strains of the graduation ceremony or the faint snatches of a speech being augmented by the mages. All of the students were dressed in their School colors, the various patches like fields against the backdrop of the grass. The amber of the shard stood out among them, along with the blunt gray armor of the War students. Devon couldn't see the stage at the edge of the quad closest to him, but he leaned his head against the wall and blinked away a few stray tears as students began to process onto it.

When the War students began their procession, he pushed away from the wall and bellowed out a shout for Dalton, knowing he was down there somewhere. His voice was ragged, torn away by the wind, unheard by anyone but himself, but he didn't care. He cupped his hands around his mouth and whooped and hollered, grinning madly even though he was crying, until his throat hurt.

Then he watched as the crowd dispersed, colors bleeding into each other, spreading out through the buildings and trees he'd called home for nearly six years. Dalton would be heading off to the army now, or the city guard, the usual two month leave the War students got before they had to report for additional training and assignment suspended due to the increasing tensions between Iandolo and Brovetto. It was unlikely he'd see Dalton again, even if the War student remained in the city. It was too risky.

He reached up and purposefully wiped the wetness from his face, his eyes dry now.

"Lane should have been there."

He glanced up toward the city's tallest towers. He didn't even know which one she'd been taken to, which had become her prison. She was out of his reach now. He was part of the lower city once again.

He turned away from it all and began descending the scaffolding. He needed to focus on survival.

He halted in the building's doorway at ground level, half in and out of shadow. The urge to reach up and tug the hood of his cloak over his head was strong, but here at mid-level that would attract more attention than leaving the hood down. He scanned the bustling street. He saw none of the city watch, nor anyone associated with the Lyceum or army, but he still hesitated. He'd taken a risk coming up to the middle city. Even if the guard no longer searched for him, Favian would have others looking.

Adjusting the satchel on his hip, he stepped out into the street and joined the flow of bodies, head slightly bowed, eyes darting toward every sharp movement or voice. He needed to get into the lower levels, where he felt more hidden, but first he needed to try to score some coin.

He crossed the street behind a horse-drawn carriage, heading away from the hub, toward the parks on the outskirts of the city. A few curved streets and a dark alley later, he entered a huge square filled with tents and carts, the marketplace a maze of narrows paths. The scents of cooked meats, fresh baked breads, spilled alcohol, and incense flooded the open space. The shouts of the hawkers vied with the hagglers and the conversations of the patrons. Devon allowed himself to sink into the rhythm of the place, nodding to vendors, smiling, but moving with purpose toward the southwestern side, so no one engaged him. With nimble fingers, he nicked a spear of grilled chicken from the edge of a fire, the meat hot and savory, then took advantage when a woman tripped and stumbled into a fruit vendor to slip an apple into his pocket. He helped the woman straighten while the vendor eyed both of them in suspicion. The spice on the chicken made him thirsty, but he saw no opportunity to snatch any of the juice or wine being sold.

The food vendors died out as he angled through the center of the market, replaced by clothiers, potters, cobblers, and other artisans. Most of these sellers kept their wares inside the draped confines of their tents, only a few pieces out on display. Devon picked up his pace. He noted two city guardsmen ahead and veered to the left, cutting between two tents. He avoided the large fountain in the center of the square where he could hear kids splashing and screaming.

On the far side of the fountain, he found the tent he was looking for. It appeared to be a tinker's shop, pans of various metals hanging from the corner stakes, clanking in the faint breeze. Devon didn't see Geral, the owner, anywhere.

He leaned down close to the door flap. "Geral, are you there?"

Nothing.

He straightened and nearly leaped out of his skin when Geral gripped him firmly by the elbow from behind and shouted, "Devon! So good to see you! Do you have something for me?"

Devon pulled his arm free. "Don't do that."

"Do what?"

"Sneak up on me like that."

"I wasn't sneaking, just returning to my humble little shop."

Devon knew not to trust the tinker's innocent, weathered face. Geral had worked with Carbolen's gang in the past, which meant he wasn't completely legitimate.

He patted his satchel. "I have a few things here that need...repair."

"I see. Step inside then. We'll take a look-see."

The interior of the tent was surprisingly tidy. Pots, pans, and cups were organized into neat stacks, separated by metals—tin to one side, copper the other, pewter in a back corner opposite a small cot and table lined with small hammers and pliers and other instruments of Geral's trade. A rug had been spread over the stone of the marketplace with a few large pillows strewn about as seating. Geral settled onto one and motioned for Devon to sit as well.

"Now what do you have for me?" He leaned forward to peer into Devon's satchel.

Devon pulled out a scattering of lucent shards, spreading them on the ornately-patterned rug. They were of various shapes and sizes, from rounded chips the size of a pea to one yellow shard as long as Devon's arm. All of them had been scavenged from the lower city, Devon rooting through abandoned shops and hovels, or crawling through alleys and niches, testing veins of lucent, hoping for the random pieces that were still active.

What lay on the rug was the result of over two weeks of searching. The lower city had long been picked clean of anything obviously worthwhile. Devon's only advantage was his affinity for the crystal. He could often bring veins of lucent that looked long dead back to life, like the purple veins in the room he and Lane had used to practice.

It was also the reason he was such a good lockpick.

Geral began humming to himself, hunched over the haul, his fingers picking through the pieces with precision. He flicked some of the smallest pieces aside, held up one shaped like a rose, long dead, with scorn before tossing it aside, then focused on what remained.

"I'll give you twenty bright for it all."

"Twenty! It's worth at least fifty."

"Hardly." He grabbed one of the pieces. "This one would be beautiful except it's shot through with that black smoke, already half dead." He flicked it with a finger and it sputtered to life, a sickly green. "Not to mention it's distorted color. I doubt anyone above will be interested, except the most desperate. It's only saving grace is I can say it comes from deep in the lower city. It does come from the lower city, yes?"

Devon nodded, but Geral had already picked up another piece.

"This one has some merit—a unique teardrop shape and a nice blue color—but it's small. Good for a merchant's youngest daughter's necklace, perhaps a bracelet. This shard of indigo will bring me maybe ten bright. These two purple chips are close enough in color to be used for earrings, perhaps, but the rest of this—" he waved at the pieces he'd discarded "—it isn't worth anything. Not to the customers I deal with in the upper city. They want large pieces, rare colors, so they can show them off at their balls and political events."

Devon clamped down on his anger—twenty would last him a few days at most. "What about this piece?" He reached for the large yellow shard, held it up, and brushed it to life. "Yellow is rare. And it has hardly any smoke."

Geral rocked back. "Yellow isn't as rare as you think."

"This piece alone is worth twenty," Devon countered. "Forty-five bright for it all. If those in the towers won't take it, you can always sell it to someone from one of the other Crystal Cities. Their lucent is dying out much faster than ours."

"True, but finding a merchant from one of the other cities isn't easy, not with the Council watching the gates as closely as they are now. Thirty."

"Forty. Last chance."

Geral grumbled and Devon started shoving the lucent back into his satchel.

"Alright, alright! Forty." He stood, mumbling deprecations under his breath as he moved to his cot. Devon scooped up the pieces he wasn't interested in and stood.

Geral reached out with the coin, but when Devon went to grab it, he closed his fist around it. "I'd pay another forty for that green shard in your satchel."

Devon reflexively clutched the pouch closer to his body. Geral's eyes were sharper than he'd thought; he hadn't meant for the tinker to see the lantern he'd taken from his room at the Lyceum. "It's not for sale."

"Fifty?"

"Not. For. Sale. At any price."

Geral's eyes narrowed, but he relented, opening his fist and dropping the coins into Devon's outstretched hand. "Let me know when the hunger changes your mind. Now get out."

He hustled Devon out through the flap, snapping it shut behind him.

Devon scanned the surrounding market, then stared down at the few coins in his hand. He sighed.

This was going to be harder than he thought.

Pocketing the coins, he skimmed through the market back into the streets, making his way to the outer edge, then descended four levels. He kept his eyes out for city guards in the first few levels, then switched to watching for gang members, especially Carbolen's gang, the lower he went. Pulling his hood close, he moved hubward on Level Twenty, deeper into the streets, until there was no sky visible overhead.

Near the hub, he halted and ducked into an alley, no more than a niche between two buildings. It reeked of garbage and shit. Satisfied that no one had followed him, he eased a section of one of the buildings aside, the makeshift door leading into a short corridor, then into a small room that he'd claimed as his own.

He tossed his satchel onto the pile of blankets against one wall, then removed the green lantern and tapped it alight, setting it to one side. Leaning back against the wall, he stared around at the scattered papers he'd brought from the Lyceum—all of the notes from his work with Lane and his research before that. Arrend's box containing his work on the Wardings sat unopened to one side.

He pulled the coins from his pocket again.

He was going to have to spend more time searching for what he needed to survive and less time here, messing with his research. Especially now that what funds he'd had when he left the Lyceum had run out.

He thought about the purple lucent tree in the practice room. As Nic had said, it was worth a lot of bright. It could feed him for months.

But he couldn't bring himself to destroy the tree. He wasn't that desperate. Not yet.

Besides, that practice room was probably being watched by the city guard. He couldn't afford to take the risk.

* * *

From the dark recesses of an alcove, Devon watched the street beyond, water dripping down steadily from the level above. He was close to the hub, two levels below where he had found the bolthole where he lived, so the street and buildings were completely covered by the levels higher up, no hint of sky. Most of the lucent here was dark, including what was used to illuminate the street. A single patch glowed a pale green a few blocks away. Most of the light down here came from candles and lanterns from behind closed windows and locked doors.

On this street, Devon could see chinks of natural light in only four of the nearest buildings and, aside from the streetlight, no visible lucent. Most of the residences and stores were abandoned.

A group of five figures skirted past. Devon drew back, hand falling to his knife, but none of them turned to look in his direction. Two of them had spiked hair, but it was too dark in this section for him to pick out the colors. He'd learned quickly that hair color did indeed indicate gang affiliations once you reached a certain level. He'd also learned the gangs he'd known when he lived down here had changed significantly, and those that did still exist had altered their alliances enough that he couldn't rely on any of his previous knowledge. Carbolen's gang was still around, but he wasn't interested in rejoining…assuming Carbolen didn't kill him outright for the failed Presidium job. He already had Favian and the city watch looking for him, he didn't need Carbolen or the other gangs searching for him, too.

Thankfully, he still had his lockpicking skills.

As soon as the group vanished into a side street, Devon darted to another doorway. He scanned the street again, frowned at furtive movement near an alley where he'd hidden before, but when no one appeared he opened the door behind him and stepped into the abandoned store. He paused long enough to eye the street again, but once his eyes had adjusted to the darkness inside he slipped past toppled chairs and broken tables, the looted counter and the space behind it, and into the storeroom in the back.

Door closed, he removed the green lucent lantern and tapped it, pale light flooding the interior. Shelving filled three walls, interrupted by a door that opened onto an office. Nothing lined the shelves but dust, cobwebs, and a few shattered jars, their contents long degraded. Based on the smell, this had been a spice shop, the amalgam of scents still lingering. He stepped through the storeroom toward the office, breathing through his nose as he kicked up dust and ancient dried spices. No one had been in here in years, perhaps decades.

It gave him a small shred of hope.

The office had even less than the storeroom. Looters had taken the desk long ago, stripped the cabinets and shelving from one wall, even pulled down placards or paintings. The rectangles where they'd been were clear. The remains of a chair had been kicked into one corner. When he stepped inside, he disturbed scattered sheets of paper beneath the dust. Crouching down, he pulled a few free, but they were full of crabbed handwriting, numbers in long columns. Ledgers for the spice shop.

Setting the lucent lamp on the floor, he began a methodical search of the room, starting with the walls. They were made mostly of wood, with strands of lucent woven into them, all of them dead. He laid his hands on each one, even though he could see the smoky threads of black inside them. He hadn't expected to find any that worked;

any buildings on this level with known working lucent wouldn't be abandoned.

His first pass finished, he began again, paying close attention to the sections of wall with the lighter rectangles where paintings had once rested. This time he looked for hidden compartments or caches, but found nothing.

He glanced down at the floor, then knelt and began shoving the scattered papers aside, revealing bare floorboards. Beneath the splintered legs of the chair, he found a loose slat.

Tossing the pieces of the chair aside, he pulled the slat free, reaching into the space beneath. He thought it was empty until his fingers brushed something in a far corner.

It took a moment to work the box out, but when he drew it into the light of his lantern, his blood thrummed. He'd searched over a dozen abandoned stores in the last few weeks, on various levels, but this was his first find. Metal, the box's edges were still sealed tight, smooth except for the rounded lucent lock on one face. One side would open with the right key. One of the better lockboxes a shop owner could get.

As he moved it around, something inside shifted.

"Definitely not empty."

Resting it in his lap, he took a deep breath, closed his eyes, and touched the lucent lock.

The skin of his fingertips prickled and then he was in, the lock's paths forming in intricate detail on the backs of his eyelids, a complex spiderweb of varicolored light. Devon's sense of location shifted, so that he no longer felt the floor beneath him or the wall at his back. He was submerged inside the lucent, part of it, although he could still smell spices, could have heard someone speaking to him if there'd been anyone around. His sense of self, though, resided in the crystal, on the pathways branching out before him. Before Arrend and the Lyceum, he'd merged with the lucent on instinct, traveled its pathways by feel alone. Now, after six years of study, he saw the paths with a different perspective. There was an inherent order to the structure, layers of threads, most of them hidden behind the surface layer where he now stood.

But he could see the threads needed to reach the next layer. All he had to do to unlock the box was reach the bottom layer by traveling the correct threads.

"Simple."

He grinned, then slid down the appropriate paths to the next layer, and the next, the paths getting less complicated the farther down he went, with fewer dead ends, until with a faint click, the top of the box popped open.

"Incredible. You actually found something."

He bolted upright to find three of the five gang members he'd seen earlier standing in the entrance to the office, the two with spiked hair at the front. He assumed the other two were out in the main room, on guard.

When he reached for his knife, tucked into the back of his pants, the leader took a step forward and said, "Don't." He held a dagger, thinner and longer than the knife Devon carried, but when Devon stilled, he lowered it slightly. "We've been watching you for the past few weeks, skulking around down here where you don't belong, searching the shops. We thought you were a joke—these shops have long been cleaned out—but you actually found something." He nodded toward the box in Devon's hand. "What is it?"

Devon glanced down and noticed with relief that the top had snicked closed, the lock reset, probably when his hand clamped down on it in shock on hearing the leader's voice. He showed it to them. "Just a shop owner's box. But it's locked."

"We have lockpicks for that. Hand it over."

"I don't think so."

The leader frowned and one of his followers gave a choked-off snort.

"We know you aren't part of a gang. You're too new here. You don't wear the colors. You don't have any support. So hand it over."

Devon stooped down, grabbed his satchel, and stuffed the box inside, slinging it over his shoulder. Then he picked up his lucent lantern.

All three of the gang members had tensed, the two in the back now with visible blades.

"What do you think you're doing?" the leader asked.

"Leaving."

Devon charged them, shoulder tucked, plowing into the leader before he could react, thrusting him back into the other two. He was out the door and into the storeroom before any of them could form a coherent sentence, but as he ran into the outer store the leader shouted, "Barter! Scorch! Stop him!"

The other two were standing on either side of the shop's entrance. The larger of the two charged him, but Devon dodged to the left and launched himself over the shop's counter, rolling across it on his back. Broken glass and pottery shards ground into his shoulders, but he landed on his feet on the far side and staggered toward the thinner woman still standing at the door, ready with a tight grin of anticipation. The skin around her eyes was smudged black with ash.

She would have skewered him with her knife, but his feet tangled in the remains of one of the chairs and he tripped and fell to the floor, satchel clutched close to his chest. Pale green light and shadow danced as he plowed into her legs, her blade slashing across his upper arm as she attempted to roll free.

Devon lurched into a crouch and threw himself out the door. He fled into an alley, tapping the lantern as he ran, plunging himself into darkness, not stopping even though he could barely see. When it branched, he glanced back, heard the gang members shouting in the street, followed by running footsteps. His eyes had adjusted, but his breath came in ragged heaves. His six years at the Lyceum had made him soft; he shouldn't be this winded yet.

Someone barked, "Devon!"

Startled, he turned toward the voice. "Nic?"

A shadow gestured from a recessed doorway in the back of one of the buildings. "Get in here! Fast!"

Devon squeezed in past Nic. The bartender from the Shandy Quad shut the door behind them as Devon spun back around.

"What in hells—"

"Shut up," Nic said. "They're coming. Try not to breathe."

Devon sucked in a deep breath and held it, his heart thudding hard in his chest.

Through the door, footsteps charged down the alley but halted at the split. Angry voices followed, then two sets broke off, one splashing past their door, the other headed away down the left branch.

The moment they passed the door, Nic motioned toward the room's interior. Devon exhaled. He followed Nic through shattered support columns, the floor littered with shards of wood. His feet crunched in splinters of lucent. Vague blocky shapes loomed up on either side and as Nic ducked beneath one he realized it was part of the collapsed ceiling. Hunched down, he half walked, half crawled to where Nic had pulled up a wide section of the floor.

"Drop down in and step to the side. There's a tunnel off to the right."

"Where does it lead?"

"To the next level down."

Carbolen's lair.

"You work for Carbolen."

"What did you think the blue-colored hair meant?"

"I thought..." But it didn't matter. "Why were you bartending at the Shandy Quad?"

"Why do you think? To keep an eye on you. We've been watching you off and on since you first entered the Lyceum, always at a distance, waiting. Carbolen wanted to see if you'd rat us out, reveal our operation to the proctors or the guard."

"If I didn't when they dragged me off to the city jail, why would I do it later?"

"He had bets that you would. Being around the proctors all the time, around those students, most of them from the upper city...it does strange things to the mind. But he lost. After a while, when we realized you were close to graduating, he thought maybe you'd be useful again, all educated and everything, that maybe you'd want to return to the fold. He sent me to the bar to feel you out." Nic shifted, and suddenly Devon realized he was close enough in the confined space he could feel his breath. "I vouched for you, Devon. Said he could trust you, even before you were kicked out. Don't make me regret it."

He should have known Carbolen wouldn't simply let him go. He'd spent six years at the college and not once had he thought he was being watched, but it made sense. His watchers had probably had orders to kill Devon the moment it appeared he'd turned traitor.

They probably had the same orders even now.

"What if I don't want to see Carbolen?"

Nic's hand fell onto his shoulder. "You know that's not an option."

"Will you kill me if I resist?"

"If I thought you'd resist, I would have left you to Saw and his thugs."

Nic faced Devon, his other hand falling on Devon's other shoulder. He moved in even closer, so their foreheads were almost touching. Devon could make out the bartender's face from the shadows now.

"Devon, it's me: Nic. You know me. And I know you. It's not going to come to that."

"I thought I knew you."

"This changes nothing. How many times did I keep watch for you while you and Lane practiced? How many drinks did we share at the Quad?"

A clang echoed through the building, followed by shouts. Devon recognized Saw's voice.

"That's the door we came through. Looks like you don't have a choice after all. They'll be through it in a second." He turned Devon to the opening of the tunnel, gave him a shove. "Go!"

Devon dropped into the opening blindly, surprised at how deep the initial shaft was. He landed hard, stumbled back into a metal wall, already feeling for the tunnel entrance. He heard scraping above, glanced up to see Nic's legs as he braced himself and slid the floor covering up and over, cutting off the scant light. A moment before he dropped into the shaft another harsh clang echoed through the building, followed by a crash as the outside door gave way with shouts of triumph. Nic's feet caught Devon on the shoulder and he cried out in pain as Nic fell on top of him. They scrabbled at each other, until Nic hissed a warning and they both stilled.

Above, muffled by the floor panel, they could hear Saw and his fellow gang members tearing the room apart.

Nic whispered, "The tunnel."

"I can't find it."

"Here." Nic's hands found his in the pitch black, guided them down to below hip level.

Devon ducked down and slid into the tunnel on hands and knees. He couldn't see where he was going, but the walls were scraping his shoulders, his head brushing the ceiling, so he didn't need a light. He heard Nic behind him, close—

And then his hand encountered empty air and he began to tumble forward.

Nic grabbed his shirt and hauled him back. "There are metal rungs bolted into the side of the shaft."

Heart hammering in his chest, Devon reached down until he felt the first rung, then twisted himself around in the cramped quarters and started down.

As he descended, he thought about all of the time he'd spent at the Shandy Quad with Lane, Dalton, and Nic, laughing, joking, drinking. He recalled the bar fight, their escape through the back room, the stacks of strange boxes he'd seen there before their first foray down to the lower levels to practice.

When his feet hit floor, he pressed up against a side wall until Nic stood beside him, then asked, "Is Arch part of Carbolen's gang as well?"

He couldn't see Nic, but he heard the hesitation before Nic shifted away. "He helps with our activities in the upper city."

"Upper city? Except for a few odd runs—" like the Presidium job, when he'd been caught "—Carbolen stayed out of the upper city."

"Things have changed."

Metal scraped against metal, followed by a click. Nic grunted as a shaft of light appeared, intensely bright after the darkness of the tunnel. Devon raised a hand to cover his eyes as Nic shifted a metal panel aside and motioned him through the hole.

He stepped into a room lit by a single candle on a table against one wall, the outline of a door to one side. The floor was made of wooden slats, the walls mostly lucent, except for the section where they'd entered. The lucent all appeared dead.

Nic ducked inside and reset the panel, slipping what looked like makeshift brackets in place to secure it before standing. "They shouldn't be able to find us, even if they do find the tunnel. They'll think the shaft is another dead end."

He retrieved the candle and opened the door.

"Ready to meet Carbolen?"

Chapter Ten

The labyrinthine approach to Carbolen's inner chamber had changed. Within a few turns and cut-backs, Devon found himself lost, his spatial orientation skewed. There were only a few places in Iandolo that messed with his directional sense; the area around Carbolen's lair was one of them.

Nic led the way with his candle, the flame guttering with any sudden movement or when caught in the few odd drafts that kept the air circulating this deep. Devon followed close behind, ducking through tunnels, doorways, or through the occasional panel Nic opened at random. They passed others in Carbolen's gang, standing guard in the halls or at intersections, most with the blue-dyed hair, all in dark tan leathers of various shades. Devon didn't recognize any of those in the outer layer; they were too young to have been part of the gang six years before. However, when he sensed they were getting closer, he began to see familiar faces—Tims, Iril, Parker. They each gave him a cold look as he passed, although Tims nodded almost imperceptibly. They were hardened, harsher versions of those he remembered, with new scars, even an ugly patch of burned skin on Iril's left temple. A few he knew should be here were conspicuously absent, although they could be off working a job. Devon suspected they were simply dead.

Then they turned a corner and Devon found himself at the arched entrance of a great hall, one both familiar and numbingly different.

It had once been a ballroom, the walls paneled in lacquered wood, striated with veins of lucent in all of the darker spectrums of color— purples, blues, greens, a few thin strands of red. The floor was blue-veined marble, cut in massive six-foot-by-six-foot squares. At the far end, the veins of lucent all converged to a single point—a circular orb the size of Devon's head that lay at the center of an intricately-carved stone emblem that no one knew the meaning of. Devon could imagine how stunning the room had been once—all of the lucent glowing, reflecting off of the lacquered wood, the gleaming floor, the vaulted ceiling.

But now, most of the lucent was dead. Only a few threads glowed along the walls, enough to light the room, exposing the cracks in the marble, the patchy remains of the wood paneling. No one had attempted to preserve the varnish on the walls or sweep the floor for decades. Hammocks had been strung in the corners, from the floor to the ceiling, and along most of the walls, interspersed with ladders. The floor was strewn with clothes and blankets, each member of the gang claiming a small area as his or her own. A few chests or wooden boxes were shoved against the wall, some with locks, not that any gang member would keep something valuable here; they would all have their own hidden stashes out in the lower city. Some would even have their own boltholes, like Devon.

Carbolen had claimed the end of the hall, set up on a makeshift dais beneath the chipped emblem and the rounded lucent that still gleamed a deep purple.

As soon as they entered, Nic blew out his candle. The general cacophony of all of those present died off, gang members on all sides halting whatever they were doing to stare at Devon. He didn't spare them a glance, focused on Carbolen, lounging in one of the worn settees that edged the dais, creating the illusion of a private space.

"Let's get this over with."

They walked toward the dais, gang members shifting out of their way, then trailing behind. The lull in the hall's activity had caught Carbolen's attention. His focus had shifted from the five gang members surrounding him—two captains Devon recognized from his own time with the gang and three others that must have risen in the ranks since then—to Devon's approach. He'd aged, hair streaked with gray, new wrinkles around his eyes, his mouth. A livid scar ran from just below his left ear across his cheek, ending near his nose. But he still had the same penetrating gaze.

They drew to a halt at the base of the dais, Carbolen standing to meet them. Devon found himself sweating, tried to hide it by stiffening his shoulders and holding the gang leader's eyes. It was easier than he'd expected.

Carbolen's chin lowered. "Six years away has made you bolder."

"I've learned a lot. Survived a lot."

"And yet now you're back in the lower city."

"I don't intend to stay long. Leave me be and I'll be gone before you know it."

"Do you really believe that? I know you've run out of what little coin you had when you were expelled from the college. I know you've been scavenging in the lower city for sparks of lucent. And I know you've been to see Geral. I'm impressed you've managed to find anything to interest him, especially since you haven't resorted to theft from the gangs who've managed to seize areas of active lucent. But you can't survive on shattered, half-dead lucent forever. You've already begun to sink into the depths of the city."

His five captains had repositioned themselves on the dais behind him, two standing to either side, the others seated. One of those seated—Went—spun a knife between his two hands, the point pressed into one index finger, the pommel on the other.

"You can feel it, can't you? The darkness. The despair. The desperation. It's already creeping into your soul, the way it crept into your father's before he was killed in that skirmish. The way it crept into your mother's afterwards, as she fought to keep you alive. I can see it in you. You fight it, but it's there. You've already started stealing—that spear of chicken at the market, the pocketed apple. Old habits are hard to lose, even after six years of relative ease."

Devon felt nauseous. "You were watching me, even at the market?"

"I never stopped watching you. I was there when the city guard released you and Arrend snatched you up for the Lyceum. I was there when you passed your first exams. We've kept our eyes on you ever since."

Devon's mouth had gone dry. "Why?"

Carbolen stepped down from the dais. "I would have killed you right there, outside the constabulary, except Arrend had already taken you under his wing. He whisked you away to the safety of the Lyceum. You were lucky they kept you busy those first few years; we couldn't watch you on the campus grounds. By the time you started venturing off campus, things down here had changed. Your skills had become more important than your betrayal."

"You mean the Presidium job." On the dais, Went flinched and Devon remembered he'd been part of the Presidium team. Except Went hadn't been caught. "I didn't betray you."

Carbolen halted directly in front of him, less than an arm's-length away. "The alarm went off when you were picking the lock."

"It wasn't me. Someone triggered it from outside. I would have seen it otherwise."

Carbolen stared hard into Devon's eyes. This close, Devon could smell the oil used to keep his leathers supple. With a small shock, he also noted Carbolen's stature—medium height, not much taller than Devon himself; broad shoulders, although not stocky; stance loose and casual, but ready.

The posture of a War student...or someone who'd been in the army.

No wonder he'd been able to retain control of the gang for so long. He'd been formally trained.

But how had he ended up in the lower city?

Carbolen glanced back at his captains. "That no longer matters. I need you now."

"For what?"

"A job that requires your lockpick skills." He leaned in closer, so they were cheek to cheek. "I don't trust you, Devon. Tread carefully." Carbolen pulled back and ascended the stairs. "Welcome back to the gang, Devon. Nic, he will be your responsibility. Watch him at all times."

"I will."

Before Devon could ask what the job was, a group of gang members charged into the hall, halting just inside the door.

"The Brovettans are attacking the wayfare gate!"

"Again?" Carbolen asked. "How many?"

"Hard to tell. At least as many as the last time."

Carbolen swore and turned back to the dais, stalking to a chest to one side. The rest of the gang members were already in motion, jumping down from their hammocks or sprinting toward their own possessions, snatching up daggers and slings, axes and hammers. Devon even saw a few spears.

"I thought the Iandolan Army had crushed them," one of the captains, Leinn, said over the turmoil.

"Apparently not." Carbolen straightened from a crouch, a sheathed long sword in hand. He strapped it to his waist as he crossed back to Leinn's side. "You and the rest, gather crews and spread out. Find out what the other gangs are doing. Keep them away from our territory. You know what happened the last time."

"Where are you going?"

"Down to the wayfare gate, as we planned."

He turned to Went. "Pick no more than ten units to accompany us," he said, then considered Devon. "And bring him. Maybe he'll see something the rest of us will miss."

Carbolen jumped from the dais, headed for the entrance, the rest of the gang falling in around him or around Leinn, who hung back, already breaking her crew into smaller groups and giving out orders. A few of the gang members whooped or laughed, but the majority of them were more somber than Devon recalled from his own time here.

"You should probably take this," Nic said, holding out a double-edged knife, almost a dagger.

Went stepped off the dais and seized Devon's upper arm in a painful grip. He batted Nic's offered blade aside. "No weapons."

Nic hesitated, then slid the blade back into its sheath. "Whatever you say. You're the captain."

Went thrust Devon forward. "Follow Carbolen. Stay tight."

"I thought Nic was supposed to watch me."

"We can both watch you. Now move."

Devon headed out after Carbolen. Most of the lair had been vacated, but he caught up to the last of Carbolen's group just outside the doors. Leinn's crews were close on their heels, but they branched out to either side at various intersections of the maze, calling out commands as they did so. Within a hundred paces, Leinn's group had completely faded away, leaving Devon, Went, and Nic at the rear of Carbolen's group.

As soon as they left the main buildings that hid the lair, everyone spread out, small groups entering alleys and side streets, paralleling their route outwards, toward the edge of the city. Devon swore the group grew as they trotted down the main thoroughfare, but Went began pushing him harder, gaining on Carbolen's position, so he couldn't get an accurate count. At least twenty raced out in front of the main group as scouts. Devon was struck by how disciplined the gang had become.

They emerged onto a platform overlooking the gate to Brovetto. The sun glared a bloody deep orange on the horizon, near sunset, wavering in heatwaves over the Flatlands. Smoke rose in giant plumes, as it had before, except now Devon was seven levels closer. The way the tiers of the city flattened out at the lower levels gave the illusion he was even nearer, though they were still too distant to hear actual fighting, only the dull thumps of explosions.

Carbolen moved to the edge of the platform, hands wrapping around the metal railing as he leaned into the brisk wind. Went pushed Devon forward, but stepped around him when they drew near, halting at Carbolen's side with one of the other captains.

"They've hit the same area," Went said. "Why would they do that?"

"Not quite the same area," Carbolen answered. "This time, they've angled farther north, toward the Bolnis gate."

Devon tried to edge forward, but Nic restrained him with a warning look. He couldn't see much between Carbolen and his captains, but he could feel the thuds in his chest from the mages battling the Brovettans, harsher than before—he assumed because he was closer.

"What should we do?" the other captain asked.

Carbolen drew back. "The Iandolan reinforcements will likely be using the Bolnis Spoke—it would be quicker and give them the chance to head off the Brovettans if they manage to penetrate any further into the city. We'll take the Corlian shaft down to Level Twelve, then River Street, come at the battle from above and east of the Iandolan Army."

"That could trap us between the Brovettans and the army," Went said.

"Not if we're above them." He gave a sharp whistle to catch everyone's attention. "The Corlian shaft!"

Everyone turned and ran to the west, some leaping from the platform to whatever lay below, most funneling into the nearest streets and buildings. The other inhabitants on this level scurried out of the gang's way.

Before Went or Nic could grab him, Devon stepped up to the edge and scanned the battlefield below.

The destruction from the first attack was clearly visible to the east of the current conflagration, but Carbolen had been correct. The thrust of the Brovettan attack was angled away from their previous incursion. He couldn't immediately pick out their goal though.

He wondered if Dalton were down there.

"Move!" Went stood a short distance away.

Devon faced him. "Why does Carbolen care about the Brovettan attack? What's in it for him?"

"That doesn't concern you. Now move!"

Nic snatched Devon's shoulder. "Are you trying to piss him off?"

They ran, through alleys and buildings, past citizens who hid themselves behind slammed doors with harsh curses. They pounded down stairs, sprinted through open halls cluttered with debris, passed through rooms with collapsed ceilings. At one point, they leapt over a jagged hole in the middle of the street, Devon stumbling on the far side, Nic steadying him. When he glanced back, he could see down at least three levels.

They emerged at the edge of the shaft abruptly, the circular hole exposed to the sky, plummeting downwards all the way to the lowest city level. Carbolen's gang was already descending the sides of the shaft using ropes, nets, and the few stairs available. The sides were composed of rectangular protrusions of rooms and balconies, stairwells and platforms, with no apparent pattern.

Nic dragged Devon to the edge and snagged one of the ropes. "Just don't look down." Then he swung out over the edge and dropped from sight.

Went prodded Devon from behind. "Go. Or I'll throw you over the side and claim you slipped."

The rope ended at a ledge, then stairs, a leap to another ledge, a net they scaled diagonally, followed by three levels of more ropes. Nic led the way, Went keeping close above him, the rest of the gang ranging out all around. They passed closed doors, gang members with flattened green hair and scarred faces peering out with obvious distrust, but they didn't interfere. On another level, Carbolen halted and conversed with another gang leader, the two facing off like rival dogs. After a few threatening gestures, the gang leader listened to whatever Carbolen had to say, then gave a curt order.

Within moments, panels and hidden hatches on all sides opened and forty members of the new gang joined Carbolen's ranks. The two leaders began to descend together, both with obvious body guards nearby.

When they finally reached Level Twelve, the two gangs merged inside a wide hangar that opened out onto the shaft. Devon stumbled up to the nearest wall, sagging against it, his arms and legs trembling from fatigue. Nic joined him, sliding down into a crouch, back against the metal wall. Went stayed close, although his attention was fixed more on Carbolen than Devon.

Nic produced a water skin, drank, and handed it to Devon. "What did you do to piss Went off?" he asked as he wiped his mouth.

"He was part of the Presidium team. I guess he's holding a grudge."

"That was over six years ago."

"A strong grudge."

"Seems like more than that."

They fell silent as Carbolen approached Went.

"What's the status?" Went asked.

"The fight is still ongoing. The army is holding its own at the gate, but the Brovettans are pushing hard. The Iandolan reinforcements are headed down from the upper city, but we're ahead of them."

"What's with the Greenbacks?" Went jutted his chin toward the other gang members.

"Starling wants in on the action."

Devon sensed there was more to it than that, but Went merely asked, "The plan?"

"Unchanged. River Street, then we get as close as we can and see what's happening."

Carbolen turned away, not even glancing toward Devon. Within moments, they were moving again, now as a solid group.

River Street was named for its winding nature. Where most streets in Iandolo either shot straight out from the hub like spokes, or curved around the hub in circles, River meandered back and forth, tending generally outwards. A shallow depression along its edge had once run with water, as if there had been a river here long ago, but now that trench only filled during the heaviest of rains. Assorted rectangular containers lined the dry river, filled with garbage and debris, hinting that this had once been a park with trees and shrubs and flowerbeds.

They rounded a corner and the sounds of fighting escalated. Carbolen and Starling halted, the entire group gathering behind them. A sharp hand signal sent scouts out into the side streets to either side.

"Something's wrong," Nic whispered. "We shouldn't be anywhere near the fight yet."

Ahead, one of the scouts ran out from a street and raced toward them. He began waving his arms over his head. "Go back! Go back, they're already—"

A spherical ball of what looked like lightning shot out of the darkness and struck him from behind, hurtling him forward. His scream shot through the crackle of the blue-white light, then cut off. His body twitched, then sagged to the floor.

"What in bloody hells?" Nic asked.

Everyone began to fidget in indecision.

"Hold," Carbolen shouted. "Steady."

Men began pouring out of the alleys, charging down River Street toward them from the direction of the lightning. They were dressed in black armor, swords bared.

"Ready!" Carbolen snapped, and all of his captains drew their weapons. Those around them drew as well. They had only moments to brace themselves.

The black-armored group slammed into Carbolen's and Starling's men, breaking into a bellowed shout at the last moment. Swords clashed and screams filled the area. As the gang members before Devon were shoved backwards, he seized Nic's shirt and pulled him close. "I don't have a weapon, only my knife."

"Here." Nic pulled his second dagger and thrust it into Devon's hand. He snagged Devon's arm as they were jostled backwards, gang members pressing in. "Stay close. We're getting out of here." He began dragging Devon away from the main part of the fight, toward the side streets.

"Who are they?"

"I don't know, I've never seen them before. A rival gang perhaps?"

Devon didn't think so. Not with that armor. He strained to look back at where the main fight raged, caught sight of Carbolen wielding his sword with cold, brutal ferocity, Went and the other captains protecting his back, their positioning reminiscent of the forms of the War students on the quad. The men in black fought just as hard, with similar training. But the bodies that already littered River Street made it clear the gang members were outmatched.

Movement far behind the fight drew Devon's attention as another group in black emerged from an alley. Four figures strode forward, halting where the scout's body lay. The lead figure stared down at the contorted remains, nudged the scout with a boot, then glanced up.

"Brovettans," Devon muttered. "How'd they get up to Level Twelve?"

Nic shoved Devon backwards, the way they'd come. "There's more of them!"

On their left flank, another group of the black-armored Brovettans emerged from the side streets. Those to the left turned to meet the charge, but those in the loose formation at the back began to fray as men and women broke and ran. Nic cursed them as cowards, then choked on his words as they saw more Brovettans moving in the streets to their right.

"They're surrounding us," Devon said, then spun to where he'd last seen Carbolen. "Carbolen! Went! They're flanking us!" He gestured toward the right.

Carbolen turned in time to see the first of the Brovettans spill from the streets on their right. Without pause, the gang leader bellowed, "Fall back!"

He didn't wait to see if anyone heard, plunging his sword into a Brovettans' side before turning to run. A general call for retreat spread through the gangs like an apartment fire, everyone racing away in the only direction still available: back toward the Corlian shaft. With the Brovettans closing in on either side, they were forced into the riverbed and hounded all the way to the hangar.

Nic grabbed onto a net at the edge of the hangar, the push from the others nearly throwing him out into the pit. "Climb," he shouted, already working his way upwards.

Devon stuck the dagger into his belt and heaved himself upward, his arms still protesting from the descent. The gang members swarmed out around them as the sounds of the fight inside cut off. Nic reached a platform, scrambled across the ledge to the far side where there were ropes, but waited until Devon caught up. He shoved Devon upwards, climbing alongside him. The ropes ended in a small alcove, both of them pulling themselves up and into it with heaving gasps. Devon glanced out over the side, trying to catch his breath.

"The gang members…they're scattering…hiding—"

"Using secret doors like this?" Nic finished.

Devon turned back to find Nic holding open a panel in the back of the alcove. "Yes, like that." He crawled forward, ducking beneath Nic's arm to enter the narrow space beyond. "Where are we headed?"

"Back to the lair. So Carbolen can rip us all a new one for having this excursion go so horribly wrong."

*　*　*

"What in all bloody shards happened?"

Carbolen's calm, steady voice sent a shiver through Devon's skin. He remembered that tone. He'd have withdrawn from the dais if he could. Everyone else in the gang—except for Carbolen's captains and Nic—were huddled at the far end of the chamber near the doors, eyes averted except for an occasional hooded glance toward their leaders. Most were nursing wounds, the more seriously injured in another room.

"They shouldn't have been there," Went said. "Our eyes on the lower levels said the Brovettans were headed toward the Bolnis gate."

"But they were there. Our eyes were wrong."

"Our eyes can't be everywhere," a woman named Toral said. "They can't see everything."

Devon didn't see Carbolen move, but a breath later he had his hand wrapped around Toral's throat, shoved up high enough her head was tilted back and her heels had lifted from the floor.

"I need them to see everything," Carbolen said. "If they aren't going to see everything, then they're worthless."

Toral's jaw worked, but Carbolen's hold was so tight she couldn't speak. He squeezed harder, muscles corded in his forearm. Toral's skin began to flush, then purple. Those on the dais fidgeted, Went staring at the floor, the others looking away.

When Toral's eyes bugged and rolled back into her head, Carbolen let go.

Toral collapsed to the floor, her gulp of air serrated and harsh. Carbolen turned his back as she broke into hacking coughs.

"Report back to your eyes and find out who these Brovettans were and how in hells they got up to Level Twelve or I'll throw you into the Flatlands with nothing but a waterskin."

Toral dragged herself to the edge of the dais, Devon shifting out of her way. He didn't reach down to help her and she didn't look up. Once off the dais, she pulled herself into a crouch, then stood and stumbled out of the hall.

Carbolen settled himself into his chair, eyes roving over his captains before settling on Devon.

"What happened?" Carbolen repeated.

Went drew breath to speak, but then realized the question had been directed toward Devon.

Carbolen leaned forward, elbows coming to rest on his knees as his attention focused. "You trained at the Lyceum, with the War students, with the mages...the privileged and affluent. Or at least their sons and daughters. What do you think happened?"

"I studied mathematics, not politics or strategy."

"They teach you more than the major subject area, especially in those first few years."

Devon got the distinct impression Carbolen had already determined what had happened. He should never had allowed Nic to bring him here. He should have found an opportunity to escape once they'd left the lair, or on the way back, but it was too late for that now.

He wondered how much Carbolen's captains had seen. He wondered what Carbolen was focused on: the attack or how the scout had died immediately before that.

Because how the scout had died carried far deadlier implications than the attack itself.

"The Brovettan army headed toward the Bolnis gates was a distraction. The group we ran into, in the black armor...they were the real purpose behind the attack."

Carbolen leaned back. "Go on."

"It was an infiltration team. They were supposed to move quickly and silently. More than likely, they were supposed to obtain their objective and get back out, without being seen."

"With that many soldiers?" Went objected.

"There weren't as many as you think," Carbolen said. "But you forget where they were as well. Anything reported by the general populace below Level Twelve would be treated as suspect at best, if not outright ignored. A secret Brovettan army dressed in black? Those in the upper city would laugh at the rumor." Carbolen's eyes didn't waver as he spoke, still fixed on Devon. "What was their objective?"

"I don't know." Devon thought suddenly of what Dalton had said about the first attack. "But whatever it was, they tried to find it once before."

"How do you know that?"

"Because some of the War students were sent down to the wayfare gate during the previous attack. One of them told me that the attack felt like it had a purpose, that the Brovettans were trying to reach something inside the city. He said they retreated for no reason, that it wasn't the Iandolan Army that pushed them back."

"So whatever they were after then, they found. But that attack was relegated to the gate level. What were they looking for on Level Twelve?"

Devon shrugged. "They changed tactics, too. Before, their entire army pushed toward their goal. This time, they sent in a smaller force and the larger army was a diversion."

"Possibly because their goal was on Level Twelve. It would be difficult for the entire army to push up that many levels. Our own army would stop them eventually." His gaze dropped and tension bled from Devon's shoulders. Carbolen hadn't asked about the scout, about how he had died.

No one spoke, everyone letting Carbolen think. Even the rest of the gang members against the far walls had quieted.

Abruptly, Carbolen stood, his captains flinching. "Have everyone but those on watch rest."

"Why?" Went hazarded.

Carbolen began walking down the hall, heading toward his own rooms, Devon assumed.

"Because tomorrow we're going to go down to Level Twelve and the wayfare gate to find out what the Brovettans were after."

Chapter Eleven

Devon lay in the semi-dark of the main hall on a blanket, staring up at the vaulted roof lit by shard-glow and shadow. He thought about the scout, about the ball of lightning, and the four figures who'd emerged after the Brovettans had attacked. At least one of them had been a mage. Nothing else could account for the lightning. But Brovettan mages…the thought twisted in his gut, brought the taste of bile into the back of his throat. He needed to tell someone, warn someone. But who? And how? He couldn't do it while trapped here with Carbolen.

Devon sat up. Nic lay beside him, but didn't stir. Gang members were spread out from his position to the outer doors, mere lumps of shadow and form. Others were slung in the hammocks strung along the walls. Soft snores filled the room, with an occasional grinding hacksaw that cut off with a snort as the member woke themselves enough to roll over. There were no guards at the entrance that Devon could see.

"Don't even think about it."

Devon glanced down at Nic, who'd opened one eye.

"I can't sleep," Devon said. "Besides, even if I escaped the hall and somehow managed to get through the maze beyond, Carbolen has already proven he can follow me anywhere."

Nic rolled onto his side, propping his head on an elbow. "Don't tell me you haven't been thinking about running."

"Of course I've thought about running. I don't want to be one of Carbolen's shit-kickers, someone he can take his anger out on. I don't want to be one of his captains either. But running isn't an option. I need to get Carbolen to let me go."

"He won't let you go."

Some of those near them stirred, shifting so their backs were to them.

Devon leaned in closer. "I don't want to be part of Carbolen's little war."

"It's too late to escape that now." Nic pulled a corner of his blanket up over his shoulder as he rolled onto his stomach. "Go to sleep, Devon. Carbolen has you in his teeth. He isn't going to let you go until he's snapped your neck and spit you out."

Devon stared into the dark with that image in his head, then lay back down and closed his eyes. Sleep came in fits and starts.

He dreamed of the crackle of lightning.

* * *

"Went, take a team and visit all of the gangs we consider allies—the Greenbacks, the Cut-throats, even the Meridians. All of them. Tell them what we ran into and that we think the Brovettans are searching for something. See if they've noticed anything that could help. Leinn—"

"Gather teams and guard the lair, I know the drill."

"Keep it secure. There have been rumblings from Saw and his gang." He turned to the rest of those gathered in the hall. "I want the Regulars with me. The rest of you, spread out into the city, all levels, normal operations. Make it look like we're back to our usual activities. But ears to the streets. I want to know every fact and rumor you hear from the gates all the way up to mid-level and beyond."

There were grumblings, but all but twelve of them began to disperse, exiting the hall after grabbing assorted weapons from their personal stashes. Nic stayed behind, motioning Iril and Parker forward. "I think you already know Iril and Parker. They'll be keeping us company today. Went's orders."

Devon mentally swore, but nodded at Iril and Parker both. "I remember some of the scars, but the burn is new."

Iril flinched, one hand rising to the mark on her forehead.

"Your skin's flawless," Parker said. "The college must have been nice."

"Not really. It's just the scars it gives you aren't visible."

Both looked confused, but before they could recover Carbolen called out Devon's name.

"I need to speak with you."

"Maybe he wants answers," Iril said, "like he did from Toral."

It was a petty comment, but Devon realized he expected nothing less from Iril or Parker or any of those within the gang really. He'd been like them before, would have been like them now if not for Arrend and the Lyceum.

Arrend. He could tell Arrend about the mages.

He strode to Carbolen's side. "What is it?"

Carbolen motioned him farther back, so that no one else was within earshot. "Yesterday, on River Street, before the attack, one of our scouts was killed. Did you see it?"

Devon stiffened. "I did."

"What did you make of it?"

"I was hoping you hadn't noticed."

"Aside from Went, my captains either didn't remember it or haven't thought to mention it yet. I didn't want to draw attention to it if they'd forgotten. Now, what did you make of it?"

Resigned, Devon said, "It was magework."

"Impossible. Only Iandolo has mages. Are you saying that it was the Iandolan Army that attacked us, disguised as Brovettans?"

"No, the army was obviously Brovettan."

"In my time in the army, I never saw magework like that."

Devon hadn't seen anything like it at the Lyceum either, on the training grounds or elsewhere, but he knew such effects were possible. His research predicted it. "Maybe it's something they learn after leaving the Lyceum."

"Is it possible the Iandolan mages are working with the Brovettans in some way?"

Devon's gut reaction was the same as Carbolen's—impossible. But then he thought about Favian, about Quinn, about how some of their actions didn't make sense. He couldn't imagine them working with the Brovettans—Favian's hatred of them was too visceral to be fake—but what if they knew there was a traitor among the mages? Perhaps someone at the Lyceum?

He fidgeted and caught Carbolen's gaze. "That's...possible."

"You know something."

"I don't. The mages are too secretive. I was a Science student."

"But your friend—Lane, was it? She was a mage. You worked with her. Closely."

"Yes, but she would know even less than me. They shut her out. They forced her out."

"Because she was Brovettan?"

Devon brought himself up short. "Maybe." He didn't like the concentrated look in Carbolen's eyes. "Something was going on with the mages while I was there. Proctor Favian, some of the other faculty, even some of the sixth years—they were all working together."

"To do what?"

Devon had thought he'd understood what was happening at the college between him and Lane, Favian and Arrend, but after Arrend had pointed out that the way Favian treated Lane may have been political, everything had been upended. If the Brovettans had mages, if Favian and the other mages knew or suspected, if...

"Mention nothing about this to anyone, even Went." Carbolen's hand dropped onto Devon's shoulder, the grip tight, fingers digging into muscle. "Understood?"

Devon jerked out of Carbolen's reach. He headed toward Nic, Iril, and Parker, massaging his shoulder.

"That looked like it went well," Iril said with a smirk.

Carbolen stepped toward the array of nine gang members who'd stayed behind. The Regulars. All of them held themselves with an edge of cocky arrogance or deadly self-confidence. All of them carried weapons of higher quality than the average gang member. And all of them had obviously earned their place among the Regular's ranks, a distinctive bluntness etched into every face among the scars. "Let's move."

They didn't descend to the lower levels using the Corlian shaft this time. Instead, Carbolen led them to the hub. Every few levels, they were halted by guards from various gangs, Carbolen stepping forward to speak with them while they eyed his escort. Most of the time, they were allowed to proceed unmolested. Once or twice, they had to backtrack and find a different set of stairs or even rappel down vertical shafts to bypass areas that rival gangs controlled.

By the time they reached the River Street level, Devon had become irritated with Iril and Parker, who kept themselves close, their hands never far from their blades. At various points, both had found time to "accidentally" bump into him, hard enough to leave bruises. The posturing was annoying.

All of that halted the moment they reached Level Twelve. Nic, Iril, and Parker closed in tighter, hemming Devon in, their attention focused outwards. The pace slowed, Carbolen sending out three of the Regulars with a curt gesture. The entire group fell silent. The streets were eerily quiet, the buildings closed up and shuttered.

Two blocks from River Street, one of the scouts reappeared, frantically motioning them into a side alley. Nic shoved Devon between the buildings, the rest of the Regulars following suit.

The scout reached them, out of breath. "The Iandolan army...is here. That's...why no one's...on the streets."

"What are they doing?" Carbolen asked.

"Sifting through the bodies...left behind by yesterday's fight."

"Where are Raven and Bitter?"

"Trying to get a closer look."

"We'll wait until they report in."

The Regulars spread out across the opening of the alley. Nic leaned back against one of the buildings on his haunches. Devon stared into the blackness behind them, a section totally devoid of any kind of light thrown from the main streets, until Parker stepped into view.

"We'd have you before you even made the next street."

Iril slid up on his other side. "If there even is another street. It may just be a dead end."

"Simply making the attempt might be worth it," Devon said. "Just to find out."

He turned to find Carbolen and some of the Regulars watching him.

"Go ahead," Carbolen said. "Run. The results might be interesting."

"Don't you mean entertaining? Why do you even want me here? Because I escaped to the Lyceum and you want to prove a point?"

"That has nothing to do with it."

"Then what is it?" Devon took two threatening steps toward Carbolen. A few of the Regulars looked at him with interest now, when before they'd been indifferent. "Why am I here? What do you need me for?"

Carbolen came in close. "I need you because you think, because you defy me, because you don't give me the answers you think I want, you give me the answers I need. Do you think the others would have understood what the presence of the Brovettans meant on River Street? They didn't think beyond the fact we'd been attacked. You saw its true purpose. Even Went mentioning the death of the scout was mere fluke. He didn't see the true ramifications. He merely expressed fear we were outmatched if the Brovettans had mages. I need someone who can look beyond the surface, who can see what's beneath. I won't find that among my followers."

"So you chose me."

"You practically fell into my hands after being kicked out of the college. Did you expect me to ignore that?"

"You expect me to believe that? You could have found someone else. If not from the gang then from one of the others you've apparently allied yourself to over the last six years. I'm not here by happenstance."

Carbolen's eyes narrowed. "Perhaps you're too perceptive." He began to turn away.

Devon grabbed his arm and twisted him back. All of the Regulars jerked upright, the closest drawing weapons so fast Devon couldn't tell where they'd been secreted. Behind, Parker swore, his voice trembling.

Devon asked again, "Why am I here?"

"Let. Go."

Devon released his hold on Carbolen's arm and the Regulars relaxed.

Carbolen leaned in. "I told you: your lockpick skills."

"To do what?"

"To pick locks."

Devon turned his back in disgust, strode toward Nic.

"Haven't you noticed the difference down here?" Carbolen said to his back. "The lower levels aren't as dangerous."

"They seem fairly dangerous to me."

"They aren't. The gangs aren't at war like they used to be. You saw the alliances we've made. There are still some who haven't seen the truth, like Saw, but most of the other gang leaders have."

"What truth?"

"That something has changed in the crystal towers. Corruption. It's like a thread of dead lucent, strung all the way to the highest tier. It's killing the city, from the inside out. It has something to do with the Brovettans and the Council. I suspect the army is involved, and after yesterday, the mages as well. Whatever it is, whoever is involved, I intend to root them out."

Devon turned back. "Why do you care?"

"Because it's destroying Iandolo and it's killing off the lower levels first. Look at all of the dead lucent down here. At this level, barely half of the lucent is still working. Lower still, even less. At the waygates, over three-quarters of the levels are in complete darkness. Entire sectors are abandoned. And the lucent is only the beginning. The streets, the buildings—it's all falling apart.

"Where do you think we can go if the city fails? Retreat to the higher levels? When the lower levels give way, the towers will fall. Maybe the other cities will take us in, but I doubt it. They're in the same situation we are. Worse, if the rumors are true. Far worse. That leaves only the Flatlands. We'll all get sick and die within months down there."

Devon wanted to argue but couldn't. He'd seen the dying crystal himself, knew it was spreading. He also remembered what Lane had said about the other Crystal Cities. "It doesn't make sense. Those on the Council aren't stupid. They must realize that destroying the lower levels will ultimately harm them."

Carbolen gave a condescending laugh. "You are too young and naïve. Those in power care only about themselves and their immediate circumstances. They would destroy all of Iandolo—all of the Crystal Cities—to retain the power and luxuries they enjoy now. They are all corrupt, as full of dead lucent as the city. The rest of those that live there don't see the danger...or at least they ignore it, because it doesn't affect their daily lives in any significant way."

"So again, why me?"

"Because I've done all I can down here. I need to find out who's behind it—who's controlling the Brovettans, who's betrayed the army, the mages. Some of the Councilors must be involved, but which ones? Do they control the army prefects? How many? Does it extend beneath them, to the captains? Lower? And what about the Lyceum? Are there proctors involved? Students?

"I need answers. And those answers lie in the towers."

"Under lock and key." It was the Presidium job all over again. He hadn't understood then why they were straying outside their normal hunting grounds, doing a job in the upper city. But it must have been the start of all of this, Carbolen's first attempts to find out what was going on. It had failed, miserably.

A sudden, sickening thought struck him. "What did you do after the Presidium job? Did you try again, with another team?"

"Why try again? My best team failed. Security was obviously better than expected."

"It wasn't the security system—" Devon began, but Carbolen cut him off.

"It doesn't matter. If it wasn't the security system, then I had a traitor among my own crew. Another attempt was futile. So I turned my attention to the lower levels, focused on what I could find out here. And I started to plan ahead."

"You began banding the gangs together."

"No. I began building my own army. But I've hit an impasse down here. I'm ready to move, but don't know who to target. I need you to break into the towers so we can figure out who has betrayed Iandolo and the Crystal Cities and how deep the betrayal goes. Access to the higher levels are restricted; I need your lockpicking skills to bypass their security."

Devon tasted bile at the back of his throat. But the two missing Regulars and a third unknown figure appeared at the alley entrance.

"For the love of all cracked crystal, shut the fuck up!" the first woman said. By her jet-black hair, Devon guessed this was Raven. She wore worn leather, stained dark, and black gloves. "Do you want the Iandolan Army to come over here and investigate? I could hear you two streets away!"

Carbolen eyed the newcomer, but motioned Raven and Bitter forward. Unlike Raven, Bitter wore more standard gang garb—shirt and breaches, leather shoes. No weapons were visible, but Devon knew she had at least three blades on her, just like Raven. She was broader of hip and shoulder as well, with a rounded face and cold eyes.

"Are they close?" Carbolen asked.

"I wouldn't have come here if they were."

"They're still out on River," Bitter clarified.

"But they aren't going to find anything."

"Why not?"

Raven pointed toward the newcomer. "Meet Rasp, one of the Cut-throats."

Rasp's hair was cut short and ragged, his face thin to the point of being gaunt. Three deep scars raked across his neck. "They aint going to find nuthin cuz the Vettans took everthing away."

"I don't understand."

Rasp waved in the direction of River Street. "After the fight, the Vettans searched the bodies, then pict up their dead and left."

"I checked," Raven said. "The only bodies out there are gang members. No signs of the Brovettans. All the Iandolan army is going to see is a turf war between gangs."

"The locals told em otherwise, but they aint listenin."

"They took Jimmie's body as well," Raven said.

Carbolen glanced toward Devon. "No evidence of anything untoward."

"So what do we do?" Raven asked.

"Where did the Brovettans go after they left the street?" Carbolen asked Rasp.

"Didnt stick around. Treated back downlevel."

Carbolen drifted toward the front of the alley, Raven, Bitter, and Rasp stepping aside to let him pass. He stared out toward the buildings blocking their view of River. "They came here for something." He turned back, eyeing Devon. "We'll head to the waygate. Maybe we'll find something at the location of their first attack."

* * *

Carbolen left Rasp with instructions to tell the leader of the Cut-throats to keep an eye on the Iandolan Army, then they retreated to the hub and began the descent to Level One. Devon had never been beyond Level Ten, but he'd assumed all of the levels were the same. He was wrong. As they descended, he realized the ceilings were growing increasingly shorter. The veins of lucent that wove through the ceilings were close enough when they stopped on Level Seven that Devon could see individual threads, over half of those dead or flickering. The buildings themselves were crude, the material used the rough formed stone called crete, glistening with mold and pocked and cracked with damage. The air grew heavier, muggy with moisture; the ventilation that cooled the interior of the levels above had failed here. Water dripped from the lowered ceiling, like a perpetual rain.

As Carbolen spoke to a gang leader, the rest of them ate the fried mushrooms and earthy broth they'd been provided, all of them hunkered down in a cavernous room Devon thought had once been a warehouse. He didn't know how long they'd been traveling—it was difficult when they stayed so close to the hub—but based on his hunger it had been for most of a day.

"So," Nic said, settling into a seat beside him, beneath the canopy that kept water from dripping onto this gang's lair, "the Brovettans have mages?"

Devon paused in his chewing and thought about the conversation with Carbolen, then swore. The gang leader had mentioned mages. He probably didn't care that the Regulars knew—he could control them—but why would he let Nic, Iril, and Parker overhear? Unless it had been unintentional. He had only mentioned mages once.

But that wasn't his problem. He chewed and swallowed before answering. "Maybe. They killed the scout—"

"Jimmie."

"They killed Jimmie with mages. Whether they were Brovettans or mages from Iandolo, we don't know."

"If the Brovettans have mages, what's to keep us all safe here in Iandolo? Our mages are the only thing keeping the other Crystal Cities at bay."

"If they do have mages, I doubt they have many. Iandolo still holds the advantage. We've been training our mages for decades."

He said it with conviction, but he couldn't keep the image of the ball of lightning streaming out of the alley and hitting Jimmie from behind from replaying in his head. He'd never seen any of Iandolan's mages using lightning on the practice field.

But again, maybe they learned that after graduating from the Lyceum. He didn't know and there was no one he could ask. Dalton might know, but Favian and the others would have him watched for certain, in case Devon showed up. The only other people he knew to ask were at the Lyceum. Lane hadn't made it far enough to find out.

He chewed on another mushroom, not even tasting it, lost in thought. He was too isolated down here, with no one to turn to.

Except Carbolen.

He grimaced and handed the rest of his broth to Nic.

"You don't want it?"

"My stomach's a little sour."

"I hear you. The mushrooms taste like mildew." But he took the broth.

Devon watched Carbolen from a distance. Could he trust him? Every fiber of his body screamed no, but he might not have a choice, especially if the gang leader intended to keep him on this short leash.

"I hear you confronted Carbolen, dared to even grab his arm."

Devon hadn't heard Raven approach. The Regular stood a few paces distant, her gaze was as intense as Carbolen's.

"I did."

"He's killed others for less. Did you not see what he did to Toral?"

"I did."

"And yet you still risked it."

"I was part of Carbolen's gang once. I won't be a part of it again."

"Yet here you are."

She sidled off, Nic easing forward. "What was that about?" he asked.

Devon shrugged, watching Raven's back.

"They say she and Carbolen had an...understanding, if you know what I mean. Awhile ago. But it ended. Badly."

"And yet here she is."

"Where else would she be?"

Twenty minutes later, Carbolen broke away from the gang's leader and approached. "Unthar says that the army presence has been increased the closer you get to the first level and the waygate since the attack. We'll have to stay off the main streets. Stay close. Cut the scouting distance by half."

The Regulars nodded and they headed out, exiting the warehouse at a signal from Unthar.

They kept to the side streets, the main thoroughfares not far away. Devon caught sight of them occasionally as they passed alleys or buildings, noted some of the army at intersections. Activity was high, groups heading in both directions—hubward and gateward, upwards and down. The Regulars detoured them around areas of heavier activity when necessary. One of them—Feral—appeared to have an innate sense of when they were being approached, bringing them up short three or four times with curt hand signals that all of them responded to instantly, without question, even Carbolen.

When they reached the first level, they stayed at least four blocks from the main streets, where active lucent was almost nonexistent. Devon quelled the urge to reach for his green shard, relieved when after a nod from Feral some of the Regulars retrieved their own shards from pockets and belts. The yellow light gave the decaying remains of the buildings at this level a sickly, diseased cast. The few people he noticed here were pale, dressed in no more than rags. They shied away from the light like animals, some reinforcing the idea with unintelligible grunts and whines.

"The main thrust of the Brovettans' first attack was this way," Raven said, motioning gateward.

After another hour, they emerged from beneath Level Two, the sunlight harsh after remaining so close to the hub for so long. Devon was surprised to find it nearing dusk; he'd lost all sense of time since his capture.

The sudden appearance of charred and collapsed buildings marked the edge of the Brovettan attack. Carbolen waved half of the Regulars out into the surrounding area, to make certain none of the Iandolan Army was stationed here. At the all clear, Carbolen ordered everyone into the heart of the battle zone.

"What are we looking for?" Bitter asked.

"Anything you think could have attracted the Brovettans' interest."

"That's sufficiently vague," Raven muttered under her breath.

"Spread out."

"What about him?" Feral motioned in Devon's direction.

"Nic and the others will keep him under control."

Iril and Parker shifted closer to Devon's side.

The Regulars broke apart, sprinting lithely up into the damaged ruins and disappearing within moments. Carbolen eyed Devon, then did the same.

"Come on," Nic said, motioning down the street they were on.

They picked through the debris from the buildings, mostly cracked stone and crumbling masonry. All of it was covered in soot, made tacky by recent rains. Devon's hands were coated within minutes.

Iril began complaining shortly after that, then kept it up, bitching about everything from the mud-ash to the heat to why they were there and what they were looking for. The deeper they moved into where the fighting had taken place, the more it became obvious that a battle had been fought here. At the outskirts, the buildings had been destroyed by fire, collapsing from the heat and flame. But deeper in craters dotted the streets, entire buildings collapsed into their centers. Lines of defense became obvious, sections where walls were blackened into a deep char, cut off abruptly by a sharp line where Devon imagined one of the mages had erected a wall of protection. In a few places, masonry had been sliced clean through and cut away as if with a blade, although not one of steel.

Even Iril quieted as the mage battle that had been waged here became obvious. The signs of blood had long been washed away, the bodies removed, but no one had made an attempt to haul away any of the debris or begin rebuilding.

Devon stepped around the corner of a building into an alley, brought up short by a shear wall of amber lucent. The Warding engulfed the buildings on either side, rising to a height of fifteen feet, a few of its facets reflecting the setting sun. He couldn't see the extent of it, but through a few of the cracks in the walls and the blown-out windows, it extended at least through the nearest buildings and beyond.

He rested his palm against the flat amber surface, then leaned in to place his forehead against it, as he'd done when he'd seen his first Warding years before. Inside, the buildings were whole, the alley running up against a stone wall with a door that was propped open with a crate of some kind, inviting him in. The stone of the street and the building looked worn but not aged. The wooden door and crate were rough and scarred, but otherwise unblemished. No rot, no decay, like everything else on this level except the gates and warehouses and army barracks. A small band of lucent ran across the top of the door, bulging out from the surrounding stone, lit a pale purple. He could see no people, but he suspected if he could step forward, through that open door, he'd find someone inside.

Above the building, a thick cloud of black smoke rose into a blue sky, lit from underneath by orange-red flames.

"Trying to get away?"

Devon turned at Parker's voice. Behind him, Iril and Nic ran into view at the end of the alley, faces locked in panic. They both sagged in relief when they saw Parker and Devon.

Nic approached. "I thought you'd run for it."

"He tried," Parker said, "but I caught him."

"I told you, I'm not trying to escape. There's no point."

Nic grabbed his arm and pulled him close. "Don't do that to me. I don't deserve it. All I did was watch you. Watch over you."

"Because you think Carbolen has my best interests at heart?"

Nic's grip tightened, but his eyes dropped.

"It's a Warding," Iril said, reaching to place her hand against it. "It's been here for a while though. The buildings inside are intact and relatively unscathed."

She pushed away, interest already flagging. "Were you trying to escape?"

"Does it matter?"

"I guess not. Bring him along. The light's fading. Let's find Carbolen and get out of this hellhole."

Chapter Twelve

"There was nothing of significance at the battle site on the first level."

"Except the Warding," Devon said.

Carbolen gave him an odd look—irritation at the interruption combined with something else. "That Warding has been there for decades."

When Devon didn't respond, Carbolen faced Went and his captains, all gathered at the end of the dais. "The devastation was appalling, but not unexpected given the descriptions we'd heard from our eyes. But none of us saw anything in particular that could have been the Brovettan's main target."

"They may have been turned back by the Iandolan Army before they reached it," Toral suggested.

"Perhaps. We had no success on Level Twelve either. The Iandolan Army was there when we arrived, searching the bodies. All evidence of the Brovettans—bodies, blades, armor, everything—had been removed."

"So as far as the Iandolan Army is concerned, this was a clash between gangs, nothing of significance," Went said.

"So it would seem. What do our eyes say, Toral?"

Toral swallowed, one hand rising toward her bruised throat but faltering halfway up. "They agree. The Iandolan Army has written off the reports of a secret Brovettan force that infiltrated all the way up to the twelfth level as superstitious fear and rumor. According to our eyes, they're already preparing a retaliatory strike, larger than the last. They're rounding up some of the general city police. There's talk of conscriptions—from prisons and the current judicial dockets—perhaps even a draft."

Everyone on the platform stirred.

"Drafts from where?" Leinn asked.

"The general populous."

"Last time they called for a draft, the army ran raids in the lower levels, grabbing everyone they could find and forcing them into their makeshift army," Went said. "If they threaten to do that again—"

"They will run into more resistance than they expect," Carbolen interrupted. "The gangs will be waiting for them."

The heightened tension in all of Carbolen's captains settled.

"Any word from our eyes in the towers about the army's plans?"

"Nothing of importance, except they intend to strike hard and fast. They're already assembling. They depart for Brovetto within two days."

"Much faster than their previous response," one of the other captains muttered.

"Someone on the Council is angry."

Carbolen stood abruptly, Went and another captain stepping back. The gang's leader paced to the edge of the dais, stared out at the array of scattered gang members in the hall. "Toral, instruct our eyes above to find out as much about how the Councilors are reacting to this second attack as possible."

"It won't be easy. We don't exactly have eyes inside the Council's chamber."

"Find out."

Toral ducked around Carbolen and stalked toward the door, those on the floor scrambling out of her way.

Carbolen singled out two other captains—Leinn and a thinner man Devon didn't know. "Double the training sessions of the gang and begin training the younger group. We're going to need the newest members to guard the lair when necessary, at minimum."

"Of course."

Devon frowned at their retreating backs—there hadn't been any training sessions when he'd been a gang member—but then noticed Carbolen's eyes on him. He stiffened. Only Went and one other captain remained on the dais.

"You've figured something out."

"What do you mean?"

"About the Brovettans. What they're after."

"I don't know what they're after."

"But?"

"But the Warding bothers me."

"I noticed. What are you thinking?"

"Nothing. I don't have enough information to form a theory. I need to see more of Level Twelve, once the army has moved out of there, possibly go back to Level One to see the Warding again."

"This is why I wanted you with us. You see things—intuit things—that none of us would." He paused. "Went."

"What?"

"As soon as we receive word that the Iandolan Army has vacated the area on Level Twelve, take Devon down so that he can look around."

* * *

Went showed up two days later.

"You wanted to see Level Twelve? Let's go."

Devon swung out of the hammock he'd been relegated to for the last day and a half. Nic stirred in the hammock above. The bartender had been trapped watching over him while the rest of the lair bustled like a disturbed ant hill. The gang had been busy, Leinn rounding up members at odd intervals for training, Toral racing in and out with reports. Devon had forced Nic to show him the training rooms, where Leinn and the other captain were drilling everyone in self-defense and knife-play. A select few were even being taught sword and spear work, the patterns similar to what Devon had seen the War students practicing at the college. The difference here was that gang members weren't training to protect mages; they were being taught to kill.

"Has the army left?"

"They've pulled out of Level Twelve."

"Back to the waygate? To join the rest of the army?"

Went crossed his arms over his chest in irritation. "No. The attack on Brovetto has been called off."

"What?" Nic lurched in the hammock, nearly fell out. "They can't! The Brovettans will attack again for certain!"

"The Brovettans have sued for peace."

"That makes no sense."

"They must have seen the size of the army the Council gathered to send against them. Did you want to see Level Twelve or not?"

Devon reached for his satchel in answer.

Nic jumped down from his hammock and brushed himself off. "I'm coming with you."

"No, you are not."

Nic gathered up his things, tugging his tunic back over his dagger, then faced Went. "Carbolen said I was to watch him at all times. Are you giving me different orders?"

Went glared, clearly considering the option, then turned away. "Come along then. It's your funeral."

Nic stared at Went's back. "What did that mean?"

"I don't know. But he's taking us out of this shards-rotten hall."

"Right."

They followed Went, already halfway across the lair. He paused outside the hall's door, considering the options presented by the outer maze, then chose a direction Devon had never traversed. It skirted the practice yard—the sounds of clashing blades, grunts, and shouted directions distinct—even though they never saw into the room. After that, the passages they took were devoid of any signs of the gang. No members passed them, no sounds came from branching corridors. Devon's sense of direction suggested they were moving counterclockwise to the hub, but he couldn't be certain, not here.

He fell back from Went, alongside Nic, and whispered, "Do you know where we're going?"

"No clue. I haven't been in this section of the lair's tunnels before." He scuffed at the layer of dust on the floor. "I don't think many have."

A moment later, Went turned a corner. When they reached it, they found him waiting at a dead end.

Devon's hand jerked toward his satchel and the dagger hidden there, but before either of them could ask, the gang captain reached out and pushed against a section of the right wall. It fell away, rigged on hidden hinges.

They stepped out into an alley, the overhead lucent lights dim. Went headed for the street to the left without comment, leaving Nic to push the door back into place. Even on this side, its presence was invisible.

Devon tried to mark where the alley entrance was, but as soon as they entered the main street he realized they were in a section of the level he knew almost nothing about. It was a dead zone, a section where no one lived, because there were few lucents working and the buildings were death traps. Entire areas had collapsed into the level below, the infrastructure sagging with rust and decay, the stench wafting up burning in Devon's nose. Went led them into the nearest buildings, passing through rooms, along narrow girders spanning pits, and over rumpled flooring that had obviously once been a rooftop. He couldn't discern any path. Went appeared to be selecting directions at random, except for the fact that he never hesitated, not even when they edged along a wall near a massive collapse, the footpath overlooking the hole a mere foot in width, no handholds available. The only light was a single thread of blue lucent high overhead.

On the far side of the dead zone, Devon was relieved to see they were at the hub, with a mundane set of stairs leading downward.

They descended two levels, then switched to a service elevator hidden deep inside an abandoned factory full of rusting machinery. It clanked and groaned its way down another two levels, juddering to a halt a knee-length below floor level in a warehouse. Devon scrambled out in relief. He'd never ridden in an elevator before and this experience hadn't made a favorable impression. Even Nic appeared shaken.

A quick jaunt down another set of stairs and they emerged on Level Twelve.

"Where do you want to look first?" Went asked.

"Let's start on River Street, where the gangs were attacked."

Level Twelve was more active than either of the two times Devon had been down here before. People were roaming the streets, conversing in small groups. A few shops were open, customers moving in and out. They passed through a makeshift market, wares spread out on thrown blankets or kept out of reach in the recesses of tents. Most of the merchandise appeared to be scavenged materials from the abandoned levels, but there was some food—bruised tomatoes, malformed carrots, cabbage, and scabbed potatoes. One vendor even had skewered meat sizzling on a scrap-metal grill, although Devon didn't believe his claim that it was chicken.

"Probably pigeon," Nic muttered, "if it isn't just rat."

"Why was there no one around the last two times we were here?"

"Because the gangs sent out a warning to keep clear the first time," Went answered.

"And the second, the Iandolan Army was already here."

Went halted abruptly. "This is it. This is where the Brovettans attacked us."

Devon glanced around. With the residents present, going about their daily lives, he doubted he would have recognized the area. There were no signs of the attack—no bodies left behind, no dropped weapons—but after spinning around, he oriented himself to the buildings and the curve of the street.

"We were about here when the scout first appeared."

Went merely grunted, although he watched Devon intently.

"The Brovettans emerged from that street over there," Nic said.

"They were headed this direction, clockwise around the hub. So whatever they were looking for must be in that direction."

Devon took off in a light jog, Went snapping for him to wait up. He slowed when he stepped off of River Street, Nic falling into step beside him.

"What are we looking for?" Nic asked.

Devon shook his head, concentrating on the buildings to either side, on the people. After a while, he dismissed the residents. The Brovettans wouldn't have come here to see a person; they'd have the person come to them. It had to be something stationary, something that couldn't be transported. He focused on the buildings, on the architecture, on what they'd once been. But here they were mostly residences, with small shops on the lower floors. The stone facades were dirty and cracked with age. Decorative embellishments on lintels had broken long ago, entire chunks missing.

He scanned it all in frustration, until he finally halted in the middle of the street.

"What is it?" Nic asked, looking around in confusion.

Went crossed his arms over his chest, his expression smug.

"This isn't right. The Brovettans wouldn't be after something mundane. It wouldn't be on a street like this, or in an ordinary building. It would have to be somewhere significant, like a museum or governmental building or a mansion or something."

Went laughed. "You expect to find something like that here? I told Carbolen this was a waste of time. You should have stayed at the Lyceum. You don't belong here. You never did."

"What about a park?"

Both Devon and Went glanced at Nic.

"A park?"

"It's more like a square now, I guess, since there are no trees left. It's this way."

The erstwhile bartender cut away from the main street, headed toward an intersection.

Devon glanced at Went, the captain's face contorted with irritation at his interrupted rant, then followed.

Three jagged blocks later, they emerged into an open square surrounded on all sides by residential buildings. Like River Street, it was littered with stone boxes, tiered in some places, that had once held flowers and shrubs and trees. Various statues were scattered among the boxes. But it was the crystalline slab of amber lucent jutting up from the ground in the center of the park that caught Devon's attention.

"That's it. That's what they came for."

"The lucent?" Went asked. "What for? They have their own lucent in Brovetto!"

"I don't know, but somehow it's connected to the Warding on Level One." He paused, turned abruptly to Went. "I need to get to my bolthole."

"What for? We've already checked it out. There's nothing there but a sleeping pallet and scattered papers."

Devon grabbed hold of Went's shirt and hauled him closer. "The papers are what I need. They may tell me what the Brovettans are up to."

"Let go of my shirt."

Devon released him and stepped back. Went pulled his shirt flat, his hands trembling slightly. The rest of his body had gone unnaturally still.

"Do you need to go down to Level One?"

"No."

"Then we're going back to the lair."

"But I need—"

"I'll tell Carbolen. He may let you retrieve your papers, or he may send someone to get them, but that's his decision."

He spun on his heel, heading out. Nic made to follow, but stopped when Devon refused to move. "What are you doing?" he said under his breath.

"Can we at least check out the lucent while we're here? I'd think Carbolen would want that."

Went slowed. "Go ahead. But make it quick."

Devon ran to the dead park, entering through a stone arch and scrambling over the boxes straight toward the amber lucent at its center. Nic and Went followed, although Went stayed back, watching from a short distance.

The amber shard was larger than the one at the center of the Lyceum and shaped differently. The Lyceum shard was mostly vertical and had numerous faces, like a cut gemstone. This one was a stark slab, jutting from the ground at an angle, the part facing upwards one flat surface, only the underside faceted. Devon placed his hand against it, felt the usual faint tingling in his skin, as if the lucent were vibrating.

"What are you looking for?" Nic asked. He tentatively touched it, jerking back at first, before running his fingertips lightly over its largest face.

"Nothing. There's a shard similar to this at the center of the Lyceum, in the quad. I've touched it a hundred times, observed it up close. This one is no different, except in shape."

"Then why demand we come over here?"

"To irritate Went."

Nic shook his head. "It's going to get you killed."

Devon patted the amber lucent. "Not while Carbolen still needs me."

"What about after?"

They rejoined Went.

"Done here?"

"I think so."

Went snorted and Devon got the distinct impression he knew it had all been a ploy.

They returned to the upper level and the elevator, using back streets, where there weren't as many people. The entire time, Devon mulled over what the amber shards could mean and about what he knew of the Wardings. But he hadn't had time to look over Arrend's notes; he'd been focused on survival. He hadn't even spent time on his own research, mostly just rearranging his papers after the frenzied packing and escape from the Lyceum. He'd been more concerned about where his next meal might come from.

He barely noticed when they clambered down into the elevator and it began its tortuous climb upwards. Nic stood off to his right, a step closer to the door. Went stood behind them.

They were three-quarters of the way up when Devon registered that Went had shifted almost directly behind him, close enough he could feel his body warmth. He'd begun to turn when Nic shouted, "Watch out!"

The elevator lurched, throwing all three of them off balance. Twisting as he fell, Devon caught sight of Went's knife, raised for a backstab. He hit the floor, pain shooting down his arm from shoulder to fingers, and rolled as Went caught himself against the back corner. The captain shoved forward, shifting his grip on his dagger in order to jab. Devon cried out and rolled again, slamming up against the back wall. He fumbled for the latch on his satchel, hand diving inside as he used his feet to skid backwards along the wall into the far corner. Went stepped toward him, breathing hard—

And then Nic plowed into him from the side, knocking them both to the floor in a tangle of punches and kicks. Went bellowed in outrage, then grabbed Nic's flailing body by the scruff of his neck and flung him aside. The side of Nic's face crunched into the elevator doors and he toppled to the floor, motionless.

Devon's fingers found the sheathed dagger Nic had given him. He jerked it from his bag, pushing himself into a crouch. His own breath came in ragged heaves.

"What are you doing?"

Went regained his feet, wiped away sweat and blood from a scratch on his forehead with the back of his arm. "Getting rid of a problem, one I thought I'd dealt with six years ago."

Devon pushed himself into a standing position, back scraping against the corner. "The Presidium job. You set off the alarms."

Went chuckled. "All I had to do was wait for you and the rest to get in deep—deep enough I knew you'd never escape before the city guard arrived."

"Why?"

"To gain Carbolen's trust and eliminate a few obstacles at the same time. But now you're back, already Carbolen's right hand, even against your will."

The elevator lurched again, grinding in its tracks.

Went lunged, knife extended, and Devon pushed off from the corner to Went's left. He didn't even try to slash at the captain, but

Went's dagger scored a slice across his upper arm. He barked out in pain, free hand clamping to the stinging wound as he struck the far wall and spun. Went was already turning. Devon launched himself forward as Went pushed away from the corner. He tucked himself into a ball and threw himself into Went's lower legs, sending the captain sprawling. A dagger rattled against the elevator doors. Devon rolled into another crouch and flung himself onto Went's back before he could recover.

Went roared when Devon's dagger sank into his shoulder. He'd been aiming lower, but he hadn't been trained at the Lyceum to fight. The blade barely punched through the leathers Went wore. Devon wrapped his free arm around Went's throat and tried to stab him again, but Went was far heavier and stronger. With a shove of his arms, he rolled onto his back, crushing Devon beneath him. The air gushed from Devon's lungs. Before he could gulp in more Went jerked into a sitting position and thrust them both back into the wall. Spots flared in Devon's vision. A hand closed around the arm holding Went's neck, another around the one holding the dagger. Went ground him against the elevator wall, then leaned far enough forward Devon managed a brief, blessed inhale of fresh air before he slammed him back again and shoved up into a standing position.

Devon attempted to stab him in the chest, but Went's grip on his wrist was far too strong. Instead, he tightened the arm about Went's neck.

Through clenched teeth, Went spat out, "Stop struggling and die, you little piece of—"

His entire body tightened and then went lax, crumbling to the floor, carrying Devon with it. Devon's forehead cracked into the back of Went's oily-haired head. He squeezed his arm tighter, but Went didn't move. Heaving in air, he rolled to one side.

"Careful, he's bleeding heavily."

Devon stared up into Nic's face. "What?"

"I stabbed him in the stomach, up under his ribcage. There's a pool of blood."

Devon jerked to the side, coming up against the elevator wall as it ground to a screeching halt. He stared at the bloody knife in Nic's hand, then down at Went's body and the blood expanding outwards from one side.

"I thought I'd strangled him long enough he'd gone unconscious."

"Ha! His face wasn't even red yet."

Devon laughed weakly, then leaned forward, hands on his knees. "I feel dizzy. And nauseous."

"It'll pass. Come on." Nic stepped over Went's body to the elevator doors, which had only partially opened. "I want out of this deathtrap."

Nic began struggling with the door. Devon remained where he was, breathing in deep, until the scent of blood and shit became too thick in the enclosed space.

Together, they pulled the doors far enough apart they could spill out onto Level Fifteen. They both lay on the factory floor, staring up at a ceiling riddled with metal rafters, lit by faint threads of nearly white lucent along the walls.

"We'll have to find another way up from here," Nic said. "I don't know how Went got through the dead zone."

Devon picked himself up off the floor, checking the contents of his satchel before putting the dagger back inside. "I'm not going back to the lair."

Nic sat up. "You have to. If you don't, Carbolen will think you killed Went in order to escape. He'll kill you on sight, if he doesn't send the Regulars after you."

"He might send the Regulars after me, but he won't kill me."

"How do you figure that? He almost killed Toral just because she didn't have the information he wanted!"

"He can't kill me. He needs me. More than he needed Went."

Nic caught his arm. "I don't think you understand Carbolen. He isn't going to take the death of one of his captains lightly. You haven't seen what he's done to some of the other gang leaders when talks didn't go his way."

"Then you go back to the lair, tell him how it happened here."

"And then tell him I let you go? Not happening. He'll kill me for not bringing you back and then he'll send the Regulars after you."

"Tell him I knocked you unconscious. You've got a serious bruise and some swelling where Went threw you against the elevator door."

Nic raised a hand and prodded the wound. "I don't think it would change Carbolen's mind, even if he believed me."

Devon began to walk away, headed toward the hub. "Then you'd better find a good place to hide."

He heard Nic grumbling behind him, the scrape of feet as he wavered in indecision.

"Where are you going?"

"To my bolthole to collect my papers. Then I'm going to find Arrend, or Dalton, and warn them about the Brovettan mages. After that...I'll deal with Carbolen then. Trust me, he'll be angry, but he won't kill me. Are you coming?"

Behind, more scuffling. Then a cut-off expletive and a sigh. "Wait for me!"

Chapter Thirteen

Relief washed through Devon as soon as he stepped into his bolthole, the familiar smells and the scattered mess of blankets, papers, and other items he'd collected since his flight from the Lyceum releasing muscles throughout his body he hadn't realized had been tensed. He immediately set the green lucent light aside and began scouring the papers, gathering them close. It was obvious someone had been through them since he'd been captured; most were out of order, the rest of his possessions out of place as well. With a soft curse, he started sorting.

"This is where you were living?" Nic asked, ducking through the opening behind him.

"Weren't you watching me?"

"I've never been here."

Devon bowed his head. "Yes, this is where I lived. It isn't big, but it's difficult to find and easy to protect."

"Carbolen found it."

"He probably had someone watching me when I ran across it."

"If he discovers Went's body and knows we've escaped—"

"He'll probably check here first," Devon finished, realizing what Nic meant.

"I don't think you have time to organize."

Devon swore and began grabbing all of the papers close at hand, shoving them into his satchel. "Grab the blanket. Use it to gather up whatever you can."

Nic began tossing items onto the blanket—papers, ink, fragments of lucent and other loose items strewn about the room. Devon crawled forward, snatching up the box containing Arrend's notes on the Wardings. He stuffed it in his satchel, then continued with the other papers. He'd told Nic Carbolen wouldn't kill him for Went's death, but he didn't completely believe it. Carbolen needed him, yes, but killing Went may have crossed a line. It was difficult to tell; Carbolen was harsher than he remembered, more violent, more driven.

Ten minutes later, a noise outside in the building caused them both to still.

Time's up, Nic mouthed without a sound.

Devon motioned toward the door, retrieving the lantern and tapping it off. Cloth rustled as Nic tied off his makeshift bundle and joined him in a crouch. Devon listened as his eyes adjusted to the faint light filtering in from the outer entrance to the building.

A ping of metal against metal and the soft crunch of gravel beneath a toe. All from the direction of the outer door and alley.

Devon tugged on Nic's sleeve and motioned down the narrow corridor to the left. He didn't wait to see if Nic understood, moving in a half crouch, half run. The hallway angled right, but he opened the door on the left and entered another, larger room. The ceiling had collapsed inwards. Nic entered a moment behind him and he swung the door nearly closed, leaving a small crack so he could see down the corridor.

Two figures appeared: Raven and Feral. Regulars.

Raven peered into the bolthole. "Shit, he's already been here. Most of his stuff is gone."

"We need to tell Carbolen. And the other Regulars."

"Maybe they'll have better luck at his other hideouts."

Raven looked down the hall toward their position. Nic flinched. Devon didn't move. They couldn't possibly be seen, not in this light. Could they?

Raven took two steps toward them, then halted. Her eyes narrowed. Devon would have sworn she was looking right at him.

"What is it?" Feral asked.

Raven hesitated, then turned back. "Nothing. Let's head back and report."

They left the building. Catching hold of Nic, Devon led him up one of the collapsed support beams to the upper floor, through a set of hallways and rooms until they stood beside a boarded-up window. He shifted one of the slats and looked down onto the alley below.

No one stood watch outside. Or at the alley's entrance.

Nic tapped his shoulder and pointed to the building on the other side.

Raven crouched in one of the window recesses, eyes on the area below. A dagger dangled loosely in one hand, as if she were bored, but her eyes latched onto any sound or movement.

Devon pulled back from the window, dragging Nic along with him. When they were safely out of earshot, Nic whispered, "What are we going to do? We can't go out the way we came in."

"I have another way out. I didn't forget everything I learned from the lower city."

"Then what? Where are we going to go? You heard Raven: they're watching all of your usual hangouts."

"I need to find Dalton. Or Arrend. Both really. We need to get up to mid-level."

"Arch would know how to reach them. But Carbolen will be watching the Shandy Quad."

"Can we send someone else in to ask him for us?"

"Who would you trust?"

They'd made their way up to the roof. Devon edged up to the section overlooking the alley, caught sight of one of Raven's legs dangling down from the niche where she'd secreted herself, then made his way to the opposite side. He repositioned the satchel and grabbed one end of a heavy wooden beam lying on the floor.

With his chin, he motioned to the other end. "Help me with this."

They carried it to the edge of the roof, then pushed one end out over the edge, until Devon judged it would reach to the lower roof of the building next door. They eased it down, then Devon climbed up onto it. The angle was steep, but the beam was rough. He walked slowly to the other side. Nic followed, with less confidence.

When Nic moved to grab the beam, Devon muttered, "Leave it. I don't intend to be back."

They dashed across the roof to the trapdoor that led to its interior. Dodging from building to building, shadow to shadow, they made their way to the hub, scrambling up the stairs to the higher levels.

They paused twice, long enough to convince themselves they weren't being followed.

At mid-level, they merged with the crowds, acutely aware that their clothing now appeared worn and grubby and out of place. They approached the Shandy Quad from the direction of the Spoke, arcing around and angling in so they weren't intersecting any of the usual paths from the Lyceum or the hub.

They halted a few blocks from the bar, at the corner of a building. Nic tugged Devon into the alley and crouched down low. "If you go any closer, Carbolen's eyes might see you."

"Do you know where they'd be stationed?"

"I know some of their locations, but not all. And they've probably changed since I was here last."

"Then what do you suggest? I need to talk to Arch." He stood, adjusted his satchel.

Nic grabbed his shoulder as he took a step forward. "I have an idea."

* * *

They stood outside a flower shop called Miriam's Blooms, closer to the edge of the city but farther from both the Quad and the Lyceum.

Devon glanced up at the sign overhead, hanging from a metal rod jutting out from the building over the doorway. It held three roses—red, white, and yellow—intertwined with the name of the store. "Why are we here?"

"Because this is a front for some of Arch's less legal practices," Nic said.

They stepped inside to the sound of jangling bells.

The interior looked exactly like a flower shop. Towards the back, near a long counter that served as a workspace, flowers separated into different kinds and colors sat in large urns, along with an entire shelf of ribbons and ties and twine. The combined scent of all of the blooms was cloying. A woman looked up as they entered and smiled. She held an assortment of flowers and grasses in one hand.

"May I help you?"

Nic moved forward to the counter. "We need to speak to Arch."

Miriam's mouth pinched. "There's no one here by that name."

"I know he makes an exchange here. It's a regular thing."

The genial glint in Miriam's eyes died and she stood upright, crossing her arms over her chest. "I said, there's no one here—"

"Carbolen sent us."

Miriam took in Nic's blue-tinged hair, gave Devon a contemptuous once-over, then stepped toward the door behind the counter. "Stay here."

Devon expected her to pass through the door, into the back rooms, but instead she pushed against a panel beside the door. Part of the wall, half as narrow as an ordinary door, swung aside. She slipped through with a parting glare, then closed the secret door behind her. It melded with the architecture of the wall and cupboard precisely, invisible unless you knew where to look.

"An exchange?" Devon asked.

"I told you Arch worked for Carbolen. He trades materials from below with those above and vice versa."

"What kinds of materials?"

"Alcohol, lucent, knives, other weapons, high-grade meat, mechanical items…anything really. Whatever Carbolen and the gang can find to trade to get what we want. You didn't think the food we've been eating for the last week came from the gang's 'farmland' did you?"

Devon hadn't thought about it. He'd assumed it had all been stolen.

The hidden door opened and Miriam motioned them toward her, mouth downturned in disapproval. As they rounded the counter and squeezed past her, she said, "Arch isn't here yet—he's not due for another hour—but you can wait with the others. Don't touch anything!"

She ducked back outside and shut the half-door with a snick.

The interior room was pitch black, but from the brief glance Devon had caught before Miriam closed the door he knew it was tight and packed with crates along one wall. Rummaging in his satchel, he produced the shard of green lucent and tapped it alight.

A man and a woman stood directly in front of them, the woman closer, holding a blade at chest level, elbow up, ready to thrust. The man behind held a similar dagger.

"Who are you?" she demanded in a coarse whisper.

Nic tried to push Devon out of the way, but in the tight space— nothing more than an aisle, wide enough for one person—all he managed to do was lean forward into Devon's side. "We're part of Carbolen's gang. We're here to talk to Arch. It has nothing to do with your business."

She appraised them, then stepped back to speak with her associate. Devon could hear the conversation, though not the words, and realized her voice was naturally that harsh, as if something had damaged her throat.

Her associate nodded.

"Stay back. You can talk to Arch after we conclude our business."

"That's fine."

Nic pulled back, the other two retreating to the far end of the aisle. Devon twisted so he could see them but still talk to Nic.

"Maybe we should just leave."

"And do what? Try to find Dalton or Arrend ourselves? Do you have any idea where Dalton has been stationed?"

"We know Arrend is at the college."

"But anyone who doesn't belong on campus is immediately identified and eyed suspiciously. That's why Carbolen couldn't get any eyes on you while you were there. Besides, everyone there knows you and knows Favian and the city guard are looking for you. Arch is the better option."

"What if Carbolen has already told him about Went and us?"

"We'll deal with that when it happens."

Devon didn't like that answer, but the crates piled up before him had caught his attention. They had no clear labels, like those he'd seen in the back room at the Shandy Quad.

The two traders had their heads bent together, backs to them.

He pried up one corner and peered inside. The green light from his lantern glinted off of curved metal—cogs and wheels, armatures, levers, mostly connected into one piece—

"Hey!" the man shouted, stepping down the aisle and slamming his hand on the cover. Devon barely had time to snatch his fingers away. "Hands and eyes off."

Devon held up both hands, palms out, and the man retreated with a grumble.

"What did you see?" Nic asked, voice low.

"Mechanical things, like those machines down in the factory on Level Fifteen."

"I wonder where they're headed."

Devon leaned back against the wooden crates behind him. They settled in to wait.

An hour and a half later—the two traders fidgeting with impatience—the hidden door opened and Arch stepped inside. The cool, scented air of the flower shop gusted in, highlighting how stuffy and hot it had gotten inside the narrow room.

Arch eyed Nic and Devon. "I'll deal with you two after I make this trade. Out."

They squeezed past Arch's bulk and stumbled out into the flower shop, Miriam waving them away from her counter with pursed lips. Twenty minutes later, scuffling and thumps sounded from the back room. This lasted another thirty minutes, then the hidden door opened again, Arch standing there, face sweaty. "Get in here."

As soon as the door closed—the room now empty of all crates— Arch turned on them.

"Tell me why I shouldn't inform Carbolen that I have you right now? He said you escaped, that you killed Went."

"Went attacked me—"

"I killed Went—"

Arch raised a hand to stop them. "One at a time." He pointed at Devon. "You first."

"We were coming back from the twelfth level, in the elevator. Went had been ordered to take me down there, to see if I could identify what the Brovettans were after. But he attacked me, came at me with a dagger. Nic tried to intervene, but Went threw him off."

"Why did he attack you?"

"To get me out of the way. He thought I threatened his position as captain."

"Devon wasn't doing so hot in the fight when I came around," Nic said. "I stabbed Went when Devon got him in a stranglehold."

Arch glanced back and forth between the two, then asked, "If that's the case, then go to Carbolen and explain the situation."

"I can't. Not yet. I needed to get some papers from my bolthole and warn Dalton and Arrend about the Brovettans. That's why we're here. We need your help. I couldn't guarantee Carbolen would let me do either of those things."

Arch crossed his bulky arms over his chest and leaned back against the wall. "You want my help to warn Dalton and Arrend... then what?"

"Then we go back to Carbolen."

More looks, followed by a sigh. "What do you need from me?"

"I need to know where Dalton is stationed. Or if he comes to the bar on a regular basis, I need to know when. And I need someone to get a message in to Arrend, maybe arrange a meeting. I can't go onto the campus at all, not without being recognized."

"That ain't going to happen."

"Why not?"

"Because the Lyceum is currently locked up tight as one of those lucent locks you're so fond of. Rumor has it the Brovettan envoy is coming, that they requested the Lyceum as neutral ground for the negotiations for peace. Their advance party is already here, making sure the arrangements are satisfactory. The Lyceum is surrounded by the Iandolan Army. Practically no one goes in or out, except soldiers and city guards. The Shandy Quad has been dead for the last two days. It's killing my business."

"Why would they demand the Lyceum as a meeting place?"

"Beats me. Middle ground? It's halfway between the waygates and the Council chamber in the towers."

"So there's no way to get a message to Arrend."

"It's unlikely."

Devon clenched a fist in frustration. "What about Dalton? Where is he?"

"Last I heard, he was stationed at the Spoke, around Level Fifteen. But that may have changed. They've been shifting the army and city patrols around due to the Brovettans' arrival."

"Does he come to the Shandy Quad much?"

"Not for months. He used to come every few days, whenever he got the chance, he said, even though they skipped the usual few months of break and put all of the new graduates right into army training. I think he was hoping to run into you."

Devon's throat seized up. The corners of his eyes burned. The reaction was unexpected and for a brief moment it overwhelmed him, simultaneously hot and cold deep inside his chest. Then he swallowed and managed a rough, "Level Fifteen?"

Arch let his arms drop, along with the stern expression. One hand fell onto Devon's shoulder. "Level Fifteen."

He gently shoved Devon toward the door. Not the hidden one that led to the flower shop, but the one through which Devon assumed the two traders and all of the crates had passed in the back wall. Devon stumbled the first few steps, then collected himself, snagging Nic's arm on the way.

When they reached the back door, Arch called out to them. "What do I tell Carbolen?"

"The truth." But Devon paused, Nic at his shoulder, anxious to go. "What did those two want with all of those machines?"

Arch's eyebrow rose. "They didn't want those parts, they were here to trade them."

Devon had assumed they were being traded down the city, not up. "What does the upper city want with mechanical parts? They're dead. The lucent in their drives doesn't work anymore."

"Spare parts. It's not just in the lower levels that things are failing. And they pay good money. Now go, before one of Carbolen's men shows up."

He shoved them out into an alley. Devon headed toward the street.

"Hold up," Nic said. "Where are we going?"

Devon didn't slow. "Level Fifteen, to find Dalton."

"We've been moving since Went found us and dragged us down to Level Twelve. Aren't you exhausted?"

As soon as Nic mentioned it, Devon felt it in his bones. His muscles ached, his knees and feet hurt, and his stomach was an empty hollow at his core.

"We'll hit the marketplace, snag something to eat, and then find some place to hunker down for the night."

Nic's relief was nearly palpable. "I know a place. It's near the hub, but we can crash there without Carbolen finding us."

"Then let's go."

* * *

Devon shifted another sheet of Arrend's research notes to the top of the stack he'd already read and glanced toward Nic's sleeping form. They were resting in the attic crawlspace of an apartment complex, after an hour of pilfering odds and ends of foodstuffs from the market. Both had collapsed as soon as Nic led him to the bolthole, but Devon had slept fitfully. Eventually, he'd given up and spent the next hour sorting the research papers they'd salvaged under the green glow of his lantern.

Then he'd begun to read.

Arrend's notes on the Wardings were fascinating. He'd detailed every Warding within the city, with notes on some of those in other cities as well, described by visitors that Arrend had interviewed. He'd drawn meticulous sketches of their shapes, including dimensions of faces and facets. Everything within view of the edges of each had been listed—buildings, people, streets. Using such details, Devon's proctor had determined a timeline for when the Wardings had been created. Most of this was guesswork based on styles of clothing and the relative deterioration of the architecture seen inside the Wardings.

After reading through five of these types of descriptions, Devon had started sensing a pattern. In each of the Wardings, when viewed from certain angles, there were signs of some kind of disaster. Smoke filled the streets of one, the people inside running from the black clouds. Reflections within the Warding on lucent and glass objects clearly showed flames somewhere deeper inside—a building had caught fire and was raging out of control just beyond sight. In another, some kind of long, segmented carriage that sat upon the elevated tracks had derailed, the lead cars strewn across the street, others dangling from the tracks. Debris was strewn around the wreckage— bricks from the buildings that had been hit, metal and glass from the carriages, shattered lucent. And there were bodies. Survivors were weeping, staggering away from the crash, blood on their faces, holding broken arms or legs. Some simply stood stunned. Based on what could be seen, part of the track had crumbled, throwing the segmented carriage into the street. This Warding had obviously been created long after the other—the buildings were cracked, facades missing in places, streaked with dirt and weathering.

The others had similar disasters—a few more fires, one with the streets flooded with water, even one with what appeared to be an intense electrical storm, bolts of lightning arcing between the buildings. There were a couple with no visible catastrophe taking place, but still, the pattern was clear. Even Arrend had noticed it:

It appears that the Wardings were created in order to contain disasters that had somehow escalated beyond control. Fires, floods, building collapses—all appear inside the earlier Wardings. In fact, there are no Wardings without visible disasters inside them until much closer to our own time. I hypothesize that the mechanism for creating the Wardings has been deteriorating over time and that these later Wardings that do not appear to contain any kind of traumatic or catastrophic event are simply malfunctions. What this mechanism is is unclear. Unfortunately, we cannot see into the center of the Wardings in order to analyze how they were formed. It should be noted that the disasters seen are almost never at the center of their respective Wardings. This suggests that however the Wardings are created, they are an inherent part of the city's structure and cannot be moved.

Devon leaned back against the pitched roof behind him, rafters on either side. "The Wardings are a safety mechanism. They were created to protect people." He closed his eyes and yawned. He was so tired, even though he'd managed to sleep a little. "So why are the Brovettans interested in them?" he mumbled to himself, feeling himself beginning to drift to sleep. The sheets of paper he held slipped from limp fingers and his head sagged forward. "Why...why are they looking for...the amber shards?"

At the edge of sleep, he found himself standing before the Warding on Level One, the destruction of the Brovettan attack behind him. He placed his hand flat against the Warding's surface, smooth and solid beneath his skin. It vibrated, a faint buzz he could feel in his teeth. When he stepped back, he stood before the amber shard at the center of the Lyceum.

...however the Wardings are created, they are an inherent part of the city's structure...

...an inherent part of the city's structure...

...structure...

The amber shard had an inherent structure, a shape defined by facets and edges. Each Warding was the same, like...like a giant crystal...like the shard...like the double pyramid needed to create the mage forms. As if they were all connected...shape and form...shard and Warding...mage and Sigil...

He bolted upright and slammed his head against the roof of the crawlspace, pain blinding him as he sank forward onto hands and knees, spitting curses. Nic jerked out of sleep and shouted, "Wher— ? Wha—?" A scramble of feet and then Nic's hand steadied him. "What's going on?"

Vision clearing somewhat, a pounding throb beginning at the back of his head, Devon grabbed Nic's shirt. "We have to find Dalton. Right now. The meeting at the Lyceum is a trap."

Chapter Fourteen

"Wait!" Nic called out after they'd dropped from a window ledge outside a building to the mouth of an alley on Level Fifteen. Nic had sagged back against the wall and now leaned forward, gasping. "Wait. I need to catch my breath."

Devon turned to face the direction of the Spoke, his skin tingling with urgency. "We need to move."

"You don't even know if the Brovettan envoy is here yet. Arch only mentioned some kind of advance team, taking care of details. If this meeting really is a trap of some kind, they aren't going to spring it until everyone's in place."

"True." He slumped against the gritty wall and watched a man and small child warily cross to the far side of the street to pass them. The man kept his eyes on them, pulled the girl closer to his side. The lucents in this area were mostly intact, although a few of the threads flickered. "My gut tells me we don't have much time though."

Nic sighed and forced himself upright. "Then let's go."

They headed straight for where the Spoke descended from the level above in a long ramp with evenly spaced obelisks of blue-white lucent on the stone walls along its length. Ten blocks away, the buildings began to improve and the number of people moving freely on the street increased. Shops and open markets appeared. Within a few blocks of the end of the ramp, the level could have been mistaken for mid-level.

Except that here, there were far more soldiers.

Nic grabbed Devon's shoulder and pulled him up short as they came within sight of the end of the ramp. It spilled out onto a wide plaza, currently filled with members of the Iandolan Army mixed with city guards. Citizens moved among them, but far fewer than usual. Most of the residents of this level were steering clear of the plaza altogether.

With Nic's fingers still digging into his muscles, Devon watched the movements of the army, tense. Then he shrugged out of Nic's grip.

"What are you doing?" Nic protested as Devon moved out onto the plaza. "They'll see you!"

"They aren't all on guard duty, most are headed up-level. Besides, how else are we going to find Dalton?"

Devon began circling, paying closer attention to the soldiers on watch than on those headed upwards. If Arch was right and Dalton was stationed here, he'd be working or at the army barracks.

Halfway around the plaza, the soldiers milling around at its center roused themselves and organized into lines at a signal Devon hadn't heard. Within fifteen minutes, they began to march up the ramp, leaving the plaza mostly empty. Devon and Nic had reached the wide thoroughfare where the Spoke continued out to the next ramp. The street was far more active, with guards posted at every intersection within sight. They crossed behind a slew of carts handled by more soldiers—supplies headed upwards after the unit that had just left—and began searching on the far side.

Devon had begun to think Dalton wasn't on duty, or was guarding one of the intersections, when Nic hauled him into a spice shop.

"He's over there," Nic said under his breath, "near that statue of the rearing horse at the corner."

Devon stepped up to the spice merchant's window, the mix of scents intoxicating. He found the statue, began scanning those in uniforms around it—

His sucked in a breath as soon as he spotted Dalton. The War student—soldier now—looked haggard, more weathered and worn than Devon remembered.

He turned to go see him and bumped into Nic, the former bartender placing his hands on Devon's chest to halt him. "Where do you think you're going?"

"Dalton—"

"—is currently surrounded by soldiers who will arrest you as soon as they figure out exactly who you are, if Dalton doesn't arrest you himself."

"He'd never—"

Nic's eyebrow rose. "Are you certain? The Dalton I remember was a War student through and through. He followed the rules."

"Not when it came to me," Devon said.

Nic's hands dropped. "Maybe so, but are you willing to risk it? Wait here. I'll see if I can get Dalton to come see you."

Before Devon could protest Nic was out the door, wending his way through the people outside. Devon watched as he paused at the statue, waiting until one of the other soldiers finished speaking with Dalton before stepping forward.

Devon could see Dalton's face as Nic spoke—confusion at first, with a wary hand on the pommel of his sword, then surprised recognition and a wide-eyed glance toward the spice shop. He looked around furtively, then stepped up to the woman who'd spoken to him a moment before, said something as he motioned to Nic, then headed toward the shop.

Devon exhaled sharply, unaware he'd been holding his breath. He wiped sweaty palms on his dirty breeches, suddenly aware of how lower-city he appeared—clothes worn and torn, stained with oil, sweat, even blood. He couldn't imagine what his face looked like.

And then Dalton was there, in the shop, standing before him, both of them frozen. His expression was unreadable—blank shock.

"Dalton—"

Devon gasped as he was crushed in a fierce hug, his face pressed into Dalton's crisp maroon and white uniform. He drew in Dalton's sweat-scent. Then Dalton was kissing him, with bruising force, but he didn't care.

When he finally broke contact, Devon's entire body was trembling, vibrating like the shard at the center of the Lyceum's quad.

"Where have you been?" Dalton demanded in a thick, ragged voice. His fingers dug into Devon's upper arms. "After you ran..."

"I couldn't come to you, although I watched. I saw your graduation. I couldn't risk anything more."

Dalton ran a hand down his face. "Of course not. And I couldn't search for you. I knew they were watching me, in case you showed up. But still." He bowed his head, collecting himself. "I missed you."

"Stop, please," Nic said dryly. "You'll make me cry."

Dalton gave a nervous laugh, then frowned. "Why are you here now?"

The urgency that had driven them to Level Fifteen seized Devon again. "The Brovettans! I came to warn you—" But he broke off, shooting a look toward the shopkeeper, who'd halted his grinding and was watching them intently.

"Hang on," Dalton said.

He moved across the shop, spoke to the shopkeeper. The old man slid from his stool—he was only half Dalton's height—shuffled to the door, locked it, then retreated into the back room.

Dalton rejoined them, arms crossed over his chest. "Now, warn me about what?"

"The Brovettans have mages and the meeting at the Lyceum is a trap."

"That's…a hefty accusation. I fought them during that first attack, when I was still a War student, and again later on. I didn't see any evidence of mages."

"During the last attack, they had a second team. Some of the gangs ran into them on Level Twelve. They killed one of the scouts with some kind of lightning bolt. I don't think they intended anyone to see."

"I saw it, too," Nic threw in. "I don't see how it could have been anything other than magework."

Dalton glanced between them. "I heard rumors something had happened at River Street, but the report back from the team was that it was gang-related."

"It wasn't. I was there. I saw the scout get fried. The Brovettans took their own dead and the scout with them when they left."

Devon could tell Dalton wasn't convinced.

"I've been training with the mages," Dalton said. "Heavier-duty stuff than what we learned at the college. None of it has involved any lightning bolts."

"You know I was working with Lane, that my research involved magecraft. According to my studies, all mages can produce lightning. Maybe those here in Iandolo have forgotten, but not the Brovettans."

Dalton pondered a moment. "Let's suppose I accept that the Brovettans have mages. How does that make the meeting at the Lyceum a trap?"

"Remember the shard of lucent at the center of the quad?"

"Yes."

"It's not just a random piece of lucent. It's a dormant Warding. I think the Brovettans plan on luring the Council to the Lyceum for this truce and once everyone is there, they plan on activating the shard."

Dalton had dropped his arms. "Which will do what, exactly?"

"It will create a Warding. I don't know exactly how it works, but if it's anything like the Wardings that we see all over the city, the entire Lyceum and the surrounding area will be engulfed in amber crystal. Everyone inside will be locked away, cut off from the rest of the city. The entire Council will be wiped out."

Dalton tensed. "It wouldn't be just the Council. All of the Prefects will be there, along with the highest-ranking officers in the army. Not to mention the most powerful mages. We'd be left with seconds-in-command at best, the lesser mages..." He trailed off, his growing horror palpable.

"You have to warn your superiors," Devon said. "You have to tell them to call off the meeting, or change it to a different location—"

Dalton's hand shot out and latched onto his shoulder. "You don't understand. The meeting...it's scheduled to start today. The Brovettan envoy is already here. They ascended to mid-level an hour ago. The force that just left here? It was sent to support the army already at the Lyceum." He swore. "Over half the Iandolan Army is there. If what you say is true, the rest of the city will be essentially defenseless."

They stared at each other, then he hauled Devon forward. "You need to come with me."

"Where?"

"To speak to my captain."

Devon pulled himself out of Dalton's grip. "He'll arrest me. Aren't there standing orders?"

"With what's been going on with the Brovettans, the importance of your arrest has shrunk significantly. We've left that to the city guard. The threat at the Lyceum is significant, but I won't be able to convince my captain of that myself. I need you there as an expert."

"I'm not an expert."

"He doesn't know that."

Nic shifted forward. "If he goes out there, you know they'll arrest him."

"They won't send anyone up to the Lyceum to warn them on my word alone," Dalton countered. "I'm a new recruit. I've barely earned the rank of soldier."

Devon didn't see any other way. "Fine. Take us to your captain."

Dalton exited the spice shop. Nic came up to Devon's side. "This is a mistake."

"I don't see that we have any other options."

"What about Carbolen? I didn't mention it before, but maybe he has contacts at the Lyceum or higher up he can use to get the warning to the right people."

"You mean if he doesn't kill us before we have a chance to explain? I'd rather be arrested. It's not much different from being captured by Carbolen. Besides—" he pushed through the door into sunlight "—I don't think we have that much time."

Dalton had wound his way onto the edge of the plaza, circling back toward the statue and the area the two hadn't covered yet in their search. He glanced back once, to make certain they were following, then halted a block farther on, near a small cluster of men in army uniforms. One of them had extra insignia on his collar and shoulders and his uniform was a little crisper, with subtle differences in cut from Dalton's.

They came up behind Dalton, who stood back respectfully, waiting for his captain to finish giving orders to the three men around him. They nodded and left, leaving the captain and two others, one of them obviously an assistant, standing a step behind and taking notes.

The captain looked to Dalton, eyes scanning briefly over Devon and Nic. "You have something to report, soldier?"

Dalton stepped forward, motions taut and precise, back straight. "Yes, sir. These two approached me with a possible threat to the Lyceum and the meeting with the Brovettans."

The captain's expression shifted, his interest piqued. He took a closer look at Devon and Nic. "A threat? What kind of threat?"

Dalton turned back and Devon stepped forward. "I think the meeting at the college is a trap."

Behind the captain, the other soldier smirked, but the captain's expression didn't change.

"How so?"

A thread of unease niggled through Devon, but he pressed on. "The Brovettans have been attacking Iandolo with purpose. The first attack was meant to get them to the Warding on Level One. The second main attack was a diversion. They had a second team, smaller, that infiltrated Level Twelve."

"What would interest them on Level Twelve? There is no Warding there."

"No, but there is a shard of lucent in what used to be a park. Their mages—"

"Wait. The Brovettans have mages?"

"Yes."

The second soldier's smirk grew.

"Go on," the captain said.

Nic made a sharp noise behind him, but desperation made Devon plow forward.

"You don't understand. The shards and the Wardings are connected. When some kind of disaster occurs in the area of a shard, it can be activated. It expands and envelopes the region, sealing it off until the disaster can be dealt with."

Nic tugged at Devon's sleeve, muttered a terse, "Let's go."

"There's a shard at the center of the Lyceum," Devon continued. "The Brovettans are going to activate it during the meeting!"

"With their mages," the soldier behind the captain said.

The captain didn't answer, simply raised a hand and motioned to someone behind Devon and Nic.

"Let's go!" Nic said more forcefully, grabbing onto Devon's arm.

Devon turned to see three additional soldiers closing in on them. With Dalton hovering off to one side, they were trapped. "Too late," he said beneath his breath.

Dalton saw the other soldiers moving forward and stepped closer to Devon. "What's going on?"

"Did you think I wouldn't recognize your friend?" the captain asked. "Devon Alamort, Science student and fugitive. Arrest ordered by Proctor Favian and Proctor Gallean of the Lyceum. I was told to keep an eye out for him specifically, since it was thought he might attempt to contact you. And here he is."

"I told him you'd listen to him," Dalton said. "The Council is at risk! Most of the upper echelon of the army!"

"I did listen. Long enough for reinforcements to arrive." He nodded to the three men, who stepped forward. "Arrest these two.

Take them to the barracks and keep watch until we have time to hand them over to the city guard."

Nic attempted to bolt, but two of the guards grabbed him and wrestled him to the ground, knocking away his dagger when he tried to draw it. He spat curses and growled as they rolled him onto his stomach and proceeded to tie his hands with twine. Devon didn't resist, the third soldier stepping in on one side, grabbing one arm, Dalton seizing the other.

"You can't do this," Dalton said. "I know him. He wouldn't make this up. Why would he risk arrest by coming forward if it weren't true?"

"Do you even know why the proctors want me arrested? It's because I studied things like the shards and magework at the Lyceum when I should have let well enough alone." The soldier yanked Devon's arm behind his back, wrested his other from Dalton, and began trussing him up, without even removing his satchel. "At least send us up to the Lyceum! Take me to Favian and Gallean. Let them decide."

The captain frowned. The two other guards hauled Nic upright and they began dragging both of them away.

"They're the only ones who can determine whether what I'm saying is the truth!" Devon shot a pleading look at Dalton as he was pulled away, struggling briefly, but Dalton appeared trapped with indecision, his horrified expression warring with his duty as a soldier. He took a step toward Devon, hand on his sword hilt—

"Wait!"

Everyone turned back to the captain. He stalked forward, capturing Devon's chin in one hand and tilting his head up so he could look into his eyes. Devon smelled his sweat beneath the stringent odor of the oil that slicked his hair. Devon made no attempt to temper his glare.

After a moment, the captain thrust Devon's chin aside and turned his back on him.

"Take them both to the Lyceum. Let the proctors deal with them."

The three soldiers stared at each other, but then Dalton stepped forward.

"We'll take them up in one of the supply carts. Over here."

One of the guards glanced toward the captain at this usurpation of control, but the captain didn't appear to care, already speaking to his second and aid.

Under Dalton's direction, they hustled Nic and Devon across the plaza to where a few wagons stood half loaded with crates and barrels. They heaved them both into the back of one of them, two guards climbing in beside them, while Dalton and the other guard took control of the horses' reins, Dalton explaining the situation to the captain in control of the supplies. He ushered them on with a wave.

"That went well," Nic groused as the wagon jounced into motion.

"Better than expected."

"How so?"

"We're headed to the college, aren't we? And we aren't walking."

Three levels later, Devon was beginning to think walking would have been less painful. Every jolt of the wagon drove nails into his joints, even though he and Nic had maneuvered themselves into sitting positions with their backs to the crates on either side. Their two guards alternated between sitting in the back watching over them and walking beside the wagon.

They rose, Devon staring out the back of the wagon, where he could see the levels splayed out before them, buildings rising into the heights until the level above swallowed up what remained. Entire sections at each level were designated farmland, usually close to the Spokes, the patches of various shades of green and yellow in sharp contrast to the sheen of metal and stone of the city to either side. Beyond the height of the waygate, the browns, reds, and umbers of the Flatlands stretched to the blue, cloud-scudded sky, broken only by the waypath to Brovetto.

On the flat sections between ramps, the only parts of the city Devon could see were the buildings on either side and the throngs of people, growing the higher they went. Those flat stretches shortened at each level. Dalton urged the horses into a fast trot at each one.

Devon knew they were close to mid-level when the proportion of citizens to soldiers on the Spoke shifted. He craned his neck around to see past the crates, toward the ramp ahead.

Dalton looked back. "The next level is mid-level."

Devon faced the Lyceum. He could see the Tower from here, its green lucent gleaming in the setting sun. Banners hung from its top, the sigil of Iridesque alternating with that of Luminesque. It had taken them nearly all day to warn Dalton and return to mid-level—longer, since they'd started out before dawn. The wagon had cut down on the time it took to return, but was it enough?

The urgency that had driven him down to Level Fifteen had been tamped down during the ascent in the wagon, curbed because they were finally doing something, and by the fact that Devon knew there was no way he could speed them up. But on seeing the Tower, it returned with a vengeance.

He needed to warn Arrend. He'd even face Favian again, if that's what it took. But he needed to do it now, before the Brovettans had a chance to—

Something in the crowds around them shifted. They were nearing the top of the ramp, where the people were thickest, Dalton forced to slow to a crawl even with the other soldiers trying to clear a path. Devon straightened where he sat, but he saw nothing happening in the direction of the Lyceum. Then he noted people pointing down-level.

His head snapped around and instantly focused on a column of smoke rising from near the waygate to Brovetto. He shifted to the edge of the cart as another column grew next to the first, then a third. More began to sprout along the Spoke, rising toward them, and then another at the barely visible waygate to the north that led to Bolnis. Flashes of blue-white lightning lit the columns from below.

"Someone's attacking the waygate," Nic said, shifting into position beside him. The crowd was beginning to grow restless, voices rising toward panic.

"Not just the waygate," Devon said. "They're attacking at every level along the Spoke and at the other waygates as well." They'd have to, he realized. If the Brovettans wanted to seize control of the city, they'd need to do more than just take out the Council and the mages.

He twisted toward Dalton. "Dalton!"

"I can't get these damn people to move!" Dalton shouted, slapping the reins against the horses' rumps.

"We have bigger issues. The Brovettans are attacking the Spoke!"

"What are you talking—" But he'd turned in his seat.

Motion caught Devon's eye: black-clad figures surging out of the surrounding streets. He swore and jolted upright onto his knees, began twisting his hands, the truss biting into his skin. "Dalton! The Brovettans!"

"Not so fast," one of the soldiers guarding them said. He stood outside the wagon, laid a hand on Devon's arm to restrain him.

"I see them," Dalton said, still looking down toward the waygate.

"Not them! Them! They're attacking on this level!"

Then the screams started as the black-armored Brovettans slammed into the soldiers guarding the top of the ramp. Blood flew in arcs as the guards were caught unprepared, at least ten falling within Devon's sight as he yanked at his bonds. Citizens shrieked, punctuated by curses, and within a breath the entire ramp and street beyond transformed into a riot of bodies and blades and blood.

"Cut us loose!" Devon shouted at the guard that held his arm.

The soldier stared at him in shock for a moment, then hardened and thrust him down into the back of the wagon. "Stay here. Don't move."

He drew his sword and charged up the ramp with their other guard, toward the Brovettans and the Iandolan soldiers who were trying to organize a defense. The third leaped from the wagon to join them, Dalton cursing, setting the brake with a yank and tossing the reins aside, ready to follow. Citizens were bolting in every direction, shouting and falling over each other to get out of the way. The Brovettans were a black wall of death, emerging out from the side streets, killing indiscriminately.

"Dalton," Devon said. "Cut us loose."

He hesitated, then cut around the back of the wagon and hauled them both out onto the ground. He drew his dagger and with a quick jerk upward, freed Devon, then Nic.

"Get out of here," he said, already drawing his sword.

Devon seized his arm. "Look."

He pointed toward the Tower of the Lyceum.

A column of amber light shot upwards, followed by a hideous cracking sound that shuddered through the stone ramp beneath their feet. The screaming intensified, a few people thrown to the ground, and then everyone faced the tower of light.

It shrank, but expanded as it did so, bulging out to the sides, engulfing the Lyceum's Tower and reaching beyond, too fast to follow with the naked eye. In a blink, it had swallowed entire blocks, the buildings inside it obscured by an amber haze. The light barreled towards them, startling enough Devon took a step back. His heart leapt up into his throat and he heard Nic mutter, "It's not going to stop. It's going to hit us."

And then it froze.

A crackling sound—like that of ice when water is poured over it—echoed off of the buildings and in another heartbeat the amber light solidified into a Warding, no more than four blocks away.

"Shards," Dalton said into the odd silence that followed. "You were right."

Then the Brovettans surged forward and the crowd fled in a wave. The maroon and white uniforms of the Iandolan Army were falling to the brutal Brovettan blades on all sides. There was nowhere to run but down.

Devon shoved at Dalton, but he dug in his heels.

"I have to help them," he shouted, the mob of people beginning to pour around them, parted by the cart. The horses staggered back, the cart's wheels screeching against the stone.

"You'll never make it back up the ramp," Devon argued. "Not against this crowd."

"Besides," Nic added, "there aren't any of your fellow army members left!"

With a sickening turn of his stomach, Devon realized it was true. He couldn't see any more uniforms through the mob. The Brovettans were now cutting viciously into the crowd.

The horses began to snort, eyes wide in fear and confusion, nostrils flared at the scent of blood. They shoved back hard, crates skidding. One of the barrels fell over and rolled off the back. Devon heard the sharp sound of the brake cracking.

Then one of the horses reared up, feet kicking, and the entire wagon began to tilt.

"Run!" Devon shouted, and pushed Dalton and Nic down the ramp. Neither one of them resisted, all three merging with the crowd as the crates and barrels began tumbling from the cart behind them. One of the horses screamed, followed by the splintering of wood, and then Devon was forced to focus on keeping his feet as the press of panicked bodies shoved at him. He caught sight of Dalton a few steps ahead, Nic off to one side, and with effort elbowed himself closer. Ahead, at the bottom of the ramp, the mob spread out onto a square, but Devon could see black-clad figures fighting at the far end, near the top of the next ramp. He snatched at Dalton's uniform, grabbed Nic's shirt, and steered them to the short wall at the right edge.

When they reached the bottom of the ramp, Dalton tried to push toward the fighting, but the crowd forced them out into the side streets of the square. Not even Dalton's raised sword deterred them. Spitting curses, Dalton was driven out of the square, but he angled toward the side of the street. Devon followed, the three of them coming up against the steps of an apartment building like flotsam in a raging river. They clung to the stone steps, Devon climbing up to the locked door, the mass of people fleeing the square roaring past.

"I have to get out there," Dalton said.

"To do what?" Devon asked harshly. "Die? I can see the square. There aren't any Iandolan soldiers left. Either they're dead—and I can see plenty of bodies—or they fled. All that's left on the square now are the Brovettans."

Dalton stared in their direction. "Where did they come from?"

"I'd guess they've been infiltrating Iandolo for months, probably since before that first attack."

"Where have they been hiding?"

"Have you seen the lower levels?"

The mob had decreased, but the Brovettans remained on the square. Dalton growled in frustration.

"They don't seem to be pursuing anyone into the city."

"No." Dalton slammed his sword back into its sheath. "They're solidifying their hold on the Spoke. They're probably doing the same at each of the waygates and all the main thoroughfares."

"There aren't as many of them as I thought," Nic said.

"They wouldn't need many," Dalton said. "Not when they caught us by surprise. And not when we'd thinned out our ranks along the Spoke and waygates attempting to protect the Lyceum and its surroundings."

The mob had thinned to a trickle. In another few moments, the Brovettans would be able to see them. Devon glanced down at Dalton's uniform. "We need to get out of here. Before they see us. Before they see you."

Dalton didn't appear to hear him. He had stilled, staring up to where the edge of the new Warding could be seen at mid-level.

The enormity of what had happened hit him, a physical blow Devon could practically see, and he sagged back against the steps. He faced Devon, swallowed.

"What are we going to do?"

Two of the Brovettans looked their way. One of them motioned to the others.

Devon came down the steps and hauled Dalton upright. He was trembling. Nic stepped up to his other side.

"They're coming," Devon said. "We need to move."

"But...what are we going to do?"

Devon didn't have an answer. "Right now. We're going to get off the streets and get you out of that uniform."

PART III

THE WARDING

Chapter Fifteen

"We have to report to someone," Dalton said.

"Who?"

"One of the captains or a Prefect. Someone!"

He was pacing back and forth in the room Devon and Lane had used to practice her forms. The purple lucent tree glowed on the back wall. It had been the closest haven Devon could think of after they'd fled the Brovettans at the ramp and square. That had been hours ago and Dalton was still agitated. Nic had gone out in search of information and new clothes for Dalton.

"If you know of a captain or Prefect we can report to, let me know."

Dalton shot him a murderous look and continued pacing.

Both of them stilled a moment later at a noise from the outer hall. Dalton slid to the side of the door. Devon reached into his satchel and rested his hand on the hilt of his dagger.

Then Dalton relaxed. "It's Nic."

The gang member burst into the room and tossed a wad of clothing at Dalton. "I did the best I could. The city is in chaos. The Brovettans are locking down all of the main thoroughfares, not just the Spokes and waygates. Apparently, they attacked the three main towers above mid-level as well. They've seized the central tower, the

Council chamber, everything. Anyone of importance who wasn't at the Lyceum for the meeting has been sealed off in the towers."

"What about the Iandolan Army? They couldn't have killed them all."

"As far as I can tell, everyone is dead or has been taken prisoner. There's a group of Iandolan soldiers being held on this level in one of the buildings near the Spoke. I didn't run into any other maroon and whites on the streets."

"And the mages?" Devon asked. "Did you see any Iandolan mages?"

"If there are any, they're being kept with the soldiers."

"Most of our mages were at the Lyceum," Dalton said. He began changing out of his uniform. "But there should have been at least six stationed at each of the waygates. A few of them were scattered along the Spoke. Why are the mages important?"

"Because I saw lightning in the smoke at the waygate to Brovetto, which means the Brovettans have their own mages fighting openly now."

That sobered both of them. Nic moved to the center of the room and knelt, rooting through the bundle he held in his other hand. He produced a broken loaf of bread, a half-dozen apples, a head of cabbage, and a few gouged carrots. He tossed an apple each to Devon and Dalton. "Better eat that quick. I'm certain it's bruised. It's all damaged a little. This is what was left behind when the hawkers in the marketplace scattered, at least what was close enough to the side streets that I dared risk retrieving it. Everyone has found a place to hunker down and wait, to see what happens next. There's practically no one on the streets now, except Brovettans."

"They can't be everywhere," Dalton protested. "They couldn't have snuck in that many of their people over the last few months."

"I didn't say they were everywhere, but they're making their presence known at all of the key locations. They've got squads of ten to twenty stationed along the ramp, others roaming the streets in their vicinity. I didn't see any of them beyond the first few blocks of the Spokes or main thoroughfares."

"Did you see any Brovettan mages?" Devon asked.

"No, although I'm not certain what they'd look like."

Devon thought back to the attack at River Street. "They seem to be styling themselves after our own mages, so battle robes I'd guess. Although they prefer black."

"I didn't see anyone dressed like that."

"Good."

"Why?" Dalton asked.

"Because I only saw lightning at the waygate to Brovetto. I'm hoping that means they don't have many mages. We've only seen evidence of two."

"Don't you mean one?"

"Two. The one at the waygate during the attack and whoever set off the shard to create the Warding. That could only have been done by a mage."

"Unless there was more than a single mage at the waygate."

"I'd wager that if they had additional mages, they would have been spread out around the city, at least at the waygates."

"They shouldn't have any mages," Nic said.

"None of this helps us with the basic problem: what are we going to do? We can't let them take over Iandolo."

"How are the three of us going to stop them?" Nic countered.

Dalton raised both hands and clenched them in frustration.

"We can't stop them," Devon said. "There are too many of the Brovettans already inside Iandolo. We'll need a small army to drive them out."

Dalton snorted. "And where are we going to find that?"

But Devon was watching Nic, whose eyes suddenly widened. "Carbolen."

"Carbolen has a small army?" Dalton asked.

Devon stood and took a bite out of his apple, then reached for his satchel. "Not an army, but he has managed to organize the gangs. All we have to do is convince him to help."

"How are we going to do that?"

"I don't know yet."

Nic began packing up the food. "Are you certain you want to go back? He isn't going to be happy about Went."

"I know, but I don't see any other option."

"We could wait and see how many members of the Iandolan Army survived and join with them," Dalton said.

"Based on what you saw, how many do you think survived?" Devon asked.

"Not many. But they couldn't have all been killed. Some of them must have escaped."

Devon moved to Dalton's side. "Do you want to go search for them?"

Dalton stared out into the darkness of the building beyond the door. "Not without you."

Devon shook his head. "I can't go. You saw how your captain reacted once he recognized me."

"I doubt whoever we find would care you're a fugitive at the moment."

"Probably not. But we don't know where the army's survivors are, or who's in charge. We do know where Carbolen is, and I'm betting he's got more men backing him than whatever's left of the army."

Nic cleared his throat. "We could simply hunker down like the rest of the city and wait it out." When both Devon and Dalton turned on him, he raised both hands, palms out. "Alright, alright, just thought I'd mention it."

"So," Dalton said, as Devon took his neatly folded uniform and stuffed it into his satchel. The former War student looked odd in street clothes, a soldier's sword strapped to his waist. "How are we going to find Carbolen."

Devon headed out the door. "Don't worry. He'll find us."

                           * * *

"Carbolen, you have visitors."

The lair was a madhouse, empty of nearly all of the gang members usually lounging or sleeping off to the sides, but bustling with people running back and forth, reporting to the slew of captains spread about. Leinn stood beside Carbolen at the far end of the dais, in deep conversation. Toral held court at the bottom, most of the runners seeking her out. There were two other men and one woman—Starling and two other gang leaders, Devon guessed. All of them wore dour expressions, frowns edged with anger and panic. They were straining to hear the reports as they came in, although there were too many to keep track of individually.

But Raven's announcement cut through all of the noise and captured everyone's interest. The cacophony died, Carbolen and Leinn turning as Raven led Devon and Nic forward. Bitter followed behind with Dalton, his hands tied behind his back, a bruise darkening near his temple. The Regular held his sword with one hand, the other forcing him forward.

Carbolen sidled to the edge of the dais.

"They gave themselves up," Raven said as she reached him. "They were waiting in the middle of street outside his bolthole. We found them on our way back from mid-level while doing our rounds."

Devon halted a few paces away from Carbolen, Nic a step behind him. Bitter jerked Dalton to a stop at least three paces farther back.

Carbolen eyed Devon, glanced at Nic, then jutted his chin toward Dalton. "Who's this?"

"His army friend, Dalton Trent. He didn't want to disarm."

Carbolen's gaze returned to Devon. He stepped down from the dais and stood a pace away. The entire room quieted.

"Went is dead. And you deserted. Again. Tell me why I shouldn't kill you both right now."

"Went tried to kill me. It was self-defense."

Carbolen's head lowered and he took a step away, halted.

Then he spun. Reaching out, he grabbed Nic by the back of the neck, thrust him to the ground in front of Devon, and knelt on the small of his back. Devon started as Nic's body brushed past him, but it happened so fast he didn't have time to react otherwise.

Nic gasped, spittle spraying, his face pressed into the grimy floor, Carbolen's fingers splayed, holding him in place. A stiletto was pressed into his neck, blood already dripping to the floor.

Without looking up, Carbolen said again, "Tell me why I shouldn't kill you both right now."

Sweat broke out in Devon's armpits and the palms of his hands. He met Nic's terrified gaze and swallowed down his anger. They'd come to convince Carbolen to help them fight the Brovettans, but based on what he saw, Carbolen didn't need convincing. He already intended to fight.

"Because you'll need me to deal with the Brovettans."

Carbolen's shoulders tensed, the blade digging in deeper. Nic flinched and closed his eyes but didn't cry out or whimper.

Then Carbolen stood, the knife suddenly gone. He wiped blood from his hand onto his shirt as he faced Devon.

"You defy me at every turn. You should have returned to the lair and reported Went's actions immediately."

"I don't report to you. I haven't been a part of your gang since the Presidium job."

"Yet here you are."

"From necessity only."

"You're alive by necessity only." He glanced toward Dalton and Bitter. "Let him go. And give him back his sword."

Bitter frowned in disappointment but sliced through Dalton's bonds and handed him his weapon, leaning in close. "I like you. Don't make me regret it." Then she patted him on the cheek and strode up onto the dais with Raven.

Devon helped Nic up off the floor. Blood continued to seep from the slash on his neck, staining his shirt.

"It's fine. It's nothing compared to what he could have done." Bitterness and hatred edged Nic's voice. Carbolen had returned to stand next to Leinn. Activity in the hall had started up again.

"No, it's not fine."

Devon stormed up onto the dais, ignoring Nic's exclaimed "Devon!" and Raven's raised eyebrow as he passed her and Bitter. Carbolen looked up from the maps spread out over a low table, his finger pointing out something to Leinn and the other gang leaders, but he straightened at Devon's approach.

"Tell me what you three know of the Brovettan attack," the gang leader said.

"Not until we reach an understanding."

Carbolen's eyes widened. "An understanding?"

"What happened just now will not happen again. I am not part of your gang. Neither is Dalton, nor Nic, if he chooses. We're free to come and go. You will not touch us while we're here. None of your gang will harm us either."

"Or what?"

"Or I disappear and you lose any chance you have of dealing with the new Warding the Brovettans activated at the Lyceum."

Leinn gasped. "You know about the Warding?"

Carbolen held up a hand to silence her. "Can you bring it down?"

"Do we have an understanding?"

Carbolen searched his face. Then, grudgingly: "We do."

Devon motioned Dalton and Nic to join him, then turned to the maps laid out on the table. There were numerous sheets, each one depicting one of the levels, more detailed than Devon would have thought possible. Sections of the maps were color-coded. Based on the one for Level Seventeen, each color represented an area controlled by a specific gang. Other sections were marked off as dead zones, or uninhabitable, or simply too dangerous to traverse. Entire sections of the three towers were missing or blank, but he did notice a few crude maps of some sublevels below Level One; he hadn't known any part of the city reached below Level One.

Leaning forward, palms flat on the table, he said, "What do you know about the Brovettan forces?"

Carbolen uncrossed his arms and pointed to two of the levels.

"Our eyes report the bulk of the Brovettan forces are forming up at the waygates on Level One, the one to Luminesque in particular, and mid-level around the bases of the three towers. They've taken over the park there and are controlling who goes in and out of the towers. We have no reports from inside the towers. The rest of their forces are spread out along the main thoroughfares, overseeing the key intersections."

"What about the intermediate levels?" Dalton asked. "Have they tried to take any other sections of the city?"

"Not below mid-level," one of the other gang leaders said. "Aside from the initial ambush and slaughter, they've left the citizens alone."

"They're hoping the brutality of that initial attack keeps the populace in order," Carbolen said. "So far, it's working. Most are staying inside. Those that venture out are being ignored unless they approach the Brovettan positions."

"How many men do they have?" Dalton asked.

"We estimate five thousand," Leinn said. "Two thousand at the three towers and on mid-level, another two thousand at the waygates—at least five hundred at the one leading to Luminesque—and another thousand scattered around the thoroughfares. We aren't certain about the number at the towers. We don't know how many entered before we could get eyes up there."

"And how many men do you have?"

"Combining all of the gangs I've managed to forge an alliance with...about half that."

Dalton swore. "That's not enough. Not with them digging into their positions and primed for some kind of counterattack. Unlike them, we won't have the element of surprise."

"Which is why I need to know if you can bring down the Warding. Are the people inside still alive? If we bring it down, will they be able to fight?"

"They're still alive. But I don't know enough about the Wardings yet to know if I can reverse what the Brovettans did."

Anger flared in Carbolen's eyes. "You said you could help. If you can't release the Warding—"

"I've only just begun researching them. I read enough of the notes to figure out what the Brovettans were up to with the shard and realize the danger, but I'll need to do more work to know how it can be reversed. And it can be reversed. The entire purpose of the Wardings was to contain a problem until it could be dealt with."

Carbolen pushed away from the table. "Then you'd better start reading. Fast."

"Do we even need to get rid of the Brovettans?" Starling asked. "Maybe we should see how this shakes out. Maybe the Brovettans will rule better than the Council."

The silence was profound. Carbolen faced the gang leader and those near drew back. "You're more ignorant than I thought. I've been to Brovetto. They rule with the same tactics they've used here— fear and brutality. Our gangs would never have survived beneath them. They would have rooted us out and slaughtered us all ages ago. If you think this first onslaught is violent, wait until they become entrenched."

He turned back to Devon. "Read." He drew the other gang leaders close and began a hushed conversation. Devon shook his head.

Leinn stepped forward. "Come with me. I'll set you up in one of the training rooms."

Devon, Dalton, and Nic followed her out of the lair's main hall, through a few convoluted corridors, and into a small room that contained two tables set against the far wall, a mostly empty weapons rack, and a crudely marked circle in the center of the floor.

"I'll have someone bring you pallets." She half-turned but paused. "If you don't bring down the Warding, we won't be able to push the Brovettans out."

Then she was gone.

All three of them exchanged looks.

"Can you bring it down?" Dalton asked.

Devon placed his satchel on one of the tables and removed the case containing Arrend's notes on the Wardings. "There has to be a way."

Dalton drifted to the weapons rack, scanned what little was there, and surreptitiously slipped something small and lethal-looking into his boot.

Two gang members arrived with pallets and an allotment of food and water, tossing it all to the floor just inside the door. Nic spread out the pallets and immediately lay down with a yawn. "You two should get some sleep," he said, closing his eyes.

Dalton moved behind Devon, his presence a comforting, solid warmth against Devon's side as he laid an arm across his neck and looked over his shoulder. "Need any help?"

Devon had already skimmed what he'd read before and found the place where he'd left off. He leaned into Dalton without taking his eyes from the notes. "I'm not certain what you could do. It's…a lot of reading. And thinking."

"And we all know War students aren't good at that."

Devon turned to protest, but Dalton was smiling. He kissed him, then held up both hands. "I'll leave the thinking up to you. I'm exhausted anyway."

He dropped down onto one of the remaining pallets—Devon noticed Nic had placed the other two close together—and promptly fell asleep. Nic was already snoring.

Rubbing at eyes that already felt thick and gritty, Devon grabbed the notes, sat down on the pallet next to Dalton, back up against the wall, and began reading.

An hour later, he caught himself nodding off, woken only by someone running past their door. He shook himself, took a brisk walk around the marked off practice circle, then sat down again, Dalton opening one eye to check on him before rolling over. Nic never moved.

He finished the notes and rested his head back against the wall behind him. It didn't make sense. Nothing in the notes explained how the Wardings were created or how to take them down. But that's probably because Arrend had been focused on figuring out what they were, not how to control them. His studies were purely academic. Scientific. Detailed notes on structure, on shape, on observed similarities and differences between them. He'd hypothesized about their purpose. But he hadn't made the connection to the shards.

"Which means the answer won't be in Arrend's notes."

Devon sagged against the wall and let the few pages he held slip to one side. He stared out into the room.

The shards were placed around the city in key locations, ready in case of an emergency, waiting to be triggered. Whoever had designed them—the Founders, he assumed—wouldn't have wanted the triggering process to be complicated. But it couldn't be too simple either, or any random person could accidentally set them off. He'd already hypothesized that only mages could trigger them, mostly due to the shards' crystalline composition and structure, so similar to—

"The mage's double pyramid."

He scrambled over to the table and his research papers, still disorganized from their frantic raid on his bolthole. He spent a moment putting them back in order, wincing as he realized pages— entire sections—were missing, probably still in his bolthole, if not taken or destroyed by Carbolen and the Regulars. But it didn't matter. The essential pages—those that described the form of the double pyramid and the conjectured structures of the four lower faces of the Source—were intact. He spread them out on the table, shoving the rest of the pages to the floor, began scanning his notations on what Lane had been able to tell him of those faces and what he'd learned by watching the more advanced mages on the practice field. There were large sections that were blank, unknown.

"But if this section controls light and its intensity, then this section here should produce lightning. On the same basis, if these regions produce structural changes to stone and metal, it stands to reason that this area here may control lucent, and thus the shards."

He stood up straight. It wasn't enough by itself. None of what the mages did relied on a single region of their primary form. It was always a combination of elements from the Source, all built to produce a single outcome. He'd have to figure out what combination unlocked a Warding.

He yawned, a wave of bone-deep fatigue washing through him. But something else about the Wardings niggled at the edge of his mind. Something once again connected to structure.

He snatched up a page of notes with a corner of empty space and began mapping out the city, the locations of the Wardings, what levels, what Spokes. It was difficult to place them on the page when they existed in three dimensions in the real world, but he could see the structures being formed already, before he'd finished drawing in half of them.

His quill skittered out of suddenly numbed fingers and he leaned heavily into the table. "It's all connected. The double pyramid for the Sigils, the locations of the Wardings, the crystal threaded throughout the city—it's all connected. They're all embedded crystalline structures. Even—" his knees grew weak, but he caught himself "— even the locations of the seven Crystal Cities."

The enormity of the complexity of the system was staggering. He couldn't even begin to fathom what it all meant. Except that everything they thought they knew about how the cities worked was wrong. The lucent dying in the perimeter cities first, the failure of the machines in the lower levels, even the Wardings that had triggered on their own—it was all related to the crystals, the mage form, and the Sigils. All of it crafted by design.

By the Founders.

But he couldn't deal with that now, not with the Brovettans seizing control. He needed to focus: the Lyceum; the new Warding. This revelation would help though. The Warding must follow the same embedded structure as the whole. That was the key.

Moving to his pallet, he dropped onto the floor and tucked his hand under his head as a makeshift pillow. Dalton snuffled and rolled into him, an arm draping over his side.

"Did you figure it out?" he asked, only half awake.

"Yes."

Dalton didn't answer. He was already asleep again.

Devon closed his eyes, body still trembling.

All he had to do now was figure out how to tell Carbolen that he couldn't unlock the Warding himself.

He was going to need a mage.

Chapter Sixteen

"We don't have a mage." Carbolen turned to Leinn. "Do we?"

"No one has ever said they were."

"What about the rest of you? Anyone have a mage?"

The others gathered—another of Carbolen's captains, Toral, and the three allied gang leaders that had been present the day before—all began talking at once.

Carbolen held up a hand to forestall them. "I'll take that as a no."

"The majority of the mages were at the Lyceum," Toral said. "The rest were scattered around the waygates and the Spokes."

"Did any of them survive the Brovettan slaughter?"

"None of our eyes have reported it, but they weren't looking specifically for mages either. They've been reporting on army personnel in general."

Carbolen gave her a look and she snapped her fingers. One of the nearby gang members ran forward, listened for directions, then sprinted for the door, calling two of his fellow runners to his side as he went.

"Assuming we find a mage," Carbolen said, "what will we need to do to bring down the Warding?"

"Think of the Warding as a giant lock. The mage isn't going to know the key. I'll have to touch the Warding to figure out that key.

Then I can show the mage and they should be able to bring it down from there."

"So you'll need time. How much?"

"It's impossible to say. Ten minutes. Twenty. Maybe more if the key is complicated."

Starling swore. "The Brovettans have the Warding surrounded with patrols. They aren't as heavy as those at the waygates or the towers, but they aren't insignificant."

"Is there a section of the Warding that we can access that's hidden from the patrols? It's only partially encased some buildings. There should be at least one where we can work on the Warding without interference."

"I'll have the eyes begin searching," Toral said.

"Even then," Carbolen said, "there is a chance you'd be discovered. I'd wager you're the only lockpick that can handle this particular lock. We can't afford to lose you."

Dalton, who'd been standing behind Devon the entire time, arms crossed, spoke up. "The rest of us should create some kind of diversion. If we can draw the patrols away from Devon's location, it would give him a better chance of success."

"You want us to risk our gangs for a single lockpick and a mage?" one of the other gang leaders asked, incredulous. "We haven't survived down here in the lower city so long by taking such stupid risks."

"You've survived because the Iandolan Army didn't find it necessary to root you out."

Starling leapt to his feet. "The Iandolan Army couldn't root us out. They tried and failed. We're too deeply entrenched." He faced Devon as Dalton bristled. "And you. What guarantee do we have that you will succeed?"

"None."

"And you expect us to follow you? You aren't even a member of one of our gangs." He leaned into Devon. "The Greenbacks will not follow this...lockpick's lead. We're out."

"Sit down."

Carbolen voice was neutral, but it cut through the gathering tension and silenced everyone.

Starling broke eye contact with Devon. "You can't possibly be considering this."

"We can do nothing until we find a mage."

"The Greenbacks—"

"The Greenbacks will do exactly as I say, as will the Cut-throats and the Meridians and the rest."

"That wasn't the agreement. We were supposed to continue leading our own gangs. All of us."

"You thought wrong. Now sit down."

Starling glanced toward the other two gang leaders for support, but neither of them said anything. He bared his teeth in a silent snarl, but sat down.

Carbolen turned back to Dalton. "A diversion only buys so much time. The Brovettans will call for reinforcements, drawing from the Spokes, the towers, possibly even the waygates given enough time."

"But if Devon is successful, we'll have our own reinforcements—the soldiers and mages trapped inside the Warding. Once they're free, they can join us."

"If Devon is successful." But Carbolen frowned, eyes shifting away, deep in thought. Even the gang leaders were nodding in consideration. All except Starling.

Eventually Carbolen stirred, gaze falling on Toral. "Tell me immediately if our eyes find one of the army mages. Leinn, take Devon up to mid-level with a small group of gang members. Search for a possible approach to the Warding—one for Devon and one for our diversion. We need options. I'll send the Regulars as well."

Leinn and the others rose at the dismissal. Starling stormed out, shoving his way through the gang members hovering at the bottom of the dais. The others followed more sedately.

Leinn snagged Devon's sleeve. "Wait for me here."

"We're headed to mid-level now?"

"Is there a problem?"

"No. But—"

"Good. I'll issue a few orders and then we'll head out."

Nic took Leinn's place as she stalked off. "What's her problem?"

"I don't think she likes our arrangement with Carbolen."

"Considering what just happened with Starling, I'm not certain how much of a lasting arrangement it is."

"It will last long enough."

* * *

"That explains what happened to all the mages," Nic said. He tried to control his gag reflex, but lost, ducking down behind the roof edge where he, Devon, Dalton, Leinn, and three other gang members were huddled, scoping out the edge of the Warding. He dry-heaved a few paces away from them, on hands and knees, back hunched.

Their perch gave them a view down a short stretch of street that ran directly into the Warding. A few Iandolan citizens were moving about below, all pointedly ignoring the group of ten Brovettan soldiers stationed a hundred paces out from the amber wall that cut through the adjacent buildings and rose upwards another fifty feet above roof level. The Brovettans had strung chains across the street, roof to roof, and had hung the bodies of Iandolan soldiers on hooks from those chains, like some kind of grisly laundry line. The bodies of at least four mages were visible at the front, not simply killed, but mutilated, more so than the soldiers that were mixed in with them. Devon forced himself to look, even though some of the remains had been eviscerated, entrails spilled out onto the street below. Others had throats slit, arms or legs severed. One had been beheaded. Carrion birds lined the chains and roofs to either side, swooping down to the corpses, disturbing those already feasting there.

"They didn't die in the original fight," Leinn said, jutting her chin out at the cobbles of the street below, where bloodstains marred the stone. "They must have been captured and were killed afterwards, strung up after being given a mortal wound. Or simply strung up and left to bleed out."

"Why?" Nic asked, his voice choked. He'd crawled back toward them, had leaned back against the lip of the roof. He wiped at his mouth with the back of his arm.

"As an example," Dalton said. "To deter the rest of the Iandolan populace. Don't tangle with us. We mean business."

"Was the fight with them at the waygate like this?" Devon asked.

"It was nasty and vicious, but not in the same way as this. That was...a fight for our lives. This—"

"This was brutal and unnecessary," Leinn cut in. "Like Carbolen said, this is why we need to force them to leave. Iandolo may have its problems—a corrupt Council, a death grip on control of the Crystal Cities because of its mages—but the Iandolan Army has never done something like this. The Brovettans are vicious and this is only the beginning."

"Then we'd better find someplace I can access the Warding," Devon said. He focused on the buildings to either side of the street, where the Warding cut them off from the outside world. To the right, the door to the building was trapped inside the Warding. They might be able to enter the building through one of the windows on the upper floors, but only if the Brovettans had been drawn away first.

The doorway to the building on the left was free, but as they watched, two Brovettan soldiers entered, two different soldiers emerging a moment later, rejoining the eight still on duty.

"They're using the building as a barracks," Dalton said.

"So unless we can get them to abandon their post, it's unlikely we'll be able to reach the Warding without being noticed." Devon pulled back from the edge. "We need something more secure than this."

"Then we'd better keep looking." Leinn motioned them all to retreat, keeping low and out of sight.

They visited five other streets that intersected the Warding, each one with a covey of Brovettan soldiers ranging in size from six to twenty, depending on the defensibility of their position. Two of them had similar displays of desecrated bodies. They skirted a park, then checked out three more streets before Dalton nudged Devon and pointed toward a building on the fourth. "It has roof access."

Devon didn't know how he could tell from street level, but he informed Leinn.

The gang leader led them in a circuitous route around three blocks before they ascended to a roof that had a view on the building.

"Shards, he's right," Leinn muttered as they settled in. She squinted down into the street. "And the door to that building is inside the Warding."

"Then there's a chance the Brovettans haven't noticed the roof access yet."

"I'll post someone to keep watch."

"That's Fulsom Street," Devon said. At Leinn's and Nic's questioning look, he added, "It's the street the Shandy Quad is on."

Dalton shifted forward. "I wonder if Arch was there when the Warding went up."

No one answered.

Leinn left two of the gang members behind and they continued to circle the Warding, looking for other options, but they found nothing better. They hadn't completely circled the Warding yet when the sun began to set, but Leinn called off the search and they descended to Carbolen's lair using the stairs at the hub.

As soon as they stepped up onto the dais, Carbolen said, "Report."

"We found a possible access point on Fulsom Street. I have people watching it now to make certain the Brovettans aren't aware of it."

"And what about the potential for a diversion nearby?"

"There's a park a few streets away. We can attack the Brovettan's position there—it's weak since the park is so open, making it hard for them to defend—then withdraw into the surrounding streets where we can set up ambushes."

Carbolen had already found the area on their map of mid-level. "Send for the other gang leaders. We'll begin strategizing."

A runner arrived at the dais, leaning in close to whisper something in Toral's ear. She asked a quick question, then turned to Carbolen. "Our eyes have found where the surviving members of the Iandolan Army have hidden themselves: Level Thirteen."

"Do they have any mages with them?"

"We can't tell. They've holed up in a complex of warehouses and have barricaded themselves inside."

Carbolen stood. "We'll just have to go and ask them then, won't we?"

* * *

Carbolen, Raven, and Dalton peered out the empty fourth-floor sockets where windows had once stood. Jagged shards of glass still rimmed the edges of the panes. The warehouse where they'd taken shelter to scope out the Iandolan Army's hideout was completely dark, the area outside lit only by a few random jags of purplish lucent. Level Thirteen had been used mostly for storage, warehouses stretching for blocks in all directions. Most were still intact, if empty, their contents scavenged long ago.

Devon stared down into the cavernous interior beside them, open all the way to the floor. He could feel the depth, even though he couldn't see it. The second, third, and fourth floors of the building were merely catwalks surrounding the outside walls, with rafters and tracks with pulleys and chains still attached above them. Water dripped down from rents in the ceiling, purple in the lucent-light.

Nic tugged his shirt and pointed toward where Carbolen and the others were pulling back from the windows. Devon had suggested the gang member stay behind, but Nic had insisted on coming, claiming, "I'm not part of this gang anymore." He'd even hacked the blue-tinged hair from his head with his knife, cutting it short enough in most places he was nearly bald.

Even stranger-looking was Dalton, dressed once again in his army uniform. Carbolen had insisted.

"What's the situation?" Leinn asked as the other three rejoined them. It was a small party: Bitter, Feral, and three other regular gang members filling out the complement. One of the gang members carried a crossbow, a sheath of quarrels hung diagonally across his chest, a second crossbow swinging from his hip.

"As reported," Raven answered, "they've taken over two warehouses, joined by an enclosed walking bridge at the third floor. The few windows have been covered, so we can't see inside. There are sentries on both roofs, attempting to stay low and hidden, but not doing a decent job of it. Something has collapsed and sealed off one of the front entrances, but the other appears open. I'll have to scout out the far side, but I'd guess that, like this warehouse, the back consists of mostly loading docks, probably sealed or barricaded in some way."

"Take two men and find out," Carbolen ordered. "We don't want any surprises here."

Raven nodded, slipped past them on the narrow walk, and faded into the darkness of the warehouse with the two gang members without crossbows.

"How are we going to approach them?" Dalton asked.

"We aren't," Carbolen answered. "You are. Along with Devon. And if anyone so much as flinches, Harsh here will take you out."

Harsh—the crossbowman—gave Dalton a genial nod.

They descended along the catwalk's stairs, Carbolen taking the spare crossbow and some quarrels from Harsh before leaving him in a window looking out on the entrance to the army's warehouse on the second floor. They waited on the ground floor until Raven returned.

"They've got the loading dock doors locked down, debris from the surrounding area piled up in front of them. I can get in through the connecting bridge if necessary. They aren't watching it closely from the roof and it has windows. I left the other two behind to give us a heads up if they try anything from the dock."

"Get into position beneath the walking bridge, but I'm not expecting any problems." Carbolen hefted his crossbow, his familiarity with it obvious, and faced Dalton and Devon. "Tell them who you are, who we are, and tell them I want to meet, here, in this warehouse, now. Whoever is in charge can bring three soldiers as escort. Don't go inside their building or you'll have a quarrel in your back. Even you, Devon. Now get moving."

Devon shared a look with Dalton, then they both exited onto the street.

"Do you think they'll listen?" Devon asked as they picked their way through the detritus strewn across the thoroughfare.

"It's going to be tough. They're on the defensive. But they don't have many options."

"We'll just have to be convincing."

Dalton put out an arm to halt Devon. They'd entered the intersection of the street fronting the army's warehouse.

"Wait until they see us," Dalton said. His stance had changed, spine rigid, shoulders back.

Devon glanced toward the roofline, saw a flicker of movement against the purplish backdrop of lucent.

Dalton lowered his arm. "Move forward slowly. Give them time to adjust to our arrival. We'll stop in the middle of the street over there, next to that crumbling section of road."

Devon found the spot he'd indicated. He took up a position on one side of the hole, Dalton on the other, then waited.

After ten minutes, the warehouse door opened wide enough to let a single person out. He strode toward them purposefully, but he was thin and his gait wasn't military in bearing. He was dressed in commoner clothes, not a uniform.

"Historian," Dalton said. "He must have been assigned to one of the units that survived in order to keep their records."

The Historian halted at the edge of the road, ten paces away. Up close, Devon realized he was their age, fresh from the Lyceum, perhaps a year or two ahead of them.

"Wearing those colors is dangerous right now," he said to Dalton. "I'd advise against it."

"I needed to get your attention. Dalton Trent, soldier under Captain Silas Hart, last stationed at the Luminesque Spoke, Level Fifteen. Is Captain Hart here?"

"Captain Hart is dead, as are most of his unit. How is it that you aren't?"

Dalton straightened. "I'd rather report to whoever is in charge here."

The Historian's eyebrows rose. "Then you should come inside. Give your report in person."

He turned and Devon drew in a sharp breath, acutely aware of the spot on his back where a quarrel was likely aimed. It burned with an imaginary pain.

"We can't," he said, biting off the words. "There are...friends watching. They want to speak to your prefect."

The Historian's eyes darted to the surrounding buildings. "And why should the person in charge be interested in you or your friends?"

"Because, with their help, we may have a way of taking back Iandolo," Dalton said.

The Historian considered this silently, then said, "Wait here."

He returned to the warehouse, the door opening for him when he was still a few paces away.

Devon fidgeted, unable to stop himself from looking toward the roof to see if there were arrows trained down on him, or back toward where Carbolen and Harsh no doubt had their fingers on triggers.

"Do you think—" he began.

But the door to the army's warehouse opened again, a tall, broad-shouldered woman stepping out. She marched forward, six others emerging behind her, including the Historian. Even though none of them were in uniform, all but the Historian carried themselves like soldiers. A sword was strapped at the woman's waist, three of the others similarly armed.

She halted where the Historian had recently stood, hand resting on the pommel of her weapon. Only a few inches taller than Dalton, she appeared to tower over them simply with her bearing.

"Captain Ilias Mannert. Report."

"Dalton Trent, of Captain Hart's unit. I bring a proposal from Carbolen, one of the gang leaders that controls the interior of the lower levels. He wishes to speak to you about coordinating an attack on the Brovettans."

"Does he?" Captain Mannert glanced toward the abandoned warehouse behind them. "How did you come to be in his company, soldier?"

"I was sent to escort Devon Alamort to the proctors at the Lyceum after his apprehension on Level Fifteen. Before we arrived, the Warding went up and the Brovettans attacked. We managed to escape and Devon led me to Carbolen, since I had heard of no other fellow army survivors."

Captain Mannert eyed Devon. "You're the Science student the proctors at the Lyceum were so anxious to find weeks ago."

Devon didn't answer. She gave a tight smile, then turned back to Dalton. "Why would I want to speak with a gang leader, especially now? And why would he want to speak with me?"

"He controls more than one gang," Devon said, "and he has no desire to see the Brovettans seize control of Iandolo."

"He wants to meet, right now, in that warehouse," Dalton added. "He said you can bring three soldiers as escort."

Her eyes narrowed. "I understand why he sent you," she said, referring to Dalton. "We likely wouldn't have sent anyone out if you hadn't been in uniform. But you—" she shifted toward Devon "—why did he send you?"

"Because I'm the one that came up with the plan to take back Iandolo. He wanted me here in case you needed further convincing."

"I see." She lowered her head. "Sergeant Oriad, return to the barracks with Carson and Vors and inform Captain Ymarell that I will be meeting with this Carbolen to see what he has to say. The rest of you will accompany me."

"Carbolen has men watching the loading docks," Dalton said.

Oriad had already turned, the Historian and one of the soldiers following suit, but he paused, looking toward Captain Mannert.

She gave a clipped laugh. "Tell Captain Ymarell not to attempt any action unless I do not return in half an hour. After that, he can burn the entire warehouse down if he wants."

Oriad left with the Historian and the other soldier. Captain Mannert waited until they'd reentered the makeshift barracks before muttering, "After you."

Dalton and Devon led the four Iandolan soldiers around the side of the building back to the door they'd used to enter the side street. Inside, Devon could see Carbolen seated at one end of a long table made from the debris scattered around the warehouse. An empty chair sat at the other end of the table, a lucent lamp of a soft yellow in the center. Bitter and the other gang members had been busy. He could see the Regular standing off to Carbolen's right, but he didn't see Feral, Raven, or any of the others.

Captain Mannert took in the scene with one sweeping gaze, her three escorts falling into place on either side of her, one behind.

She eyed Carbolen. "You wanted to speak to me?"

"Have a seat." He motioned toward the empty chair.

Captain Mannert hesitated, her eyes narrowing as if she recognized Carbolen but couldn't place him, then she moved to the chair. "Talk fast. You don't have much time."

"We have a mutual problem. Neither one of us wants the Brovettans in control of Iandolo or the province of Iridesque. Yet neither one of us has the manpower to supplant them."

"How do you know we don't have the manpower?"

"You're in my domain now. I know more than you think."

Captain Mannert leaned forward. "And you forget, my unit cannot be the only surviving Iandolan force in the city. Once we have contacted the others, we may yet have enough to push back at the Brovettans."

"I doubt it. Based on the initial reports from my gang members, approximately forty percent of the Iandolan Army were trapped in the Warding, including nearly all of the upper ranks and mages. Of the remaining forces, at least thirty percent were slaughtered during the Brovettan attack and immediately after. I'd guess more. A sizeable portion are trapped in the three towers, if not already dead. The rest are scattered throughout the city, probably in groups like your own, hunkering down in temporary havens. How many of those do you think you can contact and coalesce into a significant unit, without being exposed yourself? The Brovettans have made it clear they're hunting for survivors like yourself. It's only a matter of time before one of Iandolo's citizens confesses that they've seen suspicious behavior here."

Captain Mannert considered this, then abruptly she sat back with a slightly stunned expression. "I know you. You are—you were—a captain in the army. Captain...Coral. Captain Ben Coral. You were part of the force that was sent to Luminesque sixteen years ago that ended with the death of the Councilor's daughter—"

"Enough," Carbolen said. "It's Carbolen now. Are you interested in retaking Iandolo or not?"

Captain Mannert tapped a finger on the table. "How many men do you have?"

"With all of the gangs allied together, two thousand. And yourself?"

"Two hundred."

Devon winced.

"Not many," Carbolen said.

"You don't seem that concerned. What's your plan?"

"We attack the Brovettan forces at the Warding."

One of Captain Mannert's men snorted. "That's suicide. We'd outnumber them, but your men aren't trained and the Brovettans hold the defensive position—"

Captain Mannert's raised hand cut him off. She leaned forward again. "My sergeant is correct. But you were never stupid, from what I've heard. What else?"

"We hold the Brovettans off long enough for Devon here to bring down the Warding, thus releasing all of the Iandolan Army trapped inside."

Captain Mannert's eyebrows shot up, her gaze latching onto Devon. "You can do this?"

"There's a catch," Carbolen warned.

"I can do it," Devon said, "but I'll need the help of a mage."

"And we don't have one."

Captain Mannert glanced between Devon and Carbolen, her escort fidgeting slightly behind her. "Unfortunately," she said quietly, "neither do we."

Chapter Seventeen

"Then we're screwed before we've even started," Carbolen said. "You don't know of any surviving mages?"

Captain Mannert shook her head. "The only Iandolan mages I've seen have been strung up over the streets of the city."

"They couldn't have all been captured. There must be one out there."

Devon suddenly grabbed Dalton's arm, hard enough the soldier winced. "There is."

Both Captain Mannert and Carbolen stared at him. Dalton gave him a confused look, followed by sudden comprehension.

"Please," Carbolen said dryly, "enlighten us."

"She was only a third year—" Dalton began in protest.

But Devon stepped up to the table. "Her name is Lane."

"Your friend at the Lyceum."

"Yes. And Dalton's right, she was only a third year, kicked out before she could complete her testing. But she knew the basic forms. I'm certain she can unlock the Warding."

"She's a Councilor's daughter," Carbolen said. "Wouldn't she have been at the Lyceum when the Warding was set off?"

"It's possible, but I doubt it. Proctor Favian wouldn't have wanted her anywhere near the meeting, especially at the Lyceum. He thought she was spying for the Brovettans. And based on what she said, her mother kept her locked in the tower, almost like a prison."

"You're talking about Councilor Varenov's daughter," Captain Mannert interjected.

"Yes."

"She's been secluded in Councilor Varenov's quarters since the incident at the Lyceum doing clerical work."

"Clerical work?" Devon clenched his fist, tamping down anger.

"That's what most of the sons and daughters of Councilors end up doing."

"She's a mage. She proved that when she learned the forms."

"I try not to get involved in Council politics...or family."

Devon turned away from Captain Mannert, toward Carbolen. "She's the only option we've got."

"She's in the tower—the central tower, if Captain Mannert is correct—if she's even still alive. Remember, we have no eyes there. The Brovettans may have slaughtered everyone there."

"She's our only chance."

Carbolen dropped his head, then faced Captain Mannert. "If we can get this Lane out of the tower, are you willing to join us in the attack on the Warding?"

"How are you going to get into the tower? The Brovettans have it surrounded."

"Leave that to me."

Mannert's eyebrows rose. "Very well. I'll want to see your plan of attack."

"Of course. Are you in?"

"If you can bring down the Warding as you say, then we're in."

* * *

Carbolen's group was just about to leave Level Thirteen when he suddenly turned on Devon, grabbed him by the shoulders and slammed him up against the side of a building.

"Are you certain you can bring down the Warding with the help of this Lane?"

A fleck of spit landed on Devon's cheek, next to his nose. He desperately wanted to wipe it away, but met Carbolen's gaze squarely and lied. "I can."

Carbolen held him against the wall a moment longer, then swore and released him, already moving back down the street.

"So he was a captain, huh?" Dalton said.

"I knew he'd been in the army, or at least had been trained at the Lyceum, but apparently he was part of the same incident as Favian in Brovetto. According to Arrend, Favian was forced to retire to the Lyceum and become a proctor early. That's why he's so bitter."

"I guess Carbolen—or should we call him Ben now?—didn't like his options and fled to the lower city. He's a deserter."

"I'd suggest you catch up or he'll leave you all behind." Raven gave Dalton an unsubtle nudge.

Carbolen was quiet as they ascended back to Level Seventeen, but as they approached the outer reaches of his lair, he said, "Raven, I want you to take Devon into the central tower to retrieve the mage. Take Bitter and Feral with you, no others. You know about our entrance?"

Raven grimaced. "I do."

"Find the mage. Keep your eyes open while you're there. But bring him back alive at all costs."

"Very well."

"Wait," Dalton said. "I should go with him."

"I need you here with me, to coordinate with Captain Mannert. She'll trust you more than me."

"I can go," Nic said.

Carbolen rounded on him. "I'm sending three Regulars with him. Three. What would you contribute to the group beyond that?"

"Someone Devon could trust."

Carbolen laughed. "I'll give you that. But no. The group needs to be small if it's going to go unnoticed in the tower." He turned back to Raven. "I'll give you everything I've got on the central tower—maps, codes, everything."

She nodded, but Carbolen had already turned away. Raven glanced at Feral, Devon, then Bitter. "Wait here."

"Maps? Codes?" Devon asked.

"Carbolen's been planning a raid on the towers for a long time, remember? To find the conspirators?" Raven said. "You were the lynchpin he needed to pull it off. Now, we'll steal a mage, instead of evidence."

As soon as Carbolen and Raven entered the lair, Dalton and Nic closed in, concerned.

"Carbolen's right," Devon said, heading them both off. "You can help with Captain Mannert. I'm certain she doesn't trust Carbolen, especially after recognizing him."

"What about me?" Nic asked. He eyed Bitter and Feral. "I don't trust the Regulars."

"You heard Carbolen. They have to bring me back alive. I don't think they'll survive long if they don't."

"You'll survive, one way or another," Feral said. "Maybe a little worse for wear."

Nic didn't appear to appreciate the humor.

Raven reappeared, handing a satchel each to Bitter and Feral. "Let's go."

Devon hugged Nic, muttering a quick, "Don't worry about me," in his ear, then kissed Dalton.

"You'd better come back," the soldier said.

The Regulars herded him out through the labyrinth of corridors and rooms surrounding the lair and up toward mid-level. Devon found his chest tightening, thoughts of Dalton swimming through his head. To distract himself, he checked his satchel for his knife, for the lucent lamp, fingering through the other assorted items in the bag. It helped, but it didn't relieve the ache in his chest.

He'd lost Dalton once. He didn't think he could do it again.

Then they were two levels below mid-level. Instead of heading toward one of the ramps or even the stairwell at the hub, Raven cut away, circling the central shaft. A quarter of the way around, they emerged on a ledge, the pit dropping away beneath them, a few active lucents glowing on its sides for a few levels, but dark beyond that.

"Here," Raven said, motioning to where thick metal rungs had been attached to the stone side of the shaft. Glancing up, Devon realized he could just make out the base of the towers above, a hundred objects jutting down into the shaft, lit by lucent. Many were dripping water or oil or other less innocuous fluids.

"Move."

Bitter prodded him in the back and he realized Raven had already scaled the rungs to the next level.

He began to ascend. The rungs were slick, beaded with moisture, and spaced a touch too far apart for his shorter height, but he didn't complain.

Raven waited at the next level, at another ledge but without access to the level itself. As soon as he arrived, she moved to an even narrower path a few steps up, positioning herself so her chest pressed against the stone. The ledge jutted out eight inches, enough to fit Devon's feet. He sucked in a breath and edged out onto it, face to the wall, palms flat against its gritty surface. He tried to keep his weight tilted forward. Any shift backwards and he'd plummet into the shaft.

He started when he ran into Raven, so focused on not overbalancing that he hadn't realized she'd halted. She grabbed onto his shoulder, even as his fingers scraped the slick stone to either side for purchase. "Don't fall," she said. "You're my ticket out of here."

He gave her a questioning look, but she didn't respond. Satisfied he was secure, she motioned to a series of stones that jutted from the wall above them like steps. He nodded, afraid even his breath might push him off the ledge.

They ascended to mid-level, but still without access to the streets and buildings outside. Here there was an alcove large enough to fit all of them with room to spare. Devon stepped into its farthest recesses, pressing his forehead into the cool metal wall in the darkness to regain his composure. His entire body trembled and he started again when Feral touched his shoulder.

"Cinch this around your waist." He handed over a harness.

Devon held it up, looking at the straps and buckles. "What is this? What are we doing?"

Feral grinned. "You didn't think we'd be walking in the front door, did you? It's surrounded by the Brovettans. No, we're going into the towers...from underneath." He pointed out from the alcove, to where the struts, chains, and metal protuberances jutted down from the base of the towers. "There's an access hatch beneath the main tower, but it's in that tangle of vents and outlets and supports."

He reached for the harness and began strapping Devon into it, tightening the buckles to the point where Devon felt his circulation cut off. Devon's entire body had gone numb. As he watched, Raven climbed up the side of the alcove and grabbed onto a metal support overhead, pulling herself up onto its flat surface. She began walking down its length, casually, reaching to unlatch a length of rope from her belt. She affixed it to a pillar of metal holding the rafter up as she passed it, letting the rope out behind her, heading toward a joint where five rafters met. A white lucent lamp dangled from her belt to light the way.

Feral latched a rope to Devon's belt, tugged hard on all of the buckles, then clapped Devon on the back. "You're next."

Bitter waited for him at the corner of the alcove, where Raven had climbed up to the support. She gave him a game smile. "It's easier than that ledge."

Devon watched Raven as she slid around the column joining the rafters and began walking along one of the other four. He glanced at the wall, noticed rough hand- and footholds had been chiseled into the stone.

"We found this entry into the towers ages ago," Bitter said, "although it required a little work and a few deaths to figure out how to get to it. Only Carbolen and the Regulars know about it. And only the Regulars use it, when we need something important from inside the towers."

Devon swallowed, then reached for the first handhold.

He scaled the corner of the alcove, the length of rope Feral had attached to him trailing down behind him. Once he reached the rafter, he grabbed on and hauled himself up onto it in a crouch. The rope jerked and he glanced down to see Bitter climbing up after him. She mouthed, "Move!"

He closed his eyes long enough to catch his breath, then opened them and stood. Hands to his sides for balance, he edged out onto the rafter. The metal was wet beneath his feet, but he made it to the first column easily. He clung to it as Bitter joined him, Feral not far behind. Without a word, she attached Raven's rope to him, then nudged him after her.

He followed Raven, focusing on moving from column to support. At one point, they opened a hatch in what appeared to be a vent and he thought they were done, but they only ascended on the interior ladder to another layer of supports. The closer they got to the center of the shaft, the higher up they climbed, scaling some scaffolding, another set of rungs on the outside of a metal chimney, and one of the support columns without any handholds whatsoever, Bitter shoving him upwards from below. All three of the Regulars moved through the obstacle course as if they were rats, never hesitating, never slipping. The worst part came near the end, when they forced him to crawl hanging upside down along a length of chain stretching from one rafter to another.

They halted beneath a round hatch almost directly in the center of the shaft, Bitter and Feral collecting the ropes and harnesses and securing them in their satchels as Devon collapsed in a trembling heap. He couldn't keep his hands from shaking and his arms and legs were cold and numb. At least here there was a wide platform, supports radiating out from it. Raven focused on the hatch above, tugging on rusty latches, slamming a palm into one until it gave.

Then she turned a metal wheel, the hatch falling open toward them with a clang. A narrow shaft with rungs along one side shot up into what Devon assumed was the base of the central tower.

"And we're in," Raven said.

She reached for the first rung and hauled herself up into the opening, her shoulders scrapping both sides.

With Bitter's help, Devon managed to ascend the chimney, Raven's lucent light shining above him. The tightness of the tube eased the tension in his shoulders caused by the deep open drop of the hub below. By the time they emerged into a tiny closet, Devon had managed to control his heart and calm his nerves.

As Feral sealed the hatch behind them, Raven pulled a sheaf of papers from her own satchel.

"Where are we going?" Bitter asked.

"Varenov's quarters."

Bitter rolled her eyes. "Which are where?"

Raven consulted the pages. "Fifteen floors up. We'll take the elevator."

Bitter reached for a glowing circle of lucent in the wall as Raven stowed her papers. As soon as she touched it, a section of the wall popped out and swung away.

It opened onto a massive hall, like Carbolen's lair below, but immaculate, with glossy marble flooring, stately columns down the sides of two walls, and an intricately painted ceiling high overhead. The glow of the lucent threaded through the walls increased as they stepped out into the emptiness. Not a single thread flickered; not a single thread was dead.

"Eerie, isn't it?" Feral said. "Not a shadow to hide in."

Devon watched his back as the three Regulars moved silently across the room. He felt unclean, suddenly aware of his dirt-smeared clothes, made worse by the climb into the tower. He didn't want to touch anything, afraid he'd mar it in some way.

They reached the far double doors, Bitter and Feral standing off to either side as Raven opened one side a crack and peered out. After no more than a breath, she closed it again.

"Four guards in the hall, Brovettan. At least six servants cleaning up blood."

"The servant corridors?" Bitter asked.

Raven nodded and they shifted to the side wall, to a panel that appeared to be like all the others, except when Raven touched the wooden slat to one side it popped outwards. She swung it open enough to peer inside, then motioned everyone in.

The corridor beyond was lit with basic white lucent from above. Devon instantly felt more at ease. It was darker here, more confined.

Raven led them to the right, then through a long series of branches, obviously surrounding other rooms of various sizes. Doors into those rooms were outlined with wooden slats and simple handles. Devon lost count of how many there were and what direction they were moving, the corridors a maze. Raven paused at each intersection, but the halls were strangely deserted.

After what felt like hours, she referred to the map and pointed to a door. "That should lead into the hall outside the elevators."

Feral stepped forward, opened it, and slipped outside. Bitter sidled up, watching through the sliver of light from the hall, then motioned Devon and Raven through, following behind.

Like the hall, the hallway was pristine, urns with short palm trees accenting the marble, one of them hiding the servant's door. It was a rounded corridor, surrounding the circular elevator shaft. Feral stood before the elevator doors, watching the far side of the hallway. He'd drawn his short sword, a dagger in his other hand. Both Raven and Bitter now held blades as well. Devon hadn't heard them being drawn.

With a sigh, the elevator door slid to one side, smooth. They stepped inside, Feral coming in last, and the door eased shut.

Raven reached for the single shaft of vertical lucent inside, outlined by a faint etching resembling the tower and a series of numbers, then halted, eyeing Devon. "Give it a try."

"What do you mean?"

"I want to see what level you have access to. Touch the lucent here where it's glowing and then slide it upwards as high as it will go."

Devon touched the lucent, feeling a faint tingle, the light pulsing, then slid it upwards. The light halted at seven, even though his finger slid higher. He tried to move it upwards, but it refused to budge.

"Only level seven," Feral said.

"I can only get to four," Bitter added.

But Devon wasn't listening to them. He'd closed his eyes, finger resting on the pulsing light, and with a faint push he slid into the lucent and, like the locks he'd picked before, found himself inside the elevator's structure. After a moment to orient himself, he worked around the block.

He opened his eyes and dragged his finger up, all the way to the top.

Bitter gasped.

He faced Feral and Raven. "Easier than picking a lock."

Raven's eyes narrowed. "And you wondered what Carbolen wanted you for. Unfortunately, we aren't here for evidence right now. Take us to fifteen."

Devon dragged the light down to fifteen and let go. After a moment, his stomach dropped as the elevator began to move upwards, but without the shudders and clanks of those he'd experienced in the lower city.

Feral and Bitter edged to the door as they neared level fifteen. When it shushed open, three Brovettan guards leaped forward. Raven barked a command Devon didn't catch, but she grabbed his shoulder and hauled him back as Feral and Bitter were shoved into the back of the elevator with them, the space now cramped. Blood splattered Devon's face as blades clashed and knives slashed. He could see nothing but flailing arms, heard nothing but grunts and curses, Feral's back shoving him up hard into the wall.

Then the tussle ended, Feral lurching forward clutching his upper side, the rent in his shirt already stained with blood. The three guards lay sprawled in the elevator and across the opening, Bitter to one side, her cheeks flushed, eyes bright. Raven stepped over the bodies into the hall.

"It's clear."

Bitter grabbed a body and threw it outside the elevator. Wincing, Feral did the same, Raven pulling the one across the door out by his leg.

"Not much we can do about the blood," Bitter said, looking at the stains in the elevator.

"Are you good?" Raven asked Feral.

"Stings like a thousand fire ants, but I'll be fine."

Raven didn't argue, already facing the three corridors that branched off the foyer and the doors beyond. She pulled out the map again, pointed down one of the halls. "The doors at the end. The suite."

Bitter approached and touched the lucent circle on the right double door. Nothing happened, although it did pulse brighter. She tried the left with the same result. "It's locked."

All three Regulars turned to Devon.

Stepping forward, he placed a hand on the right circle and sank into the lucent. The corner of his mouth twitched. "It's more complicated than the elevator. And it's been locked from the inside."

"Then someone's in there." Raven gestured to the other two, both of them sliding into defensive positions on either side of the door. "How much longer?"

"Not long. It's got multiple layers of protection, more than it should. But not...enough."

The lock clicked and the right door eased open a crack. Devon stepped back fast, but no one burst through.

Raven edged in front of him and peered inside, then entered, the others following.

It opened onto a sitting room that felt more like an audience chamber. Couches and chairs were artfully arrayed into conversational groups between low tables and tall urns. Lucent sconces lined the walls. Two sets of doors opened off to the right and left, the room extending all the way to a single clear lucent floor-to-ceiling oval window that stretched wall-to-wall, framed on either side by thick sky-blue curtains. Devon was drawn immediately to the window, his gut clenching when he looked down upon the flat circle of mid-level below, broken by smaller towers and wide circular swaths of parks and rectangular fields, crossed with swatches of roads, the thin lines of aqueducts and cisterns reflecting the harsh sun. Lifting his gaze, he stared out across the barren Flatlands, able to see much farther at this height than he ever had below. The burnt earth stretched to the horizon, broken and shattered, a hundred different shades of brown and red and yellow. Plinths of craggy stone rose from below, some wide enough to be plateaus. The city of Brovetto glinted in the distance, far closer than Devon had imagined, although he knew the perspective at this height was deceptive.

"This door is locked."

Devon turned from the window to see Feral at the near set of the doors on the right. Raven emerged from one of the other rooms shaking her head, Bitter a step behind her.

They congregated around the second set of doors, Devon reaching for the lock. "This won't take long."

As soon as they heard the click, the doors slammed outwards, throwing Devon backwards into a table. Wood splintered and ceramic shattered beneath him as he fell. He caught a fleeting image of two Iandolan guards, swords raised, and then a blinding orb of fire roared from the room at chest height. Heat seared Devon's face as it passed overhead and exploded against the far wall into sheets of flame. Blades clashed and a figure appeared over Devon. He raised an arm, fumbling for his dagger, but the figure abruptly knelt at his side.

"Devon?"

Before he could answer, Lane twisted and yelled, "Stand down! They aren't with the Brovettans!"

A few clangs of metal answered her, but then the room fell silent but for gasps and some panting. The three Regulars had backed off, the two Iandolan guards stepping toward Lane protectively. All of them were tense. Wary.

"What was that?" Devon asked.

Lane looked toward the scorched wall, then reached down to help him up. "Don't you remember our practice sessions? I haven't been sitting idle up here, you know. What are you doing here?"

"Saving you."

"I don't need saving. We had ourselves locked in. The Brovettans couldn't get to us."

"And you couldn't get out."

"We were working on that."

"Less talking," Raven said, pushing forward. The two Iandolan guards bristled. "More fleeing. Is this the mage?" They both stared at her, the smell of char in the air. "Right, stupid question. Tell your guards to follow us."

The three Regulars ran for the outer corridor. Devon started to follow, but Lane grabbed his arm, then motioned toward one of the two guards. He stepped back into the room they'd just left, returning with three satchels.

"Who are they?" Lane asked as she shrugged into one of the satchels.

"They're Regulars, part of Carbolen's gang. We're here because we need a mage to collapse the Warding and you're the only one left. As far as we know."

"You're back with the gang?"

"Carbolen didn't give me much choice. But technically, no, I'm not. I'm only helping them. We need to get moving."

"What does that mean?"

Devon was already at the door to the suite. Lane hadn't moved. "It's complicated. I can explain later."

From down the hall, Raven shouted, "Devon!"

Lane shared a look with her two guards, one of whom shrugged and said, "It's as good a time as any. And they've already cleared out the Brovettans in the hall."

"Then let's do this."

She joined Devon, the two guards bringing up the rear.

"It's good to see you."

Lane shot him a sideways look. "You, too."

"What have you been doing?"

"Surviving. You?"

"The same."

He didn't understand her coldness, but Feral suddenly called out, "We've got company!"

Before any of them could react, Devon heard the shush of the elevator door and then Brovettans spilled out into the hall ahead of them. The Regulars leapt into the fight as Devon, Lane, and the two Iandolan guards raced forward.

"There are too many of them!" Lane shouted. "Back off to the left!"

She halted in the middle of the hall, one of her guards hauling Devon back as she began the hand gestures of the basic form. Her motions were tight and controlled; Devon could practically see the double pyramid shape. He sucked in a breath as she jabbed a specific Sigil in the Source without hesitation—

A vortex of fire whirled into being in front of her, coalescing from thin air, a backwash of heat flinging Lane's hair back and turning Devon's skin waxy. Then it surged down the hall, straight at the elevator and the covey of Brovettans clustered before and in it.

One of them shouted a warning, but the streak of flame struck, exploding into sheets of fire as screams reverberated down the hall. Lane was already running toward the scent of seared flesh and burnt hair. One of the guards shoved Devon into motion. Lane stalked through the charred meat, a few of the bodies moaning, then ducked left. Devon followed, breathing shallowly through his mouth, to find Bitter and Feral finishing off the few Brovettans that hadn't been caught in the fire.

"Now what?" Raven asked.

"I'm not getting in that elevator," Bitter added, one arm covering her mouth. "Blood is one thing, but burnt flesh..."

"We don't have to. There's a servant's elevator."

All three Regulars moved to the side as Lane stepped over the three dead bodies before them without a glance and pushed through a single door behind the main elevator shaft that led to narrow servant corridors.

"How did you intend to get out of the tower?" Lane asked as Devon and the rest followed.

"If you can get us to the first floor, we can get you out," Raven answered.

Devon didn't want to think about reversing the path they'd used to enter.

"I can get us to the first floor." She halted at the end of the corridor and touched a lucent button. "After that..."

"How were you going to get out?" Devon asked.

She met his gaze squarely. "I was going to fight my way out."

The elevator chimed and the door rattled open. They all stared at the small space.

"I don't think we're all going to fit," Bitter said.

Chapter Eighteen

"We got her," Raven announced as soon as they entered Carbolen's lair. Her voice echoed throughout the chamber, followed by cheers from the few gang members present.

On the dais, Carbolen stood, Leinn and Toral turning to face down the hall. Devon was surprised to see Captain Mannert in the group. She leaned back, two other Iandolan soldiers behind her seat.

"Were there any problems?"

Raven came to a halt at the base of the dais, Bitter beside her. Devon stayed near Lane, who stood back, spine rigid, the coldness he'd noticed in the tower still present. Her two Iandolan bodyguards fanned out to either side, both giving Captain Mannert confused looks. Feral had broken off of the group as soon as they entered Carbolen's domain with orders from Raven to prepare the Regulars.

"Lots of blood. Fewer Brovettans. No issues."

"Anything of note to report about the tower?"

"Nothing. All we saw were Iandolan servants cleaning up the mess and Brovettan soldiers. They must have removed everyone they could find from the tower. Or killed them."

Carbolen's gaze fell on Lane. "Yet you eluded them."

"With help."

"And you're a mage?"

"She's most definitely a mage," Bitter said. "She fried a bunch of Brovettans so we could escape."

"The only reason they didn't find us was because I was a mage. I kept us hidden when they came for everyone."

Captain Mannert stood, brushed off her uniform. "You forget who you are speaking to, Carbolen. She is the daughter of a Councilor."

"That's more a detriment here."

Mannert stepped down from the dais and approached Lane, who shifted her gaze warily from Carbolen to the captain.

"Are you hurt? Did the Brovettans—"

"I'm fine. As soon as we realized it was an attack, my guards locked me in my quarters. I never even saw the Brovettans until after."

Lane's irritation at this was clear, but Mannert flicked her gaze toward the two guards for verification before she continued. "Have they told you what they—what we—intend? Why we need a mage?"

"Only in a broad sense. Devon said he needed me to bring down the Warding and release everyone there."

"That's the gist of it. The Iandolan Army has been gutted, mostly because a significant portion of our soldiers and command staff were sealed away inside the Warding. The rest of us were either killed in the Brovettan attack or have been scattered into groups like the one I control. There aren't enough of us left to break the Brovettan hold on Iandolo. They've seized the waygates and the towers."

"Which is why you've resorted to consorting with gangs."

Mannert stiffened, but said, "Yes."

Carbolen moved to the edge of his dais. "And now that you're here, we can finally put all of our plans into motion. Raven—"

"Feral is already readying the Regulars and spreading the word to the rest of the captains and gang members."

"Good. Captain Mannert, I suggest you return and prepare what's left of the Iandolan Army under your command. I'll do the same with the other gangs. We'll meet your men at the rendezvous."

Carbolen motioned to Raven and Bitter, who trotted up to the dais. Orders were given, Leinn and Toral sweeping by them on their way out of the hall. Mannert watched silently, then turned back to Lane's bodyguards.

"Stay with her. Keep her safe, no matter what Carbolen proposes."

At their nods, she shifted to Lane. "Have him explain the rest of the plan. Only agree if you think it has the potential to succeed. There are always other options."

"Such as?"

Mannert didn't answer, mouth pressed into a grim line, then turned and stalked out of the hall, her own escort scrambling to fall into place around her.

The rest of the hall began to buzz with activity, like a disturbed wasp nest. Lane shifted restlessly.

"Come on," Devon said. "There's someone I'm certain would like to see you."

* * *

"Dalton!"

Lane sprinted across the room Carbolen had given Devon, Dalton, and Nic, throwing herself into Dalton's startled arms. Her two bodyguards situated themselves discreetly outside the door. Nic watched as he sidled toward Devon.

"So you found your mage."

"She didn't give me such a warm welcome. She tried to kill me with a ball of fire."

"A warm welcome of a different sort."

Devon couldn't help a small smile.

Lane broke away from Dalton. "Where's your uniform? You're still part of the army, aren't you?"

"I am. But for now, I'm here with Devon and Carbolen. A uniform makes me conspicuous."

"You weren't caught in the Brovettan attack?"

"I was carting Devon up to the Lyceum when it happened. He was under arrest."

Lane glanced toward Devon, the first real, considering look she'd given him since they'd found her in the tower. Something broke through her stoic expression: a flash of concern, there and then gone. "Why are you here, Nic? Aren't you a bartender?"

"He's part of Carbolen's gang."

"I was part of Carbolen's gang. I was only a bartender so I could keep an eye on Devon while he was at the Lyceum."

"Meaning you were spying on him." She stepped close, Nic edging back before standing his ground. "I thought you were a friend."

"I was. I am!"

Lane dismissed him, faced Devon. "Tell me about the plan to retake Iandolo."

Devon drew a deep breath and launched into the details. Then Dalton took over, relating what Captain Mannert and Carbolen had cobbled together as a diversion, what they hoped would become a significant retaliation once the Warding came down and the rest of the mages and Iandolan soldiers were freed.

"And that's your plan?"

"That's the plan. We need you. Captain Mannert hasn't found another surviving group of Iandolan soldiers with a mage. If you don't—"

"I'll do it," Lane interrupted.

A tension Devon had held inside his chest since they'd found Lane inside the tower eased. "I thought—"

Lane faced him. She had hardened since he'd last seen her at the Lyceum, in the Inner Sanctum. "You thought what? That I'd refuse? Because of what happened with us at the Lyceum? Because of what they did to us?" She laughed, the sound unpleasant. "If it were just Favian and Quinn trapped inside the Warding, then maybe I would. But it isn't. The entire Council is in there." She hesitated, then added, "My mother is in there."

"I thought you were angry. With me. When we burst into your rooms in the tower, you were cold. Removed."

"Oh, I was angry. At Favian and the other mage proctors. At Quinn and her petty hatred and clumsy politics. And yes, at you, for befriending me, for helping me learn the basic mage form, for drawing me into your own battle with Favian and getting me kicked out because of it. Even though I went along with it willingly, eagerly."

The harshness in the planes of her face faded and he saw the Lane he remembered from the Lyceum again.

"But then I realized that Favian and the others were never going to let me continue on and graduate, no matter what I did. His hatred of the Brovettans, his bitterness over the botched attack and how the Council forced him to retire and become a proctor, was too great. He would have sabotaged my studies eventually. Quinn would have helped. She desperately wants my mother to be displaced from the Council, denounced or at least embarrassed politically, so that her father can take my mother's place. He would have had the position if my mother hadn't returned from Luminesque when she did."

"How do you know all of this?"

"Did you think I went back to the tower and sulked in my luxurious prison? They wanted me to do clerical work, to be productive, to forget about being a mage. So I dove into it. And on the side I began asking questions about Favian, about Quinn, about her father, about everyone. I learned things. And I practiced the mage forms in secret. They couldn't stop me. I knew more than most third years, because of what you taught me."

"How is Carbolen involved?"

Lane frowned. "In what?"

"In the botched attack on Brovetto. He was there. Captain Mannert alluded to it. He was part of the Iandolan Army until then."

"I don't know. His name never came up."

"He wasn't called Carbolen then. He was a captain. Captain Ben Coral."

Lane shrugged. "The soldiers that were part of the force were demoted and absorbed back into the army as far as I heard. Maybe he wouldn't accept the demotion and fled."

Devon stood silent a moment, adjusting to what Lane had said. "Doesn't it seem odd to you?"

"What?"

"How everything seems to all stem from that failed attack in Brovetto sixteen years ago: Carbolen, Favian, your mother, Quinn's father. They're all related to that attack. And now, abruptly, the Luminesque are aggressive again, attacking our waygates, seizing control of the city."

"What are you saying?" Dalton asked. "That the attacks now are related to the failed attack sixteen years ago? How?"

"I don't know, but..." Devon turned to Lane. "Are you certain the entire Council was trapped in the Warding?"

"As far as I know. They were all supposed to be there, for the treaty signing. Why?"

"Because Carbolen is convinced someone on the Council is a traitor, that they're the ones orchestrating all of this. He thought we'd find them in the tower. Or working with the Brovettans."

"I didn't see any other Councilors in the tower, but that doesn't mean much. We managed to scavenge a few supplies in the first few hours. After that, the Brovettans had men stationed on our floor. We couldn't leave the suite."

"What about Quinn's father?" Dalton asked. "Could he be the one working with the Brovettans?"

"He isn't on the Council, so he wouldn't necessarily have been at the treaty signing," Lane said.

"But we know that Favian was working with him, and Favian would never ally himself with the Brovettans."

"Maybe Favian doesn't know Quinn and her father have a deal with the Brovettans. If they do. We're basing this all on supposition."

It didn't make sense. Not if Carbolen was right about corruption in the Council. Unless Quinn's father had a deal with the Brovettans that Favian wasn't aware of. If the Brovettans took over, Quinn's father would presumably get a place on the Council—if there was a Council under their rule. Favian might be willing to overlook Brovettan rule if he could escape the Lyceum. Assuming the Brovettans ever released the Warding in the first place. Based on Iandolan and Brovettan history—an aggression between the two cities that was decades if not centuries old—the Brovettans were unlikely to let the mages and army out, no matter what deals had been struck between Quinn's father and Favian.

He shook himself. "It doesn't matter. We need to focus on our part of the attack, on bringing down the Warding."

He turned to where Lane's two bodyguards were waiting, but Lane grabbed his arm, caught his gaze. The old Lane was there in full force, the one he'd met at the Shandy Quad, the one who'd risked the lower city and expulsion to learn the mage forms from him. "I'm glad you came to find me. I'm not certain I can do what you want—I never finished third year after all—but I'll try. Show me the form that will bring the Warding down and I'll start practicing."

"I don't know the form."

"What do you mean?"

"I won't know the form until we reach the Warding. It's a lock. And I'm a lockpick. I won't know the shape of the key until I reach the lock."

Fear flickered through Lane's eyes, but then the hard edge returned. "If that's the way it has to be."

"It is."

"Then so be it."

* * *

The gangs gathered in the streets at mid-level outside the park where they intended to attack the Brovettans, converging from all directions, coming in singles and pairs and groups. It happened slowly, over the course of the morning. The citizens on the back streets began to notice when they were only at half strength. Most grew uneasy and retreated into their houses, shutting windows and doors with fearful backward glances. But some of them strode purposefully away and returned with weapons and friends, sidling up and mixing with the gang members loitering in the streets.

Carbolen said nothing about these additions, barely acknowledged them.

When the streets began to get crowded, a group of seven Brovettans arrived. Their leader obviously sensed the animosity in those gathered, but he'd been sent to disperse them. He ordered them to break up and go home, threatened them, but no one made a move on him or his men until one of them drew his sword. By then they'd been surrounded, men subtly shifting position until their escape routes had been cut off. They died cursing, the fight short and brutal, their bodies dragged into a nearby house.

When nearly three-quarters of the gang's forces had assembled, Carbolen turned to Devon and Lane. "Captain Mannert's soldiers should arrive shortly. Time for your group to get in position." He gripped Devon's shoulder, squeezed hard. "We'll all die beneath Brovettan blades if you don't bring that Warding down."

Then he walked away, calling for Leinn and Toral, men beginning to gather around him like flies to meat.

Raven stepped forward. "Let's go."

Raven and Bitter led the way, Devon, Lane, her two bodyguards dressed in gang clothing, Dalton, and Nic behind, Feral bringing up the rear. They pushed through the still growing number of gang members who were all beginning to move toward Carbolen and the park, finally breaking free at an alley. Raven picked up the pace, trotting through the darkness between the buildings, skirting the last few people they ran into that were headed toward the coming brawl. The heightened tension of the gathered mob fell away. Yet Devon couldn't relax. The closer they came to Fulsom Street, the more knotted his shoulder muscles became.

One street away, Raven ducked into a narrow passage barely wide enough for one person to walk abreast until she reached a section of the brick wall and began climbing. Someone had removed bricks, leaving spaces for hand- and footholds. She ascended the four floors quickly, her shadow disappearing over the roofline above within a matter of minutes. Bitter held Devon and the rest below until Raven reappeared and gave a signal, then she began ushering them all up the wall.

Above, they gathered at the edge of the roof, the Warding reaching into the sky three rooftops away, birds circling overhead.

The nearby streets were quiet, a few people bustling about on their daily errands, although there were fewer than normal. The Brovettan guards stationed near the Warding on Fulsom Street hadn't noticed yet. They couldn't see the park where Carbolen and Captain Mannert must be close to starting their attack. Looking at the sun, Devon realized they had little time to get into position.

As if reading his thoughts, Raven gestured sharply and they all crawled over the wall to the adjacent roof, running to the next roofline hunched low so that the Brovettans wouldn't see them from the street. The Warding loomed higher and higher above them. The largest drop was to the last roof, the one with access to the building below. Fleeting pain spiked up through Devon's legs as he landed, Nic giving out a muffled grunt beside him, and then they were through the trapdoor and inside the building. Bitter was a vague shape ahead in the darkness as Devon blinked rapidly, his eyes adjusting from the harsh sunlight to the darkened stairwell. They descended two floors before Bitter shoved them through the open door of an apartment and they ran into the amber face of the Warding.

Lane gasped, the sound eerily loud after the utter silence of their run across the roof. She stepped forward and lifted a hand to the amber, but did not touch it. It cut through the back of the sitting room at a slight angle, the door that led deeper into the apartment sealed inside it, along with a wall cabinet filled with dishes and glassware, a narrow table, part of a sofa, and a set of chairs. The rest of the room, outside the Warding, had been cleaned out. Only a dusty table remained, a pair of windows looking down onto Fulsom Street to one side.

"Do what you need to do," Bitter said, her voice barely above a whisper. "Fast."

Devon took in everyone in the room. "Where are Raven and Feral?"

"Guarding the roof and the stairwell below. I'll be right here, to warn you if anyone is coming and to give you as much time as I can buy."

"What about us?" Dalton said.

Bitter gave him a careless grin. "You, Nic, and the bodyguards keep them safe as long as you can."

Then she stepped away from the door. They heard the creak of the stairs as she settled into position.

Nic, Dalton, and the bodyguards shared a glance, then turned toward Devon.

"Right," he said and shifted to the Warding, reaching out and placing his hand flat against it. His skin prickled, then he closed his eyes.

He heard the others shifting behind him, the floorboards groaning.

"Why isn't anyone here?" Lane asked.

"Would you live here if that thing was cutting off half of the building? Besides, the Brovettans probably kicked everyone out."

Dalton responded, but Devon had already sunk into the Warding, their conversation fading. The layers of the Warding's structure rose up around him, far more complicated than the elevator in the tower or the lock on Lane's suite. He swore beneath his breath.

Dalton appeared next to him. He felt him more than heard him, a comfortable warmth. "What is it?"

"It's going to be more complicated than I thought."

"But you can still do it?" Nic asked from farther away.

Devon didn't answer. Instead, he dove into the layers.

At first, it was as if he were falling through water, the crystalline structure glowing in pathways around him, flaring and pulsing with power. But the farther he sank into the tangled lines, the more he began to sense patterns. Like the double pyramid of the mage's basic form, the Warding had an inherent outer structure. Through the complexity of pathways, he began to notice certain ones were thicker, more stable, and glowed brighter. The smaller paths vibrated with tension, as if locked in place, but straining to reach another state.

And all of the patterns matched the larger structure of the Wardings and the city.

Reaching forward, he seized on one of the thicker paths, steadied himself, then began to trace it, racing along its length until it branched in two different directions. He hesitated, then chose one of the branches at random, streaking down its length to another branch, then another, some of them intersecting with ones he'd already traversed. For each one of those, he chose a different path, when possible.

Even before he finished mapping out the pathways, the shape they were forming became familiar: the shard at the center of the quad at the Lyceum. And the size of the Warding could be controlled. Whoever had released it had pushed it out to its maximum dimensions, to capture as much of mid-level within it as possible.

Settling into one of the intersection points, he paused to collect himself, aware that outside the building Carbolen and Mannert had probably already attacked the Brovettans at the park.

He needed to find the key.

Someone touched his shoulder, the sensation electrifying, pinpricks of tingling pain cascading from the touch into his chest, drawing him back into the real world. "How's it going?" Dalton asked. "The fighting has begun. The Brovettans in the street below have become agitated."

"I've mapped the structure. Looking for the lock now."

"I don't know what that means, but good luck." Dalton's fingers squeezed once in reassurance, then retreated.

Focusing on the lines mapped in his head, Devon began untangling the structure within, searching for the mechanism that had allowed that lone shard in the quad to expand into the Warding. None of the smaller threads appeared to be tied to the mechanism used to create the Warding. They were all attached to the shard's outer structure, straining to pull it back, to pull it down and inward.

Shifting his mental position, he stared down toward what would be the base of the shard and saw a harsh, glowing amber light.

"There you are."

He dove for it, slowing as he drew nearer, the smaller threads around him growing dense, more tangled. But he could see the base, where they all originated from.

And he could see the access point.

Moving carefully, he sank down through the lattice of the shard and slipped into the lock.

In the room, Nic suddenly swore, his voice muted, as if Devon's ears had been covered in thick cloth. "I don't know what you're doing, Devon, but you'd better do it fast. A large group of Brovettans just arrived on the street. They're conferring with those already on guard." He swore again, more violently. "They're breaking into groups. They're starting to search the buildings!"

"Dalton, cover the door." Bitter's usual light tone was gone. "I'm heading down to warn Raven. You two, come with me." Devon assumed she meant Lane's bodyguards.

Another touch, this time to Devon's back. "Devon?"

"I've found the lock. Picking it now. Get ready, Lane."

Her hand withdrew. Devon concentrated. The principle was the same as the box he'd found in the abandoned shop: a certain key released each layer, allowing you to advance to the next level. Find the right sequence and the layers would crumble and the lock would pop. The only difference here was that each layer was a node in the mage's double pyramid structure. He found the first part of the key and slid through the first double pyramid, revealing another, then another and another and another, all nested within each other.

"How many damned levels are there?" he muttered to himself.

Then he slid through the last layer and found himself at the center of the shard. He hovered there, in the utter calm at the deepest part of the amber, somewhat stunned. He'd done it. He'd found the key.

But the Warding still remained. He knew the pattern, but he wasn't a mage.

With a grunt, he surged back out through the lock, through the threads, and dove back into his body—

His eyes snapped open as Nic grabbed the front of this shirt and pulled him close. "They've reached our building!"

Devon heard Raven yell, swords clashing immediately after, all coming from the first floor.

"How'd they get into the building?" Lane asked. "The door was inside the Warding."

Devon gently pushed Nic away, the ex-gang member reluctantly releasing his grip. "It doesn't matter. I have the key." Devon turned to Lane. "Are you ready?"

"Show me the pattern."

"It's more complex than any we worked on in the lower city."

The planes of Lane's face hardened. "Just show me."

Dalton appeared in the doorway. "Nic!"

Devon began the sequence for the mage's basic form as Nic sprinted for the door. Lane watched intently as the sounds of fighting intensified below.

"Your form is off," Lane said.

"I haven't been practicing like you." But Devon forced himself to focus. Taking a deep breath, he started again, moving a little slower, trying to hit the exact sequence the first time. Beside him, Lane watched as he repeated it twice more, then she began to mimic him, the two of them standing side by side. Her first few attempts weren't even close, her sequence mixed up. Once she had the right sequence, it came down to precision. On a few attempts, the air before them shimmered or sparked, but her focus grew more intense with each try.

She had been practicing, Devon realized. Her basic form was perfect, her motions confident.

"You've almost got it," he said. "But you'll have to be touching the Warding."

They both reached back, their motions almost in sync. A shudder passed through him and he realized they'd sunk into the same connection that had bound them when they'd practiced in the lower city. He could sense her heartbeat, nearly aligned with his own. Their breathing matched, slightly accelerated with tension. Every swing of an arm and jab of a finger happened almost simultaneously between them. In another few moments, they'd be perfectly bonded.

Someone screamed outside the room, followed by the splintering of wood and a sickening crunch. Men bellowed out orders. The sounds were getting closer. Feral appeared in the doorway, reached forward, and hauled Nic back, throwing him to the floor inside the room. Then the Regular darted forward, Dalton stumbling back at the same time, a slash across his upper arm, blood soaking his sleeve.

Dalton glanced into the room. "Devon, it's now or never!"

But Devon didn't react, couldn't react. The connection between himself and Lane had solidified, the world receding, all sound overlaid with their combined breath, the rush of their blood, their perfectly attuned bodies.

They began the sequence again. Dalton dodged forward, out of sight, was thrust back into the room almost immediately along with Feral, Raven, and one of Lane's bodyguards. The two Regulars blocked the door, Raven bleeding heavily from a wound on her thigh, Feral's face splattered, a cut along his neck. The Brovettans pounded at them, crowding forward into the hall. One of their blades slid through Feral's chest, point jutting from his back. He staggered, blood gushing from his open mouth. Nic, Dalton, and the bodyguard sprang forward as he fell, Dalton slicing open the man who'd killed Feral before his sword was completely free of Feral's body. There was no sign of Bitter or the second bodyguard.

Then Devon and Lane finished the sequence.

Devon felt it click into place through the skin of his palm, the entire Warding shuddering. Lane snatched her hand back, their odd connection snapping like taut rope.

In the space of a breath, the solid wall of amber slicing through the room shimmered into brittle white light and began to retract.

Both Lane and Devon stepped back, but it was gone before their heels landed.

They shared a stunned glance, then Dalton cried out and Devon spun back to the door.

Dalton staggered back from the fight, hand clutching his side, as Nic punched a Brovettan savagely in the chest with his knife. The bodyguard fell with a blade through his throat. Devon grabbed Dalton and dragged him deeper into the room as Nic stepped over the guard's body to fill the gap next to Raven.

"It's not as bad as it looks," Dalton gasped.

Then his knees gave out beneath him. Devon swore, catching him beneath the shoulder, his weight almost taking them both to the floor. He hauled him into the back of the room that had been enclosed inside the Warding and lowered him into a chair. Dalton groaned, the hand holding his side slick with blood. Devon tried to pull it away, but Dalton shoved him back and through clenched teeth said, "Go help them!"

"And what exactly am I supposed to do to help? Spout mathematical equations at them?"

Before Dalton could answer, Lane yelled, "Drop down!"

Raven twisted, snatched hold of Nic, and threw him to the floor.

Fire swirled from Lane's hands and blasted into the lead Brovettans, flinging them out into the hall and scorching the door on all sides. Screams followed, the stench of burning flesh a breath behind a draft of hot air. But Lane was already moving forward, her hair flaring behind her, her hands in motion. Flame launched into the hall again as she stepped over Feral's scorched body, splattering against the soldiers who'd already been hit once and fanning out to either side. Three men collapsed, their chests nothing but charred meat and bone. Those behind bolted toward the stairs. Orders were being shouted, unheeded, as Lane flung more fire in their wake, turning to face the stairwell, her hand crooked, her face intent.

Raven scrambled to her feet, shot a glance at Lane, then Feral. "Devon, get Dalton out of here." She stepped through the door behind Lane.

"Can you make it?" Devon was already tucking his shoulder into Dalton's armpit. Nic surged up from the floor and took Dalton's other side.

"I have to."

With a moan, they lifted him up out of the chair and stumbled toward the door, Lane throwing another swirl of fire down the stairs. Devon tried not to gag at the burnt flesh as they stepped over Feral and Lane's bodyguard, then the three far more charred men in the hallway. Raven motioned them toward the stairs leading to the roof.

"Why can't we—" Nic began, but cut off with a curse.

Devon glanced behind.

The hall and stairs before Lane were an inferno, at least four more Brovettan bodies strewn out before her, the walls, floor, and ceiling all on fire, wood crackling. Smoke billowed overhead, funneling along the ceiling above them as Dalton staggered upwards as best he could with their help. Raven called for Lane, the mage retreating only after sending another flare of fire down to the first floor.

They fell out onto the roof, smoke swirling out around them. Raven herded them toward the next building, the roof beneath Devon's feet already growing hot.

As Dalton struggled to haul himself up onto the next roof, Devon and Nic supporting his feet, Raven turned to Lane. "You saved our asses down there. I can see why the mages are so useful to the army. I don't understand why they let you go."

"It had nothing to do with her," Devon said. "It was my fault."

"You provided them with an excuse. They would have found another without you, eventually."

Something deep inside the building cracked and the roof shuddered. At the same time, the noise of fighting from the streets escalated. In the distance, an explosion echoed from the direction of the Lyceum, thumping in Devon's chest.

"Those released from the Warding have joined in the fight," Devon said.

Raven shoved him to the wall. "Climb. Before the building falls away beneath us. We'll join up with Carbolen and the others as soon as we can."

"We?"

But Devon leaped for the lip of the roof, Lane on his heels. On the second roof, he shrugged Dalton's arm over his shoulder again and they limped toward the next building.

Behind, from the direction of the Lyceum, the battle cry of the War college rose up, followed by the thud-thud-thud of mage castings and a surge of screams.

Chapter Nineteen

"He won't make it."

Nic and Devon dragged Dalton another four paces before Lane grabbed Devon by the shoulder and swung him around to face her.

"He won't make it! You have to leave him here. He'll bleed out otherwise."

From farther ahead in the alley, Raven turned back. "Let me take a look."

Dalton gasped, his entire body trembling, but he removed his hand. Blood spilled out and Devon's stomach clenched, but Raven knelt, ripping Dalton's shirt away. Dalton hissed as she prodded the wound before standing.

"She's right. He can't be moved much further and he needs to be seen by a healer." She scanned the neighborhood. "We're not far from the Shandy Quad. We'll take him there."

"You need to see a healer yourself," Nic said.

Raven glanced down at the wound in her thigh and the still-wet bloodstain, now reaching all the way down past her knee. "It's nothing. This way."

They ducked into an alley, cut across another street, this one littered with a few bodies but otherwise empty, then found themselves back on Fulsom. The sounds of battle increased as they drew nearer to the Lyceum, which appeared to be the focus of the fight. Plumes of smoke rose into the air along an entire stretch from the park where Carbolen and Captain Mannert had started their attack all the way to the college. A short time ago, new fighting had erupted closer to the towers. The Iandolan Army must have sent a contingent to break the Brovettans' hold there. Men had probably already been sent to the waygates, if there were any to spare.

They burst through the doors of the Shandy Quad without encountering any forces in the streets. As soon as their eyes adjusted to the darkness inside, they found themselves staring down five blades and three spears, Arch at the forefront.

"What in hells are you doing here?" he asked, lowering his spear as he recognized Raven. "The streets have gone mad. You shouldn't be out there." Then his gaze flicked toward Devon, Nic, Lane, and Dalton's sagging body. He swore and spun. "Clear a table! Ryck, get your ass out that door and find Mindell. Don't protest, just do it! This man needs a healer. Fast."

Four of Arch's men—Carbolen's men, Devon was willing to bet—scrambled to clear a space around the largest table in the bar, a fifth man darting outside after a cautious glance down the street in both directions. Lane shut the door behind him, plunging the room into darkness. Arch swore again, his voice changing direction as he ambled behind the bar. A moment later, lucent light began to flood the room as he tapped the chips reserved for drinks alight and began spreading them around the room.

He ended at the table, Dalton lying still, his breath coming in short gasps. Arch plucked his hand away from the wound, examined it, then clucked his tongue. "Deep, but not mortal if we can get it tended to and it doesn't get infected. Aron, fetch towels. Lots of them. And boil some water. Mindell will need it."

He glanced around at the rest of them. "Any of the rest of you injured?"

"Raven," Lane said.

The Regular rolled her eyes. "It's nothing."

But Arch was already headed her way. He knelt and, to Devon's surprise, she let him take a look.

A rumble sounded deep in his chest. "Not as bad as Dalton's, but it should at least be tied off. Aron, bring me one of those towels."

Devon hadn't heard Aron return, but he set a bunch of rags down on the table beside Dalton, then tossed one to Arch.

The bartender began cinching the rag around Raven's thigh, eliciting a breath sucked in through her nose when he jerked it tight. Devon crept up to Dalton's side, reached down to brush the matted hair from his sweaty brow. Dalton's eyes were glazed, but they focused on him.

"You have to go," Dalton said, voice ragged. "You and Lane. You have to do what you can." He coughed, grimacing at the pain it caused.

"I know." Devon leaned down and kissed him, tasting salt and sweat and blood. "Don't die on me."

Dalton smiled, then moaned. "Shards, what are you doing?"

Aron didn't even glance up. "Prepping the wound." He tossed a rag aside, already soaked in blood, then ripped Dalton's shirt away.

Dalton cried out as it jostled his body, cursed, then latched onto Devon's arm with a shockingly strong grip. "Go." He shoved Devon toward Raven, Lane, Nic, and the door, Arch joining Aron at the table.

"He'll be fine," Raven said, "especially if Mindell watches over him. He's part of Carbolen's network."

Before they could step outside, the doors opened again, Arch's other four men bristling, weapons raised, until one of them said, "Mindell," and ushered the healer inside, leading him to the table. Devon wanted to wait to see what the healer said, but Raven and Lane gently forced him outside into the harsh sunlight.

The sound of close fighting greeted them, Raven immediately pulling them back up against the outside of the building.

"That's no more than a street away."

"Shouldn't we see who's fighting?" Lane asked.

"You're a mage. I want to get you as close to the real fight as I can. That's merely a skirmish, probably between Brovettan soldiers and the gangs or some of the citizens that have decided to fight back. It could even be simple looting. We can't waste you on that."

"You overestimate me."

Raven looked at her, gaze harsh. "As Bitter would say, you fried those Brovettans to a crisp in that house, without any help from us. Not to mention brought down the Warding."

"The fire is my only trick."

"It works. Keep it ready." She paused to listen. "Best guess is the worst of the fighting is at the Lyceum. Let's go."

She led them down Fulsom, kept them close to the buildings. Devon's skin prickled as they moved, the general noise of blades and screams punctuated by odd silences and the echoes of more intense fighting farther away. Three blocks later, Raven froze as a large group of thirty Brovettans ran across Fulsom from a cross-street, headed away from them. None of them turned, attention fixed forward. A block beyond that, the door to the apartment building they'd just passed opened up and a group of three families spilled out, children clutched close to their parents. They stared in fear at the four of them before one of the women issued a curt command and all of them bolted down Fulsom, away from the Lyceum.

More bodies began to appear, one entire intersection filled with them, both Iandolan and Brovettan, carrion birds already feasting. A few thieves ransacking the bodies scattered as they appeared, although Devon doubted they'd gone far. They picked through them, Devon trying not to look down. Nic made gagging noises from slightly behind him. The stench of blood was thick, almost physical. It coated Devon's throat, slick and viscous, unmitigated even with shallow breaths.

At the next intersection, Raven peered around the corner, then pulled back. "Fighting in the streets. The Brovettans have pushed the Iandolan Army back to the edge of the college."

"What about our mages?"

"I don't see any of them."

Devon edged forward and crouched down to look.

At the far end of the street, the plaza before the two massive buildings that served as the college's practice fields was under siege. The Iandolan Army—about two hundred—held their ground against a Brovettan force at least twice their size. The Brovettans threw themselves against the wall of men, but the Iandolans had the advantage: they were defending the narrow passage between the walls and they weren't trying to advance. There were no mages in sight.

"They can hold them off indefinitely," Raven said. She'd shifted to Devon's side in order to see. "They're using shields to form a wall. The Brovettans may wear them down, but it will take time."

"I don't think the Brovettans are going to wait." Devon motioned to where a fresh contingent of a hundred Brovettans emerged from another street. It was a solid block of soldiers, marching in sync. They halted and turned to face the plaza, starting a march forward. But as they moved, the front ranks began peeling away in a maneuver Devon recognized from the Lyceum quad.

"They've got a mage," he said sharply, already turning to Lane.

"What do you mean?" Raven asked.

"In the center of their formation. Lane, get up here!"

Nic and Lane stepped out around the corner, Raven two steps ahead but out of Lane's path—

Devon felt a thrum in his chest, like a drumbeat, and the center of the plaza erupted with a juddering crack of thunder, stone fountaining upwards from in front of the advancing Brovettans. But it didn't stop, another shuddering crack splitting the air, then another and another. The stone of the plaza spewed up and out, chunks as large as Devon's torso crashing to the ground on either side. Orders were shouted, both the Brovettans and Iandolans caught in the plaza hastening to scramble out of the way, but it was too late. The line of destruction drove straight through the plaza, men screaming as the ground heaved beneath them and tossed them into the air. Devon's gorge rose as he realized some of the men were being torn apart by whatever force the mage was using.

Raven snatched at Lane, grabbed the front of her shirt. "Do something!"

"I don't know how to counter that!" Lane yelled, her eyes wide. "I don't even know what the mage is doing! I never saw anything like that at the Lyceum!"

The sound of shattered stone and shrieking men escalated as the mage tore the Iandolan line to shreds, the Brovettans advancing into the breach slowly, the tight formation loosening only enough for them to step around stone debris or the occasional mutilated body. Devon caught a glimpse of black robes through their ranks, but then the Brovettans who'd been in the plaza before the reinforcements arrived fell in behind the new ranks and cut off his view. The Iandolans at the back of the line were bellowing orders to fall back, retreating into the corridor between the two practice fields, but the mage didn't stop, the sound of destruction changing as it entered the narrower street, echoing off the buildings on either side. Parts of the walls crumbled with each explosion, the noise becoming so deafening Devon clamped his hands over his ears, the others doing the same. Lane hunkered down next to Devon, as if that would help.

They stayed in position, huddled against the wall of the corner building, until the echoes began to fade. But the attack hadn't stopped. Down the narrow corridor, fresh explosions and screams arose, muted by the practice yard walls.

"They're attacking whoever's left at the Lyceum," Raven said. She spun on Lane. "Why didn't you stop them?"

Lane bristled. "How?"

"Scorch them all from behind!"

"It doesn't work that way. I only know how to create a whirl of fire about three feet across at chest height. It works well in hallways and confined spaces. Not so much in a wide-open plaza. I'd maybe hit about ten or twenty of them before the rest circled around and cut me down."

"The rest of us could have protected you."

"Out here?" Devon countered, motioning to the street before them. "Three of us against five hundred?"

"The Iandolans—"

"That's why the mages have so many soldiers to protect them. They need that many to keep everyone else at bay!"

He stood and stepped toward the shattered plaza.

"Where are you going?" Lane asked from behind.

"To the quad! I'm not going to let that mage and the Brovettans destroy the Lyceum!"

He heard the rest of them catch up as he hit the first part of the demolished plaza, entire chunks of flagstone ripped up in a swath six feet across, shredded bodies on either side, moans coming from those who'd been farther out. A few were moving, attempting to sit up, to stand, but he ignored them, gaze locked on the pocked stone of the corridor ahead. He felt more than saw Raven fall in on his left, Lane and Nic on his right.

They entered the quad and utter chaos.

Battles were being fought on all sides, Brovettans attacking Iandolan soldiers and gang members and citizens in groups of two up to twenty. Larger groups were scattered throughout the grass, centered around mages. Fire shot out from a few of these groups and walls of wavering light shimmered across the quad. Forces Devon couldn't see knocked Brovettans back or flung them into the air, Iandolan soldiers closing in to finish them off. All of the formations he'd seen practiced on the field were being put into practice, but without any of the precision and uniformity witnessed at the college. Here on the battlefield, it was madness. And not all of the mages and soldiers were from the army. Some were clearly students, swinging swords and crooking hands in desperation as they advanced across the grass.

"There!" Raven shouted, pointing toward the center of the quad, where the amber shard of the Warding jutted up into the sky, exactly as it had before it had been activated. Iandolan soldiers surrounded the shard, protecting a contingent near their center.

"The Councilors," Lane said. Her eyes darted back and forth. "They have at least five mages in their ranks to protect them, but they're being attacked by four Brovettan mages."

"Four?"

"One from each quarter."

"I was hoping there were at most two."

Four Brovettan soldiers noticed them hovering near the entrance to the quad and charged. Lane raised her arms, hand crooked, but Raven took out three as Nic finished the fourth.

"What's the plan?" Raven asked, cleaning her blade on her sleeve.

"We have to take out their mages."

"How? There are only four of us. Their mages are surrounded by at least forty soldiers. Not to mention there's an entire battlefield between us and them."

"We have a mage."

"Have you not been listening?" Lane exclaimed. "I'm not even a third year! I can barely produce fire in a limited capacity! And these mages from Luminesque are doing things I've never seen before."

Devon turned to face her. "But I know the structure the mages use better than anyone else."

"How is that going to help? You can't access it. You don't have—" She halted, her eyes opening wide in sudden understanding. "The bond. You want to use the bond."

"What does that mean?" Nic said, voice irritated. He and Raven had taken up defensive stances before them, discouraging anyone from approaching.

"We used it with the Warding," Lane said. "He knew the key, I didn't, so we aligned ourselves so that everything one of us did, the other mimicked. He provided the sequence for the key, I provided the connection to the Source—"

"And the Warding fell," Devon finished. "We can do the same thing here."

"We aren't close enough. My fire extinguishes itself after twenty feet."

"I know how to augment the distance."

"What about their mages? They know things we don't."

"They know things our mages don't. But I never learned under those conditions."

"Whatever you're going to do, do it," Raven snapped. "We'll protect you as long as we can."

Lane chewed on her lower lip, eyes drifting toward the intensifying battle. Then she nodded.

Devon spun to face the quad and the Warding. Beside him, Lane raised her hand, crooked her fingers, and began the steady motions of the basic form.

He began to mimic her, their motions nearly matching up. But that sense of connection wasn't there and Devon could tell they weren't quite aligned.

"Devon—"

"I know. Just keep going through the basic form."

On the quad, lightning suddenly lashed down from the cloudless skies, the bolts snaking into the Iandolan soldiers surrounding the Councilors. The army's line wavered, screams of terror lancing through the general roar of the fight. Men and women cowered away from the bolts, those closest clapping hands over their ears or reeling away, those at the edge flung backwards.

Closer at hand, another group of Brovettans gathered and headed towards them.

"Devon!" Nic shouted.

"I can see."

But he and Lane weren't in sync. What was wrong? Why wasn't it working like it had during the practice sessions or at the Warding? What was different?

He hadn't been trying to form a connection then. He'd been focused on something else. He'd been relaxed.

Sucking in a deep breath, he steadied himself and closed his eyes, pushed the cacophony of the battle away, drained the tension from his arms, his shoulders, his back. It flowed down through his gut and into his legs, his head sagging forward. And as the last dredges seeped away, the faintest of connections began to form with Lane, strengthening as he drew himself inward, as he lifted his head, as he opened his eyes.

They snapped into perfect alignment a few moments before the band of twenty Brovettans arrived.

Without his volition, Devon's crooked hand began to move from the basic form into a secondary form, but he didn't fight it. With assured motions, Lane flew through the Sigil, fire swirling into existence in front of her. With a final flourish, she sent it spinning out into the Brovettans between Raven and Nic, even as they both engaged them with their blades.

Men bellowed in pain, fell back in flames, and Lane and Devon stepped forward into the gap as one, Nic yelling, "Careful!" as he slashed and ducked.

But Lane was already completing the form again, fire roaring, splitting the Brovettans into two groups. Seven of them were already down, moaning from burns or dead. Raven had taken out four more, Nic another three. The remaining six turned to flee. Lane sent a surge of fire at their backs.

They didn't have far to run. Some of the Iandolan soldiers nearby had noticed the skirmish and were rushing to meet them.

"Ah, reinforcements," Nic said.

"It's about time," Raven grumbled. She faced Devon. "You're up."

Devon nodded, Lane doing the same, then he lifted his arm and crooked his hand. "Time to reap what you've sown," he and Lane said together.

His first attempt sent a blast of wind across the eastern part of the quad, so violent it knocked men off their feet and sent them rolling. But he hadn't meant for it to be wind nor in that location. "The order was wrong," Lane and he said together, although the thought had come from Lane. "And the plane in the Source," he added with her.

He tried again, a sheet of flame falling out of the sky like fiery rain, pouring down on the Brovettans surrounding one of their mages. The screams were horrific, but Devon was already shifting his attention, repeating the form, altering it only enough to change the distance and direction. Another sheet of fire, twice as large, fell on the western part of the quad. But this time it struck an invisible wall ten feet over the Brovettans' heads, the flame cascading down the surface to the side, spilling out into the random fighting scattered around the quad and scorching the grass. Devon swallowed down bile, aware that some Iandolans had been caught in the carnage, perhaps even students, but Lane had already begun the basic form again. He dragged his attention back to the main fight.

"They're already adapting," he and Lane said together. "We'll have to try something different this time. Perhaps something from their own arsenal."

When the form completed, jagged bolts of lightning lanced out of thin air, arcs splintering off, striking into the heart of the group that had defended against the sheet of fire. The biggest bolt struck the center, at least seven others riddling the soldiers surrounding the mage. Men and women were flung backwards, away from the charred husks of those that had been directly hit. As the bolts died out, only afterimages on the backs of Devon's eyes, those husks fell.

"Two down, two more to go," Lane and he said.

They shifted their focus to the closest group.

But the battlefield had changed. Raven and Nic were no longer alone. At least thirty Iandolan soldiers had formed up around the four of them, a formation similar to that used by the Brovettans.

And the Brovettans—

"You've caught their attention," Raven shouted over the noise of the fight. "They're turning toward us. I suggest you start thinking about defenses."

"Defenses?" Lane and he said together.

But Devon already understood. He started the form, Lane forced to copy him, but he rushed it, because he could see the mage headed toward them, could see her face, her hand, the form she was already completing.

"Get down!" he and Lane screamed.

Ahead, the ground heaved and earth and grass exploded upwards in a line headed straight toward Devon and Lane's position, just as it had out in the plaza. Except that had been stone. This was dirt, easier to move, so the path of destruction struck much faster.

Men and women bellowed, tried to throw themselves aside, but it hit too fast. Those in front were ripped apart as it gouged through the quad and shot into their formation. Those in back had a few seconds to shift, but even then it caught those near the center and flung them high. Lane and Devon screamed simultaneously and then Devon was wrenched by the invisible force to one side, the connection to Lane snapping as they were thrown apart. He landed in the grass on top of someone else's body, an edge of armor or pommel of a weapon digging hard into his side, then rolled, the breath knocked from his lungs. Gasping, he lurched to his feet, found Lane already completing a Sigil, her hand thrusting forward at the end. He staggered toward her as a wall of shimmering blue light formed between the scattered Iandolan forces and the Brovettans charging to meet them.

"Lane!"

She spun toward him, wincing, although Devon couldn't see any obvious wounds. "I thought it would buy us some time."

Raven was screaming at the Iandolans to reform their ranks, soldiers dragging themselves to their feet, Nic racing around helping them up.

"We have to reform the link," Devon said.

As one, they faced the shimmering blue wall, already beginning to fade.

The link came faster this time, snapping into place of its own volition, as if it had been waiting.

"We need some kind of shield," Lane and he said as they began walking forward into position behind the ragged Iandolan line. "Something that will protect those of us left."

Devon was already thinking, his hand moving into the basic form. Something that could stop the lightning and the fire. But what about the earth attack? How could he stop that?

They finished the form, but Devon didn't take over to start a secondary form.

"Not yet," he and Lane said, in answer to Lane's unasked question. "I need to see what the Brovettan mage is planning. Be ready to start the base form immediately after I finish."

The blue wall had died down enough they could see movement on the far side.

"They're close!" Raven yelled. "Be ready!"

The shimmering blue wall vanished, but the Brovettans didn't move.

At their center, the mage began a form. Devon watched. As soon as she began the secondary form, he and Lane shouted, "It's the same attack! Scatter!" and he crooked his hand and began a counter.

The earth exploded in front of them, but neither Devon nor Lane moved. The Iandolans, Raven, and Nic were already clear. The force plowed toward them, a gust of wind preceding it.

Thirty feet away, Devon finished his form, he and Lane's hand falling to close it off.

With a heave, the earth exploded ten feet in front of them, sod flung higher and wider and with more force than what approached. Within seconds, the two met.

A thunderclap of power rocked the air, a second concussive gust—much more powerful than the first—shoving hard against Devon's chest and flinging Lane's hair behind her. Both squinted against the grit it carried, raised an arm to shield their eyes. Anyone closer was thrown backwards, even the dead that littered the ground.

Lane and Devon started the basic form again, began moving forward, hitting the mangled earthen path they'd created within a few paces, then the crater where the two forces had met.

On the far side, the front ranks of Brovettans had been caught in the blast, their men—those still conscious—moaning and picking themselves up off the ground. But it was the mage that lay exposed near the center that held Devon's attention.

"She's not Brovettan," Lane and he said.

"Do you recognize her?" he and Lane asked.

They shook their heads. "No one I know."

They raised their crooked hands, the mage mirroring them. The Brovettans still alive and mobile behind her scattered at a sharp command.

All three of them finished the basic form at the same time, then held. Devon and Lane came to a halt forty paces from her. Dressed in black with leather accoutrements, she glared at them both, her hair trailing out from the sides of the black hood she wore. Devon guessed she was nearly forty years old, her eyes sharp and filled with hatred.

"Who are you?" she demanded. "No one here knows how to create an air cantrip. No one anywhere has been able to counter mine."

Neither Devon nor Lane responded. They held their hands steady.

Both of them flinched when the mage began her secondary form.

"What is she doing?" Lane and he asked.

"I don't recognize the form," he and Lane answered. "Some kind of barrier. Some kind of shield."

A mostly translucent wall shimmered into existence as movement caught Devon's eyes. An Iandolan soldier had knelt to one side, had sighted a crossbow.

The bowman fired, but the bolt shattered when it hit the mage's wall, a mere ripple radiating out from the impact point. Devon and Lane spun around. The wall surrounded them, a half sphere of shimmering light that distorted everything outside, as if they were looking through a waterfall. Even so, Devon could tell the Iandolans had seized control of the quad. The fourth mage was either dead or subdued. Those near the Warding were now running toward the three of them. A few of the Iandolan mages were gathering around the wall's edge, Favian among them.

The mage in black shot a scathing look at Favian, even as the proctor forced everyone to step back and began a form.

"He won't be able to break through," she said. "Not in time anyway."

She began the basic form again and Lane and he shouted, "Devon!"

Devon finished the secondary form for Lane's fire at the same time the mage finished her basic form. But she'd been watching and dodged to the right, the flames hitting the shimmering barrier and bursting outwards without touching her. Devon and Lane swore, already starting the basic form as the mage began her secondary; she hadn't lost her hold on the basic form she'd already created.

This was why mages didn't fight one-on-one, why the Council always sent them out in groups, so that one mage could be completing the basic form and preparing for the next strike while another was attacking or defending with a secondary form. One-on-one, he couldn't complete a defense before the mage could attack. The only option was to—

"Run!" Lane and he shouted. Both of them raced away from the mage as she completed her air cantrip. The familiar sounds of exploding earth followed them, gaining ground, as they charged toward the far end of the barrier.

At the last minute, the barrier only ten feet away, they angled left, pushing hard, pain burning in Devon's side where the pommel of the sword had dug into his ribs. He felt the cantrip crackling across his back, attempting to suck him into its shredding vortex—

But it hit the barrier. A sound like ice shattering cascaded upwards as it dissipated, the barrier unaffected.

Devon and Lane turned, but they'd lost the basic form, lost their advantage. The mage had already begun again. Devon and Lane cursed, began their own basic, lagging behind. The mage finished first, sent another cantrip at them across the length of the barrier's dome. Lane and Devon tensed.

"Should we—" Lane and Devon began.

"Hold," Devon and Lane said.

They finished their secondary form moments before the cantrip struck. Their own cantrip formed directly in front of it.

The thunderclap echoed a thousand times louder inside the dome. The concussive wave snatched both Devon and Lane off their feet and flung them into the barrier behind nearly ten feet off the ground, snapping their bond. Devon's breath whooshed from his lungs as he hit, the back of his head cracking into the barrier. He landed face first in the grass, dazed, but rolled onto his back. Lightning sparks flashed across his vision. His head pounded with each pulse of his blood. He moaned, but twisted onto his side and blinked in Lane's direction.

She wasn't there.

"Lane!" he shouted, dragging himself to his knees. He tried to stand, but the world tilted. Gasping, he hung his head, forced himself to focus, then staggered to his feet. "Lane!"

She stood over the mage on the far side of the barrier, hand crooked, face locked in concentration. The mage had backed herself up against the barrier, one hand raised to ward away Lane's attack.

Devon stumbled toward them. "Lane, what are you doing?"

"Who are you?" Lane demanded, hand poised in threat, like Quinn's hand so long ago back at the Shandy Quad. She'd already completed the basic form, Devon realized, was primed for the secondary. "Who are you and why have you done this?"

The mage laughed, her hand dropping slightly. Like Devon, she looked dazed. The concussive wave must have flung her against the barrier as well. She was breathing in short, harsh pants, a touch of blood flecking her lips.

"You don't even know." She licked her lips and swallowed, wincing. "Don't even know why we came. Why we fought." Her gaze focused on Devon, then shifted back to Lane, the amused expression giving way to a hard, cold, determined despair. "Ask your mother. Ask Favian."

Then she started the basic form.

"Not this time, bitch," Lane said, and began her secondary.

Devon surged forward. "Lane, no!"

The fire struck the mage full in the chest, licking outwards and singeing Lane. The mage's scream reverberated in the dome, but Lane didn't flinch—from the fire or the shriek.

When the mage's body collapsed backwards—the scent of charred, smoking meat slamming into Devon's senses—Lane sagged. Devon lurched forward and caught her before she could fall. She leaned into him heavily.

"It's my ankle," she gasped. "I twisted it earlier, when we were thrown aside by the first cantrip."

Before he could answer, a sound like rushing wind filled the dome. Both of them hunched down, even though there wasn't even a breeze. The sound faded as the barrier that had locked them in with the mage appeared to change into shimmering light and stream upwards into the sky, almost like how the Warding had expanded and retracted. As soon as it lifted, Favian stepped forward, a few proctors—including Arrend and Gallean—crowding in behind. Raven, Nic, and an entire contingent of Iandolan soldiers rushed forward from the opposite side to check the bodies of the Brovettan soldiers that were scattered across the dome's field. Behind the proctors, surrounded by their own entourage of soldiers, were the Councilors.

"What happened?" Favian demanded. "What have you done?"

Lane straightened beneath his angry glare. "We stopped her." Her posture tensed as she looked toward her mother, Councilor Varenov. "I killed her."

Favian halted a few paces away, gaze shifting to the dead mage. His entire body stiffened in shock. The others edged forward, Lane's mother pushing through the soldiers, proctors, and mages to Lane's side. It appeared as if she wanted to pull her daughter into a hug, but she restrained herself, her expression torn. They were markedly different—Lane clearly Luminesque, her mother Iridesque—but Devon could see similarities in the planes of their faces and chins.

Around them, the stunned whispers had already begun.

"She's not from Luminesque," Varenov said sharply. "Who is she?"

Favian's teeth clenched, the muscles in his jaw tensing. "Her name was Terrial, the daughter of Councilor Martov."

"We thought she'd died during the raid on Brovetto sixteen years ago," Gallean said.

Chapter Twenty

Most of the Councilors had hung back with the proctors, but now an older man with gray hair, dressed in rumpled finery, shoved his way forward. Devon recognized him from the entourage at the end of the army's first march on Brovetto months before.

"Terrial? Did you say—"

But then he reared back from the scorched body and charred ground. One hand rose to cover his mouth, whether in horror or at the stench Devon couldn't tell. He stared at the body from his position at the edge of those gathered, tears gathering in his eyes. They did not spill over.

Instead, he steadied himself with effort, schooled his features with flat appraisal, devoid of emotion. He lowered his hand with a sniff.

"This wretched soul attempted to destroy Iandolo, nearly succeeded with a coup. My daughter would never have made such an attempt." He glanced around those present. "This...this is not my Terrial."

He moved away stiffly, the crowd parting, until he'd faded behind the general entourage of guards, clerks, and others surrounding the Councilors.

Varenov cleared her throat. "We've captured the fourth mage and the Brovettan envoy who lured us into this trap, along with most of their guards. Have we seized control of the Lyceum, Proctor Gallean?"

"I believe our forces are subduing the last of the Brovettan army within the Lyceum now, Councilor."

"And what about the rest of the city? The waygates and the towers?"

"We've received no official reports, but Captain Mannert—who led the Iandolan soldiers that freed us—has taken her command to the towers, along with the gangs that helped her."

"Gangs?"

Arrend answered. "It would appear some of the gangs from the lower city offered to help Captain Mannert free us from the Warding and push the Brovettans out of the city. They were under the command of a man named Carbolen." Arrend glanced at Devon. "In fact, she claims that he came to her, that it wouldn't have been possible to free us without their aid."

"Really. I believe the Council will want to speak with Captain Mannert and this Carbolen, once things have settled down."

"Of course."

"According to the men we've placed on the Tower here at the Lyceum," Gallean continued, "the waygates are currently being wrested from the Brovettans. The city rose in revolt as soon as the Warding collapsed. I'll need to wait for official reports, of course, but I'd wager that we'll have the city back under our control by nightfall."

"As soon as we have control of the waygates, double the guard there. Triple it if you can. If I were the Luminesque, I'd have a secondary force already on its way to Iandolo to solidify control of the city. They should almost be here. We'll want to greet them appropriately upon their arrival."

"I will inform the prefects, although we are significantly short on men at the moment."

Varenov waved around the quad. "The students of the Lyceum have more than proved themselves worthy. Recruit from the fifth and sixth years if necessary."

"Very well."

Favian suddenly stepped toward Devon and Lane. "And while you are issuing those orders, you may as well arrest these two."

That caused an immediate protest from nearly everyone surrounding them—the soldiers who'd joined them as they pushed into the quad beneath Raven's orders, the Council's entourage, the students, and a few of the proctors. Even Varenov frowned in disapproval.

Arrend pushed forward, placing himself between Favian and Devon. "What are you doing, Favian? You saw what these two did."

"I don't know what they did," Favian snapped. "What I saw was two former students—one of whom has an arrest warrant out on his head and one of whom never completed her third year—using mage forms that are unknown to us but are apparently known by our enemy. You cannot tell me that does not give you cause for concern." When Arrend simply stood, teeth clenched, Favian raised a hand. "Proctor Gallean?"

Gallean motioned the soldiers closest to him forward. They surrounded Devon and Lane, a discontented murmur growing steadily on all sides.

"Take them to the college's War dormitory for now," Gallean ordered. "Place them in one of the empty supply rooms."

"Put them in separate rooms," Favian said. "We don't want them talking to each other. And tie their hands. I don't want them using any mage forms to break free."

Two of the soldiers snagged their wrists and tied their hands behind their backs with belts someone pulled from two of the dead. Then they shoved them toward the War students' building.

Lane twisted toward her mother. "Are you going to let them do this? We saved you from their mages. Without us they would have killed all of you!"

"We would have overwhelmed them eventually," Favian said.

Lane spat on the ground at his feet as she was thrust by him, then ripped herself from her guards' grip, straightened her shoulders, and stalked toward the barracks on her own, with only a minor limp.

Devon glanced back, locked gazes with Raven, who tapped a furious Nic's shoulder. Both of them faded back into the ranks of soldiers around them. He glanced toward Arrend, who said, "I won't let them do this. Not this time."

Then Devon followed in Lane's wake.

As the ragged remains of the army and students parted before them, Devon heard Councilor Varenov say in a stern voice, "The Council would like to speak with you, Proctor Favian. With all of the proctors of this school."

* * *

Arrend was the first person to come see him.

He'd been sitting on the floor of the storage room for an indeterminate time, hands still tied behind his back. They hadn't provided him with a chair or a cot or even a glass of water. Three War students guarded the door. Devon hadn't bothered to check to see if they'd locked it. The room smelled of oil and metal, with an underlying hint of some kind of spice, like cinnamon. It was lit by a narrow band of lucent above the door. He couldn't hear anything, the walls thick, made of stone and mortar. He'd dozed off at one point, jolting awake with a crick in his neck that still hurt when he twisted his head too far to the left.

When the door rattled and creaked open, he didn't bother standing.

"Devon."

"Proctor Arrend."

Arrend smiled—wistful and a little haunted—then faced the guards outside the door. "No need to enter. I won't untie him, you have my word."

They might have protested, but the words were laced with Arrend's professorial tone. One of them murmured something and Arrend closed the door.

He didn't even look around, merely stared at Devon. "What did you do?"

"I unlocked the Warding. I'm a lockpick, remember? Your notes helped, of course."

"What about in the quad? Did you—?"

"I did nothing. It was all Lane. Her power, anyway. Keeping my hands tied is useless."

"But how did she know those forms? She didn't learn them here, and Councilor Varenov swears she's been kept inside the tower since her expulsion from the Lyceum."

"I guided her in the forms."

"Even the ones that Proctor Favian does not know?"

"Once you understand the basic structure, it isn't that difficult to extrapolate."

"The structure you discovered while studying here."

"Yes."

Arrend shook his head. "Favian suppressed your research, your proposed final challenge. He had it sealed and banished to the Library, no one but mage proctors allowed to look at it."

"Even though it's only a set of questions?"

"He didn't want anyone reading them and creating questions of their own. The path that would lead to is too dangerous, he said."

"What do you think?"

"I think that path has already been traveled, by you, by Terrial and the rest of the Brovettan mages. Ignoring it now is pure hubris."

"Favian brought this upon Iandolo."

"What do you mean?"

"He's the one that started it, with his failed raid on Brovetto. Whatever happened then, he and Gallean and whoever else was part of it thought Terrial was dead and left her behind. She's the one who trained the other Brovettan mages. She's the one who brought them here."

Arrend raised a hand to stop him. "The Council has already discovered all of this. We managed to subdue the fifth Brovettan mage. She's been cooperative. Proud of what they did here, even."

"Fifth mage? I only saw four on the quad."

"The one who activated the Warding. Gallean saw her break protocol and make for the shard at the beginning of the treaty ceremony. He didn't understand the danger, but he sent soldiers to grab her. They almost had her when the Warding went up. As soon as it came down, they seized her and knocked her out. That was before anyone realized what had actually happened, of course. It took us a while to figure out we'd been trapped for days already, if not longer. The sound of the fighting nearby is what drew us out and woke us up. That and the fact that the envoy from Brovetto tried to kill us all."

"Why did they do it? Not Terrial—she obviously had her own personal vendetta—but the others."

"Because the Crystal Cities are falling apart and the Council is doing nothing about it. Luminesque is probably the worse off of all of the other six, but there is the additional animosity between our two cities, one that has existed since the Founding and been revitalized over and over again by both sides through the years. Iandolo has always been in control, a control that has only increased over time, and Luminesque has always resented it. The Council thought the recent attacks were instigated by the rebel underground in Brovetto, but it's becoming clear that they weren't. Terrial and her mages broke off from them years ago. They approached the government Iandolo had in nominal control instead, led by those in Luminesque who secretly hate us. That's why they had so many soldiers under their control, why they were so organized and well-supplied. Their betrayal of those in power in Luminesque is a shock."

"The Council can't ignore them now. They'll have to do something."

"They've already declared the entire governmental leadership in Brovetto—men and women they placed in control—traitors. A retaliatory strike set to seize control is already being organized."

"I meant they can't ignore the true rebels, those protesting the declining conditions in the cities. They'll have to do something about the dead lucent, the decaying infrastructure eventually."

"I don't think the Council knows what to do. The lucent is failing everywhere, even here in Iandolo."

Devon said nothing. He didn't know what to say.

Arrend shifted. "What about you, Devon?"

"What do you mean?"

"Are you hurt? Did you need anything?"

Devon heard the question Arrend truly wanted to ask: how have you been?

"I could use something to drink."

"Of course." Arrend turned to the door, but paused, one hand on the handle, looking back. "They're arguing over what to do with you. You and Lane. Some want to parade you around the city as saviors, reinstate you at the Lyceum, make you a proctor."

"And what did Favian have to say about that?"

"Favian wants you arrested, maybe even executed for trespassing on the mage's domain, but he knows no one would accept that now. He's considering keeping you at the Lyceum—so that he can keep a close eye on you, I'm certain. He's afraid of you. Of what you've done. Of what you might be able to do. I came to see if you'd accept a position here, but I don't even have to ask."

Devon met Arrend's gaze. "It would be a prison sentence."

"Yes, it would."

He left. Shortly after, a guard came in with a pitcher of water and a glass, but refused to untie his hands. He poured the water and let Devon drink, but his hands trembled and he withdrew as soon as Devon said he was finished, leaving the half-empty pitcher and glass to one side.

Favian and Varenov came next, Favian flinging the door open, already halfway across the room before Varenov stepped inside.

"How did you do it? How did you become a mage?" He halted a few steps away, looming over Devon.

"I'm not a mage. I'm a mathematician."

Favian knelt. "Don't feed me shards, you thieving wretch. We saw you on the quad, you and Lane. You halted whatever it was that gouged up the earth and tore our men apart. You killed two other mages with fire and lightning. You killed their head mage—"

"Terrial," Varenov interrupted. "A mage you trained."

Favian waved her statement aside in disdain. "You killed their head mage without any soldiers to protect you. Don't tell me it was all Lane. She never finished her third year!"

"Because of you."

"Bah!" He stood and paced away.

Varenov took a single step forward. "How did you do it?"

"I provided the forms, Lane provided the power."

"That's it?"

"That's it."

"And how did you break the Warding?"

"The same way."

"How do you know the forms? You weren't trained as a mage here."

"I'm a mathematician. I was trained to recognize and manipulate structure. The mage forms and the Wardings are nothing but structure."

She leaned slightly forward, locked eyes with him. "And is it true that the proctors here actively interfered with my daughter's education?"

Favian lurched forward with a sharp, "Councilor!"

Devon didn't let his gaze waver. "Yes."

Varenov straightened, while Favian fumed to one side. The Councilor looked troubled. "What are we going to do with you?"

"He cannot be allowed to roam free, Councilor. He's too dangerous. We must keep him and Lane here at the Lyceum, under careful watch. Perhaps he can contribute to the Mage school, explain this structure he sees within our Sigils. We can reinstate Lane as well, continue her training as a third year."

Varenov faced Favian. "Continue her training as before?"

Favian stilled. "She would be trained as all other third years are trained."

"So I would hope."

Varenov looked back toward Devon. "Have you gotten all of your answers, Proctor Favian?"

"Not all, but enough. For now."

"Then we should return to the Council meeting."

They departed, Favian closing the door with a hard thud.

Not long after, all three guards entered, one with a tray of food. They untied his hands and left the tray. After the tingling of retreating numbness faded from his fingers, he ate the steak they'd brought, dipping chunks of bread into the mashed potatoes and gravy. He saved the cheese for later. When they returned for the tray, they left his hands untied.

He paced the small room, twelve steps across, twenty forward to back. He glanced at the door, at the lock, but it was mechanical, not lucent. The guards would hear him attempting to pick it. If it were even locked in the first place.

Eventually, he sat again, hands in his lap this time, and fell asleep.

* * *

Devon woke with a start, blinking at the darkness. The band of lucent had dimmed, but as soon as he started moving it brightened again. He sat forward, winced at the sharp pain in his neck, then stilled.

Something bumped into the door, then scraped down its length to the ground. Devon lurched to his feet as the door opened and a body slumped through the opening. One of the guards.

Raven stepped into view. "Don't worry, they wouldn't let me kill them. They're only unconscious."

"They, who?"

"Your mentor, for one," Arrend said, appearing over Raven's shoulder, along with Nic.

"We're getting you out of here," the ex-gang member said.

"But what about—"

"Both of you. Now come on."

Devon moved into the hall, stepping over the prone bodies of his guards. Three more lay in the hall outside another door farther down, two others with Councilor Varenov's colors standing over them. A moment later, Lane stepped outside, followed by her mother. Devon's eyebrows rose in question.

"I will not have my daughter attend this college again, under any circumstances, much less what amounts to house arrest," Varenov said stiffly.

"Even if it means setting us free?"

"Even then. I trust you and my daughter more than I trust Favian and the proctors. Present company excepted, of course."

Arrend merely nodded. "We should leave, before one of these guards rouses or someone notices us."

"You and the councilor should lead," Raven said, "at least until we're out of the building."

Arrend and Varenov took up position in front, the rest trailing behind, Varenov's two guards last.

Devon sidled up to Nic. "Where's Dalton?"

"Still recovering. We'll see him once we're safely away."

"What about Carbolen and the rest of the gangs?"

"They fought the Brovettans along with Captain Mannert and the rest of the city until it was obvious that the Iandolan Army and the citizens would overthrow them, then Carbolen ordered a fading retreat," Raven said. "They vanished into the woodwork, as we do. Captain Mannert didn't seem too concerned with capturing us, although she made a token effort."

"How many died in the fighting?"

"As many as it took to win."

Devon didn't like that answer, but they'd reached a stairwell. Arrend went up first, then motioned them to follow. The halls and rooms beyond looked like those in the Science dormitory, except these were decorated with various weapons and shields and banners. The dining rooms and great room were the same, but the books lining the shelves were on tactics and forms, brawling and swordplay. They only caught glimpses of the main rooms, Arrend taking them through the vacant kitchens, the savory smells making Devon's stomach growl, then through servant corridors and out a side door into the area between the War school dormitory and one of the practice yards. Devon was surprised to find it dark out; he had no idea how long he'd been kept in the storage room.

Arrend turned to Devon. "This is where the Councilor and I leave you. You'll find the guards placed at the quad's entrance rather distracted tonight."

"Why's that?"

"Because not everyone—councilor, proctor, soldier, or student—agrees with keeping you under the college's thumb. And right now, that appears to be the direction the argument is turning."

"They want to use you, of course," Varenov said. "Force you to reveal your secrets, to teach them, so that they can either bury the knowledge or use it against the other Crystal Cities. It's a way to muzzle both of you, while pretending to honor you. They attempted to muzzle my daughter once. I will not give them another chance."

She caught Lane's shoulders. Lane appeared too stunned to respond. "Go. Learn what you can from Devon. You don't need the Lyceum anymore. And you don't need my protection. I can't keep you here, safe in our towers. You'd never survive it. You have too much of your father in you."

She drew Lane into a hug, which Lane hesitantly returned. When they released each other, Varenov wiped at her eyes, then looked sternly at Devon. She stalked up to him, imperious, then leaned over and whispered in his ear.

"Favian's right. You two are the most dangerous people in Iandolo right now. In all of the Crystal Cities. Don't make me regret this."

Then she snapped her fingers at her guards and withdrew without looking back.

"Stay safe," Arrend muttered, then drifted off in the direction of the Science dormitory.

Raven stepped up to Devon's side. "Well, that was heartfelt. Almost made me blush. We should probably leave now. For real."

"I agree," Nic said, already moving into the shadows near the practice yard. "That was just uncomfortable."

"For you, maybe."

Raven ushered Lane and Devon after Nic, all of them crouched low. But when they came out from behind the War dormitory, Devon stopped short.

"What is it?" Lane whispered from behind.

"Look at the quad."

Half of the quad was gouged up by the fighting, the grass churned and trampled. Craters and trenches marked where the air cantrips had ripped it apart, while charred stretches outlined where fire and lightning had struck. But in the sections farthest from where the main battle had been fought, near the scriptorium, Library, Tower, and Inner Sanctum, the quad was covered with bodies, figures moving among them, bending down occasionally, either tending to the wounds or pulling a blanket up over the head before rising and moving on.

"There are hundreds of them."

"More than we saw after that first attack, when they sent the students down to the waygate," Lane said.

"And there are more out in the city," Raven said, prodding them forward. "They ran out of room to house the wounded everywhere. It will take days if not weeks to burn the dead."

They entered the lane between the two practice fields, although nearly all of it and the walls to either side had been destroyed. Glimpses of the practice yards could be seen through ragged holes.

Halfway down its length, someone called out, "Who goes there?"

Nic and Raven tensed, both drawing weapons, but Devon stepped forward. "Itch, is that you?"

Itch moved forward until Devon could see him in the sparse light coming from overhead and from the quad behind. "I'll be damned. If it isn't the master mathematician himself." He checked out the others, nodding politely toward Lane, barely giving the two gang members or their weapons a glance.

"Why are you on guard duty? Shouldn't there be War students here?"

"They're all out in the city. They pulled a bunch of the Science and Merchant students for guard duty. The rest are helping the Humanities students with the wounded."

"Some of the War students are here," someone said, stepping out of the shadows. She was young, with pock marks on her face. There were four others behind her, ranging in age and school.

"Third year or less," Itch said to Devon with an exasperated eyeroll.

"Are you going to let us through," Raven interrupted, "or do I have to kill you all?"

Itch gave a start, glanced back toward the quad, then motioned them forward. "Let's get you through before anyone notices. Oh, and Arrend said you'd probably need this." He handed Lane a robe with a hood. "No one in Iandolo is going to take kindly to Brovettans for a while."

They all stepped back, the pock-marked girl giving Raven and her black leathers an appreciative once-over. The rest merely gave them furtive looks or pretended they weren't there.

Once in the demolished plaza beyond, Raven broke into a sprint.

They worked their way through a traumatized city, dead still lining the streets where they'd fallen, groups of citizens working to collect them all on wagons or carts. Most of those they ran into were on edge, so they stayed in the shadows and kept their distance as much as possible. The number of dead increased as they reached the area where the Warding had stopped, but not far beyond that it decreased dramatically, most of the fighting centered around the Warding and within, or along the Spokes and near the waygates and towers.

Raven led them toward the hub, but didn't dare risk trying to pass Lane through whoever was on guard there. Instead, she used one of the gang's tunnels down to the lower levels, passing from level to level, building to building, until they reached Carbolen's lair.

Like the quad at mid-level, the main hall of the lair and many of the surrounding rooms were filled with wounded, although none of the gang members here looked significantly hurt. Devon guessed that anyone seriously injured had been left behind, to be dealt with by the Iandolan Army, if they survived long enough to be found. Regular gang members appeared to be binding up wounds, staunching blood, and stitching together cuts. Alcohol was flowing freely. Scattered among them were a few healers, Mindell included.

They passed the healer on the way up to the dais, picking their way through those lying or sitting on either side. Devon grabbed a handful of his shirt as he stood.

"Where's Dalton?"

Mindell extricated himself before answering. "The man I helped at the bar?"

"Yes, that man."

"He's resting in your room. We brought him down here as soon as I halted the bleeding and Arch thought it was safe to move him. He should be fine." The healer looked exhausted, eyes sunken hollows, his skin smeared with dried blood and sweat.

"Should be?"

"As long as he doesn't get an infection."

Mindell shifted to the next wounded gang member.

"Let him work," Raven said. "You can see Dalton after you've spoken to Carbolen."

Devon almost refused, relenting only when Lane put a hand on his arm and said, "Let's just get it over with."

They wound their way to the dais, where Carbolen sat with Leinn, her arm in a sling, and Toral. All but Carbolen looked as haggard as Mindell; the gang's leader appeared energized.

"—with half the city in turmoil, we should get our gang members out there, see what we can manage to scrounge while their attention is elsewhere. This is a prime opportunity. We may even be able to get something from the towers—"

He broke off at Toral's nod toward the four of them waiting at the edge of the dais. Carbolen sat back, hands on knees, eyes latched on Devon. "So you did it."

No exaltation, no awe, not even a taint of respect. Just a statement of fact lined with sharp edges.

"We did it, as promised."

Raven shifted out from behind them, moving toward Carbolen's end of the dais. Nic pressed a little bit closer.

"From what I hear, you managed to do a bit more as well. At the Lyceum."

"The stories are probably exaggerated."

"Perhaps."

Raven reached Carbolen, leaned down to murmur something to all three of them, too low for Devon to hear. Then she stood, shot Devon a warning glance, before stepping to the side.

"Regardless, you present a problem. Toral tells me that the Council and the Lyceum have taken a strong interest in you, and Raven informs me that you've just escaped imprisonment. Where were you planning to go?"

Devon honestly hadn't thought that far. All he wanted to do was see Dalton. He and Dalton and Lane could plan after that.

"I thought the lower city—" he began, but halted as soon as Carbolen shook his head.

"You can't stay in the lower city. Once the Council and the proctors at the Lyceum realize you're gone, they'll turn the lower city upside down to find you, regardless of how indebted they are to the gangs for their release. They can't afford to look the other way. Not with you two. Not after what you've done. And unfortunately, neither can I."

"What does that mean?" Nic asked.

"It means we're too valuable for him to simply let go," Lane answered.

Carbolen smiled. "I see you've inherited your mother's quick grasp of events."

"You promised we could come and go without your permission, that we weren't part of your gang," Devon protested.

"You aren't. But after what happened at the Lyceum, I can't have you roaming around freely either, not as naïve as you both are. You need protection—from the Council, from Favian and the other proctors, from the other Crystal Cities once they hear rumors of what has happened here." He faced Lane. "Some of you will even need protection from the citizens of Iandolo themselves, because of your race. I intend to offer you that protection."

"Whether we want it or not."

"I'm glad we understand each other." He turned his back on them. "Raven, allow them to see their friend. I'll make arrangements while you're gone. I'll want you to accompany them. They need to stay hidden from everyone, including our own gang members and the Regulars. Only Leinn, Toral, and myself will know their location."

"Very well."

Raven motioned them off the dais and back through the wounded, out into the corridors.

As soon as they were outside the hall, Devon said, "He can't do this. He—"

"He has done this," Lane said sharply. "And to be honest, I'd rather have him protecting us than to be stuck back there at the Lyceum, or worse, secreted back inside the tower somewhere under Iandolan house guard."

"But all we've done is trade one prison for another."

Lane gave a bitter laugh. "That's all I've done my entire life. At least with Carbolen we know he's protecting us because he's protecting his own ass."

Still fuming, Devon pushed through the door to their assigned quarters. He stopped dead when he saw Dalton asleep on a cot, face pale, snoring slightly. His chest was wound with bandages.

Lane prodded him from behind.

Anger forgotten, Devon moved to Dalton's side and knelt. He reached forward, but didn't dare touch Dalton's face. His hand trembled.

Then Dalton flinched and snorted, shook his head, brow furrowed, and opened his eyes.

They stared at each other a moment, then Dalton smiled. "You made it."

Devon leaned forward and kissed him, hands on both sides of his head. When he finally pulled back, he said, "That was supposed to be my line."

Dalton chuckled, then glanced around at Lane and Nic, hovering just behind Devon, and Raven standing by the door. Eyes on Raven, he said, "Time to go?"

"Everything's all set."

"Then we'd better get moving, before Carbolen catches on." He winced, but dragged himself up into a seated position.

"What do you mean?" Nic asked.

"I didn't think Carbolen would simply let you go," Raven said.

"So she came to me," Dalton said. With help from Devon, he pushed up into a standing position. "We came up with our own plan. Are the supplies in place?"

"Ready to go."

"But…what are you going to tell Carbolen when he finds us missing?" Lane asked.

"I don't plan on telling him anything. I'm coming with you."

Nic look stunned. "Just like that?"

"Just like that. You'd better help Dalton. We need to move fast."

With Nic and Devon's help, Dalton made it out the door. They wound through the labyrinth surrounding Carbolen's lair, Raven scouting ahead, using corridors Devon didn't think had existed two weeks ago. They came out onto Level Seventeen's streets at the end of a dark alley, then picked their way down to the dead zone where Went had used the elevator to take them down to River Street. Here, Raven cut off in the opposite direction, winding them in toward the hub. They paused to give Dalton a rest every so often, but kept moving as much as possible.

When they were only a street away from the hub, most of the structures here still intact, Raven pulled them into a large, empty building, the ceiling a cavernous opening overhead. At the far wall, adjacent to the wide pit of the hub, were four elevator doors. One gaped into nothing, its doors half open. Another opened up into an elevator cage, but the doors were stuck, a large hole punched through the elevator's floor.

The other two appeared functional. Raven moved to the one on the right, pressing the lucent node beside the door. It lit, flickered briefly, then held steady.

She gave them all a reassuring nod. "It's stable. Trust me."

The cage arrived with a shriek of grinding metal, worse than the elevator Went had used. The doors slid open, catching only once, and Raven ushered them inside, where five hefty satchels waited for them. One of them was Devon's own. He cried out, nearly dropping Dalton as he snatched for it.

"Easy," Dalton said. "We've got time."

Ripping it open, he looked up at Raven. "My notes. My lucent light."

"I salvaged as much as I could from what you'd left behind at your bolthole and in your room at the lair."

"But why?"

She looked away, silent long enough that Devon thought she might not answer. But then: "I've been a gang member and a Regular a long time, long enough to learn to respect Carbolen, to follow him fervently, to fall in love with him, and then to be cast aside. I thought I could ignore him, continue to be a Regular, follow his orders. But I can't. I needed to find a way out. But leaving the gang isn't that easy. You already know that. When you returned, I saw an...opportunity. Something I could exploit. You wanted out; I wanted out. You needed protection; I'm trained to protect.

"And now you've become even more valuable, even more dangerous. Both of you." She glanced toward Lane. "You need me even more."

She reached forward to the elevator controls, her hand pressed to the bar near the top, the lucent lighting up a pale blue. The elevator only went up to mid-level, Devon noted.

"Where are you taking us?" he asked. "River Street? Level Seven? Level One?"

Raven faced him, a grim smile touching her eyes. "Oh, no. We're going all the way down. Into the Flatlands."

She pulled her finger down the bar to the bottom and the elevator began to move.

The Epic Saga Continues
in the second novel

CRYSTAL REBEL

Find it and the third novel

CRYSTAL WAR

In ebook and trade paperback now
wherever you buy your books.

Or pick it up at:

www.zombiesneedbrains.com

About the Author

JOSHUA PALMATIER is a fantasy author with a PhD in mathematics. He currently teaches at SUNY Oneonta in upstate New York while writing in his "spare" time, editing anthologies, and running the anthology-producing small press Zombies Need Brains LLC. His most recent fantasy novel, *Crystal War*, concludes the fantasy series begun in *Crystal Lattice* and *Crystal Rebel*, although you can also find his "Throne of Amenkor" series, the "Well of Sorrows" series, and the "Ley" series still on the shelves. He is currently hard at work writing his next fantasy and designing the Kickstarter for the next Zombies Need Brains anthology projects. You can find out more at www.joshuapalmatier.com or at the small press' site www.zombiesneedbrains.com. Or follow him on Blue Sky at joshuapalmatier.bsky.social or on X as @bentateauthor or @ZNBLLC. And check out the Zombies Need Brains Patreon and online magazine ZNB Presents at www.patreon.com/zombiesneedbrains.